A Turbulent Crown

A Timeless Falcon Dual Timeline Series

Volume Three

PHILLIPA VINCENT-CONNOLLY

Copyright © 2023 Phillipa Vincent-Connolly.
Copyright © 2015 Cover photography Richard Jenkins
Copyright © 2023 Cover design by Megan Sheer: sheerdesignandtypesetting.com

First Edition

The author has asserted their moral right under the Copyright, Designs and Patents Act, 1988, to be identified as the author of this work.

All Rights Reserved.

No part of this publication may be reproduced, copied, stored in a retrieval system, or transmitted, in any form or by any means, without the prior written consent of the copyright holder, nor be otherwise circulated in any form of binding or cover other than that in which it is published and without a similar condition being imposed on the subsequent purchaser.

This book is a work of fiction. Names, characters, businesses, organisations, places, and events, other than those clearly in the public domain, are either the product of the author's imagination, or are used fictitiously.

Any resemblances to actual persons, living or dead, events or locales are purely coincidental.

A CIP catalogue record for this title is available from the British Library.

❧ Gina Clark ☙

Thank you for your incredible friendship, love, loyalty, witty one-liners, naughty, and inspirational encouragement, extra-ordinary tea-making, continuous supply of champagne, and laughing together until we both could barely breathe; I love you.

One

THE NATIONAL GALLERY – PRESENT DAY
FOUR YEARS SINCE MY FIRST TIME-SLIP

Trafalgar Square is packed with tourists in the autumn sunshine. Live-performance artists stand statuesque, hoping Jessica and I will deposit money into their little coin receptacles as they pose. I fumble in my bag to find my purse at the bottom and drop a pound coin into the performer's pot at his feet. He looks down at me with a twinkle in his eye but makes no other show of appreciation. Jess yanks me by the arm.

"Come on!" She frowns. "You'll make us late."

I don't know why she's worrying because, as we make our way through the hustle and bustle of the crowds, I know we've a half-hour to spare before the talk we're due to attend starts. She dragged me along to this event because she thinks the subject matter will be useful in supporting us both in our up-and-coming PhD studies at St Mary's University, Twickenham.

When I returned to Carshalton after my time-travelling adventures, having fallen down the steps after the episode with George, I was relieved to discover that the train accident Mum thought Dad had been injured in, wasn't the one derailed after having failed to stop in time and hitting a fallen tree. Dad was on a later train, delayed by the incident. Having heard the news on the local radio station, Mum presumed the worst. Once my iPhone acquired sufficient charge, it sprung to life and pinged non-stop with missed calls, message notifications, and voicemails, because Mum and my friends had been frantic in their efforts to contact me. Not knowing, of course, that I was in the sixteenth century, she'd phoned all my friends trying to get messages to me about Dad, which is how Rob came to relay to Professor Marshall what she thought had happened, just as I'd time-slipped back into the professor's office.

I was so relieved Dad hadn't been on that train. However, even without it being an emergency, it didn't mean I'd go back to the Boleyns. Far from it. After sleeping with George, and the mess that likely followed, I vowed that I'd never go back to Tudor England. I took too many risks, and even though I might miss him, my fear of messing up the Tudor history of this country with my stupid meddling had floored me. The professor tried to question me on numerous occasions, but I refused to be coerced into sharing anything intimate about George and me.

Sometimes, I wonder if Professor Marshall's allowing me to find the cypher ring, and all that followed, is a flouting of the student/teacher relationship in terms of safeguarding. But, come on, what history student in their right mind wouldn't want to time-travel? It's a conversation my friends and I've had on many occasions, discussing what we might actually do. But experiencing a time-slip is another thing entirely. They have ideas on what events they might like to witness, but always as a somewhat distant observer. The possibilities were endless. But, for me, to experience the Early Modern period in real time, and close-up, was something else. And I couldn't even hint at my reality.

Though I haven't used it since, I was fortunate with the way the cypher ring and time-slipping worked for me. While I may have been away for months or years in Tudor England, it usually meant I was only absent for hours or days in 21st century time. It's mind-blowing. I didn't question things too much, in case I jinxed it, but I'm glad the cypher never sent me awry. Each time, when I didn't use the portal, I thought about when and where I wanted to go, and it took me there. And while my time in *Tudorville* was a fantastic experience, it can't be denied that I meddled too much. It took enormous effort and time to fix the history, and I don't want to risk messing it up again, to the detriment of our present day, not to mention Tudor times. Anyway, it doesn't matter if I want to return – I can't. I left the cypher ring in the top drawer of Professor Marshall's desk, where it's safe, and out of my hands.

It's not just about messing up the history. I'm afraid of returning to the Boleyns again because of what I feel for George, and because of how far things went between us. If Professor Marshall knew what happened, he'd go crazy. I have no doubt he would never give the cypher ring back to me, or allow me into his office, taking away any opportunity to return to George, even if I wanted to. It's been best to keep my mouth shut about our tryst, not to mention our being disturbed by Henry VIII himself. I blush at the thought. No, I'm not prepared to give up my innermost secrets to anyone. Not the Professor. Not Rob, either. Those two know enough but, from now on, I will only share with them what I think they need to know.

Jessica, while being my best friend, will never know what went on, and I'm never ever going to tell my parents *anything* about what happened since Professor Marshall gave me the cypher ring. All they need to understand is that I'm getting on with my studies, and that's it. Some things are best left unsaid. It's not that I can say *'By the way, Mum, Dad, I spent a few years in the sixteenth century, where I was best friends with Anne Boleyn, made passionate love to her brother, and formed enemies at the Tudor Court.'*

No one would ever 'get it', unless they'd seen these people from the past with their own eyes, as Professor Marshall and Robert Dryden have. Indeed, the whole scenario is better left alone. It's not the kind of experience to share with anyone because it's so sodding unbelievable. People might think I've gone mad – maybe even pack me off to the nearest psychiatrist. Besides, four years has passed since my last time-slip. I finished my degree, completed a History MA, and am now waiting to start a PhD. I'm fortunate Professor Marshall is going to be one of my supervisors, which is great because he knows me so well already.

The few times he asked why I stopped time-slipping, the only explanation I could give is that I wasted enough time interfering in the lives of the Boleyn clan, messing things up through my meddling, and that my education and career is more important than anything else. In the end, he seemed to accept my *excuses*. I expect he didn't push it because he didn't want to lose one of his more enthusiastic students.

Even with the passing years, I still miss Anne, and at times my hearts pangs for George and his sweet kisses, but, for my own sake, I must remain steadfast, accepting the reality that my time with them is over. Whilst my periods away from 21st century England were short, Rob didn't waste any time, hooking up with Georgina, another girl on our degree course. That fizzled out soon enough, but it didn't take him long to latch onto a series of new ones, seeing me well and truly side-lined. His current fling's name is Hannah. He's not far ahead of us now, outside the National Gallery, walking hand in hand with her through the crowds. We still say hello, but that's about it. I'm fine with it, though sometimes I regret what might have been.

"This should be good," Jessica says, jolting me from my thoughts.

"Yes, I'm looking forward to it. We didn't cover much on art history during our previous courses, did we?"

We make our way up the stairs and into the auditorium where the talk is taking place. As we take our seats two or three rows from the front, I see Rob and his girlfriend taking adjoining seats on the front row. She cuddles up to him, his arm around her, and I wince inside at the public show of affection.

Jessica huffs. "Take no notice of them. I've heard it's not that serious, anyway. And they're always arguing."

"Honestly, I'm not bothered." I keep the lie from my eyes and pull out a bottle of water from my bag.

"Did you bring a notebook?" she asks as she grabs a pad and pen from her bag.

I unscrew the lid and take a sip. "Of course. Making notes at these talks is essential. Professor Marshall has always thought so too. Probably why he encourages us to do it, right?"

"Yep, it's no fun trying to decipher notes made a few months after an event." She laughs.

"Especially if you can't keep up with what's being said, and you can't write shorthand!" I pull out a biro and notebook, its cover patterned with nice flowers – one of several I purchased a few years back from Hampton Court.

A woman, who I presume is the head of events, steps up onto the small stage and stands behind the podium. She taps the microphone once, then clicks on the buttons of a laptop in front of her, which brings up the first power-point slide showing the title of the talk and its speaker. The overhead lights dim, and she glances at her watch.

"Ladies and Gentlemen, I would like to introduce our special guest speaker for this morning, Doctor Janina Ramirez, a cultural historian, broadcaster, and author based at the University of Oxford, with a passion for communicating ideas about the past. Please give her a very warm welcome!"

"Hello!" Janina says as she walks out in front of her enthusiastic audience. Dr Ramirez looks wonderful in a bright red dress, lace pashmina, matching scarlet lipstick, Goth-black shoes, and tights, with elegantly straightened raven hair and kohl-rimmed dark eyes. She is already miked up and raring to go.

"Hello, and welcome to this morning's lecture!" she says, beaming, arms open wide, as if trying to hug the audience. "I'm Janina Ramirez – an Oxford Art Historian, Art detective, and writer. Primarily, I'm a chief investigator of images." She stands in the middle of the stage, making sure there is no barrier between her and her audience, taking the relaxed approach of not using the podium. I get the impression she has memorised all she wants to say, or perhaps it's the fact she's a bloody good visual arts' historian and knows her stuff.

"Today, we are looking at one of my absolute favourite artists from the sixteenth century – HOLBEIN." She raises both eyebrows, taking in her audience.

"This is exciting!" She looks at a self-portrait of the artist, which has come up on the screen behind her. "We are going to discuss the portrait of Holbein's family." She looks out at us again, soaking up our attention. "When we think of Holbein, we think of the paintings of the Ambassadors, or those depicting Henry VIII, and at least two of his wives,"— she smiles — "but the image I have chosen to talk about today, is the painting of his wife and their two oldest children."

She stands sideways on as the slide changes to the image so she can look at it as she talks.

"This is perhaps a counter-intuitive choice because we always think of the nobility he painted in their silks and satins while he was at the Tudor Court." She changes the image to more well-known examples before bringing it back to the previous one. "I have deliberately chosen this painting, as it shows his wife and children as ordinary people – the kind of work he didn't do very often. It gives us a glimpse into his personal life, which we rarely get to see. This is dated fifteen twenty-eight."

She walks back and forth across the stage, and every so often catches my eye.

"What is interesting about this image is that it was painted on paper. Not panel. The paper was pasted onto panel later. Holbein was born into a painters' family in Augsburg, a city in Bavaria, Germany. His father, Hans Holbein the Elder, was one of the most famous painters of the Tudor period. Holbein the Younger did not stay in Germany but moved to Switzerland because The Reformation made patronage of artists difficult, so he looked for patronage abroad. We know he went to France, hoping to get in to see the king, but that didn't work, so then he went to England." She smiles.

I wonder, if I had stayed, whether I might have met Holbein. He never seemed to be working at the Tudor Court when I was there – or our paths just never crossed.

"He first went to England in 1526," Janina continues, "and spent two years there before returning to his family for four years. Then he left them again and didn't return but for a brief visit in fifteen thirty-eight. He was an absent father!" She giggles.

I know he had several illegitimate children. He must have led his wife a merry dance, and not given her a happy life. I've heard that geniuses are often wrapped up in their work and their personal life always seems to suffer.

"Holbein is living proof of the impact that the Reformation had on the arts. The chief attraction for England is that he wanted patronage from nobility and the court."

She flicks the slides to show Holbein's painting of Sir Thomas More. What fascinates me about the portrait, is you can see the hairs growing out of the man's chin – and from what I have seen of him in real life, it's a close likeness.

"He first painted the portrait of Thomas More and his family," Janina continues, her eyes wide with enthusiasm, "and then, when More was executed, he realigned himself between the church, royalty, and different courts, because he kept losing patronage. He never fell from grace at the English Court, even when his sitters did, with the likes of Thomas More and Anne Boleyn being executed. Nor was he blamed when he painted the miniature of Anne of Cleve and later the marriage of her to Henry failed. Painting her image was a crisis point for Holbein, and he continued to be an important player on the stage of art. The image of Anne of Cleve was almost abstract and idealised in style in comparison to his other works, and maybe Henry should have realised that it would not have been the same as the sitter. It was not as natural."

She knows what she's talking about, and Jessica and I are scribbling notes as fast as we can.

"Imagine having to paint someone's portrait like Holbein did, with the woman concerned sitting in front of you, and all the officials at her court watching exactly what you are doing – judging your ability. You aren't going to paint an ugly depiction of your sitter, are you?" Laughter rises from the audience. "He'd have to get out of the Cleves' court alive, so he sugar-coated what Anne of Cleve may have actually looked like – and that whole process would have put him in a very difficult position." She nods to emphasise the point.

"This portrait I've chosen to talk about is very different from other Holbein works, as it doesn't idealise his wife and children." She uses a pointer to bring our focus to specific areas on the painting. "There is a lot of colour in her face, which you don't usually see. This composition reminds you of the image of the Virgin and child and is a very powerful image…"

She carries on delivering her talk for over an hour, which includes ten minutes of questions, and the opportunity for photographs and to buy a signed copy of her latest book. We go over to where she is now sat, waiting patiently with sharpie in hand. Jessica picks up a copy of her book, *'Julian of Norwich'*, and hands it to her, whereupon Janina signs it.

"Janina, thank you for your wonderful talk," she says, smiling. "Holbein is one of my favourite artists too."

"Oh, I'm so glad you enjoyed it!" Janina beams from ear to ear. "It is so wonderful to be able to share my enthusiasm with so many people who appreciate Holbein's work." She then looks at me as I hand over her new book, *'Femina: A New History of the Middle Ages, Through the Women Written Out of It'*. She opens it and places it flat on the table in front of her. "What is your name, Lovely?"

"Beth. I'm a reader of history at St. Mary's University."

"So, Beth, you could say we are colleagues of sorts!" She starts to write my name in the inside page. "What period are you researching?"

"The Tudors." I watch her write *'Beth, To a fellow historian, Best of Luck with your PhD – Best Wishes, Janina.'*

"Ah, no wonder you looked so interested during my talk." She nods. "Did you enjoy it?"

"Very much, thank you. It is lovely to meet you."

"And you, Beth."

I take the book from her, and Jess and I make a move. A queue of people are waiting to talk to her, and I don't want to take up any more of her time.

When the event finishes, we go down to the little café on the lower ground floor to find a table. It's a small, quirky space with modern black and white tiles and industrial styling – the perfect place for us to grab a sandwich and a cup of tea. We purchase what we want to eat, find a free table, and sit down.

"What did you think of the talk?" I ask Jessica.

"I thought it was brilliant, but then I love Janina, and I love Holbein. I mean, who doesn't?"

She talks about what her research entails – it's a different period to me, mostly Medieval but sprinkled with Tudor, so it's no wonder Janina Ramirez is one of her favourite historians. Jess is one of those girls who is extremely intelligent yet shows that side of herself in an understated manner. A dark horse. She listens a lot, as she knows you don't learn too much from talking and isn't the type you want to get on the wrong side of. If you are on the right side, and have earned her trust and loyalty, she's a friend for life.

I take a bite of my sandwich, then notice Rob and Hannah sat in the corner. The conversation looks heated, and she doesn't look happy. I watch from the corner of my eye as she gets to her feet and chucks stuff onto her tray, her exasperation clear as she gesticulates to Rob in frustration. He keeps shaking his head and sits there with his arms folded, until she gives up, grabs her handbag from the chair, and walks away.

"I wonder what's going on there then," Jess says as she finishes her piece of cake.

"God knows!" I reply. As I gulp back the dregs of my tea, Rob walks towards us.

"Play it cool," Jess whispers, not looking at him.

"Girls, would you mind if I join you?" he asks, putting his hand on the back of the chair beside me.

"Yes, why not?" Jess says, getting straight in there before I can reply. She looks at me, then at him, smirking as she ignores my glare.

"Did you enjoy the lecture?" he asks, checking his phone before putting it into his blazer pocket.

"We thought it put Holbein in a new light," I reply. "But then, you know I love his work."

He runs his hand through his hair, a trait I remember is a nervous habit. The lad must be feeling it after Hannah's walkout. He looks smart today, in chinos, a crisp shirt, and a navy blazer.

"You dressed up, didn't you?" Jess says, her sarcasm dripping.

"I had to." He grins. "Just in case I got a photo with Janina in the meet and greet."

"And did you?" I ask.

"Yeah. Take a look." He pulls his phone from his pocket, taps and scrolls, and hands it to me."

I scan it. "It's a nice photo. She's lovely, isn't she? Doctor Ramirez, I mean – down to earth."

"One of the most approachable public historians I've ever met," he says.

I can't help but swipe across to check out the pictures of him and his girlfriend stood together at the Tower, Hever, Hampton Court, and other historical sites. It looks like they've spent a lot of time together. I hand him back his phone, which he stuffs back in his pocket.

"What happened with Hannah?" Jess asks, brave enough to ask him what I'm already thinking. "I saw her storming off."

"Hmm – that." He stuffs his hands into his trouser pockets. "I don't want to talk about it."

"That's good," I say, staring daggers at Jess. I wouldn't want him to think I was interested in his love life – he hasn't been on my radar for a long time now. "We don't want to hear about it."

Jessica's phone starts buzzing, and she picks it up and answers it.

"Mum?" She raises her eyebrows at me. "Where are you?" She nods at the ceiling. "But why so early?"

Oh, no, I know where this is going.

She stuffs the remaining morsel of cake in her mouth and carries on the conversation. "Okay, no problem. I'll meet you outside Selfridges. Give me half an hour?" She gets up and puts her bag over her shoulder. "Yes, wait for me on the seat outside the Oxford Street entrance." She nods twice, purses her lips, then nods again. "Yes, okay, I won't be long." She ends the call and stuffs her phone into her handbag.

"I'm so sorry, guys – I've got to go. I promised my mum I'd meet her later, but she's come in early." She shrugs at me. "Clothes' shopping, you know how it is. I need her advice, and the use of the 'Bank of Mum'."

With that, she hugs me, says goodbye to us, and leaves me sitting alone with Rob. This is not how I expected my day to go.

As I glance at Rob, I realise I haven't really got over George, which is probably why I haven't had a serious relationship with anyone since my return. I've had one or two flings, even made mistakes – the odd one-night stand I'd rather forget – but nothing serious.

"Would you mind coming with me upstairs to the gallery?" he asks, running his hand through his hair. "It's part of my research to critique representations of male gender in Early-Modern Masters, to see how royalty and nobility, along with the yeoman tried to place themselves within the political and religious swing of the Reformation through art." He half smiles. "I need a sounding board, and..."

His pained expression tells me enough to understand the situation; his first choice is no longer available after walking out on him. I can think of better company, but at least the conversation will be academic. Why not?

"If you like?" I shrug. "Art history is something I've always had an interest in, but my academic knowledge is limited. I only did an art history module for my degree, so don't rely on me for succinct responses to any questions you might have." It's a credible reason for him wanting company, isn't it? I doubt he has an ulterior motive. After all, there's no way he's interested in me now, other than as an acquaintance.

We take the escalator up to the floor where the sixteenth-century portraits are on display. Even though I'm not interested in Rob anymore in a romantic sense, and we are no longer really friends, I do still care about him. Yes, I did have a thing for him, but then George stole my heart. Rob can be a bit of a dickhead at times, but I do feel sorry for him, especially after seeing Hannah walk off. I'm going to try and be a friend, rather than being sharp. It costs nothing to be nice.

We stand in front of the National Portrait Gallery portrait of Anne Boleyn. It feels strange staring at her image when I know what she actually looks like. Whoever the artist was, did not capture a great likeness. Anne's eyes are far more striking in real life. On the other hand, even a talented painter could never capture the essence of the woman within. Rob stares at her, as she glares stony-faced back at him, keeping her secrets.

"It doesn't look like her in real life, does it?"

"No, not really." I frown, not altogether happy that he's qualified to make such a statement. "It's sad that Henry destroyed all the likenesses of her."

"You never know, there might be some paintings out there yet to be uncovered. You saw that portrait art historian Graeme Cameron discovered of her a few years back, didn't you? Well, he assessed that it was her."

"No," I reply, giving him a curious look. "That's one research paper I must have missed."

We carry on walking around the gallery, looking but not really talking, until he stops dead in his tracks on coming to a Holbein sketch of a young, unknown Tudor lady. I do a double-take when I look at it, squinting at the eerie resemblance. Why is it I can recognise myself? It's like looking into a five-hundred-year-old mirror. I can't take my eyes from it, and the whole experience sends a queer shiver down my spine. No one has ever drawn a likeness of me during my Tudorville escapades, so when could this have been rendered?

Rob stares at the pencil sketch, then looks at me, then back at the drawing. "You know, this could very easily be you." He scrutinises the sketch all the more, his nose so close, I'm afraid he'll set the alarm off. "I don't remember you saying you sat for Holbein."

"I didn't."

"Well, the lady in the drawing has your features – you must be her doppelgänger."

"Stop, Rob, I think I'd remember if I met Mister Holbein. It can't be me."

"Well, the likeness is uncanny."

As we move down on, I take a last glance back at the drawing. It is me – I know it. And it means one thing: I went back. My goodness, I went back. My tummy flips and a shudder runs through me. I'm fated to return to my beloved friends in Tudor England. I follow Rob to the next painting, the butterflies fluttering around my stomach making me feel like I'm on a big dipper.

"What did George Boleyn look like?" he asks, his tone rather impertinent as he stands at a painting of two Tudor noblemen on horseback.

"Why do you ask?"

"Well, you would know, wouldn't you? You did get…close."

I dig my hands into my coat pockets, not meeting his gaze. "Well, let's put it this way – his best features couldn't be displayed in a painting in a public gallery."

His mouth hangs open, and I have to hold back a wry chuckle at my success in shutting him up. However, as I walk into the next room, I wonder if I've implied too much about my relationship with George. Methinks, I need to be more careful with my comments in future. But he did deserve it. I look back at him, unable to smoother a victorious smile.

"That's what you get for being a smartarse."

He stiffens. "What do you mean by that?"

"You were trying to make a fool out of me."

"No, I'm not."

"I told you what I told you about the Boleyns in confidence. I wish I'd never introduced you to Anne, or the portal. I didn't share the experience with you for you to use it to belittle me. I may not be a cactus expert, but I do know a prick when I see one."

"That's quite obvious," he says, his cheeks reddening.

"Look, I'm not hanging around here for you to insult me – I've got to start planning my research. See you later, maybe!"

I leave him standing there, stunned. We may have almost had 'a thing', but it didn't happen. While I sometimes wonder how that might have been, I'm now living my life, doing my own thing. Maybe it's his ego that won't let me go? I shake my head. I don't want to hang around with someone who wouldn't know how to treat a real woman unless it bit him on the scrotum. And that's not going to happen where I'm concerned. No, there are much better men than him around. I know there are. Well, not so much here, but there's definitely one, in Tudor England. And I know I went back – that sketch proves it – so what's to stop me being proactive and returning to see how things are? How George is? There can't be any harm in a quick visit, can there? Better than staying around here with smarmy Rob. Yes, my mind's made up – I'm going back to George. And it would be so lovely to see dear Anne again.

I pull out my mobile and call Professor Marshall.

"Sir, it's Beth Wickers."

"Hi, Beth, how are you?"

"Good, thanks. I…need a favour."

"Oh? What is it?"

"I need to check the front cover of the Ives' book, just for my own peace of mind, you understand?" I sigh. "Something's happened and I need to confirm that the book is back to its original state." I glance around to make sure nobody can hear. "If there's a problem, I'm going to need the cypher ring from your desk drawer."

"Are you serious?"

"Yes, sir."

"Why? I thought you'd rectified everything – according to that book."

"Professor, I need to be certain, you understand?" George's smiling face comes to mind.

"What's happened to bring this on?"

"What?"

"You said something happened. What?"

Yikes! My mind races. "Erm… I saw a Holbeinesque pencil sketch in the National Portrait Gallery."

"Why is that significant?" At this point, I can imagine his perplexed expression. "The NPG is full of portraits!" He chuckles, and I can almost smell the cigarette smoke I know is billowing around him.

"Sir, the Tudor pencil sketch is one done from life – it's a drawing of me!"

"Good grief," he says. "Erm…let me think."

A tapping sound comes down the line, and visualize him with a pen in hand, knocking it off something as he ponders the potentials.

"Beth?"

"Yes, Professor?"

"Can I meet you outside Saint Mary's at two p.m.?"

"That would be great. I'll see you then."

Two

PRESENT DAY – CARSHALTON, SURREY

Standing in my bedroom, looking down at the cypher ring, I have no idea what I need to do to rectify the cover issue. Maybe it's just about keeping Anne on the right track, and observing history as it happens. Not sleeping with *anyone*. Perhaps my mission is an easy, simple one: To pass my days in *Tudorville* observing Anne's life.

I'm nervous, but excited at the same time, as I push the cypher ring onto my middle finger. Professor Marshall didn't give it back to me at first, which isn't surprising, until we got to his office, and he realised how things really were.

I stood there in silence, and he just stared at me.

"You are not going to like this." He frowned, leant against his desk, a lit cigarette in one hand, his copy of the Ives' book in his other.

"Why?" I asked, my tummy in knots as I watched smoke circle above his head. No wonder the ceiling was an awful yellow rather than pristine white. I coughed into my hand. "I thought we'd sorted out the book and it was back to its original state?"

"I thought so too, but…"

Hmm, not like the professor to be lost for words.

"Sir, let me see it," I demanded, and snatched the book from his hand. Rather rude, but I couldn't help myself. I stared at the front cover, my face going cold. The title was the original, but not the image. The portrait on the cover was me, again! Why did it keep changing, reverting to a new history, when I thought all had been rectified? I flicked through the pages. The contents' page seemed as it should be. Parts I – IV were all there, as expected. The illustrations' list, the same. And the preface. All the text read as it was meant to read. It was puzzling, to say the least, that just the image on the front wasn't right. The rest of the book seemed to be okay.

"Crap," I said. "Now what?"

"Beth, between that sketch and the changed cover image, you have enough reason to go back." He sighed. "It's a sure sign that not everything with the history is as it should be." He pulled on his cigarette and rolled his eyes.

I shrugged. So much for just wanting to go back to see George. "How should I know what's going on with this book, or even the sketch? You are the academic, Professor. This is your territory."

"That may be, but I'm not the one who changed Tudor history, am I? I'm not pictured on the cover of the Ives' book, am I? Nor does a Tudor portrait of me hang in one of our national galleries."

He nodded at the book in my hand, his eyebrows raised. I supposed seeing the sketch was a credible reason to go back to the 16th Century. Everything might be okay with Anne but, as a good friend, I knew I needed to check things out. So once again I had a mission, not just to reacquaint myself with George.

Trouble is, the cover of Eric Ives' book. Why has it a portrait of me on the front? What did I do to change the history? I know I haven't been back, but the pencil sketch proves I was. It's confusing, and not good, so I'm standing here now, preparing to time-slip, but not just to see George. No, I need to go back to correct the history. Again.

I check the date on my calendar to mark the exact day to jump to on my return, and as I look down at myself in the Tudor clothing, I wore last time I came back, I realise it still smells of the Tudor Court – of wood smoke, sage, cinnamon, nutmeg, wine, and George. My heart swells at the thought of him. But is the dress decent enough to wear? I could've tried to wash it, but the fabric is so expensive, and old, but yet not, and I didn't want to risk spot-cleaning it. I've hidden it away for so long under my bed, I was worried it wouldn't fit me anymore. But here I am in it now, after such a struggle to fasten it by myself. No one but Rob and Professor Marshall know of my time travels so I couldn't ask Jessica to come round to help me. It's times like this I miss dear Agnes. Anne always helped me, too, for that matter. Both of them were always so kind to me.

After a mental shake, I check my hair is okay, then run through everything I need in the linen holdall – I don't want to look conspicuous. Yep, everything looks good: Toiletries, perfume, Paracetamol, mascara, and tampons – in case my implant stops working. It seems I'm ready. I look out of my bedroom window, and normal life looks, well…normal. Far from my own life. Rutterkin meows outside my door but I'm not going to let him in, not now. He

can use his cat flap to go outside when he needs to. My parents are at work, so if I miss any of my time in the present, the hope is they won't have noticed – fingers crossed. Just in case, I leave a note:

Mum,
   Doing research in the library, preparing my bibliography, ready for my PhD.
   Don't worry about dinner – I will sort myself out when I get back.
   Love you,
   Beth x

Rooted to the spot, my heart pounding under the reed boning of my gown, I adjust my gable hood, then tie my cloak around my neck as I gaze at my reflection in my dressing-table mirror. I smile. Considering I've rarely dressed myself this way on my own before, I haven't done too bad a job. I've watched enough of The Tudor Dreams Historical Costumier's Facebook Live videos to have a reasonable knowledge of the way Tudor women dressed. On top of that, I've been fortunate to have Anne Boleyn dress me, with the help of her servant Agnes. Poor Agnes. She may be gone but I will never forget her. Anne and I were devastated when we lost her to 'the sweat'. I shouldn't be thinking about Agnes – it will take me too far back in time, with the possibly that I might bump into the version me when I first jumped. What a concept, and a Hall of Mirrors. That would be a bad flash. I need to think of Anne, and George, but movement through the broken patterns in my net curtains distracts me, and I peer out to see schoolkids walking on the pavement, laughing together, huddling in their little gangs on their way to school.

I should be doing history research but excitement bubbles in the pit of my stomach as I grip the cypher ring, thinking of the sixteenth century and Anne. But I can't get George out of my thoughts. Not that I mind thinking of him – it's the initial reason I wanted to go back.

With a whoosh, the blood pounds around my head, my ears buzzing as I slide through a maelstrom before my feet pound on stone cobbles, and I have to work to gain my balance on the undulating surface. The time-slipping experience is like a mental, emotional, and physical car crash. I'll never get used to the feeling of my brain rattling inside my skull.

My head hurts as I open my eyes and glance down at my knuckles, white from gripping the raised cypher on the ring. At least I've landed out of sight of anyone. I realise it's a warm day and laugh at myself for initially pulling my cloak around me. It's a reflex. A form of protection, as I clasp my cloak, and the linen bag tightly to me. Clamping my nostrils shut, I feel nauseated by the smell of horse manure and damp straw, mixed with God knows what. It makes me gag. The clatter of hoofs filters in from a nearby street, and a scruffy dog presses his nose to the ground, no doubt in the hope of sniffing out scraps. I look around me, regain my composure, and pull the hood of my cloak about my face in case I'm recognised.

Right now, I need to find Anne and get back to the familiar surroundings of the palace. I keep my wits about me as I walk through the courtyard of what appears to be a coaching inn for travellers, until I'm standing within a crowd, which is surging around me, their momentum carrying me along as they make their way up a hill ahead of us. Where am I? I look over my shoulder, and my face goes cold on seeing the Tower of London behind me, looming over all the other Tudor buildings around it like a four-headed giant.

The stone walls, with the sun hitting them, look like blocks of gesso painted against a backdrop of blue sky. Judging by the clear blue, and sunny sky, I have to assume that it must be spring or summer. I've no idea of the events going on around me, but I know I'm in amongst a huge crowd near the outer walls of the Tower, so something momentous must be afoot. I know where I am but not when. It isn't where I expected to time-slip.

"He wants more than his head cutting off!" a man ahead of me shouts.

"What is it they say?" another man says to him. "Incest is best?"

With that comment, unease wells into my throat.

"They should cut his cock off!" someone else snaps. "Fucking his own sister – it is ungodly!"

A ball of fear fills my chest. The crowd moves onwards up the hill, dragging me with it. All I want to do is retreat, out of this hungry murmuration. I grip a woman's arm.

"What day is this?"

She stares at my hand on her arm, then meets my gaze, frowning. "It is, Lady." She shrugs me off.

"And the…date?" I almost choke on my words. "What is the date today?"

"The seventeenth day of May."

I swallow back rising bile as I glance about. "W-what's going on?"

"Have you been asleep, my dear? 'Tis the execution of the queen's brother – that Viscount Rochford."

"George Boleyn?" I can hardly say his name.

"That be the one." She nods. "Along with those other dogs, Norris, Weston, Brereton, and that musician – what's his name?"

"Mark Smeaton," I just about whisper.

"Yeah, that's him! They have all had a ride on that dirty mare. Those men will all get what's coming to them."

A giant of a man, walking close by, buts into our conversation. "Yeah, and the queen took all what were coming out of them!" His words drip with sarcasm. "Let's be having them traitors." He's so tall, a bit like Geoff Capes, and his chest is that hairy, he looks like he's wearing a sweater. His hands are as big as shovels, with grubby fingernails, and arms big and thick enough to pick a Shetland pony up and carry it around like a pup. What he's saying makes me cringe, but I dare not say anything to the contrary for fear of offending him.

"Eh, Paxton, will we have a good view?" his friend beside him asks.

"It'll take a bit of pushing, but I'll be getting us right to the front, do not be worrying."

"But I can't see over your big head!" a woman who is linking Paxton's arm says.

19

"You can sit over my shoulders, Joanna!" he suggests.

"You only want to get up me skirts. Your clothes need a good wash by the looks of thee."

"There would never be enough piss to wash his clothes, eh, Joanna?" Paxton's friend says. "Did you wash the king's clothes in piss?"

"Never! Do not say such things. The king was good to me when I was in his service."

"Yes, I heard how good he was to you – your daughter is by the king is she not?"

"Paxton Merrill, that be treason, what you are saying. You may be built like a barnyard door, but I'll need all of London's piss to clean your clothes!"

Joanna smells of urine. She must be the local laundress. I wonder what Paxton meant about the king. Weird. Did the king take commoner mistresses? Would Henry have bedded a mere laundress? I can't believe what is happening, or that I've somehow landed two years ahead of my destination, at my beloved George's execution. Whatever happens, I can't afford to lose it, though I don't know how I'm going to cope with seeing what I believe is about to happen at this place today.

"You lot are starting to piss me right off now!" someone shouts.

Paxton's friend chuckles. "Best get a bucket, Joanna, to catch the piss flowing off the scaffold, 'cause that's what'll be running when all those nobles' heads roll!"

"Them all be talking of rolls, Mary – did you bring the bread with you?" a man walking next to me asks a woman at his side, who I presume is his wife. His breath is putrid. "These executions may take some time, and the entertainment will give you one hell of an appetite."

She smiles, revealing blackened teeth. "Yes, I did, John – and the pies!"

"Enough for the children?" he asks, picking a little boy up and hefting him onto his shoulders.

"Of course!" she replies, holding hands with a young girl.

"Father, I can see the scaffold!" The boy points ahead.

"It be an early start, but 'tis a good day out!" Mary says.

Panic grips me at what's to come but the crowd pushes ahead, and I have no choice but to go with it. Then the scaffold, draped in black, looms to my right. The morning sun is so hot on my cheeks, and my heart is racing, matching a rhythmic tattoo of drumbeats bouncing off the walls of the Tower. A trudging of heavy boots slides into the mix as guards from inside the prison push past us, the light reflecting off their shiny halberds dazzling me.

"Out of the way!" a yeoman warder shouts.

The deafening thuds on the drums beat out their death knell as the guards march past. THUD! THUD! THUD!

"Move aside!" another bellows.

THUD! THUD! THUD!

The crowd around me is pushed left and right, and I try to hang back, hoping I can somehow get away from witnessing what is about to happen. I hide behind the taller and broader men in the crowd, feeling like Judas Iscariot, not wanting anyone to recognise me as a friend of the Boleyns.

"Get out of the way – we are on His Majesty's business!"

THUD! THUD! THUD!

The yeoman guards continue pushing past people. Citizens gather in groups around the scaffold, nudging each other for the best view. Some perch on the viewing platforms, shuffling along, pies and handkerchiefs in hand.

THUD! THUD! THUD!

Yeoman guards line up around the scaffold, halberds faced outwards to the crowd. Through the gaps between onlookers, I see another group of guards escorting their prisoners up the hill. More thudding drums.

THUD! THUD! THUD!

Then my worst fears are realised when I spot George, walking, the first in line, followed by Henry Norris, Francis Weston, William Brereton, then Mark Smeaton, who has to be carried along by guards on both sides. Mark is a pitiful sight. Eyes closed and swollen, his back hunched, his feet dragging along behind him. The narrative, popular from history, seems to be correct – he must have been tortured. A man would confess to anything under such pressure.

More guards bring up the rear. The thudding of their drumbeats resonates in everyone's ears.

THUD! THUD! THUD!

I think they do this to drown out the jeers of the crowd, and to stop the convicted from conversing with onlookers. The burly guards march in time to the accompanying drumbeat, its heart-shaking rhythm reminding their charges not to make a run for it.

My heartbeat synchronises with the thud of the drumming, my blood pounding in my ears as George takes tentative steps up the shallow scaffold steps. Beneath his open doublet, I notice his embroidered shirt marked by sweat, tears, and soon, it will be marked by his blood.

THUD! THUD! THUD!

George knows he is going to be dispatched first, because of rank, and stands closest to the block, and his executioner. The rest of the condemned follow suit and line up behind him. They all stare at their feet, to avoid looking out into the crowd.

THUD! THUD! THUD!

Peering between the men in front of me, I see Sir William Kingston, with Thomas Cranmer next to him, holding an open bible. Kingston steps forward and speaks to George. Then the crowd hushes as George steps around the block and approaches the edge of the scaffold so he is closer to the watching, waiting crowd, who crane their necks in anticipation.

THUD! THUD! THUD!

"Dirty knave!" someone shouts out before he has a chance to say a word.

"Get on with it!" another man roars at the axeman.

George looks ashen but still handsome. He scans the crowd, as if looking for someone – I hope it's not for me. Can I bear to watch? Fear and foreboding grab at the back of my throat, and bile burns my tonsils as I try to hold back the sheer terror. But I can't move – frozen to the spot – unable to look away.

As he takes a deep breath, he places his right hand over his heart, pressing his doublet. I frown, wondering why. Is he hoping that by doing so, what he's about to say will come across as genuine and sincere? I don't know. For the life of me, I can't remember anything I've read about this horror. My head is so muddled. As I strain to watch him, beads of perspiration prickle my brow. I want to stop this but am unable to move, paralysed by the sight of my dearest, darling George about to meet his end. Everyone around me is waiting with bated breath as he prepares to speak.

"Gentlemen and Christians," he says, his voice confident and loud, the crowd listening in stony silence, "I was born under the law, and I die under the law, forasmuch as it is the law which has condemned me."

The whites of his eyes look bloodshot as he scans the faces of the crowd, but he surprises me at how confident he sounds. His voice doesn't break, and he doesn't flinch as he continues to hold his hand firmly over his chest.

"Gentlemen here present," he continues, as if he is a wise man, "I come not hither to preach at you, but to die. Nor do I now seek for anything, in the sorrowful plight in which I here stand, save that I may soon bathe my dry and parched lips in the living fountain of God's everlasting and infinite mercy. And I beseech you all, in his holy name, to pray unto him for me, confessing truly that I deserve death, even though I had a thousand lives – yes, even to die with far more and worse shame and dishonour than has ever been heard of before. For I am a miserable sinner, who have grievously and often times offended. No, and in very truth, I know not of any more perverse or wicked sinner than I have been up until now. Nevertheless, I mean not openly now to relate what my many sins may have been, since, in such, it can yield you no profit, nor me any pleasure here to reckon them up – enough be it that God knows them all."

He looks around at those waiting for his death, probably hoping his words will not fall on deaf ears. I clench my fists at my sides as he takes another breath.

"Therefore, masters all, I pray you take heed by me, especially the gentlemen of the court, the which I have been among, I beseech you all to take heed by me and beware of such a fall, and I pray to God the Father, the Son, and the

Holy Ghost, three persons and one God, that my death may be an example to you all. And beware, trust not in the vanity of the world, and especially in the flattery of the court. And I cry God's mercy and ask all the world forgiveness of God. And if I have offended any man that is not here now, either in thought, word, or deed, and if you hear any such, I pray you heartily on my behalf, ask them to forgive me for God's sake."

He stops speaking, and the vomit rises at the back of my throat as the seconds tick away until the axe strikes its lethal blow. My palms are sweaty, and my heart thunders beneath my bodice. I wish I could get away, but I am cornered on all sides – hemmed in, with three or four lines behind me. I'm too short to notice who is watching with me. All I can see is the back of men's bonnets, the feathers in their caps fluttering in the breeze where some haven't taken them off in respect. I push through towards the front row, needing to get closer. Some people cough, and others stay silent, listening and waiting.

"And yet, my masters all, I have one thing for to say to you: men do common and say that I have been a setter forth of the Word of God…"

I turn my head, looking about me, and see some women nod in agreement, with others sighing.

"…and one that have favoured the Gospel of Christ – and because I would not that God's word should be slandered by me, I say to you all, that if I had followed God's word in deed as I did read it and set it forth to my power, I would never have come to this."

He scans the crowd again, and my heart breaks at his bravery. All I can do is try to stop myself from being sick when the moment comes, and do my utmost not to faint. Even at the thought, my head grows light, and I have to press my toes into the ground to steady myself. I'm so close to him, it would take just a second to dash up there and help him. Take him away to safety. Protect him. But there's nothing I can do. And I don't feel as if I can physically stand here and witness my one true love be decapitated before my eyes, let alone save him. I want to scream at the top of my voice so they stop this barbaric act, but I can't interfere with history. I have been warned often enough. It would be catastrophic to more than myself. But all that keeps going through my head is losing my darling George. I love you! Dear God, why couldn't you stop this?

"If I had," he says, his beautiful, strong voice carrying to me on the breeze, "I had been a living man among you. Therefore, I pray you, masters all, for God's sake stick to the truth and follow it, for one good follower is worth three readers, as God knows."

He stands still, looking out over the crowd, but then Kingston steps forward and leads him back around by the elbow, behind the block. My legs are shaking so much I'm sure the people around me notice. George looks to his left as the executioner steps forward.

"Forgive me for what I'm about to do, Viscount Rochford?"

George hands him a leather purse full of coins. "You have my forgiveness but not my consent, for I still had so much living to do."

The executioner takes the purse, stuffs it in the pouch on his belt and instructs George to kneel in the straw. He does as he's told and rests his neck in the arc of the block, facing in my direction. The drummers start their short drumroll in unison.

George closes his eyes and stretches out his arms. Inside, I want to scream out *'George, I am here, I will always be with you!'* but watching the sequence of events as they unfold, no sound escapes my lips. My brain won't work. I can't form the words. A victim of sensory loss, your eyes cry out with no voice – an innocent voice. A silent call. What have I done to you? The silence around me is deafening. I'm one of the dirty guns. Kill and run. As if I fired a bullet through your heart. In this shocking moment, his eyes open, and for a split second his gaze meets mine. I see the trace of a smile as he realises it's me, and my heart lurches as a tear rolls down the side of his nose. If ever there was a time when I could willingly change the course of history without the thought of consequence, it is now. I mouth *I love you*, but his eyes widen, petrified, as he feels the axe blade rest on his neck.

In one swift move, the executioner swings the axe, and its blade embeds in its target. I close my eyes, unable to watch, but I hear something going on and reopen my eyes to see the executioner place one foot on the block to gain leverage so he can release the blade from the gristle and muscle of his victim, to take a final, definitive chop into the vertebrae. How George stops himself from crying out, I don't know? This time, I witness the next blow, and in the following millisecond, flinch at the thud as his head drops into the waiting straw. The executioner grabs George's dark hair and shows the crowd his bloody trophy. They cheer. As his head is held high, bloody ribbon-like threads hang from his neck, and within two or three seconds of being held aloft, his beautiful eyes close. I watch in horror as his corpse judders, with arterial spray from his neck splattering those of us at the front of the crowd.

A piercing pain rips through my chest, and I fail in my efforts not to fall to my knees. People next to me stare as I let out the most horrendous sound. But even in the midst of my despair, I pull out a handkerchief from the purse on my girdle belt and wipe away the still-warm spots of blood on my nose and cheeks. I look down at the scarlet stains on the fresh white linen, shaking my head in disbelief, then stuff the blotted fabric back in my purse. When I raise my head, I realise I fell forward, closer to the scaffold, and I can't miss the look of horror on Henry Norris's face as servants of the Tower slip and slide in the blood under their feet. My heart thuds as hands reach out around me, trying to push between the guards to dip their own handkerchiefs in what remains of George's blood, now pooling on the scaffold platform. A biting anger surges in me, and I'm sickened by the barbaric nature of the human race. To them, it's like a day out, like going to a football match. To me, it feels like the end of my world.

Liberty takers are shooed away by the guards, and George's body is lifted off the scaffold into a waiting barrow, his head placed back above his neck, as if the executioner is preparing to repair his grim handiwork.

The drumrolls start again as the executioner's next victim steps forward, ready to give his speech to the crowd who are growing silent again. For a split second, Henry Norris stares at me. He says nothing but his expression seems strange – as if he is disgusted with me. Why would he look at me that way? He doesn't look glad to be yielding himself up to death, which is what traitors were expected to do, to avoid persecution of other family members.

I turn away, unable to watch any more. Tears stream down my face as I'm pushed back into the on-looking guards, in the wrong direction. Thinking fast, I dart between them, lift the black cloth that drapes the edge of the scaffold and hide underneath it in the darkness, out of potential danger and away from the mockery of the watching crowd. This situation is like nothing I've ever experienced before, and I hope never to again. I look up at the slits in the scaffold floor and listen to the scuffing footsteps as the shadow of Norris moves to the front of the platform. He's victim number two, and I try to block out the sound of his voice.

What I have witnessed will remain with me forever, and I have to get away if I am to survive it. I secure the linen handles of my bag on my shoulder, clutch the cypher ring, and think of Anne in the hope I will time-slip to my intended destination. With my eyes clenched shut, it happens, and I'm falling into the darkness of oblivion.

When I open my eyes staring into dim light, I blink away a heavy feeling, like I've been unconscious for hours. Ah, I'm in a bed, and the canopy appears to be a familiar Tudor four-poster. It takes a moment to realise that I'm lying on a linen sheet and pillow, and I'm in a shift. Okay, I have no memory of undressing, so someone must have removed my kirtle, petticoats, and gown. I look to my left, through the slight gap in the drapes, and see my clothing laid out over a chair. A shiver runs through me, and I reach down and pull a coverlet up over my chest for extra warmth. Have I landed in winter, having jumped from spring? Am I in Anne's bedchamber? If so, I have no idea what palace or house I am in.

Movement outside the drapes catches my attention. I don't know who or what to expect. On seeing a shadow at the foot of the bed, I bolt upright.

"Who is it?"

More movement – I clutch the coverlet against my chest.

"It is I, George."

My heart leaps on hearing his voice. I can't believe it. Did I dream about his execution? No, it was real. I'll never forget the horror of it. My time-slip error, leading to me observing his death, is a clear warning not to meddle with the correct outcomes of history. But how did I end up there? I know I was a bit distracted before I jumped. Hmm, perhaps the ring was putting me to some kind of test? I shiver at the memory of what I witnessed – the scene like something from a film I shouldn't have watched.

A dim glow appears, then George walks around the side of the bed, pulls the drape open, and leans in, bringing the flickering candle to my face.

He frowns as he leans closer. I'm trembling, and I realise that I must be in shock. It hasn't been long since I saw his beautiful eyes close in his decapitated head. I flinch when he touches my hand, and I'm unable to speak.

"How do you fare, sweet Beth?" he asks, giving me a curious look.

Is he for real? If he only knew the half of it.

He half smiles. "You have been asleep for hours, and I have been vexed for you."

I still can't find the words to answer him. It's like I'm conversing with a ghost.

But he's not a ghost, because his touch on my hand is warm. He smells of woodsmoke, sage, and cinnamon – familiar fragrances I have missed. When he sits on the edge of the bed, I reach out to rest my hand on his shoulder, his flesh firm beneath. No, this isn't an apparition sat before me – he's really alive. I swallow back a lurking sob. How I'm not an emotional wreck, God knows. He can't know – ever. I can never divulge what I've witnessed. Because what I saw was real, and not a dream – an unforeseeable blip with the cypher ring. All I can hope is that it won't happen again. It is my lesson to stay focused on the time I need to go to, when I prepare to jump.

"I wanted to see that all is well with you." He smiles. "Will you not speak?"

"I-I am s-so sorry, George," I stammer.

"Anne found you collapsed in a passageway, and one of the king's physicians was sent for, to treat you."

It's then I notice a burning in my forearm. Indeed, my arm has been bandaged in linen.

"What did the physician do to me?"

"Bled you," he answers.

Before I have a chance to ask more questions, we look towards the sound of footsteps in the passageway outside. The latch on the door lifts, and someone enters the chamber. George gets to his feet, protecting the flickering flame with a cupped hand. He steps out beyond the drapes and walks around to the door to see who is there.

"Anne!" he says, and I lay back against the pillow, pretending to sleep.

"Brother, mine, what are you doing here?"

"I had come to see how Beth fares."

"Well, I had come to do exactly the same thing."

"She sleeps, Sister."

"Then, George, leave Beth to sleep."

Out of the corner of my eye, I see him wink at me as Anne escorts him from the bedchamber. While I'm devastated by what I witnessed at the Tower, my heart is eased knowing that I'm back with George and Anne, in safer times. I hope.

FEBRUARY 1532

The chapel bell tolling in the distance, resonates, and thunderous hooves clatter on cobbles as visitors come and go, in and out of the palace courtyard. With a good night's sleep behind me after time-slipping from witnessing George's execution, I look out of the casements and have to remind myself that this isn't a film set. I'm not part of a costume drama being shot for a TV streaming channel. I hope I will fall back into life at the Tudor Court like a duck to water, as if I've barely been away. While it's difficult, I try to put the horror of that misaligned time-slip at the Tower out of my mind and do my best to continue as if it never happened. In the future, I need to be specific when I think about my destination, and to whom I need to go to.

It goes without saying that Anne is pleased to have me back with her, but I have no idea why I've slipped back to this moment in time, to 1532. No matter, life will undoubtedly go on, with the days playing out in their colourful patterns, so long as I don't meddle.

"Why did you leave me – leave Court as you did?" she asks out of the blue, when I see her in her chambers. She screws her nose up under her furrowed brow. I've been waiting for the question, which she hasn't broached up to now. "You left no word. No letter. Nothing!"

A lady-in-waiting, who I have never seen before, enters the room, and Anne watches the young woman go to the fireplace and encourage the flames around the logs to dance as she pokes the burning wood.

"Mademoiselle Joscelyn come over here, would you?"

She walks over and stands still with her hands clasped in front of her. "What can I do for you, Lady Anne?"

"Firstly, I would like you to meet my good friend, Mistress Elizabeth Wickers." The young woman smiles at me as she curtsies. "This is Anne Joscelyn, a gentlewoman of my chamber – but we call her Nan."

"'Tis a pleasure to meet you, Mistress Wickers." She gives me a curious look, then turns to Anne. "Would you need me for anything else?"

"Yes, Nan, will you fetch us some wine, please?"

"Yes, Mistress Anne." She curtsies again and leaves the chamber, shutting the door behind her.

"Who else serves you here?" I ask, feeling somewhat out of the loop.

"Well, as I could not rely on your presence, I had to appoint other gentlewomen to serve me, in case you never came back." Her lip curls in a sarcastic smile. "The ladies, besides Mistress Joscelyn, are my mother, of course. Then there's Margaret Grey, who is Dowager Marchioness of Dorset. Next is Anne Stanley, the Dowager Countess of Derby." She rubs her brow, as if trying to grasp a name. "Then there is Mary Howard, and Jane Boleyn, both relations. Erm…Dorothy Stanley, Countess of Derby – another of my relations."

"Goodness, what a family affair!" I laugh, the heat from the flames in the grate warming our bones as we sit opposite each other.

"The list does not end there, Beth, for there are others. I am expected to do favours for my family, and even distant relations, now the king has set his heart on me. Sometimes, the politics of my privy chamber gives me a headache." She shakes her head and laughs.

Talking of the king, I wonder where things stand with him, and that history is exactly where it's meant to be. How much have I missed? Judging by the design of Anne's chambers, the list of gentlewomen serving her, and the sumptuous gown she's wearing, not to mention the jewels and diamonds around her neck, it is clear her star is still in ascent, and she continues to be a mistress, even if she hasn't yet reached the zenith of her power by being crowned Queen. I reflect on the intriguing flip, where I have been away in my time for four years, yet hardly any time seems to have passed in Tudorville.

"How is His Majesty?"

"Impatient to get the matter of our marriage decided. He is sometimes frustrated by our lack of support."

"It *may* happen, Anne – as sure as I sit before you." I follow this with a reassuring smile.

"You are sure you do not lie?" She peers at me, one brow down.

"Take what I say with a pinch of salt, my sweet friend, because this is all I will share with you."

"I suspect you have known who the husband of my future life is since the first day I laid eyes on you, but you were too selfish to share."

"Anne, that is unkind!" I realise I've raised my voice. "You know I cannot tell you of your future. Well, not every detail – you would never believe me if I did."

She scowls at me.

"It will not make any difference. Besides, we have had this conversation many times before." I can't allow her to see my exasperation. "Be content that I am here with you, in your company, yes?"

"I suppose so," she replies, pouting like a petulant child.

With that out of the way, my thoughts wander to George. I shift, resting my elbow on the arm of my chair.

"I apologise for my behaviour." I stare past her, thinking of the last time I was here, the night George and I – the time we made love. Christ, when I say it in my head, I can't believe it happened, but it did. In some ways, I'm sorry for it, and feel guilty for Jane Boleyn's sake, but not for me or George. He wanted me, just as much as I wanted him. And it was damn good, even if we were interrupted by Henry.

It's not long before Nan Joscelyn comes back into the chamber, carrying a tray with a flagon and two Venetian wine glasses. She sets it down on a nearby sideboard.

"What are you sorry for?" Anne asks me.

"The way I left Court." I keep my voice low. "I did not say goodbye."

Nan walks over to us. "Mistress Anne, would you like me to pour you some wine?"

"That would be lovely, thank you, Nan." She smiles.

Nan turns to me. "And you, Mistress Elizabeth, would you, too, like some wine?"

"Nan, please call me Beth." I nod towards the flagon. "I shall help myself should I want some, thank you." I'm surprised the Tudors haven't got a serious problem with alcohol – however, I know they drink so much of it because of the low water quality.

"Very well," she says, and walks to the sideboard and pours Anne a full glass of wine, which she brings over. "Will that be all, Mistress Anne?"

"Yes, that is all." Anne waves her away, and she leaves us alone again.

She eyes me above her glass. I can tell she's working through questions she wants to ask – to tease my secrets from me – but I must guard my thoughts against her beguiling ways. It's cold outside and I'm thankful the fire in the hearth is roaring. I stare into its flames, feeling Anne's gaze burning into me.

"What is it?" she asks.

"Nothing." I fold my hands in my lap.

"You lie," she says, putting her wine glass down on the table beside her. "But then a few lies have been told around here concerning you."

I frown at her, wondering what she means. She doesn't look happy, and I hope George hasn't told her about us. He wouldn't, would he? I fiddle with my girdle belt.

"Do you know how difficult it is for me when you go back to your time?" she whispers, leaning forward. "How hard it is to explain your sudden absence? And you do not leave us for just days or weeks. No, often years, though this time only eight months have passed. – you left in June 1531!"

"I apologise, but sometimes I can't control when or where the ring time-slips me back to." I shrug. "I finished the course I was attending, and achieved my qualifications. I've not wasted my time. I'm nearly twenty-five now."

"Twenty-five?" Her brows furrow and she folds her arms across her chest. "How can that be? When I first met you, you were near-abouts the same age as me – I am now thirty."

"Mistress, I cannot explain, except to say that when I am time-slipping, I barely age. Please don't, erm…do not ask me why, because Professional Marshall gave me no explanations for any side effects that might happen when using the ring.

"For all your experiences with me, it has not awarded you better manners. What woman leaves her best friend without a word?"

"Anne, forgive me," I plead. "Do you really need me now that you have the king's protection?" She scowls at me, as if doubting my genuine apology. "But there is a good reason for my absence. I promise."

"It has something to do with my brother George, does it not?" She keeps her arms folded across her chest and sits back, glaring at me with what looks like more than a hint of suspicion. Crap. This isn't good.

"Why would you think that?" I ask, hoping I don't blush.

"When I told him you had gone back to your family, he thought I meant your 'family' in our time. He was adamant about going to find you, to bring you back to Court."

I wince, thinking how my sudden absence would have hurt him.

"It took all my strength and cunning to persuade him not to go to Surrey."

"Did he tell you why he was so upset about my leaving?"

"No, he refused to, but by the way he was vexed over your absence, it seems he still has strong feelings for you."

I shift in my seat again and rub my forehead, wondering how much she knows about us getting physical.

"How is he?"

"With your absence, he resigned himself to his path in life – learning to be a diplomat." She gives me a gentle smile. "And…he resolved himself in getting a son and heir on Jane. He had hoped she'd be pregnant by now, at least." I can't help my eyes widening, but Anne just shrugs. "Do not look at me like that – he is doing what is expected of him. You remember, he now has a title as Viscount Rochford, and has been on diplomatic missions to France."

"I am glad he is happy." I try not to be selfish and think of my own feelings.

"I do not know how he will be now you are here, Beth – but, as I have said on many occasions before, please do not encourage him."

"Anne, I don't – I never have!" I must lie. It's not all my fault, though – George did seduce me, albeit over some time. He didn't need any encouragement, being a walking groin.

"Good. I shall say no more on the matter." She sips her wine. "I have other news."

"Excellent," I respond, unable to hold back a smile, knowing she always has a grasp on what's happening at court. "I need to catch up on all the gossip."

"Thomas More has resigned from the House of Commons."

"Really?" I pretend not to know a thing about it. "What reason does he give for his resignation?" I get up and walk over to the sideboard to pour myself a glass of wine.

"I am uncertain," she says. "However, I imagine it is his disapproval of Henry's recent disregard of the laws of the Church, and the king wanting an annulment from Katharine."

"Well, you know that Thomas More does not support the king's relationship with you, although he would never say so outright – and I suspect the king does not view this opinion in a kind light." I take a sip of my wine, hiding my grimace at its sharpness. It won't take long to get used to it again.

"I have a feeling that Henry's vengeance towards one of his longest and closest friends will be imminent." Anne watches me take my seat.

"Why do you say that?" I ask, as if I don't know. "Being the way he is, it doesn't surprised me that Henry appointed one of his oldest and most trusted friends to be his chancellor. After all, Thomas More has been a centrepiece of Court for many years, has he not?"

"Yes," she says, "Thomas has been in Henry's life since he was a boy, and the king has always respected him." She nods once. "Until now."

"Everyone knows More is a great intellectual, who follows in the footsteps of his father." I take a sip of wine. If I drink it slow, hopefully it won't go to my head. I still don't know how the Tudors can drink so much alcohol and not even seem tipsy. Perhaps it's been diluted? It's not as strong as some of the German wine Dad drinks with his dinner, which has to be a good thing. It tastes more like mead. The distillers must use honey instead of sugar to ferment it. I nurse the glass in my hand, wondering whether I need to remember every minute detail of my time here. Sometimes, I get lost in the moment, but I need to keep reminding myself of my mission. I need to figure out how I went wrong last time, rectify events by setting things in the right direction, then leave before the inevitable happens. And then there's George. I have a plan, which I need to stick to.

"Henry told me Thomas More would have preferred to enter the Church, becoming a monk, but he loves to be around people, and as the number of his offspring shows, he is a man who enjoys sex!" Anne lifts her eyebrows.

"Like any other man." I giggle, covering up my grimace, not wanting to have a mental picture of Sir Thomas More having sex.

"He may be a good family man, Beth, but the trouble with him is he cannot detach himself from what he thinks a good religious man should do." She says this matter of fact, then gets up and looks out through the window.

I put my half-empty glass on the table beside me and join her. As we look out into the gardens below, we see the king walking with More by his side. It's a blustery day, with the naked tree branches swaying in the wind as heavy clouds scoot across a white-grey sky. The feathers in Henry's bonnet mirror the dancing branches. His dogs run free, playing 'fetch' with a ball, and digging in the herbaceous borders. Henry calls them to heal but they are too intent on their play to obey.

"The king told me Thomas More fears he missed his calling, not going into the Church." Anne looks at me. "And I have heard rumours that he wears a hair shirt next to his skin, as does Queen Katharine."

"It's rituals of the old faith – did you expect anything less?"

"No, not particularly." She sighs, watching the men walking away.

"To me," I say, "Thomas More appears like a modern man, despite his Catholic faith, especially to those who do not know him. He is a humanist, after all." I look down at the small group below, and Anne and I laugh when Henry bellows at his dogs as they try to bury their ball.

"The other problem with More,"—Anne gesticulates with her upturned hands— "is he supported Wolsey until his fall." She frowns, leaning her hands on the windowsill. "Then he became ferociously hateful when the cardinal was arrested."

"Wolsey was always prone to winding, erm… I mean, vexing people." I need to remember to speak Tudor. "From history, I know that More is an excellent hater – he puts Christian charity aside, for his favourite pastime since becoming chancellor has been to persecute evangelicals of all persuasions, has it not?"

"He detests Lutherans," Anne says. "And likes to use the most abhorrent violence towards them."

I watch Thomas More walk with Henry, knowing that such violence will soon be coming for him. Even though I long to, I say nothing of this to Anne. It would give her comfort if she were to know that Thomas will no longer be as close to Henry, and therefore unable to influence him. However, she might not be pleased to learn that he will die a hideous death. Beneath her ambition, she has a gentle heart, and I'm certain she would not wish death on anyone. It's unfortunate that she will be blamed in the future, by the masses, for Thomas's horrific demise.

14TH APRIL 1532 – GREENWICH PALACE

I look back at Greenwich Palace, its turrets and towers looking glorious in the Easter sunshine. It's easy to understand why this place is Anne's favourite residence. We promenade through the knotted gardens, listening to the sparrows talking to one another as they pop in and out of the hedges and nests, feeding their young.

Even though the sun is out, it's not too warm, and I pull my cloak about me as the wind whips around us.

Anne seems impervious to it and smiles at me. "I have asked the king to appoint Thomas Cromwell as *Keeper of The Jewel House*, jointly with Sir John Williams, and, in his wisdom, Henry has agreed."

"Your family's patronage of Mister Cromwell is admirable." Our leather soles crunch the gravel of the pathway. I'm aware that Henry likes to surround himself with able, low-born courtiers. Hmm, perhaps that is why he likes me? Everything we are, everything we possess, will come from the king. With such power, he can make or break a man.

"Henry is so amenable," she says.

"Unless he is disagreed with, and then he becomes changeable."

"Not with me!' She laughs.

"He's never disagreeable with you, and he never will be." I lie, knowing well that she will not always be untouchable – as she is now – if history still plays out as it should, so long as I don't meddle. Mention of Cromwell makes me nervous because I'm aware that, even if Anne's execution is a direct result of the king's wishes, Cromwell will still have something to do with it.

As we take a turn about the manicured gardens, bordered with low, green, and white fencing, vines and high hedges, the wind chill hardens.

"I think it wise that we go inside, Beth, warm some mead, and heat ourselves by the fire less we catch a cold. What say you, friend?"

"It is a good idea," I reply, a shiver running up my spine, as if someone has just walked over my grave.

The atmosphere is strained as Anne, Henry, and I, along with a handful of courtiers sit or loiter in the king's privy chamber. Henry is spitting blood because of the recent sermon preached at the convent of Greenwich on Easter Sunday. Being present at the time, he was not best pleased.

"That preacher implied that the unbounded affection of princes and their false counsellors deprived them of the knowledge of the truth!" he bellows from his dais.

Anne sits next to him, her hand over his. I'm not sure her gesture is helping as his face has turned puce.

"The preacher's words did not please me!" he continues, his voice louder. "The provincial told me clearly that I – I was endangering my crown!"

Anne takes a sharp intake of breath, no doubt because she's all too aware of the great and little murmuring at Henry's alliance with her.

The king grunts to himself. "I caused my chaplain to contradict what the provincial had preached, daring to say that all the universities and doctors were in favour of the divorce!"

"Henry, my love – let men grumble." Anne taps the back of his hand. "Do not let them dampen your spirits, for I like you better when you are light of heart."

"A king cannot always be light of heart, my darling – it has no reflection on my love for you, but it is the crown I wear that bears the weight of the responsibilities of our realm."

Norfolk, like a twig about to break, bows, viewing his niece with his beady eyes. He approaches Henry. "Your Grace, you were good to arrest the warden who said your chaplain was wrong."

Henry thinks it will benefit his cause by allowing preaching in favour of the divorce, but his cause grows worse, for his people murmur. Anne still waits with patience on opinions by lawyers from across Europe in aiding a resolution to the king's Great Matter.

Life at court continues to roll along at its spectacular pace, despite the political setbacks for Anne and Henry. Tonight, to lighten the mood, he has arranged for his musicians to present new music at a court dance, just for everyone's enjoyment. Heady, primaeval theatre, designed for us all to play the pretence of courtly love – to feast – and to take our minds off the political problems that roll around the throne.

After Henry and Anne have dined in private, they come out to fanfares into the Great Hall at Greenwich, where the musicians in the gallery begin to play the opening introduction to a galliard. But Henry sends word to them to play the music to a recent composition of his own. Anne takes a sidestep and nods to him, making a low curtsy. He bows and offers his right hand to raise her from her deference, and as the music starts up, he puts his left hand upon his hip and leads her before all the gathered courtiers to a clearing made between the banqueting tables and the dais. Anne's movements are graceful and precise as she floats around the floor like a deity – even her hands are graceful. All eyes are upon them, and Henry knows it. He rises to their attention, giving an even more spectacular show.

"Come, come! I am not just here for your entertainment." He laughs, looking around at his admirers. "Mistress Boleyn and I have shown you how the dance is to be done, now you must all join in and try it."

With that, the floor becomes a bustling hive of activity. All ages, shapes, and sizes of people swirl around in a kaleidoscope of colour that engulfs the parquet flooring. The rustling of taffeta and silks can be heard with every swish and swirl as the sweet music resonates in the ears of everyone assembled.

I'm stood on the periphery of the dance, somewhat nervous about who might ask me to partner them. Anne has taught me well to dance but there is a big difference in practising within the privacy of her chambers and displaying my incompetent technique in front of a hall full of spectators. I flinch at the caress of warm breath on the back of my neck, just below where my gable hood rests. When I turn my head, my heart leaps on seeing George, the candlelight catching the sparkle in his eyes. He looks happy, healthy, and handsome, yet a little older, probably about twenty-seven. I banish a flashback of his eyes before they closed for the final time at his execution and reflect instead on how he has avoided me these last couple of months, both in Anne's chambers and in public. Until now. Hmm, I wonder what has changed.

"Is this a ghost before me, or is she flesh and blood?" He laughs. "May I have the pleasure?" This comes with a wry smile.

"I think you have already had that long before now, sir – after a dance such as this." I lean closer. "You know I am not the most proficient dancer."

"Your lack of experience in the dance is made up for by the intimate delights we have savoured when we have been alone."

Heat flushes my cheeks as he takes me by the hand and leads me to the floor. Does he still have feelings for me? I hope I haven't hurt him too much, disappearing for eight months, yet in my time it was over four years. I sense all eyes upon us as we start to dance. Sir Thomas is watching, his gaze showing some nervousness. I hope he approves of me dancing with his son. Thomas Howard, the duke of Norfolk, doesn't seem to approve, but he doesn't like anyone, unless him knowing them helps his advancement. He approves of Anne's relationship with the king – I know this. I heard he encouraged his niece as her relationship with Henry blossomed. Indeed, he has never been politically sensitive, but is by no means stupid. I remember how allegiances shifted towards the Howards and the Boleyns, as Anne's star began to rise, and how Howard thought Wolsey was an upstart, too close to the king, and was glad when the cardinal fell from favour.

As I move about the floor, I feel his gaze following me. George is proud as a peacock, showing me off at every advantage. I glance at Norfolk, his attention making me feel uncomfortable. The times our paths have crossed, I have always felt uneasy. He's not a pleasant man, and I understand why Anne dislikes him, even though he is her kin. However, he is on her side, because what helps Anne, helps the Howards. The man is self-serving and knows the best way to get what he wants, which is to do what the king desires. Sadly, for Anne, I know Norfolk's association with her and the Boleyns is a temporary one, rather than a united, permanent, political alliance.

Sir Thomas looks as uncomfortable as I feel, as he stands next to Norfolk, his brother-in-law. The old tensions between these conflicting personalities, which created differing agendas, are still there. I follow where Sir Thomas is looking – towards his daughter as she dances with Henry. His face is pale, his eyes tired. Maybe he isn't as accepting of his daughter's rise at court as I thought he might be? He looks uneasy. The tables appear to be turning as Anne moves closer to wearing a crown. Now, she seems to be the defacto head of the Boleyn family. I have no doubt her father is aware that the fate of the Boleyns lies in her hands.

He looks like he is suffering sleepless nights. Does he feel uncertain about the future? Perhaps he's wondering what will happen with Anne. Will she be Queen of England or discarded as a mistress? Now that he has lost his agency with her, maybe he's worried about his own position? Perhaps I should try to speak with him alone when I can – to reassure him, but not give too much away. I almost trip over my toes as my thoughts tumble through my head. I need to focus on George.

"Mistress Wickers, how do you fare?" he asks, holding my hand tighter.

"I am such a poor dancer," I reply, glancing about at the people staring at us from the edges of the hall. Many a disdainful look tells me the attention given to us is not all friendly.

"You do well. You underestimate your abilities."

The Boleyn's ally is Thomas Cromwell. He stands at the edge of the dais, watching all that goes on tonight. His rise at court is a shadowy one. He is an MP for Taunton and has been for some time. He's also a member of the Privy Council, and since the fall of Wolsey, he has risen in the king's estimation. The Boleyns know a potential ally when they see one. Anne has told me she thinks he is the answer to her prayers. From her point of view, Cromwell is discreet and full of ideas, dedicated to reform, and getting Henry an annulment so she can marry him. And because Cromwell is neither noble nor gentry, she considers him no threat. This is a man she thinks her family and the king can do business with.

As the dance comes to an end and George leads me off the floor, I'm aware of Cromwell watching Anne, then George and me. I shudder inside, knowing he could be the man behind the eventual fall of the Boleyns. George's arm about my waist snaps me out of my thoughts.

"Are you well, Beth?" He looks down at me, concern in his eyes. "You look like you've seen a ghost."

"I have been deep in thought, is all." I try to look away.

"What is it?" he asks, edging closer.

"Do you see all eyes on your sister, and on us?" I give him an expectant look. "Your father looks ill. I am worried about him. Are you not?"

"Father fares well – you worry too much." He chuckles.

"George, your family have scandalised most of Catholic Europe by by-passing the pope to help Henry become Head of the Church in England." He frowns at me, his surprise at my outburst clear. "It should not surprise you how half of the court despise us? To some, you are dangerous iconoclasts, smashing a thousand years of religious tradition to get what you all want."

"What?" He looks shocked, and leans down to me. "I thought you supported Anne, and us?"

"I do!" I look around me, hoping no one has overheard our conversation. "But I worry about the stress this has on your parents – I care about you all." I grab his arm. "I've watched your father tonight. He doesn't look happy. Without Wolsey as an ally, your family have struggled to help bring about an end to the king's Matter, and I can see it is putting a great strain on you all."

"Beth, you worry your pretty head too much." He releases his grip my waist and grabs two goblets of ale as an usher passes by. I accept one from him and he takes a gulp of the golden brew from his.

"Your father has become more assertive of late, knowing he may become the father-in-law of the King of England. Do you not think he must be frustrated that concluding Anne's marriage to the king, and securing her place on the throne, seems a long way off for him?"

"He has assured me he will support Anne and ensure that she takes her rightful place by the king's side." He leans closer. "I heard it from his own lips." His voice is barely audible beneath the music from the minstrels' gallery.

"Your father expects everyone else at Court, besides his immediate family, to support him, but there are still so many people here who are on the side of Katharine, the queen. George, I think he is painfully aware that you and Anne are beginning to make enemies here, and he doesn't like it. He worries. I haven't told your sister but much of the vitriol is aimed at her."

"Anne?" His eyes widen, as if he is wholly innocent of the goings-on at court.

"George, you are no fool – there's always mutterings about anyone who holds the power here. You cannot say you haven't heard what 'they' say about Anne?"

"Of course, I have, but every time I mention it to her, she dismisses it and tells me not to talk of such dangerous things. What am I to do?"

"Protect her. Protect yourself! It will only get worse."

He straightens, his frown showing his puzzlement. I've said too much. I know it. Me and my big mouth. Hmm, methinks it's best to retire for the night. I turn to walk away.

"Mistress Wickers! Beth?" It's the first time I've heard real uneasiness in his voice.

I turn around. "Do not follow me, George. You know what happened last time we left a dance together."

As he stares at me like a wounded stag, I know my words have pierced his heart. I turn away and depart, giving him no opportunity to follow me.

SUNDAY 1ST SEPTEMBER 1532 – WINDSOR CASTLE

"Madam, the time has come for you to get up."

I open my eyes to see Nan Joscelyn standing over us. Anne hasn't budged beside me.

"Wake the Lady Anne – her brother is here."

My tummy flutters to life and I nudge Anne's shoulder twice, lifting her from her slumber. She blinks at me, and I'm sure she sees my excitement in my eyes. The argument George and I had months before has all been forgotten, and my heart leaps at the prospect of seeing him this morning. I have not been in his company, properly, for such a time. That's the trouble with being in love with a married man. Nan glances over her shoulder, and I follow her gaze, my skin prickling at the sight of George standing out in the antechamber.

Anne rouses and smiles at me, no doubt recalling what this day is about to bring. She lifts herself onto one elbow, her tousled mane of hair hanging about her shoulders.

"Are you not dressed yet, Sister?" George calls, as excited as we are. He peers around the chamber door. "I thought you would have been up and ready hours ago, seeing as this is your special day." He smiles as he teases her, then glances at me, knowing full well it will make me blush.

Anne groans, rubbing her eyes. "I have hardly slept at all, and now you all come here to preen me!"

"That is the job of your ladies, Sister. 'Tis not mine." He chuckles. "I am here to make sure you are not late – Father and the king are impatient to see you."

Everyone seems happy today, but Anne flicks her hand at Nan, bidding her get on with the task of picking up the clothes from the chair. I watch her, as, despite Anne's silent reprimand, from time to time she casts an eye in George's direction. Understandable – he is easy on the eye. However, today, his full attention is on his sister.

"Anne, have you seen my ring?" I ask, realising the cypher ring is not on my nightstand where I left it last night. Panic rises in the pit of my stomach – if I don't find it, I may never be able to get back home.

"Which ring?" she asks.

"The ring I always wear!"

"Oh, *that* ring." She grimaces as she looks around.

"Are you sure you do not, have it?" I ask.

"I am sure."

"It will turn up," George butts in. "It has probably dropped off the nightstand and rolled under the bed." He smiles. "Besides, my Lady, a woman of your beauty does not need such adornments."

I scan the floor near the nightstand. However, there's no time to look for it now. We have too much to do getting Anne prepared, dressed, and on time for her ceremony today.

"George, flattery will get you everywhere," I say, wagging a finger at him. While I jest, I'm hoping to God he's right and the ring turns up.

I can't worry about its whereabouts at this minute because, today, in this historical palace, Anne is being created the first Marchioness of Pembroke and is to become the first female English commoner ennobled in her own right, without inheritance or marriage, which will make her the most prestigious non-royal woman in the land. Everyone here seems to be petitioning for her favour, yet George and I are in her inner circle, already benefiting from her patronage, and that of her fiancé, with titles, lands, and monies bestowed mostly on George. I insist that I am not interested in titles, so long as I have gowns befitting a lady who serves the Lady of Pembroke.

The purpose of the granting of the title is to *fit* Anne for the European stage, in readiness for the couple's upcoming meeting with King François I of France. Despite years of trying, Henry's Great Matter has not been resolved, and his marriage to Katharine of Aragon has still not been annulled, so Anne is still Henry's queen-in-waiting. In the light of his predicament, he believes it important that she be given a status befitting England's future queen and be recognised as his consort.

In preparation for the ceremony, Elizabeth Boleyn and Mary Carey arrived at Windsor yesterday. Anne's apartments are now filled with family and the women who make up her growing household; everyone seems to be in such exceedingly high spirits. George is ushered out of the bedchamber by Nan. A table has been set in the adjoining room with ale, fruits, cheeses, and bread, which I'm sure George will pick at.

Anne shrugs her dressing gown over her shoulders and follows me into the wardrobe where her ceremonial gown and cloak hang in anticipation of its human mannequin. I take in a quick breath upon seeing the ensemble in the clear light of morning, and Anne is silent as she takes in the splendour of the garments the royal wardrobe masters have prepared for her. They are exquisite to the eye, as both the gown and cloak are made of sumptuous, deep-pile velvet in a crimson hue, which gives off the most opulent of sheens. The kirtle is made from a cloth of deep gold, accompanied by red petticoats, and the bodice is in matching crimson velvet encrusted with gold-work and ribbon embroidery. Its neckline is trimmed with a delicate array of rubies, pearls, and diamonds, and the sleeves are cut in a slender fashion, straight and long, ending in a point set with extra gold-work embroidery. The surcoat is crimson velvet lined in a deep crimson satin, which has a long flowing train bordered by the most sumptuous pure-white soft ermine.

Anne brushes her hand over the ermine and sighs. "What if the ceremony does not go well?" she whispers. "What if I say the wrong thing, with everyone watching?"

"If the king thought you unworthy, he would never have imagined such a day for you. He certainly would not be taking you to France as his potential bride. Think about it."

"But what if I fail in my duty to perform this task today, what then?" Her voice is shaky. I wonder if she has imposter syndrome. She can't feel like that, surely. Anne is too confident to feel inadequate.

"Nothing will go wrong, Anne," I say, resting my hand on her shoulder. "This is your destiny."

"You knew this would happen, did you not, and on this very date? Remember the engraving inside you cypher ring of fifteen thirty-two? It signifies me becoming Lady Pembroke, does it not?"

"Perhaps." I lie, knowing well what the ring must signify. I don't know why I didn't put two and two together before. Maybe I did, subconsciously. Who knows?

"Perhaps?" She looks at me under a lowered brow. "You knew, you just chose not to tell me."

"Anne, you would never have believed me, even if I had told you."

"No. Not in the beginning."

"See! So why accuse me of not supporting you?" I smile. "I have helped encourage you to get to this point in your life where you needed to be. Yes?"

"Yes."

"Then be grateful and be glad. Do not press me for answers about—" We are interrupted by Nan Joscelyn and Nan Gainsford coming in and busying around Anne, trying to hurry her along in readying herself for her special day.

As her ladies prepare her ensemble, I'm stunned at the quality of each garment. "You will look magnificent in this, Lady Anne!" Nan Joselyn exclaims.

"Regal!" Nan Cobham declares.

Looking at each garment, it's obvious they must have cost hundreds of pounds – the equivalent to thousands of pounds in 21st-century money. I can scarcely believe such beautiful and intricate handmade apparel exists. If I only had my mobile phone on me to take photographs, but I hid it away with my personal belongings and some of my modern toiletries when I returned to Tudor England. The bag is stuffed in the bottom of the trunk Anne gifted me when we first arrived at court. Being in possession of the only key means I'm confident it is safe from prying eyes.

As I open the bedchamber door, I see that George still lingers outside, while the other gentlewomen of the chamber prepare a bath for Anne. It isn't long before other servants besides me are scolding him for hanging around when his sister is being groomed for the day's ceremony.

"Is there anything else to eat?" he asks, grinning at me as I look through the gap in the open door.

I'm having none of it, closing Anne's bedchamber door behind me and shepherding him towards the outer doors. "I will summon you when your sister is ready."

"Promises, promises," he says, chuckling. He glances over my shoulder, then places a protracted kiss on my cheek, inhaling full and deep, as if I am a rose in shallow bloom. "Mmm, you smell heavenly." He bows, and I can't hold back a smile as I watch him leave.

"Lady Anne, your brother is fearless and incorrigible!" I protest as I walk back into her bedchamber, wishing George was not such a magnet to my vulnerabilities.

She laughs at me. "Well, Beth, I have told you before not to encourage him."

"Anne, you know he came to see if *you* were ready." I smile to myself as I prepare the water in her bath, ensuring it is piping hot and scented with rosewater. She throws her dressing gown onto her bed, and her shift falls at her feet before she steps into the wooden tub, sinking into its inviting depths, letting the water wash over her body to rinse away the dreams that consumed her through the night.

The rough soap is rubbed over her olive skin, cleansing her, and preparing her for the prestigious events of the day ahead. When she gets out, Nan Gainsford brushes and dries her hair in front of the hearth fire, applying a touch of lemon oil to enhance its shine. I grab some of my modern makeup from my chamber and assist her with a little blusher without anyone knowing, before pressing the mascara wand into her hand so she can apply it without her gentlewomen seeing. But Nan spots her brushing the tips of her lashes with the black magic.

"What is that, Mistress Anne?" she asks, puzzled by the strange-looking device.

I warn Anne not to apply too much, as her face should be radiant on a day like today and she is beautiful enough without it. She shrugs Nan off.

"It is a new fashion for the eyes that my father brought back for me from France." I snatch the mascara wand from her as soon as she's finished with it, so Nan doesn't get the opportunity to inspect it.

Once Anne has been warmed by the roaring fire, Nan retrieves a freshly pressed and embroidered shift from the clothes' chest, fits it over her, then laces her into the red silk petticoat. Anne stands there in her bare feet as I secure and fasten her into the boned kirtle, which shimmers golden in the firelight. The voluptuous, crimson skirts are fastened against her waist, and the matching bodice is tight around her breasts, which swell against their firm binding - the pearls and rubies on the neckline glistening as the beautiful sleeves are attached and laced up, finishing off the whole ensemble and making Anne look every bit the titled Lady she is to become.

We leave her hair brushed loose and it shimmers as it flows to her waist. I pass the casket to Nan, and she fits the emerald ring Henry gave Anne for her betrothal, then attaches ropes of gold chains and diamonds about her slender neck. The jewels were Queen Katharine's but now her diamond rings decorate the first and last fingers of Anne's left hand. She looks resplendent as the flickering firelight picks up the carats of the diamonds.

"Lady Anne, the king will be astonished by your great beauty and magnificence today!" Nan declares.

"Oh yes, Mistress, you look striking!" another gentlewoman chimes in.

Anne says nothing, standing before us with an air of dignity, as if she is already a queen. Gainsford kneels as Anne pokes one foot then the other out from the hem of her dress, sliding each one in turn into the crimson silk slippers that match her incredible gown. She shuffles on the spot, spreading out her skirts and train before straightening her bodice so she feels as comfortable as she can in such heavy fabrics.

We accompany her through to her privy chamber, where Lady Elizabeth Boleyn and Viscount Rochford are waiting with other personages of the court in their finery. George looks magnificent, clad in his striking crimson-red coat. I notice little else, wanting to forget myself – that he is married – and rush forward to throw my arms about his neck and kiss him with a burning passion. Indeed, I want to tell him how much I love him. But I can't – I must remember that I cannot meddle with the history or the lives of him or anyone present. I must only observe, keeping to my specific mission of ensuring that the Ives' book cover, and England's history, returns to its proper form.

As we stand in this large, spacious room that connects the audience chamber with the privy chamber, we are surrounded by people of great rank and notoriety. As I watch the event of the year start to unfold, all I have on my mind is not knowing where the cypher ring has got to. Without it, there's no way I can get back to my time, unless I travel all the way back to Hever to try the portal, and even then, there's no guarantee it will 'work' for me. I have to try to focus on the here and now, and on Anne's future, not mine.

I take a deep breath, then release a long quiet exhalation. Time to be more Tudor. The chamber is flooded with light from a large oriel window adjacent to where I stand with George, and the natural light illuminates his features, and his beautiful, richly decorated clothing. He looks even more spectacular than usual if that's possible. In fact, everyone present is well turned out, resplendent in their finery.

Further up from where I stand, along the same wall, are two mullioned windows overlooking the small courtyard. I'm in awe of my surroundings and can't believe I'm standing in Windsor Castle, at this time in history. I know these chambers will be elaborately refurbished in the future from their sixteenth-century state, and my heart breaks for its lost history, and the internal decorations that will be irrevocably changed in my modern time – especially after the royal family, and particularly Queen Elizabeth II, had to orchestrate the rebuilding of sections of it, due to that 'annus horribilus' of a fire in 1992.

I can't fail to notice how this particular room is so lavish. Partly covered with wainscoted oak panelling and set about with decorative pillars, which are worked in the grotesque style and painted in rich reds, blues, and gold leaf. All the colours blend together like a rainbow, with the apparel of those gathered. An elaborate frieze depicting religious scenes is set around the upper third of the room, similar to Wolsey's closet that still exists in modern day Hampton Court Palace.

Silhouettes of the gathered throng blend in with the fine tapestries and oil paintings that hang on the walls, their depictions of significant and dynastic importance. A large stone fireplace dominates the left side of the chamber and remains unlit in the warmth of this Indian summer. Yet I must confess that, despite the dazzling grandeur, I am startled by the number of people gathered. When we moved to Durham house, Anne was permitted four ladies-in-waiting, besides me, arranged according to her rank and status. These ladies are Margery Wyatt, now Lady Margaret Lee, Nan Gainsford, Mary Norris, and Joan Champernowe. A maid, and an equerry – George Zouche – and a single page of the chamber had all been appointed by Henry to wait upon Anne. The rest of the time she spends in the quiet company of her mother, who acts as a chaperone.

As I survey the room, I realise just how high Anne has been elevated at court and the exalted position she has come to occupy as consort-in-waiting. Now, attending her are eight ladies of noble birth, all of whom I recognise from my time at court. George leans into me, whispering details about this one and that one. He nods in the direction of the diminutive thirty-six-year-old Eleanor Paston, explaining that she is the Countess of Rutland, the daughter of his cousin, Bridget Haydon. Near her is the 'kindly' twenty-three-year-old Dorothy Stanley, Countess of Derby. He explains that she is one of the youngest of seventeen children born to the late Duke of Norfolk and the much younger half-sister of his mother, and because of the age gap, he tells me that his mother enjoys acting as a surrogate mother towards Dorothy, which is touching to know.

Far less pleasant, he suggests, is the sight of the rather dour and formidable Elizabeth Wood – Lady Boleyn – his aunt, who, despite the family connection, makes it clear through her manner that "she disapproves of his 'chit' of a sister". Her imperious and brittle manner is difficult to witness, but Anne is tactful, and we watch together, as she tries to show no hurt by the woman's disdain and rejection. In the future, I know this aunt will be one of the five women to attend Anne when she is first committed to the Tower in 1536, to spy on her and report her every word to Master Kingston.

"There is no love lost between these two," George whispers.

"It is not surprising," I whisper back, "that the sight of your aunt makes Anne recoil in distaste. From her manner, it is clear that she is not a supporter of your sister, even though she is family."

"Pfff!" George scowls. "My aunt can go hang, for all I care." It seems there is also no love lost between George and his aunt.

"George!"

To my left is the sour-faced Jane Boleyn, and, sadly, George and I are well aware of her foibles. She watches the sweet and easy affection between me and her husband with pursed lips. Of course, she holds me in disdain, having witnessed my closeness to him. A woman to keep my eye on.

Near the door to the distant presence-chamber, two ladies in discourse stare at Anne with turned heads. One is Honor Grenville – Lady Lisle – the middle-aged wife of Arthur Plantagenet, uncle to the king. Although ambitious, I find her to be a cheery and pragmatic character, who is ever wanting to ingratiate herself into Anne's good graces. The other is a dear friend of Anne's, Bridget Wiltshire – Lady Tyrwhitt – who I first met at Allington Castle on that idyllic day when Anne, Thomas Wyatt, George, and me, whiled away an hour or so chatting beneath that large tree in the golden sunshine. A happy memory. It was a glorious day until that evening, when Thomas stole that trinket from the pocket of Anne's gown, which, some weeks later, caused Henry's serious altercation with George about Anne's honour.

Bridget is close to Anne's age, and, according to George, grew up in Stone Place in Kent, where his family and the Wiltshires were neighbours, sharing common fealty. Of course, I have met her on occasions when she visited Hever.

"Bridget has long been a friend to Anne," George whispers. "Their paths have crossed often at Court, for she has long been in the service of Katharine, and has passed many happy hours with Anne."

"Yes, George," I reply. "Often in a pleasurable dalliance with the gentlemen of the king's chamber when they used to stop by to pay their respects to the queen. You remember, for you were a witness to the goings on."

"Indeed, I was." He chuckles. "This was before Henry removed Anne from waiting upon his wife, and although Bridget's friendship with my sister seems to remain firm, with Anne's elevation, it means they see each other less often."

How am I going to keep up with all these changing faces and rank? I don't know how the king does it, but he seems to remember everyone's title and name, as if he is a walking encyclopaedia.

"Today is to be an intimate affair," he says, "with my sister surrounded only by members of her extended family and close Kentish friends."

I see Margaret Lee giving Anne a supportive smile.

George approaches Anne with me. "God bless you, Sister mine," he whispers, leaving a tender kiss on her forehead. "I am so proud of you, do you know that? I swear, it makes me want to weep." He looks like he has tears in his eyes.

"You do look regal today, Anne," I say, "and you carry yourself with dignity."

"I congratulate you, my sister. Father is no opportunist, but he always said you were a golden key that might open any door."

Anne looks a little nervous as she smiles at me, then reaches out and grasps George's hand. "Thank you, Brother. Father is glad he did not engineer this day. He never wanted it, but I wish him to be blessed because of it. And, George, I cannot imagine this day without you."

With that, we all step into the procession formation as the dukes of Suffolk and Norfolk, attired in doublets of Tudor green velvet, lead the way. Following them is Anne's father, now the earl of Wiltshire, accompanied by the French ambassador Gilles de la Pommeraie. A trail of earls and viscounts follow them, in order of rank.

Anne's garter bears her patent of creation as Marquess of Pembroke. Lady Mary Howard carries the coronet of Anne's marquisate on a crimson velvet cushion. Following Lady Mary are the countesses of Derby and Rutland, who, between them, carry the twelve-foot-long crimson velvet mantle trimmed with ermine that will be placed around Anne's narrow shoulders.

In her moment of public glory, she looks exhilarated. I'm relieved as the procession leaves her privy chambers, with the spectacle helping me forget about the lost cypher ring, albeit temporarily.

With nervous excitement, and trying to appear regal, I join this magnificent party of men and women, trying to gracefully step in time with everyone, one step after another, as we make our way along the queen's presence chamber, past lower members of the court who will not be permitted into the king's presence chamber to witness the ceremony. They doff their caps, curtsy, and bow at the passing group, as protocol dictates. The Tudor court is a complex web. Anne must feel such an asset to her family now that her star is close to reaching its pinnacle of power.

We all turn left when our turn comes, walking halfway along the even grander Watching Chamber, before following Anne, like marching mice following the pied piper. Next, Anne and her party turn in through a doorway on the right, which leads along a light and airy gallery. I cannot believe I am about to watch Anne Boleyn become the premier lady in the land. As we approach the heavy, gilded oak doors that lead into the king's presence chamber, the excited buzz of an expectant court filters out to us. She turns her head to find me, offering me a huge smile of excited expectation, even though she knows she enters the lion's den, a pit containing some of her most implacable enemies, all of whom hold sufficient status to be gathered for the ceremony within. Even for them, this is history in the making.

While I know what is to transpire today, I cannot help but observe this woman with awe. Courtiers are all too aware that this is an auspicious day for Anne. Even her enemies cannot fail to be impressed by how she has caused the country to be turned upside down; it is only the Catholic supporters amongst them who are against such an elevation in her power and prestige, as is the event they are about to witness today.

We wait with bated breath to be admitted into the chamber – to be received by its central axis, the king himself, around whom all power-hungry courtiers pivot. Those gathered, watching, and waiting, jostle for position. I stand amongst them as Anne awaits her announcement, and I feel so proud of her – a self-made woman before the word feminism is known. No man has brought about this astonishing elevation, not even her father. At best, Thomas introduced her to court but did not support her relationship with Henry – he never has. It is Anne alone who is responsible for where she now stands, as she is far too astute to be a pawn in the political games and aspirations of anyone, including her uncle.

I am all too aware, from our conversation years ago, about her writings in her book of hours, that she has always had a strong sense of destiny and faith, which she puts down to God's benevolence. She is shrewd, intelligent, as well as ambitious – I will give her that. Thomas Boleyn is not the cause of her rise or her later fall, and any suggestion otherwise discredits Anne's dedication to her own destiny.

The Garter Throne room, as Henry's presence chamber is known, is packed to capacity – thronged with eager faces – all striving to catch a first glimpse of Anne. Onlookers gasp when she enters the room. She is a bringer of light to a once-grey world, and I know she feels as if she has been appointed by God himself to establish the true gospel of faith, to reform Catholic belief.

She will now preside over her own shadow court, creating a second household, alongside that of the king. The remnants of Queen Katharine's household only exist because of the stragglers from her court, who follow Anne and her entourage with reluctance and clear begrudgery. All the invited English nobility are elegantly dressed in their ceremonial clothes, some entering the spirit of the event, if only for the king's sake.

I spot the only courtier who matters to me, George. He now stands by the dais, at the front of those gathered. His face lights up with a radiant smile as he looks in my direction, then his gaze falls upon his sister. He is so handsome in this moment of quiet contemplation. Everyone now worships at the altar of Anne Boleyn as she stands before us in solemn dignity. She is the golden goose, and the entire court knows it, even if some of them don't like it.

Thomas Wriothesley reaches the foot of the dais and bows low to the king. He is flanked on either side by the dukes of Norfolk and Suffolk. Norfolk appears skeletal, gaunt, and hawkish. However, even he has broken his stony expression to show a smile, which is a miracle, as he is a grumpy old git who usually has no time for anyone unless they are doing him a service. Charles Brandon has gained a little weight since I last saw him, along with a few extra grey hairs in his beard, and I must admit it makes him look rather distinguished. But he's still not my type, and he's never made a play for me – thank the Lord!

Thomas Boleyn stands next to George as they take their places at the fore of the leading noblemen to the left of the Canopy of Estate, next to Giles de la Pommeraye, the French ambassador.

A clarion sounds as Wriothesley steps forward to announce the arrival of Lady Anne Rochford to the king and all those gathered. The procession glides into his presence with great dignity, nobility, and grace. Having bowed to the king, Wriothesley steps aside, leaving Anne standing in front of Henry. Since I entered the presence chamber, he hasn't taken his eyes off Anne, and she has met his intense gaze. In carrying out this ceremonial elevation of his mistress, he is confirming his obsession with her. I do wonder, though, if she is in love with him as much as he is with her. However, throughout the ceremony, her attention remains locked in the delicious intimacy of his gaze, her expression so full of hope and expectation. His generosity shines upon her, like the shafts of sunlight that spiral through the stained-glass windows in a kaleidoscope of colours. His magnanimity knows no bounds. The king's favour can be capricious, yet here Anne stands beneath its full radiance. His support, and eventual lack of it, will shape a destiny that will come under the dark shadow of his wrath, and of the Tower, unless I were to take a hand in it and steer her on a different course. But, I know all too well that I can't do such a thing, can I? It's bad enough that I have to tweak how things are, to correct the Ives' book cover. According to Professor Marshall, it's all about making sure that Anne's life story plays out exactly as history recorded it. It's that simple. Simple, he said! Yeah, right. I sigh to myself, wondering if he has a true understanding of what it means to be living out this experience.

Anne kneels upon a crimson velvet cushion, embroidered, and fringed with gold. She raises her head as Henry towers above her in his incredible majesty. With his throne behind him, he is framed by a red velvet canopy, one of the finest, richly embroidered pieces of fabric I have seen in the castle. It has been worked intricately with gold thread, wrought into a pattern of twisting vine leaves, and edged with a geometric border design. Just above the throne is the royal coat of arms: a red Welsh dragon and white greyhound supporting the royal shield of England, itself quartered into a pattern of a golden fleur-de-lis and English lions. The shield is surmounted by a gold crown with the letters HR VIII worked in gold thread.

I watch Anne in awe as her patent is presented – read by the Bishop of Winchester. Bishop Gardiner is a man who sets his sails according to the direction in which the wind is blowing, as he has already shown himself to be a turncoat in the matter of Henry's divorce, first supporting him and then swinging behind Katharine, only to realise that he looked to be on the losing side. Luckily for him, Stephen Gardiner managed to salvage some shards of trust from the wreckage of his disloyalty, and Henry took him back into royal service, but he will never trust his servant in the same way again. Besides, the bishop has a true devotion to the Roman Catholic faith, and on that account alone, he will never be a real friend to the new marquess.

In a deep, clear voice, he begins to read aloud the patents that are being conferred upon Anne and her offspring, in her own right. I breathe a sigh of relief as she is awarded lands of the Lady Anne Marchioness in Wales, the house at Hunsdon, and Estwyke in Hertfordshire, manors of Stansted, and trumpets fanfare as the king gives her two patents: one of her creation as Lady Pembroke, the other of one thousand pounds a year.

The event appears to be going well, but the cypher ring is never far from my thoughts. Where the hell has it got to? What am I to do if I can't recover it? And what if I don't get to travel back to Hever to try the portal? What then? My tummy flutters as a thought crosses my mind: what if someone has stolen it? But who would be so bad as to do such a thing? A flurry of faces whizz through my mind, almost throwing me off balance, and I have to stop myself turning to scrutinize those around me. It could be plausible. After all, Anne's letters from Henry were stolen. History told the world where they'd end up – in the Vatican Library, in Rome, of all places. Personally, I think they should all be returned to 21st-century England, because they are important historical artefacts that belong to the British. But that's an argument for another day. I need to recover the professor's lost cypher ring; I'm responsible for it while it's in my custody. But who could have taken it? I go through a short list of potential suspects in my head, then shake it all out as I drag myself back to the current proceedings. Whatever about the ring, I don't want to miss witnessing every detail of this auspicious occasion.

A deep silence fills the chamber as Henry steps down from his dais. He puts Anne's mantle around her shoulders before nodding to Lady Mary, who passes him a gold cypher ring, which looks the same as mine. My face goes cold, and Anne looks surprised as Henry slides it onto her middle finger. I shudder inside. Why has he given her my cypher ring? How did…? I join the dots, remembering the engraving on the inside of the band; 1532. How did I not realise the ring's significance before this moment? Call myself a historian? Get a grip! Seeing Henry give Anne this ring, and marrying the crown and cypher on the ring to this event, is the exact reason why I time-slipped back to this year.

I stare at the king. How on earth did he get the ring? No wonder I couldn't find it. Goosebumps erupt across my shoulders as I consider the consequences of Henry VIII discovering the ring's secrets. Good God, what disasters might have been created in English history had he time-slipped elsewhere? My mind boggles at the idea but I can't help smirking, and I enjoy an inner chuckle thinking about the possibility of King Henry time-slipping to a 21st-century London, going to Buckingham Palace, and being caught out by security as he sits on our current monarch's throne.

It's not easy to hold back a smile. He's no Michael Fagan, who, in the summer of 1982, managed to break into Buckingham Palace more than once, and even ended up in the queen's bedroom, sat on her bed, and spoke to her before being taken into custody. Hmm, what would happen to someone who might break into Henry's bedroom now, to sit on *his* bed and talk to him? I suspect, much the same as happened to the Lord High Admiral, Thomas Seymour, in January 1549, not many years from now, when he broke into Henry's son, Prince Edward's bedchamber when he was king, and was executed for it. At least Michael Fagan never suffered that fate!

Whatever about how the ring got to be on Anne's finger, I'm relieved I now know where it is. She understands its significance and will never let anything happen to it. I'm sure she'll return it to me. I just need to find the right time to talk with her about it.

Lady Mary then passes the king a gold coronet, and with great reverence, he sets it on Anne's head. In full view of the entire gathering, he leans forward and places a gentle kiss on her lips, sealing once and for all her exalted position at court.

I can imagine the weighty presumption of the king that now rests on her shoulders, a requirement that she must hope to accomplish. He is fiercely proud of his fiancée – he told me so in Calais. As he stands before her, his cause, of receiving a long-awaited male heir from her, must feel like an unspoken mounting debt around her neck. I shudder, because I know what's coming in the future, if I don't interfere, and I've already seen what will happen to my beautiful George.

The king's unconditional love is now expected to be reciprocated and may take on a different form: that of the demanding, perhaps, even, controlling husband. He will expect her to repay her promise in full. Sadly, we women always have to pay the piper. I know I swore not to meddle but if I have anything to do with it, she will not pay for it by the spilling of Boleyn blood. Hers, or her brothers. I'm glad Professor Marshall isn't here to try and read my thoughts.

After the ceremony, I wait as Anne thanks Henry before he goes to St George's chapel at the side of Giles de la Pommeraye, his honoured guest. They are followed by much of the court, all of whom are eager to play their part and bear witness to the rest of the day's spectacle. It's a great day but I cannot help worrying about the cypher ring, and the fact it's on my friend's finger, not mine. Knowing what lies ahead troubles me, and I'm finding it so difficult not to meddle, struggling with my inability to allow my dear friend and her brother go to their grisly deaths.

In the privacy of Anne's bedchamber, Lady Margaret Lee and Elizabeth Wood are helping me to remove Anne's ceremonial robes and coronet when there is a knock at the door. George, his mother, and Mary Carey are full of smiles as they enter the chamber, and Anne is overjoyed to see them, throwing her arms about them all as they congratulate her on her peerage. I sit on a nearby stool, smiling to myself as I witness their excitement as they gush over Anne, proud of her achievements and what it could mean.

"Did I not look marvellous, Mother?" Anne beams. "Have I not made the whole family proud, even Uncle Norfolk?" She sits so Margaret can plait her hair to be ready to wear a French hood.

"You have indeed, Daughter. Your father has been stuck for words and does not know what to make of all the splendour."

Mary sits on a stool beside Anne, passing the comb to Margaret as she creates sections for plaiting Anne's dark hair.

"Imagine what you will look like as Queen!" George exclaims to the crowded chamber. Anne blushes, looking down at her hands in her lap. "This is all preparation for that moment." He steps over and leans closer. "Sister, many people will be affected by jealousy. Do you remember when we used to play kings and queens – do you remember that long summer at our aunt's house in Erwarton?"

"You were always the king," she says.

"And you were the queen."

Anne glances at her sister. "And you, Mary, were always the lady-in-waiting."

Mary rolls her eyes, as if to say, 'Don't I know it!', but remains silent and just nods at Anne.

"Yet, look at me now!" Anne proclaims. "It will not be long that all assembled here will address me as *Your Majesty!* Fancy that?" She laughs, that unforgettable laugh, and looks at me, her eyebrows raised. I suspect she is struggling to believe what is happening.

Mary is trying to look happy for her. Is she 'over' Henry by now? She must be.

"Lady Pembroke, please stop moving your head!" Margaret snaps.

Anne giggles. "Forgive, me. I am all excitement!"

I'm buzzing with my own excitement. "And soon, Anne, as you say, you shall be the real queen!"

George and Anne both smile at me, but she doesn't look away, and I wonder if she suspects that I knew of her destiny all along.

"Did you see the king?" I ask, uncomfortable under her scrutiny. "He could not take his eyes off you!"

"But did you see the Duke of Suffolk?" Mary interjects.

"No!" Anne and I reply in unison.

"Did you not see the look on his face when His Majesty kissed you in front of the entire court?" She raises her eyebrows.

"I did not, Sister. What did Suffolk do?"

"He frowned most emphatically! He looked most aggrieved."

"Suffolk does not like me, Mary," Anne says.

I consider how powerful, invincible, and regal the king looked, so full of adoration for Anne at that moment. This man, who is almost a god to his people, has seen fit to endow Anne Boleyn, whom the court considers a nobody from Kent, with his heart, but not his hand in marriage. Not yet. Anne has sworn to me that when Henry makes of her a good offer, she will be a good wife, a noble queen, and knows she will be blessed with his son and heir. If only she knew.

She scowls a little before turning away to admire Margaret's work on her hair in a small hand mirror.

Today has been a special day, for it marks Anne's ascendency to the nobility, and her new title of Marchioness of Pembroke will not only offer her new property and vast wealth but also marks another step along her path from commoner to queen. I wonder if Catherine Middleton felt how Anne now feels, in her transition from commoner to Princess of Wales.

Like Princess Catherine of Wales, Anne has never been more popular with her family, who shower her with many gifts, some from her closest kin, but unlike the Princess of Wales, who is both popular and supported by the public and royal family, Anne, it seems, is not. She has received gifts from cousins she has not spoken to in an age, but they have an agenda – most of them use their show of support as a way of angling for preferment. Of all the gifts, the one presented by William Brereton is her favourite. It is a puppy, an Italian greyhound she has named Urien, from the tales of Arthur. He is a timid little thing who, when he cannot seek the warmth of my or Anne's skirts, hugs the hearth in search of comfort, chewing on a jewelled slipper that is part of a gift presented to Anne this morning by the French ambassador. The whole chamber is piled with sumptuous and frivolous gifts.

Much later, when everyone is beginning to retire to their chambers, I sit with Anne. She has kicked her slippers off, removed all regalia from the day, and relaxes in her dressing gown and shift, sipping a small glass of wine.

"Have you not had enough?" I ask, wondering if the intoxicating beverage has gone to her head after the day's celebrations.

"I am used to it." She giggles. "It is you who is not!" She sets the Venetian glass back on the table beside her. Her clock strikes one a.m. as Margaret Lee pokes the slumbering fire back to life.

"You should go to bed, Margaret. It's late." She gets up and pats Margaret's shoulder as she places the wrought-iron poker back in its stand. Out of the blue, a gentle tap sounds on the chamber door. The usher, a sensible young man, has already gone to his room, leaving us alone.

"Who would be here at such a late hour?" Anne asks.

"Shall I go?" I ask, but Margaret is there before me. She opens the door and George smiles at her, then gives us all a flourishing bow. He looks a little worse for the drink, too, not slurring his words but more high-spirited than normal, if that's possible.

"Evening, Sister!" he says. His doublet is unbuttoned, and his hair is unkempt. He's probably been arm-wrestling with Wyatt or teasing Patch, the fool. He looks around the chamber and blinks in the low light.

Margaret stares at him, no doubt wondering why he's here so late, then turns to Anne. "Madam, would you allow me to turn in for the night?"

"Of course, I said so – now go." Anne beams. "And, Margaret, thank you for all your kindness today." Margaret bobs a little curtsy and leaves the chamber.

"Brother, you should not be here at such an hour. Go to bed!"

"With Lady Lee?" He chuckles. "Heavens, no! She is the sister of my dearest friend."

"George, don't be foolish – I think you have had a little too much wine."

"Oh, Sister mine! Or should I say, my Lady of Pembroke?" He smirks. "Do not scold me – I came to see you." He walks over to her, lifts her hand, and kisses it, then steps over to me, pulls me out of my seat, and draws me closer before planting a kiss on my neck.

"What do you want, George?" Anne asks, and I imagine she's trying to distract him from me. "If you have come for Beth, then be quick, for your wife is asleep in the next chamber."

How I wish for George to have come to whisk me away. My face heats at the thought of it. Get a grip, Beth, you're not a child anymore.

"Sadly, I have not come here to lure Beth away, and I do not want to wake up my wife." He frowns. "I have come to give you a present!"

"A present, Brother?" Her face lights up. "Let me see it?"

He walks back over to her and hands her a small, exquisite book with a brown embossed cover he's been holding all this time. She opens its delicate, illuminated pages, and I realise what it is. George has translated a religious book of writings from the French as a gift on this day for his sister.

She runs her forefinger across the title. *"Epistres et Evangiles des cinquante et deux sepmaines de l'an, by Jacques Lefèvre d'Étaples."* She flicks through the first few pages, enthralled, then turns to what I see is the dedication.

"To the right honourable lady, the Lady Marchioness of Pembroke, her most loving and friendly brother sendeth greetings."

It is clear from those words that the manuscript was produced especially for her by George. He takes the book from her. "Let me read you the rest." He holds the page up to the candlelight.

"Our friendly dealings, with so divers and sundry benefits, besides the perpetual bond of blood, have so often bound me, Madam, inwardly to love you, that in every of them I must perforce become your debtor for want of power, but nothing of my good will. And were it not that by experience your gentleness is daily proved, your meek fashion often times put into use, I might well despair in myself, studying to acquit your deserts towards me, or embolden myself with so poor a thing to present to you. But, knowing these perfectly to reign in you with more, I have been so bold to send unto you, not jewels or gold, whereof you have plenty, not pearl or rich stones, whereof you have enough, but a rude translation of a well-willer, a goodly matter meanly handled, most humbly desiring you with favour to weigh the weakness of my dull wit, and patiently to pardon where any fault is, always considering that by your commandment I

have adventured to do this, without the which it had not been in me to have performed it. But that hath had power to make me pass my wit, which like as in this I have been ready to fulfil, so in all other things at all times I shall be ready to obey, praying him on whom this book treats, to grant you many years to his pleasure and shortly to increase in heart's ease with honour."

He hands the book back. "What think you of my words?"

"Brother, I think they are beautiful. What a lovely book!"

It is a useful dedication for historians and researchers like me, because it makes it clear that George produced the manuscript at his sister's command, and it shows their joint interest in evangelical literature. However, I think it's important because it gives historians a glimpse of the relationship between the siblings. George has captured the affection he has for his sister in this dedication. I look on in silence, astonished to have witnessed this wonderful happening, realising he has given Anne a gift not of gold but something for her mind, for her soul and her spirit.

"Within those pages is a brother's love." He smiles. "See, I had it translated especially for you. I hope you do not think me so bold to present unto you these writings of mine, which humbly desire you to overlook the weakness of my dull wit, and instead see the strength of faith that drives them, which I know you share."

As Anne skims some of the script, I recall coming across this priceless book at the British Library and was sad to see the pages were water damaged. I remember when I first opened it, there was something mesmerising about the blurring of its hand-painted illuminations.

Anne stares at the pages where her Pembrokeshire coat of arms can be found opposite a full-page miniature of the Crucifixion, featuring the Virgin Mary, John the Baptist, and Mary Magdalene.

Every now and then, George points to certain sections. "I had the book made specifically for this day. See, your initials 'A.P' for Anne Pembroke can be found throughout." He smiles. "I hope you like it."

"Oh, George, it is wonderful!" she cries.

He kisses her cheek and bids her goodnight. The giving of this gift, and this conversation, speaks volumes for the relationship between these two siblings, who are so similar to each other, with many comparable interests. This one particular interest is their faith, and the religious reform of the Catholic Church. George startles me by placing a hand on my shoulder, snapping me out of my thoughts.

"I would kiss you Beth, but I think it might get me in trouble." He smirks. "I shall see you both on the morrow!" He bows, then walks out. His rise at court, because of Anne, has been meteoric. He appears to be coming into his own, rising from the lowest rungs of the court into the king's most inner circle.

Anne walks over to me, sliding my cypher ring from her finger. "Now George is gone, I can give you this back?" She hands it to me, and I look at the date inscribed inside it. '1532'. It's my ring. I knew it must be significant to Anne being made Lady Pembroke.

"You had the ring all along, and didn't tell me?"

"No, Mary Howard took it."

"Why would she steal my ring?"

"Never steal." She shakes her head. "Henry wanted his jeweller to see it – to make something similar for me. He admired the ring on you and thought I had originally given it to you."

"And?"

"He asked Mary to fetch it, as he wanted me to have it for the ceremony today. Although, he did wonder why your ring had this year engraved on its inside."

"How did you explain that to him?"

"I told him that, as soon as you knew he was going to give this title to me, raising me to the nobility, you wanted to commemorate the event with the engraving inside the ring."

"I see. He believed you?"

"Yes, of course. Why would he not?" She smiles. "He has commissioned his goldsmith, Cornelis Hayes, to make a copy, which Thomas Cromwell, as Keeper of the King's jewels, will deliver to Windsor in but a fortnight."

I look at the ring. "Then we must make sure both rings don't get mixed up."

"They will not," she says with confidence. "My ring is set with diamonds that are slightly different."

I look down at my ring again, relieved as I twist it back on my finger, where it belongs. It feels better to have it back in my possession. "That is good." My anxiety has eased now that my time-travelling device has been returned to me. I can't imagine how bad my experiences here might have become if it had been lost for good, or, worse still, one of the Tudors found out its secret and managed to travel anywhere they liked with it. Professor Marshall would have killed me if I ever made it back to my time. Is the creation of a copy a good idea? What if Anne's ring held the same powers as mine?

SEPTEMBER 1532

Standing in the Great Watching Chamber, I observe the assembled courtiers and their women, trying to overhear their conversations. Some stand idly around waiting for a glimpse of Secretary Cromwell, or even the king himself, who will enter from the small door of the privy and presence chamber at the far end of the room. Sunlight streams through the stained glass of the window, spraying rainbows of colour over the already astonishing tapestries and artworks. The duke of Norfolk stands with his cane holding court, speaking to those at his shoulder and squinting across the room as each new personage is announced into the chamber. Others sit and play Nine Men's Morris, trying to pass the time until the king may grant an audience with the waiting petitioners. Women whisper behind their hands, admiring the men, hoping their favourites might catch their eye and smile back in flirtation. George stands a few feet away, with his father, discussing politics, no doubt, along with Sir Thomas Wyatt and the handsome musician Mark Smeaton.

Mark began his career with an exceptional singing voice in the service of Cardinal Wolsey, and was then transferred to the Chapel Royal to sing for the king once Wolsey was dismissed from office. Like Wolsey, Smeaton has lower-class origins – his father is a 'mere' carpenter. However, he is embarrassed by his working-class background and has since dropped the use of his surname, preferring to be referred to simply as "Mark". The king, who always appreciates great musical talent, showers him with a large salary and royal favour. In preparation for the state visit to Calais, Mark has received a bonus of £1,250 for organising much of the musical entertainment, and by 1536, at the end of Anne's reign, he will be on a salary eighteen or nineteen times higher than that of the average court musician. To put it in 21st-century terms, plain old Mark is the Reg Dwight of his day, better known as Elton John, and Anne is his candle in the wind. He proves this by dressing well and has his own horses and a few servants; he doesn't seem to be the kind of man who needs the favour of the future queen, nor to slip between the linen sheets of a queen's bed for royal favour, as he already has the ear of the king. He's a man's man, unlike Sir Elton John. His arrogance has escalated as he adopts the mannerisms of an aristocrat, which have opened him to criticism and mocking within the insular world of the Royal Court.

The Countess of Worcester and Lord Thomas Percy have confided in me that they think Mark has ideas above his station, and Nicolas Bourbon, a French *émigré* and scholar, thinks him insufferably pretentious, and, in his poetry, Wyatt characterises him as a shameless social climber.

The palace is often full of gaiety and decadence – a place in which religion and politics mix with luxury, art, fashion, and music. Some of the most graceful and lovely flowers of the English nobility are amongst its constellation of players, but nothing outshines the captivating beauty of Anne, who Henry regards as the epitome of the ultimate English rose. Other players are like thorns – ambitious, duplicitous, and malignant, like a cancer on the skin of the monarch. When handsome and ruthless men haunt Henry's corridors, its halls and audience chambers, I make a point of observing them. Considering how, soon, they will await death on Tower Hill for having come too close, like moths to a flame, whilst some of their fellow-revellers will be the ones arranging the details of their executions. I shudder at the thought, as George Zouche strides towards me and holds out a small square-shaped letter, sealed with a red wax 'P' crest and ribbon.

"From the Marquess of Pembroke, Mistress Wickers." He nods, urging me to take the letter. From over my shoulder, I notice his Excellency, Eustace Chapuys straining his neck to see what I'm holding. He hides his intentions by standing beside a table laid with foods, picking at a lump of cheese while I open the sealed parchment. As he circles closer, pretending to strike up a conversation with a nearby courtier, I scan Anne's delicate script.

Beth,
I bid you come to my chambers as we need to make haste in preparing for my journey and interview in Calais, for all must be perfect for Henry and me when we make our visit to the King of France. You must know that the thing I have most been longing for will surely be accomplished during this most important diplomatic visit.
Anne, Marquess of Pembroke.

George Zouche bows and walks away. I fold the letter as Nan Gainsford glides toward me. She looks radiant and beautiful today, admired at court by many men, but not as much as her mistress.

"Did you get the request from the Marquess?" she asks.

"Yes, Mistress Gainsford."

"Are you not excited to be going to Calais with the king and Anne?" She tilts her head to one side as Chapuys nudges closer, my ears burning at the thought of being overheard. However, fiction has painted him in the future, he is no misogynist or fanatic but his manner at times does wind me up. I glare at him.

"Chapuys, why don't you just come over and ask to read the letter, instead of all this cloak and dagger, pretending you are talking to someone else when it's quite evident that you are not?"

He gawps, as if slapped in the mouth with a wet haddock, then scoots off, not impressed with my candour, the feathers in his rather large hat fluttering after him.

Nan looks at me. "Ought you to have said that to the Spanish Ambassador?"

"I'm sick of him following me around like the smell of a bad fart. If he has something to say, or wants to interrogate me about my mistress, why does he not just come right out with it?"

She sighs. "I know."

I turn at the sound of steps behind me to see Chapuys, ever bold, and not about to give up, approaching. He removes his hat this time, then makes a bow.

"I have heard it said that there will be no ladies present at the interview between the kings of England and France, with the Lady Anne." He purses his lips. "But it seems the Lady Anne is insistent on you accompanying her on this visit." He gives me a wry smile. "And I've heard the king has agreed."

I can't believe he dares to address me so. To hold my temper, I close my eyes for the soothing length of a slow breath. When I look at him, it's without the urge to slap him.

"Are you, Mistress Wickers, preparing yourself to visit France?" He sucks in a sharp breath, his eyes narrowing. "Is it you who will be attending the concubine?"

"Ambassador, that is none of your business."

He goads me further with a sarcastic grin, showing his elongated incisors. With teeth like them, I'm surprised he goes out in daylight. He wants to discover my mistress's secrets so he can relay them back to the courts of Europe. But he will get nothing from me. He licks remnants of cheese from the corner of his mouth, snaps his chin up, then walks back to the table to continue pretending to choose food.

Nan puts her hand to her mouth and laughs. "The audacity of the man. He seems to me to have every resemblance of a rat! Fancy him calling Anne Boleyn a concubine?"

"I know, the cheek of him."

She smiles. "Let us hope he does not go down with a headache or have too many nightmares after eating all that cheese."

"Never mind him," I say. "He may work for the emperor but is of little consequence to me." I lean closer. "Did the marquess tell you of a great secret that will be accomplished in France?"

From her expression, she already knows what I mean by this.

"I hope our mistress is not under some strange delusion, for she considers herself so sure of success, I do not wish her to succumb to dissolution. I know you are her principal friend and favourite, whom she holds as sister and companion, but can you not offer her some caution?"

"Nan, it is not my place to suggest caution – the Lady Pembroke does as she desires." I take her by the elbow and pull her out of Chapuys' earshot, for I know he will transcribe almost every word we utter when he reports to his master, Charles, the Holy Roman Emperor. I give him a backward glance before ushering Nan towards the antechamber and away to Anne's apartments. There is much preparation ahead of us before we embark on our journey to France.

Three

11TH OCTOBER – DOVER TO CALAIS

I stare up at the early morning sky, the frosty wind whipping around us as we prepare to travel by barge to Gravesend. I have been told we will then transfer by ship to the Isle of Sheppey before journeying overland via Canterbury and onwards to Dover. Whilst awaiting our departure, I watch from the south-facing windows of the privy apartments as the main cavalcade sets off. It passes out through the gatehouse on the south side of the palace precinct and snakes its way up the hill to join the main London to Dover Road. It is a magnificent sight to behold, with so many ladies and gentlemen of Henry's court bedecked in rich fabrics, furs, and a dazzling array of jewels. The procession is flanked at intervals by Henry's yeomen of the guard, so distinctive in their vibrant red, gold, and black livery. Each one carries a halberd at his side, and, from time to time, the morning light catches the steel edge of its axe-shaped head, casting a flash of brilliant white light, sending a shiver down my spine as it reminds me of when I time-slipped to the wrong day and had to suffer witnessing George's execution.

The steel-edged axe heads make the procession shimmer like a rivulet of water, stretching as far as the eye can see. It is an auspicious event, promising the splendour that is to come in Calais.

Anne and I are accompanied by thirty or so ladies who have been appointed to attend on her during the trip, and they make their way through the palace towards the privy stair. There, our barge waits to take us on the first leg of our journey. As we stand at the steps of the Water Gate, there is a good deal of commotion; a whole flotilla of barges is required to convey the three-hundred-strong party on its way. The air is filled with shouts as the boats are directed one by one into position to collect their prestigious cargo.

Henry has placed the queen's barge at Anne's disposal, and she takes her place under a canopy of arras and cloth of gold, whilst I am followed on board by several of the other ladies, including Margaret Lee, Nan Cobham, Jane Boleyn, Mary Carey, and the Countesses of Rutland and Sussex. Soon, we cast off and our oarsmen slip into a steady and hypnotic rhythm. Just ahead of us, the king's barge leads the flotilla eastwards along the Thames, the royal standard fluttering in the gentle breeze.

I am becoming accustomed to travelling in this manner, and there is nothing more delightful or comfortable than sitting in a sumptuously furnished barge as it glides along the shimmering surface of the Thames. It is fascinating to watch the many fine sights of Tudor London slip by. From my position, I see Thomas More's London property, then Thomas Cromwell's Austin Friars residence, its rooftops ascending towards Heaven the more he is elevated in the service of the king. I'm overawed by the simplicity of the city in comparison to its modern-day equivalent.

Anne smiles at my expression as I drink in the atmosphere. Her fool, Jayne, is being serenaded by Mark Smeaton. Jayne amuses us all as she joins in with one of his latest ditties. I lift my chin, taking in a deep breath of clean, fresh air, relishing the chill of this glorious autumn morning as the river breeze pinches at my cheeks with her icy fingers. Anne seems filled with a sense of vibrancy and anticipation at the enormous adventure ahead of her as, for the first time, she will step out onto the international political stage of Europe. The flotilla makes good progress at a steady pace dictated by a drummer aboard a nearby barge, whose beat echoes across the surface of the water, compelling the whole procession to move as one living, breathing organism.

A young gentleman – Thomas Culpeper – approaches Anne. He is no more than fifteen, and bows courteously before addressing her.

"My Lady Marquess, I have been sent thither from his most gracious majesty to entertain you and your ladies on your journey. I am to sing while Mark Smeaton accompanies me on his lute with gentle music."

Margaret and Nan smirk as he introduces himself to the rest of the assembled ladies, covered in their furs and huddled on cushions. He is a handsome fellow, with an unusual, magnetic aura – a combination that has not gone unnoticed in the court. For someone so young, he seems to have a high opinion of himself. The ladies are relaxed, flirtatious, and at ease in his company. I believe he is a distant cousin to Anne, on the Howard side of her family, and, as I know too well, is related to a little girl, called Kitty Howard, who will later be the fifth queen to our king, so long as I don't change history from what it is meant to be. I feel a little sorry for him, and shudder at the thought that his youthful neck will one day be on the block, like both his distant cousins.

His blue-eyed gaze burns into the onlookers, who respond to his smooth manner and velvet voice with coquettish giggles. Margaret blushes at the brazenness of this dashing youth.

Anne raises a brow at Margaret, then sits back in her chair and takes in the spectacle. Mark Smeaton, like Thomas, is a young man full of devilish charm, and grins back at Anne with a cocksure spirit. He and Anne are worlds apart in terms of their position in life; the traits they share are the same impish spirit and enticing sexuality, and it is not difficult to see how their passion for life and the arts may be a dangerous chemistry that might be fatally misconstrued by Cromwell's men of logic, or by those who will in the future seek to use it brutally against them. I think about my potential power to save all these men and women who will be marked and executed as traitors, if I did go against Professor Marshall's advice never to meddle.

EN ROUTE TO CALAIS – ENGLAND'S LAST FOOTHOLD IN FRANCE.

It's getting late, and England lies somewhere behind us as Anne, and I stare out to sea from the flotilla. The waters are choppy, the wind blustering around us as we consider all the people we have left behind. I'm not great with sailing, and my stomach feels like a washing machine on full spin. It gets too much, and I hang onto the side of the boat, my face over the side, just in case.

"Who is for cold meats and pickles?" George asks, arriving on deck carrying a wooden board. I can't think of anything worse, and I'm sure my face shows how green at the gills I'm feeling.

"Can you not have a bit of compassion, Brother?" Anne snaps. "Beth is unwell." She puts her hand on my shoulder. "Can you take Beth below to my cabin? Perhaps pour her some wine?"

"I am not certain wine is the answer," he replies. I wonder if he thinks he is the answer, as he takes my arm and guides me towards the stern, passing some of the ladies who are talking between themselves. I cover my mouth with a handkerchief and slow my pace to catch snippets of what they are saying.

"…how does Henry think he can pass her off as his consort when they are not even married?" one of them says.

"Henry is still married to Katharine," Elizabeth Wood replies. "He's a bigamist!"

"You cannot talk of his Majesty like that?" another responds.

"Do not worry, he's down below playing cards with Suffolk and some of the other men."

Silly girls. It would only take one loyal courtier, or George, to report back for them to have all their privileges removed. George glares at them from the corner of his eye and guides me to the stairs leading below deck.

The main purpose of this trip is for Henry and Anne to gain King François' public recognition and approval of their relationship. Henry wants François to then meet with the pope and push the case for the annulment of his marriage to Katharine. The circumstances of the Calais interview will reinforce Anne's stance as a political player. She will re-enter the world of the French Court, and I hope she will dance with François and talk with him – she has told me that is her wish, and she can convince him of the significance of her position.

George holds me steady as we enter Anne's cabin. It's empty, thank goodness. He hands me a small goblet of wine, but I refuse it, still nauseous.

I sit back on a cushioned bench of sorts that is built into the cabin, and he sits next to me.

"I would kiss you, Beth, but looking at your face, I think the time is not right!" He chuckles.

I grimace. "Did you not know you make me feel sick all the time?"

"What?" He stares at me. "Lovesick!"

"No, silly!" I lie.

"Foolish, am I?" He shakes his head. "I think not, sweet Beth. For we have both been struck by cupid's arrow for many a year, and you know it."

"You are always full of yourself, sir."

"Always have been – ask my father."

I get to my feet, pull my French hood off and throw it to the floor. "George, quickly, I fear I am going to be sick!" I press my hand over my mouth.

"You do look rather green." He laughs again.

"This isn't funny, I really am going to vomit!"

He leads me by the elbow to a small window, some kind of Tudor porthole, which he opens and encourages me to lean out. The waves undulate beneath us, their murky blue-green hue and choppy white foam making me feel worse. Trust me to get seasick. George is rubbing my back between my shoulder blades, his touch gentle. If anyone came in here now, this wouldn't look good. Thank God Jane Boleyn is above deck, gossiping with the other gentlewomen.

"Let it out – you will feel better for it!" he whispers.

Being sick is the experience that keeps on giving. As the contents of my stomach rise, I gag, then remember I must look at the horizon. Isn't that good for relieving seasickness? The ship rises and descends through the waves, and I stay focused on the skyline as George keeps rubbing my back, his warm hand reassuring. I exhale, then suck in the salty air, deep and slow before exhaling again. I think it's working. Yes, I'm beginning to feel a bit better.

Seeing my improved state, George steps away, and I turn and pick up my hood from the floor.

"Thank you for being here, but I fare much better now. Perhaps we should go back up on deck." I smile. "We will be missed."

"My sister will think we are up to no good." He chuckles.

"I'd rather we didn't give anyone that impression."

He takes my hand and leads me to the cabin door.

Some hours later, our grand flotilla is poised to enter the harbour at Calais, making a vibrant and colourful spectacle. In the crisp sunlight, every ship is hung about its sides with a myriad of St George flags, along with at least two flags of the royal standard, all fluttering in the gentle breeze, attended by those gentlemen and ladies of the court who travel with us, like the duke of Richmond, Henry's bastard son. Henry is trying to help Anne bond with the duke so they can establish a positive relationship, and she can be a good stepmother to him. Anne, however, is more interested in bearing Henry a son of her own and feels she will have no time for the duke then. Richmond often moves between royal palaces to be near his father, but his principal residence is at Richmond Palace. He is with us on this trip for a special reason.

Henry and Anne are standing proud as everyone marvels at the sight of the magnificent medieval town of Calais and the many people who have gathered to greet them. As we approach, the seamen on our ship set about navigating our vessel past the castle of Rysbank, an ancient stone fortress that guards the entrance into Calais' natural harbour, a remnant of the vast empire of England's Plantagenet dynasty. Over the two hundred or so years that Calais has been occupied by the English, the marshy area to its west has been drained and cultivated – a vast network of watercourses, dykes, and canals stretch back from the town – keeping the earth from becoming waterlogged and providing rich, fertile pastures for growing crops.

On the right-hand side of the town is a tower known as the Water Gate, which guards the entrance to the inner harbour of the citadel. However, it is the Lantern Gate, the principal gate of the town, that dominates my first impressions of Calais. In front of it, by the side of the harbour, a splendid procession of knights and soldiers form to accompany the mayor and the Lord Deputy, both of whom wait on the quayside to greet the king and his mistress.

Henry glances across at Anne, then me, and smiles, excited at the sight of the townsfolk gathered to welcome our arrival, with many cheers of "God save the king!"

I am relieved to set foot on dry land, and to leave my seasickness behind me. Anne seems elated as Henry takes her by the hand, leading her with pride by his side, whilst all about us, a thunderous roar of cannons signals our safe arrival. Anne's time with Queen Claude groomed her for the position she now occupies as queen-in-waiting beside one of the most powerful kings in Christendom.

CALAIS, OCTOBER 1532 – THE MEETING WITH THE GREAT MASTER OF FRANCE

Led by the mayor, with Henry following behind, the royal party ride in magnificent procession down Lantern Street and into the breathtaking central Market Place. Henry is a picture of gracious majesty, and I feel proud to be English as I ride behind him and Anne. This is her first state occasion and, from time to time, voices cry out from the crowd with "God bless the Lady Marquess of Pembroke!"

The people of Calais have taken her to their hearts in a way that, sadly, is not often the case on the other side of the Channel. I do my best to carry myself with dignity. Here, in the heart of the English Pale, I feel important as I am smiled at by people in the crowd. All my cares about Anne's future, which so often stalk me like menacing shadows, dispel amid a sea of good wishes. Our procession makes for a glorious sight to the ordinary townsfolk who stare out from little windows above us that jut out over the narrow streets.

Behind us ride the premier nobles of the land: the Dukes of Richmond, Norfolk, as Lord Treasurer of England, and the Duke of Suffolk. A little further back rides Stephen Gardiner, Bishop of Winchester, and the bishops of London, Lincoln, and Bath. Adhering to the strict hierarchy of Tudor society, then follows the Earls of Exeter, Derby, Arundel, Oxford, Surrey, Rutland, and Thomas Boleyn, now the Earl of Wiltshire and Ormond. The parade stretches back almost as far as the eye can see, and while I can't make them out, I know it includes George Boleyn, Sir Thomas Wyatt, Sir Thomas Cheney, Sir John Wallop, and three of Thomas Boleyn's brothers: Sir William, Sir Edward, and the youngest brother, Sir James Boleyn. It is unfortunate that his attendance guarantees the presence of Elizabeth Wood – Lady Boleyn – who, as George told me, Anne does not get along with.

Once in the Market Place, I gasp at the magnificent sight of the Town Hall, which dominates the southern side of the square. We cross to the right of Staple Hall before turning into the long and narrow High Street, which runs east to west through the town, towards the towering edifice of the church of St Nicholas, a magnificent Gothic building where, in the fourteenth century, the young Richard II was wed to his eight-year-old bride, Isabella of France. To celebrate our arrival, the court and the townsfolk of Calais stop at the church to hear a Solemn Mass.

In front of the beautiful altar, Henry and Anne kneel in prayer, giving thanks for their deliverance. An hour later, we leave to a deafening peal of bells that sing out their song of celebration before Henry and Anne arrive at their lodgings at the Exchequer, a fine mansion opposite St Nicholas's, which has been newly enlarged and refurbished for our visit. The king is to wait at Calais for a full ten days before riding out to meet King François.

While he and Anne lodge in Calais, the Duke of Norfolk, Earl of Derby, and a group of gentlemen will meet with 'The Great Master of France' and his men at the English Pale, which is six miles outside of Calais and the last English outpost before the rest of the European continent. Within its fortified walls is a grid-like network of narrow streets, packed with fine medieval houses owned by affluent merchants. No doubt the streets are decorated with a multitude of colourful banners and flags to welcome the eventual arrival of the king.

Henry showers Anne with a bounty of jewels purchased from grateful local merchants, and spends a good deal of time discussing the refurbishment of Whitehall. He has ordered no expense to be spared in completing the remodelling of Wolsey's original palace. Messages arrive regularly, updating him with developments. The plans are spread out on a huge table in the Exchequer Great Hall, where he and Anne discuss and debate how works will progress. The two of them seem closer than ever.

On the third evening after our arrival, I sit in the window seat of Anne's privy chamber whilst she plays cards with Henry, George, and his wife. The apartments are hung with cloth of gold and arras – the tapestries surrounding us depicting dramatic scenes from the Battle of Agincourt. The floor is laid with expensive carpets that have been shipped from Greenwich and are strewn with roses, lavender, and other sweet herbs, the scent of which is diffused by currents of warm air emanating from the welcoming fire in the large stone fireplace.

They are laughing during a game of Primero, a sort of sixteenth-century version of poker. Anne has a knack for it and often beats the king, much to his dismay. Great cries of disbelief and playful accusations of skulduggery are cast about when one of us acts out a particularly convincing bluff or snatches victory from an overconfident opponent. In the background, Mark Smeaton serenades us on a virginal with tender songs of love and chivalry, smiling across at me on occasion, which irritates George as he tries to conceal his frustration at being ignored by me. Instead, much to his annoyance, he has the full attention of his wife.

We are served fresh, sweet cherries, grapes, and pears – a present from Anne de Montmorency. The king is in excellent spirits, having enjoyed three glorious days already of hawking, gaming, and dancing. He has given Anne all he can bestow, for now. I'm not surprised that she has fallen head over heels for him. The plan she originally designed, to disentangle herself from him, has truly backfired, just like I hoped it would. I'm glad, as it means I do not attract his attention anymore, as it appears that any smouldering, lustful thoughts of me in Henry's heart are now mere embers.

I cast a glance at Jane Rochford, who so often seems miserable and put out. She is a creature of slight frame, narrow-waisted, with a bosom not much raised. Like most women of nobility, she has fashionably pale skin, which is as translucent as porcelain, mousey-brown hair, and clear, blue eyes – similar to her sister. Her beauty is only flawed by her eyes being set a little too wide apart, giving the permanent impression of her being startled at her surroundings. Otherwise, her face is a slender, oval shape, whilst her nose is well-proportioned, and she has full, rose-coloured lips. The woman is difficult – often prickly – but is not evil and heartless unless, of course, she talks of me. Anne says she slanders me behind my back at every opportunity, but I can't help how her husband feels for me. I hope I won't be the cause of her turning her back on George and Anne. Maybe her disloyalty will be due to her wild jealousy of Anne's close relationship with George. Is that what will drive her to be vindictive? On the other hand, will she be intimidated by Cromwell during his intense, relentless interrogations of Anne's ladies-in-waiting during the investigations of the Privy Council before Anne's arrest?

George loves life, and although he takes pains to hide his feelings for me, I know he adores me. Since time-slipping, I have a newfound confidence in myself, but I still feel different to how I imagine other ladies here feel about themselves. George brings out my sexy, vivacious, and challenging side – a contrast to most other women at court. The only crime he will have committed is having been poorly matched with a woman who is hopelessly ill-equipped in temperament, needs, and sex drive to ever satisfy him or hold his attention.

To compensate for what she lacks, she armours herself against the world, not allowing anyone close because she is ill at ease with herself. She shares nothing of her childhood with anyone. Hmm, did her family neglect her? That could explain her craving attention in adulthood, looking for satisfaction in marriage, thinking it would make her feel important – the mistress of her household, adored by her husband and surrounded by doting children. However, she has been married to George for over six years and is aware through confidences with Anne that she has never captured her husband's heart, and no precious Boleyn heirs follow. I tried to touch on the subject with her at Hever, but she brushed me aside as if it mattered little to her. She hides her pain well, which must be deep and raw. To be honest, I feel guilty. Her haunted look hurts me, and I wish I could understand her.

Even though George has told me he loves me more than life itself, it won't save him, and I may have to help Jane, so she won't feel the need to implicate her husband and sister-in-law in the short few years to come. If I can do that, and change their fate, despite what Professor Marshall has advised, then I should. But then history will be changed forever, won't it? Oh God, what am I to do? I am pulled this way and that by my dilemma, and I'm not sure what the best route is to take.

For the time being, though, I turn my attention to the game. Jane and George have turned in their hands in defeat – George with more than a little disgruntled but good-natured frustration. I have to turn away from looking at Jane, switching my focus to the courtyard outside. The gravel crunches under horses' hooves as dispatchers arrive. Cromwell stands in amongst them, issuing orders and directing them this way and that.

The game is now left for Henry and Anne, and she smiles at him from behind her hand of cards. I'm fascinated by the way she flirts, and sometimes

I have to pinch myself to remember who I am witnessing first-hand. If her leg goes any higher beneath that table, she will turn it over, ruining the game by running her foot up the inside of Henry's leg. I believe she's doing her best to distract him from his turn of hand. His eyes widen and his cheeks redden, and I assume Anne's foot has touched his codpiece. To divert her from her provocative move, I cough into my hand.

"Mistress Wickers, are you unwell?" Henry bellows as he drags his gaze away from Anne face.

"Just a slight cough, Your Grace." I dip a curtsy, fighting back a coy smile.

"Perhaps my Lady needs a cup of wine?" Anne beckons to a servant standing against the wall surveying all that's going on.

She giggles as I accept the wine, and I roll my eyes back at her as I take a long sip. Henry attempts to keep a straight face as he struggles to concentrate on the game. We all know he wants to win the good deal of money placed in the centre of the table. However, in truth, he is in so jocular a mood, I suspect he cares little about the wager, and is thoroughly enjoying playing along in earnest with Anne's under-table game. He raises a brow at her, and it's clear that he's trying to weigh up whether her bravado is true or not. Anne mirrors his gesture in reply, yet holds her counsel, saying nothing.

After careful consideration, Henry places another wager on the table, 'Primero!' he says as he lays his cards before him.

Anne fakes disappointment, and he smiles with satisfaction and reaches to take the winnings piled high between them. As bold as brass, she swipes at his knuckles with her cards, causing him to halt in confusion before she declares her hand, with some delight.

'Chorus!'

Henry throws his hands up, crying out in mock despair at her possessing yet another winning hand. Everyone is laughing, and George shakes his head.

"Anne, how do you do it? You are the luckiest minx I have ever known. We shall all be bankrupt if we keep playing you at this game!"

"Bankrupt indeed, my Lord!" Henry chimes in. He turns to speak over his shoulder to the keeper of his privy purse, Sir Henry Norris, who stands close by in attendance.

"Sir Henry, be sure to give my Lady Marquess her winnings."

"Thank you, Your Majesty," Anne says, her tone playful.

The joyful game is interrupted as the arrival of the Duke of Norfolk is announced.

"Ah, Norfolk. Come here – rescue me from your niece, lest the Privy Purse be soon empty!" He sits back in his chair, still chuckling.

"Anne, you will ruin the king if you continue beating him at cards." He bows to Henry.

"Uncle Norfolk, the king's purse is deep, and besides, I do not always win against the king." She smirks.

"Madam, you do!" Henry bellows out a raucous laugh, looking her up and down, glaring in pretend anger at her impertinence. It seems she can get away with anything.

"Lady Anne, Lady Rochford, Mistress Wickers," Henry announces, "I have plans for the masque to be celebrated on Sunday next. I need to go and speak with Norfolk and Norris about it."

All curtsy and bow as he leaves the room, taking his male courtiers with him. With winnings banked, the game ends.

"Jane – Sister, dear – and Beth, would you accompany me?" Anne asks. "I think to take a walk in the gardens."

Taking advantage of our privacy, she guides Jane by the elbow, walking ahead of me to see if she can find the underlying cause of the woman's usual, intractable sadness. I listen in as we meander our way through the queen's presence-chamber and out into the gardens.

"Jane, I am glad of your company with us at Calais. It is a pleasant town – do you not think?"

Jane turns to smile at Anne and looks less melancholy. "Indeed, Madam, I think it is the most agreeable town that I have ever known, and it is good to see his grace in such fine health and good spirits. He loves you dearly."

Anne smiles at the truth of Jane's words as we continue to walk along.

"Tell me, Jane, has my brother been buying you gifts?' She nods towards the beautiful carcanet with diamonds and sapphires which hangs about Jane's neck, complementing the pretty green gown she is wearing about her tiny frame.

Jane raises her hand and touches the necklace. "Yes, my Lady, he thought it befitting of the great celebrations ahead of us." Her smile is wistful, hinting at sadness behind her words.

"'You always look as if you carry the weight of the world on your shoulders," Anne says, her probing gentle to dig beneath the surface of Jane's obvious unhappiness. "Is there anything you need to tell me? How are things between you and my brother?" She touches Jane's elbow. "You know he loves you, Jane, don't you?"

Jane looks away. In an instant, I see that Anne has reminded her of a painful truth she wishes not to be reminded of.

Anne stops and faces her sister-in-law. "Come now, Jane, we are sisters, are we not?" Her eyes widen in emphasis. "I want to help you if I can."

Jane hesitates, unable to meet Anne's gaze. Perhaps she is weighing up the wisdom of confiding in Anne because of me being in earshot. I step between them and lay my hand on her shoulder, which causes her to look me straight in the eye.

'My Lady…Wickers… I want so much for George to love me, to treasure me more than he does anything else in this world. Indeed, I would give my life for him. I adore him! But it seems you are my rival for my husband's affections. Have we not had disagreements on this matter before?"

"Yes, but—"

She brushes my hand off her shoulder. "I am used to George not always being in our bed because he is chasing ladies of the court, like you, but there is nothing I can do about it."

My jaw drops. Has Jane witnessed a stolen moment between George and me?

Her eyes fill with pain, but she straightens. "I fear, because of you, that he loves me not. I try to be a good wife, but George… Well, he… Oh, it is difficult to speak of it!"

"I'm sorry," I reply, turning to walk away.

"I cannot bear to look at you – even less, say your name."

"Sister, dear," Anne says as Jane looks away from me. The other ladies, who still follow us, are within earshot of our conversation.

A burning shame fills my chest, and I need to leave, to find some privacy, but Anne waves her other ladies away, indicating that they should keep their distance. She takes Jane by the hand and leads her into the privy garden, while I'm thinking I'd like to take her by the throat and bury her in the undergrowth. Everywhere we go, Jane is always causing drama, and it gets tiresome after a while.

"Do not upset yourself, Jane. Mistress Wickers has never taken your husband to her bed." How little she knows. "I assure you, Beth has spurned his advances and there is nothing between them – they are friends, and no more." Jane takes a sideways glance at me, assessing me in that split second. "Do not judge Mistress Wickers. You have my word and that should suffice."

I feel sick hearing Anne giving her word on the back of what I know to be a lie.

"However," she says, her tone changing, "if George takes a mistress, then isn't it better that it is someone we know, trust, and love, than an enemy of the Boleyn's who would use their closeness to George to hurt us all?"

As crazy as it sounds, it eases my conscious. She is trying to cover all bases by being diplomatic. Oh yes, she'd make for a fabulous politician.

Jane bristles. "Anne, I cannot believe you would suggest such a thing – a woman who knows how true love can hurt!" She's probably thinking about how Anne was once hurt by Henry Percy. With that, she storms off, like a petulant child. But this is no childish matter.

I look at Anne in disbelief. "That may cause an issue in the future."

"What do you mean?"

"Well, an unhappy wife and sister-in-law might tip up an apple cart, if you give her the chance. I suggest you keep your family members close and potential enemies even closer."

She looks dumbfounded, not realising the bees' nest she may have disturbed.

"The trouble with my brother," she says, "is that he is a man of great passion and lust, like most men, and every time he sees a new lady at Court, he wants to take out his manhood and piss all over her pretty face, to mark his territory – just like Henry!"

"Anne! I cannot believe you have just said that." Have I been just another pearl on George's codpiece?

"I hope not? But you know what men can be. I fear that what George asks of Jane…in bed…is sinful, in Jane's eyes, and, more importantly, in the eyes of God."

"No, I do not believe that of him – he has only ever been a gentleman to me." If my experience with him is anything to go by, I guess Anne is insinuating that his sexual appetite is rapacious and his open-minded attitude to sex is too much for her self-conscious and conservative sister-in-law to bear. I hope Jane doesn't turn around to look at us, because I'm already gripped with guilt. "Let us not talk of George, my Lady. Men can be selfish creatures. As women, we all must learn this fact and must never forget it." I speak from what I know lies ahead for Anne. "It is a woman's lot in this life to endure as best as we are able." This is certainly true for the 16th-century wife, who is, in the eyes of the law, society, and God, the property of her husband. Thank God, at least, that has changed, and I realise how lucky I am to taste a kind of freedom unknown to the women who surround me.

———— ❄ ————

Later, I feel a little lightheaded after my supper, and realise that the French wine is stronger than I'm used to. I rise from my seat at the table.

"Anne, I am so sorry, but I have a headache. I need to go to my bed. Do you mind?"

She looks up at me and smiles. "I see no reason why not."

Henry overhears. "Mistress Wickers, I thought you would be well used to French wine!" He chuckles. "But if the revels are intolerable for you tonight, and your mistress has given permission for us to no longer have the enjoyment of your company, then we shall see you on the morrow." He nods.

"Thank you, Your Grace." I bob a curtsy. Out of the corner of my eye, I see George watching me. He goes to rise but I direct a discreet shake of my head at him. Anne notices our interaction and I know she keeps her eye on me as I make my way from the hall.

I make my way back towards Anne's chamber through dimly lit passageways, the only sound being the hem of my skirts brushing the rushes on the floor. When I'm nearly there, I pass an open door to find Jane Boleyn sitting alone on a settle in the candlelight.

"Do not loiter in doorways, Beth," she hisses. "People will question your upbringing."

"I do not know why you have to be so sharp and vicious, Jane. No wonder no one seems to ever want to be in your company."

"Obviously, that is how George feels about me too!"

"See, there you go again." I shake my head. "If you could just change your attitude, just a little, you would see such a different reaction from people when they are in your company."

When she lifts her head and looks at me, I see the pain in her eyes.

"I'm so sorry, Beth, I do not mean to snap at you." She pats the cushion next to her. "Come and sit with me?" Her expression is full of sorrow.

"I am so sorry, too. I do not mean to pry."

She pats the cushion again. "Methinks it is about time you and I talked. What say you?" I walk into the chamber and sit beside her. "It would be nice to have an ally at Court for once."

"What ails you?" I ask.

"My past and present have made me this way."

"Whatever do you mean?"

She takes a shaky breath. "I hope to God if I tell you what I am about to tell you, you promise you will never repeat it, because, if you did, I fear I would have to call thee a liar!" She rings both hands. "Everything gets repeated at Court, in a chain of whispers, and I never want what I am about to tell you to be part of the gossip."

"I'd never repeat a word," I say. "I am not that kind of woman."

She sits back with her spine pressed against the settle, and stares into space.

"I know you don't like me, Jane."

"Do not say a word. Please listen to me." She turns to look at me. "I am very much aware that you are attracted to my husband, and he to you." She places her hands flat in her lap. "Mistress Wickers, what you do not realise is that I have seen George pursue new and pretty women of this court many times before, so him favouring you, and showing you attention, is nothing new to me. You are just the most recent of several."

Why is she saying this? Is she trying to hurt me? Put me off George? Make me leave court? I knew she was jealous – she has shown her true feelings on many occasions before now.

"Jane, you forget, I knew George before you ever married him – I've known the man since he was just seventeen!"

"Mistress Wickers—"

"Please, Jane, we are past such protocols – call me Beth."

"Beth, what you do not know, and what no one else knows, was that before my marriage to George, I was in love with someone else."

"In love?" I say, as if it seems impossible that she could possibly be in love with anyone else but George.

She jerks her chin up. "Do not look so shocked. I too can be attractive to the opposite sex. I was once like you – everyone wanted to be around me. Everyone loved me, men especially. I was once the life and soul of my family estate. I was noted for my sense of fun, my laughter, my love of life. I may not be a beauty like the widow Mary Carey, or a woman of great wit and sophistication like Anne, but, like them, I do have my charms, even if they cannot be seen by you."

"You are loved by other men?" I say, trying not to sound too shocked. I stare at her.

"Not just by men but by one man in particular. I loved him, and he loved me back."

"What went wrong? Are you saying you had improper relations with this man?"

"Of course, we did. We thought we were to be married. When I found out I was to be pre-contracted to George Boleyn, Robert and I planned to elope. But my father, Lord Morley, being cousin to the king, insisted that marrying into the Boleyn family, an up-and-coming name, with Thomas Boleyn being a man of mark, would be a good match. When I saw George at Court, I willed myself to like him. I watched him many a time, trying to work him out. It was not because I had taken a fancy to him, but that I was expected to fancy him, as my husband to be. I noticed how he was with you, and I realised he'd never love me in the same way. I decided then and there that I did not want to marry him. He was not the man for me, but my family had paid a substantial dowry – the king had helped with monies towards the marriage, too, and I was powerless to do anything. I was bought and paid for."

I nod my understanding. "Women have no say in this world and are at the whims of man – so much is expected of us." Indeed, not much has changed in five hundred years.

"My time with Robert in the country all seems like a dream now, when I think about it. I was so different then. I would have given up everything to be with him."

"Where is he now?"

"I have not a clue. My father and his family banned us from being together. It was too much of a liability for me to be near him, especially once I had been pre-contracted to George."

"I think you have a broken heart."

"I do not want to be here at Court and would never have been if it were not for the Boleyns. I'm afraid that my sadness means I do not want to see other people happy when I am not."

These revelations make me look at her in a whole new light, knowing she was not a maid before her marriage. I dare not say this to her, but why didn't George notice she wasn't a virgin on her wedding night? The chastity of a Tudor man's bride is important to him, right? I try not to show any reaction in my expression, and she carries on the conversation.

"The fact that I have never had the ability to bring a child from my womb at the due time is but a clear sign that, in the eyes of God, George and I are completely incompatible. But it does not stop me caring for him or wishing things might be different."

I remain silent, not knowing what to say. In her own way, she loves George, but her heart never belonged to him, and I know he never wanted to be with her. No wonder they seem unhappy. I feel bad for her, but I shouldn't feel guilty, because I cannot help that George has feelings for me.

"Beth, will you stay away from George for me?" she whispers.

"I will try my best, but I cannot make such a promise on George's behalf that he will stay away from me." I get to my feet, and she looks up at me.

"I thank you for that, and I thank you for your honesty, but it does not mean to say I am content."

I don't answer her as I go to the door and walk out.

CALAIS, FRANCE, 16TH OCTOBER 1532

The conversation with Jane has been playing on my mind. To distract myself, I decide to go with Henry and Anne on a hunting expedition, using birds of prey. For me, hawking will be a new experience, and, like all things Tudor, I am mesmerised by the sight of these majestic birds as they take flight. A party of close friends and confidantes accompany us, such as Thomas Wyatt, Henry Norris, George, Jane, Anne's cousin Mary Howard, and Anne's mother. Many of the other great nobles and gentlemen, including Thomas Boleyn, have left Calais this morning to meet Anne de Montmorency within the English Pale to finalise arrangements for the forthcoming meeting between Henry and François.

The earth is flush with a palette of autumnal colours on this bright morning, and we have all dressed to compliment Mother Nature's mood, choosing gowns of plain crimson velvet, green velvets, and amber wools – our sleeves turned back with miniver, fox fur, and wolf. Anne's jewels wink in the sunlight with brilliance, alerting us to her growing stature next to the king's side.

Before we left, I pinned a beautiful pendant to the front of her gown, set with the cypher 'AB' in gold, and from which hang three large teardrop pearls. As we spend the day hawking, several of Henry's falconers and cadgers attend us, the latter of which carries six or seven hooded birds on a large wooden frame slung about his shoulders. One of the birds is a rare and fabulous white gyrfalcon imported from Russia – the most expensive of birds – presented to Anne by the king. I remember him gifting it to her. Robert Cheeseman, his master falconer, has been training his birds. Anne confides in me that this gyrfalcon was a gift to her from a Russian prince, and as she does so, I yearn to laugh aloud but have to keep my thoughts to myself – only Anne could receive such a gift from a member of Russian royalty.

The bird is a magnificent creature, much like its owners, with his breast unblemished and white as virgin snow. He is an aloof beauty, and the king has warned Anne that such birds are notoriously temperamental, highly-strung, and difficult to fly. Perhaps he admires Anne so much because she and the bird share similar characteristics: rare, capricious, and dangerous. The falcon's pedigree has aroused her curiosity.

As I watch the silent nature of this wild and unyielding creature, I hope Anne will allow me to try him for myself. I have learnt much about the ancient art of hawking and falconry at re-enactments, and watching falconry displays at National Trust properties such as The Vyne, in Berkshire, and I even got to hold a couple.

Peregrine and gyrfalcons are the most prized birds, yet Henry prefers to work with native goshawks, sparrow hawks, and merlin. He is a practical hunter and chooses to use birds that fill his larder. The hawk is affectionately known as 'the cook bird', and after a day in the field with these exceptional hunters, we often return with an abundance of rabbits, hares, and ducks for the table. I am most acquainted with the merlin, a small type of falcon, which, because of its size, is well known as the bird of choice for a woman. These are expensive, though, and prized by the nobility as a symbol of status and wealth.

As we parade through the town, the king carries the most splendid of his hawks upon a gloved hand for all to see. He looks as majestic as his bird, and so handsome – every inch a magnificent prince – dressed in a riding coat of black satin with two cut borders of black velvet and a russet partlet also of black velvet, lined with black sarcenet. Once we reach an area of open ground, several miles southwest of the city walls, he turns to Anne.

"My Lady, do you not think that this is an ideal spot for hawking?"

She seems touched that he has asked her opinion on something which, in truth, he knows the answer.

"'Tis a good spot, indeed, Your Majesty. You have chosen well."

"Would you care to fly your bird first?" he offers, and she nods in agreement.

"Master Cheeseman,' he calls out, and he is handed a fine hawking glove embroidered with red silk. I watch as Henry fits the glove on Anne's hand.

I turn my horse about and retreat a distance, sidle up next to George, and watch his sister excel at the art of hawking alongside Henry. George dismisses his serving man and I'm able to speak to him with a degree of privacy.

"Forgive me that I have not had a proper chance to speak with you this day. I trust all is well?"

"Thank you kindly, Beth. I am indeed well." He leans over in the saddle so no one can overhear us. "And you, I must say, look beautiful this morning."

I can't hold in a coy smile. George, as ever, has a way of making a woman feel desirable. With some sadness, though, I think for a moment upon his wife and the misery she feels from her husband's rough neglect. And even though they don't share deep love, I suspect she longs for such a compliment from him. It spurs me on to raise a delicate issue I cannot defer any longer.

"George, I need to talk to you about an important matter." Before he has the chance to say anything, I go on, "It is about Jane."

He raises his brow, his curiosity piqued, for it is a subject that never comes up between us.

"She is sorely aggrieved, for she thinks that you care not for her," I say, remembering to speak Tudor.

"She is right!" he replies. "I—

"No, George." I flick my fingers on the pommel just enough to silence him. "First, you must listen to me. I think she has guessed about your love for me – she is a woman, and we have a sixth sense about these things. I know how it is between you and Jane, and in truth, neither of you is to blame." He stares at me. "I am to blame. I should have left your family home when it was obvious you were to be married."

"I could never have put up with that," he says, looking pained. "It is a sad fact that I am poorly matched." He sighs, looking at me in earnest. "But to be without you, would be even worse."

My heart melts at his words. "Jane is not a bad woman but one who is ill-equipped to cope with your lusty appetite. I fear that you ask things of her in bed that she cannot in all good conscience give herself over to."

He flushes scarlet, not used to a woman addressing him about such intimate matters. Despite his discomfort, I push on, leaning closer.

"I know that she cannot fulfil your needs – she has told me so herself."

He turns his head away; I suspect because he cannot meet my gaze. The man cares little for the opinions of others, except Anne's, and perhaps mine. While I hate to be so harsh, he needs to be told, even if my message is difficult for him to bear. I forge on with all the compassion and love I can muster. For his sake, and Anne's, I need to be tough on him.

"George, you must realise this. Very soon, your sister will be Queen of England. You must know that the Boleyns have so many enemies who will use anything they can find against your family to bring you all down from high favour. Until she has borne the king a son, we are all vulnerable. Do not make your wife our enemy because of your selfish and foolish desires. Especially not because you want me." His eyes widen. "I beg of you, be a good husband to your wife. Treat her kindly and with respect, and if you do have to find your pleasure elsewhere, for God's sake be discreet and be careful. Do not bring ill repute to your family. I say this out of love and respect for you."

The longest silence lies between us. For the first time since I have been in Anne's world, I have taken George to task, but only out of the great love I feel for him. I know the dangers that lie ahead for my beautiful friend Anne and her somewhat-irresponsible brother, and I want to keep them safe. While I still hope to change the course of history, for now, I hope I have done my bit to calm a storm that may become a hurricane.

He has no time to respond, however, as the hunt has begun. Beaters with hounds flush a petrified rabbit out from the undergrowth. Judging the moment precisely, the king removes his bird's velvet hood and releases its foot bond from the glove, allowing it to take flight. From our vantage point, we watch the hawk lock onto its prey and swoop down upon it with deadly accuracy. The hawkers shout as they rush to retrieve the kill before the hawk tears it apart and spoils it for the table. We all cheer and applaud the king's good fortune before he turns and smiles at Anne, his face alight with boyish excitement. He basks in her acknowledgement of the success of his bird. As I observe the party, and despite all I know, I wish it would never end.

When I turn around, George has gone but his mother has come up next to me atop her beautiful black mare. She seems to sense there is something wrong, and I'm grateful she doesn't ask me about it. As it turns out, she has something else on her mind. From our mounts, we watch as the hawker covers the prey with a rough cloth, coaxing Henry's falcon back onto his hand and feeding it a morsel from a pouch of ready-cut treats in reward for its work. As the first kill is bagged, Lady Boleyn turns to me.

"The king looks well and happy. How are things between him and Anne?"

"Very well, indeed," I answer in truth. "The king shows her daily ever-greater affection." I wait for her to continue, sensing her line of questioning is leading somewhere.

"Has he spoken anymore to her about marriage?"

Ah, now I understand her concern. With some heaviness of heart, I give a gentle shake my head. "Anne speaks nothing of it due to her fear of provoking a vicious argument with the king. I have avoided asking her about the subject entirely."

I know Anne yearns to end this long wait. After all, she is not getting any younger.

"Beth, unfortunately, men do not often show the same measure of decisiveness in matters of the heart as they do in issues of power, wealth, and revenge."

Her intense gravity has taken me off guard, for she has always been cautious about remaining chaste and virtuous. Anne's physical relationship with Henry has been about urging her to maintain her good name, and her virginity above all else. Hmm, there is something in the way Elizabeth Boleyn addressed me that leaves the statement pregnant with unspoken meaning.

"What are you saying, my Lady?"

She never taking her eyes from mine as she leans closer. "Sometimes a man needs to be left with no choice. Sometimes, Beth, we need to make that decision for them."

"What would you have me do?" I ask, suspecting her intention.

"You will speak to my daughter? I know that you have her ear."

"My Lady—"

"Beth, I think it is your turn to watch me fly my bird."

I turn to Anne's loud voice. She is awaiting my response, and there's nothing I can do but walk my horse closer to the action.

In short order, the falconer passes the bird up and it steps onto her glove, and he stretches out and flaps his mighty wings. It is the first time I have witnessed Anne's skill with her bird, and I admire his beauty, yet all I can feel is the pressure of having to speak to her regarding consummating her relationship with Henry.

A rook circles close by, the perfect quarry for Anne's bird as, with her right hand, she slips off his crimson velvet hood, releases his foot bond, and he takes off, his steely resolve clear to have his way and make his kill. He climbs above his prey, chasing and turning until the rook begins to tire and loses height. The falcon puts in a few short swoops to confuse the bird before it makes a last, desperate attempt at escape. Breaking free from his circling, in one long flight and without hesitation, Anne's bird pitches into a vertical dive and takes but a few seconds to descend upon his startled prey, crashing into the back of its head with a 'thwack' that echoes around our small valley.

I need to tell Anne the time for prevarication is done. She already knows she must take matters into her own hands and carve out her destiny. Right now, she needs security, and Lady Boleyn is telling me in her way that it will be the consummation of their relationship, and the king's child within her belly, that will finish this never-ending stalemate. I am shocked that the final push comes from her mother. This is a fraught and contentious situation for the Boleyns. The pope hasn't officially sanctioned any relationship between the king and Anne, and the court is not wholly unified in accepting her, even as a mistress. Yet the dye is now cast, and I resolve to support the family, and urge Anne to act decisively before we return to England.

Four

19TH OCTOBER 1532

Lost in my thoughts, I trace my fingers across the page in the book I'm holding in my lap. The words are clear and vivid, but I don't take in what I'm reading. Reminders of Professor Marshall's warnings replay in my mind. His words are etched into my brain and have stopped me developing my physical relationship with George. I don't want to upset Anne, or for that matter, George's wife. However, I need to lay down some ground rules with Anne about the future, but how to do that without giving too much away?

The door to my chamber opens and Lady Fitzwalter, one of Anne's women, enters.

"My Lady, Madame La Marquise is here to see you." She curtsies and steps aside, allowing Anne to enter with Nan Cobham and Margery Horseman following.

"Where is a bible?" Anne asks, her impatience clear in her tone and manner. "I need Henry to swear on a bible." She sweeps around looking for a copy, pulling some of the precious books off the shelf in her haste.

"Why do you want Henry to swear on your bible?" I ask, watching her frantic search. "You do not need a bible, as I've heard from George that Master Cromwell can recite the whole of the New Testament!"

"I want the king to swear on a physical book, the word of God, before witnesses, that he will marry me as soon as we get back to England and make me his queen!" Her resolve seems strong, and she is set on her course. I leap up from the window seat and grab her hand.

"Anne, I need to speak with you alone before you go back to Henry."

She turns the bible over in her hand and looks at me. "What is it? You look distressed." She ushers the other women from the room and sits with me on the window seat.

"I have warned George from me and urged him to return to Jane, to treat her as a wife should be treated – for his sake and yours, Anne." I grasp her hand tight. "I hope I have done the right thing."

"George is his own master, and whatever he wants, George will no doubt decide without our help. Besides, you cannot blame him for loving you. Look at you, with your perfect skin, soft hair, and white teeth – you never seem to age a day."

"You can talk," I say. "You have fared just as well. You are as radiant as the day I met you. And you have held the king back for years, with great success."

"You allow me too many compliments but, yes, I did hold back His Majesty – it has been a mission. However, I have had to make allowances for him, letting him pull my shift down so he could kiss my breasts. We have done most things, except for the actual act of love." She looks to the door, as if hoping no one stands behind it, eavesdropping.

"That is a concession," I say. "And you have done well to preserve your maidenhead."

"It has not been without its trials." She smirks. "Because once you stoke his fire, it is very difficult to quell his ardour." She stares into the distance for a moment, then sits up. "I would not chide nor blame you anymore if I were to hear you have ended up in George's bed. If he had a long-term mistress, it may make his marriage to Jane a little more bearable."

"Anne! I cannot believe you've suggested such a thing – especially when you were so against the idea of me having any relationship with George when he first relayed his feelings for me." I try to act as shocked as possible but, inside, I feel ecstatic because she has now, more, or less, given us the green light.

I glance at the door, hoping there is no one behind it, listening in. "If your feelings have changed about your brother and me, then please let him know because it is not my place to make advances to him."

After all we witness at court, with men and their wives, she must be aware that husbands stray from the marriage bed when couples are misaligned. Look at her Uncle Norfolk. Indeed, nothing changes throughout history, especially if men are unhappy in a marriage. Look at Henry, Katharine, and Anne's triangle, and in my world's recent history, the Charles, Diana, and Camilla debacle – and now, George, Jane, and I are inextricably linked. Hmm, men always have their way in the end. It seems, however, that Anne will also have her way in everything with Henry, as she knows the hold, she has on him.

"Anne, are you in love with the king?"

"What an absurd question!" She wrinkles her nose at me. "You are aware of my feelings for Henry. Why do you ask me such a thing?"

"I want to know if you truly love him in your heart."

"At first, I was unsure. Remember my plan?"

"To dissuade his advances? Yes. You thought he would never try to annul his marriage."

"Indeed. Who would have thought we would be here in Calais, and me now a Marquess?"

"Do you think the king will now make you, his wife?"

"Well, I have the emerald as a promise." She smiles, looking down at her left hand. "But I think I have to push Henry to secure my position as his wife, sooner, rather than later."

"Your mother spoke to me about this very matter and is concerned that you tarry by not inviting the king to your bed. How do you intend to persuade him, to bring matters to their swift conclusion?"

"I do not think the king will need much persuasion – once he sees me naked and willing, the deed will be done." Her cheeks redden as she smiles again.

I nod once to myself. "Then I can assure your mother that she does not need to worry."

"I do not know why you are asking me, Beth, when you know what is going to happen." She scrutinises me. "You know *everything* about me."

Her emphasis makes me nervous. The responsibility of changing events through my actions weighs heavy on me. What to say?

"Anne, you would upset God's divine plan for your life and for Henry should you know the whole truth of your future. Doesn't God say in his word not to worry about tomorrow as tomorrow will look after itself?"

"But Beth—"

She cuts herself off when Lady Fitzwalter opens the door.

"Madame La Marquise, the king summons Mistress Wickers for an audience with him."

Anne gets up and makes for the door, but Lady Fitzwalter stops her in her tracks. "Just Mistress Wickers, Madame La Marquise."

As I turn towards the door, Anne's brows are furrowed. I'm not sure if she's more angry than concerned.

I pass through the private gallery connecting Henry's privy closet – his innermost sanctum – to Anne's, thereby avoiding the public gaze. When I make to curtsy in the usual fashion, he stops me, holding up his palm, and beckons me to come and sit beside him.

"Norfolk, I wish to have an audience alone with Mistress Wickers." He ignores the other men about us, speaking with warmth.

"Very well, Your Grace." Norfolk bows, then flicks me a suspicious look before pushing everyone out of the room. When he closes the main doors behind him, their footsteps fade down the passageway outside.

"Do not be alarmed, Mistress, stay just as you are, for I wish to discuss the Marquess of Pembroke with you."

The softness in his voice and his warm informality indicates that he wishes to confide in me, and I am somewhat flattered, to say the least. I can imagine Anne grinding her teeth along the hallway, wondering what we're discussing. But she must know my loyalty is with her. It is early evening, and the king is casually dressed, clad only in his hose, nether stocks, garters, boots, and a finely embroidered linen shirt that is open at the neck.

"I watch you, Beth. You are a great support to Lady Anne. I admire your loyalty." His eye contact is intense.

"Thank you, Your Grace."

His gaze holds firm, and I know he is working up to whatever he needs to say. "I believe I can speak frankly with you?"

"You can, Your Grace." I allow a gentle nod with this.

"I have known passion with Anne, but not to fruition. I have tried other women, to take the edge off my longing for her, but the plum is sour with others in comparison to the sweet nectar that lies within my love for her. She drives me to a distraction that I have to shake whenever she is near me."

He takes a long breath through his nose, looking pensive. "I have read Wyatt's poems and she is the hind who takes me off the path and into the woods – into darkness – into an unknown world of my own making. I do not want to be thought of as an infidel and do not want to make a breach in the walls of Christendom, but I need all loyalty to make her mine. Cardinal Wolsey did not go far enough in dealing with my Great Matter, but now Master Secretary Cromwell says he has things in hand."

"Yes, My Lord, I am aware of this." I keep my eyes downcast so as not to incriminate myself in religious matters.

"But, you see, I need my marriage to Katharine annulled, and quickly."

"No one should stand in your way, Sire. You are the king of England. I believe you have read the works of William Tyndale, have you not?"

"Ah, The Obedience of a Christian Man? Yes, that great book – a book for all kings to read. It came to my notice through the Dean, who had lifted it from young Master Zouche. Anne had marked passages suggesting that I would find them well worth reading. And so, I did."

"The king is in the person of God," I say, "and his law is God's law. Hence, you, My Lord, are accountable to God alone, and the obedience of the subject is an obedience required by God. Indeed, when the subject obeys or disobeys the prince, he obeys or disobeys God. Simply ask Bishop Cranmer to declare your marriage to Katharine null and void and marry the Lady Anne."

"You are well equipped with wise words, for one so young, Beth." His voice is soft. "You make me dare to hope that which I have never dared dream before. But Rome will never allow it!"

"Maybe not, Your Grace, but you must put yourself off from the shackles of Rome. Anne, Tyndale, and many others believe that, as head of the Church in England, you can do whatever you wish in both religious and political matters."

"Hmm, you speak with admirable clarity."

"Then, My Lord, be the king you are meant to be, and do as you will."

A wide smile lifts his expression. The lion is beginning to understand his strength.

I flinch when a clarion announces Anne. Henry walks towards her with fierce intensity, never taking his eyes from hers. He takes her chin in his gentle hand and turns her face up to him.

"You look so incredibly beautiful, Madam." His voice is imbued with great wonderment.

"What bothers you so, Henry? Why did you need to talk to Mistress Wickers alone?" Her voice is equally soft.

He shakes his head, the action slow. "'Tis nothing, Anne. For how could anything be wrong when you are in this world, and at my side? Yet, I declare I know not what spell you have cast upon this heart of mine, which remains bound unto you above all others."

Despite these great words of love, I shudder inside as I watch them together, for I know of the accusations of treason that will be made against Anne during the terror of 1536. He thinks she has somehow enslaved his heart, bewitching him by her magnetic allure. I hope the king, even in his anger and self-pity, will be reminded of moments like this, including his intense feelings for this woman, and repent of how he will treat her.

"As you know," he says after a long moment of silence, "I leave for Boulogne tomorrow, and I find that I'm missing you already."

He hangs his head in sadness in a rare display of raw and tender vulnerability. Anne takes his hand in hers and gives it a gentle squeeze, reassuring him of her presence. He lifts his head to look at her.

"Anne, I love you with all my heart. There is no other woman in the world like you – you are life itself. I do not think that I could breathe without you in my world." He sinks to his knees, looking up at her with intensity. "Swear to me you will never leave my side…"—Anne makes to speak but he shakes his head and continues—"and I swear to you, as God is my witness, that, come what may, from this day forth, I am bound to follow, love, and to serve you until the very end of time itself."

"Will you swear it on the bible?" She holds the small Latin bible outstretched to him, and he places his huge paw over it and beckons me closer as a witness.

"I swear before Almighty God and upon his holy bible, that I, Henry the Eighth, King of England, promise that I shall make Anne Boleyn my wife on return to Dover, and thereafter, Queen of England."

I swallow back a dry tightness in my throat. There it is — the vow that is to bind these two lovers together for all eternity. It has come unexpectedly. Yet, with a flash of lucid insight, I understand all the feelings they have for each other, and their desire to do what is right before God. It has all been born of this moment. In the back of my mind, I visualize the Ives' book cover changing for the better in the professor's office.

They hold each other for the longest time, with tears of wretched longing and raw tenderness flowing down the king's cheeks. When Anne kisses his lips and waves me from the room, a great pity and compassion for their souls overwhelms me as, for the first time, I realise how their love has transcended time and is still with us five hundred years later.

It's clear that I have worked my magic advising Anne and Henry. I hope I haven't overstepped the mark by doing so. Will Anne think I have overstepped the mark if I act upon her advice concerning George? How will Jane react? I am bothered by how developing my relationship with George may affect history. And even though it's a relief how things have turned out, might it have a detrimental effect on how Jane views it, if it comes to light? A woman scorned, and all that. I'm aware of the potential repercussions of my meddling – it's always in the back of my mind.

I am mired in responsibility, which, in truth, should not be mine to take, but here we are. If Anne could only give the king a healthy son, or if the son she carries in 1536 could be full-term, and be born healthy, then history could be rewritten. Henry would not have to betray her, nor would he break this vow. Perhaps then, the two of them could finally be free.

20TH OCTOBER 1532

Henry has left Anne with her orders. He smiles at her with admiration, and not a small amount of relief at her measured reaction.

"When François and I return after completing our state visit, you will reign over the celebrations as if you were my wife, and queen. While I am away, please oversee our plans so the French will not soon forget their stay in Calais, as hosted by the English king, and his queen-in-waiting. I trust in your style and ability for detail, and with Master Cromwell to assist you, I can be certain that François and his nobility will be duly impressed."

"I will do precisely as you have asked, Henry. You will be proud of me, and your court in Calais." She lays her hand on his cheek. "Do not tarry overlong, my darling, for I will miss you."

"And I will miss you, too, my love. I miss you, already."

Henry and his company of noblemen take leave to meet with François and his courtiers for a stay, hosted by the French, in Boulogne. He has risen magnificently to the occasion and is dressed in rich, russet velvet, with borders of goldsmith's work and a myriad of the finest quality pearls sewn into his coat. As he leaves Calais, an impressive escort of one hundred and forty velvet-clad men of the court, forty guards, and a vast retinue accompanies him on six hundred horses. The remaining English company look forward to reports forwarded from the meeting of the great kings. We know only men will attend it, and that there will be frequent pauses in conducting business to allow for entertainments, which will include bull and bearbaiting, cards, and gambling. There will be ceremonial giving of gifts – fine horses, jewels, and clothing – and the awarding of honorary titles. The sons of the respective monarchs will officially be presented to the other king, being advised that they now have a new royal 'Father', and must always honour, respect, and obey him.

With the king's departure, the palace falls into relative quiet, and Anne and I retreat into our private rooms. My encounter with Henry a few days before has left me pensive. I feel as if a spell has been cast from which there is no escape, and I find myself slipping deeper into a dark hole of despair. Since then, I have been haunted by my knowledge of the fate that lies ahead for Anne. The oppressive responsibility of my role bears down on me, and I am tortured by the prospect that I may never save her.

Troubled by these thoughts, and desiring my own company, I have excused myself from Anne and seek refuge in the queen's garden chamber, sitting at a fine mullioned window that looks out onto the gardens below. For almost half an hour, I have struggled to concentrate on a book, with stillness failing to come. Frustrated, I toss it to one side and lean back in defeat against the window, my gaze coming to rest on the most vibrant and beautiful tapestry that is hung on the opposite wall. I am amazed when I realise that it depicts the marriage of Henry's sister, Princess Mary, to the aged Louis XII of France in 1514. By some quirk of fate, in my time, it has come to rest at the Boleyn family home, and I remember seeing it during my last pilgrimage to Hever. That day, I stopped in profound astonishment when I recognised the face of the young woman I have come to know so well – Anne Boleyn – shown as one of the ladies in attendance upon the new queen. It seems fitting that the tapestry should begin life here at the Exchequer in Calais, for it must have been here when Princess Mary first rested on her way to Abbeville to marry King Louis.

A soft tap at the door pulls me out of my reflections, and Anne enters.

"May I join you, Beth?" she asks, with her usual gentle smile, and I indicate that she should take a seat beside me. I continue to gaze at the tapestry, somewhat lost in my own world.

"Your memories of Calais, when you were here as a girl, must be so carefree, my Lady."

"Yes, I was unencumbered by weighty matters of marriage or dynastic duty." She sighs and touches my arm. "Are you well, Beth? You have been so quiet since the king's departure, and I am concerned for you."

Ever maternal, it did not take her long to touch on the matter. I do not look at her but continue to stare at the tapestry, wondering where I would begin to explain what troubles me so sorely.

"Are you not happy for the king and me?"

"Of course, Anne."

"I beg you, Beth, please do not be vexed, for you have witnessed how the king simply adores me – he says he cannot live without me. As we speak, our great friend and most loyal supporter, Doctor Cranmer, returns from the continent to be consecrated as Archbishop of Canterbury, and Master Cromwell works tirelessly to ensure that legally no one may challenge the validity of my marriage to the king. When all this is said and done, Henry will make me his wife."

Her being so upbeat may have to do with Henry swearing on the word of God, for to do so and not mean it, in this religious age, would be a dangerous thing. At this moment, it troubles me to imagine how her heart will be broken by the tragic events due to befall her, and her family, if fate takes its course. In that moment, I want to warn her, to toughen her up and protect her, in case I could get away with changing the history. I turn to face her.

"Anne, my dear friend, you must listen to me. As your mother has warned you about Court before, the Boleyns make a nest in a bed of vipers and…" I clench my hands together, not knowing how to explain what I should not know. "You must not speak of this to anyone, but if you cannot give the king a son, then…then things may happen – terrible things – and if they do, I promise you this,"—I take both her tiny hands in mine, squeezing them, entreating her to listen to my every word—"I cannot be more specific, but if what I speak of comes to pass, then you will know that what I have spoken of now, is the truth, and you must, dear Anne, get away from Court as quickly as you can, and stay away – do not think to return, for you have your life to think of, and you will need to retreat to a nunnery."

"A nunnery?" Her eyes flash with fear. "Beth, you're frightening me! Of what terrible things do you speak?" We both flinch at the sound of a forceful knock at the door. "Are you suggesting the king will push me aside?"

"No!" I lie, taking the opportunity to say it before the door opens. "The king loves you." I shake my head. "My Lady – think nothing of what I've said, I was being foolish!"

She is perturbed but I feel compelled that, come what may, I must make her safe, though I don't know how to do it. There's so much I want to change, but I'm terrified of changing anything, in case the Ives' book cover remains the same. Yet, I'm desperate to change everything, just to save Anne and George. Of all the Boleyns, she and George deserve it. Neither has a malicious bone in their bodies – not really. All they try to do is protect their own positions and try to influence Henry towards reform of the Catholic faith. Anne believes in that cause. Yes, she has a sharp tongue and can say cruel things at times, and George loves to joke at other people's expense – but don't we all say things in the heat of the moment?

Anne nods but fear is plain in her eyes. She lets go of my hands and turns towards the door. "Enter!"

Her aunt, Elizabeth Wood, steps in, with her hands clasped rigid as ever in front of her stomach. "My Lady, Master Farlyon has sent word that he is ready for the rehearsing of the masque and awaits your presence."

"You are performing a masque for King François, and Henry?" I ask.

"Of course!" She half-smiles. Her connection to the King of France, to his court, and his circle, means she can offer her relationship, with Henry as a lure, as a way of engineering the situation for the better, with her in the middle. I know she has confided in Henry that she can speak to the French because she knows their customs and their language and what to do in matters of diplomacy. I've heard her tell Henry that she can bring François around, and once he accepts her queen-ship, she believes all of Europe will accept her as Henry's wife.

Even though I have not been able to convey all my fears to her, it has been a blessed relief to share some of the load that has weighed on me in recent days. As we make to leave, she appears confident, because of her mission, and I'm determined, for her sake, to forget my worries and throw myself into the courtly celebrations planned for Sunday, October 27th. When Henry returns from Boulogne with François, she needs to be at her glittering best, for he will expect her to shine like a diamond, captivating the court above all others as his intended wife and queen. I must be at my best, too. At this stage, I can't let him, or Anne, down.

Five

THE EXCHEQUER, CALAIS, 25TH OCTOBER 1532

I shift from one foot to the other, feeling as if I cannot wait for another second to see Henry and François come into view. Just inside the Mile Gate, thronged soldiers of the garrison and the entire remaining English force are on their toes to gain the first glimpse of the glittering parade of French and English nobility soon to arrive. I almost jump at the deafening roar of cannon, followed a few seconds later by the stinging smell of gunpowder as smoke fills the air. When it clears, I can't help smiling at the sight of their Majesties, riding side by side at the head of the brigade, both dressed in gleaming white.

As they approach the town, what must be hundreds of cannon shots are fired, the sound reverberating around the narrow streets and marketplaces. The kings and their retinue ride to Staple Hall on the market square, in which lodgings have been prepared for them. Henry will be pleased when he tours the housing readied for François and his sons, since Anne has personally reviewed every detail during the king's five-day stay in Boulogne. The Duke of Richmond, Henry's illegitimate son, has been joined by a great company of noblemen who have not been at Boulogne, and Anne and I watch as he greets his father and salutes the French king again, embracing him in a most honourable and courteous manner.

The rooms at Boulogne are lavishly decorated and François' chamber has been draped with a fantastic fabric of damask, embroidered with silverwork and colourful silks to emulate flowers and vines growing from the floor. His presence chamber is hung with silver tissue, his cloth of estate finely wrought with red roses trimmed in pearls. The privy chamber, grandest of all, is a vision in green and crimson velvet embroidered with branches, flowers of gold bullion, and noble beasts and golden coats of arms. Throughout the room, the drapery is adorned with precious stones and pearls.

Anne awaits Henry back in their apartments within the Exchequer – the Staple Inn. When he arrives, Monsieur Pierre Viole, the Provost of Paris, accompanies him. Monsieur Viole presents Anne with a gift from his own king, with a note accompanying the package saying: *Madame la Marquise, j'attends notre réunion.* Within is an ice-white, impeccable diamond, the largest Anne or I have ever seen.

That Sunday evening, her wardrobe chamber is alive with chatter and laughter as she and I, along with a few select others, don costumes for the masque that is to take place after the grand banquet in François' honour.

"Lady Anne," a melodious voice calls out, "you would be well-advised not to feast too abundantly on the tempting dishes served at the banquet this evening!"

Anne peers over the heads of the ladies-in-waiting who are swathing us in red tinsel satin, to see Lady Lisle levelling an impish grin her way. The woman's irreverent brand of humour is in full play.

"Why so, Honor?"

"Since your costume is so spectacular, my Lady, and the fabric hugs your body just so. In fact, it clings to you. If might be presumed that rather than you having ate very large portions at a state banquet, it may surely be misinterpreted as none but a baby? Courtiers might be so bold as to think a prince is boldly showing himself on the evening of his mother's presumed marriage? Just imagine how quickly the gossip would reach Dover, and then London!"

Anne's volley of laughter at her crafty reply hinders my attempts to swaddle her in silk. Only Honor could be audacious enough to joke about the persistent rumours that Henry and Anne have secretly planned their wedding for today, instead of a masque.

"You know," Anne whispers to me, "I am sorely tempted to round out my stomach with a cushion, to encourage the gossips, and to measure the speed of their whisperings. What say you?"

I wink at her as we continue to be adorned with the gossamer silver cloaks, which will only partially conceal our crimson undergarments. The diaphanous capes are to be drawn together by a delicate cord of gold, which is woven loosely in a sensual pattern, leaving enough of an opening in the front that the body-tight crimson tinsel can be observed.

"I'd rather you did not. Your heir will come, but at the right time." Anne stares at me, knowing there must be some truth in my remark.

"Tell me more, Beth. I hate the way you keep secrets from me."

"No, Lady Pembroke. You will never know *all* my secrets. Just some."

"You tease me so!" She sighs. While we talk,

to add a final, and vitally important touch to Anne's costume, she instructs me to retrieve a specific piece of jewellery from a chest in her suite. After I place it around her neck, she studies her reflection in the mirror, a wicked smile showing she has something in mind.

"Just for this evening, I plan to indulge in a personal act of revenge." She steps back out to join the other women, only to be met by wide-eyed stares at the sight of the Occitan cross hanging between her small breasts. Made of heavy gold, it has dark rubies in the centre and on each of its four points, with large, pear-shaped pearls suspended from three of those points. It had been Katherine's favourite jewel.

She leans closer to me. "Do you remember her wearing it?"

"I do. The piece is not at all to my liking – much too heavy and ornate – but it is instantly recognizable as the royal jewel Katharine favoured, and always wore."

She smiles at her gentlewomen and sweeps from the chamber with a flourish. As Henry's mistress, she is not formally invited this evening. However, she cares not if she will cause any scandal, and is prepared to steal the show. Eager guests are being served from an astonishing array of over one hundred and seventy dishes, including a huge variety of meat, game, and fish. The masque, which is just getting underway, includes, as ever, music, dancing, singing, and acting, with many of the latter parts played by the king's professional actors. These actors often perform allegorical plays, which pay homage to their sovereign lord. Such masques are hugely popular at Henry's court, for they provide a great spectacle of entertainment and allow noble lords to participate and show off their mastery of courtly pastimes. Tonight, the banqueting hall is alight with speculation, for amongst the English nobility are many of King François' noblemen, all of whom are eager to catch the first sight of Anne Boleyn, and some of whom remember the lady from her time at the French court, some twelve years earlier. She is under intense scrutiny, and she knows it.

I cannot resist the temptation to take a peek at what lies beyond the curtained doorway, as this is my first experience of performing in a royal masque, and with the finger of one hand, I draw the curtain back a couple of inches to catch a glimpse of our audience. It is a celestial vision that takes my breath away, for the walls have been hung with silver and gold tissue and adorned at intervals with gold wreaths that glisten with precious stones, and each of the twenty silver chandeliers bear close to one hundred wax candles. The light cast from these illuminates the faces of several hundred courtiers as they eat, drink, and make merry with old friends and new.

To complete the glittering spectacle, on the far side of the room, close to the dais where the two kings dine, is an enormous seven-tier buffet, gleaming under the weight of the Tudor gold plate. It makes for an impressive display of princely wealth and status. The evening's revels are well underway and will soon reach their climax with our dancing. King François sits at Henry's right-hand side as his guest of honour. Henry is dressed in violet cloth of gold, the noblest of colours, reserved for the king and his immediate family, plus Anne since her elevation to the peerage. What is most eye-catching about the king this evening is the magnificent collar of fourteen rubies and fourteen diamonds that hangs about his shoulders, the smallest ruby being the size of an egg. These stones are separated by two rows of pearls, with one rare and precious stone hanging from this collar, being The Black Prince's ruby. It was one of Henry's favourites, apparently. The stone is a magnificent jewel the size of a goose egg, given to Edward of Woodstock, the Black Prince, in 1367, and even worn by Henry V in his crown at the Battle of Agincourt. It has been in the possession of every English king since, and I long to tell Henry that, in the 21st-century, it would be set into the Imperial Crown of England, perhaps one of the best-known jewels in the world. But, of course, I can't share that because it would give my truth away.

By wearing it today, King Henry is reminding François of England's magnificent victory against the French at Agincourt, almost to the day, one hundred and seventeen years earlier, in 1415.

I have seen enough, and let the curtain fall back into place, then turn to face Anne and her women who are chattering with nervous excitement. This night reminds me of the masque at York Place, when I first time-slipped, which feels so long ago now. We eight ladies complete our costumes by raising glittering masks to our faces and fastening them behind our heads with satin ribbon. At a signal, we sneak into the banquet chamber to the plaintive beat of a single tambour. All conversation stops, and every eye is fixed upon us as we wind our way about the head table.

From the notable guests there, we each select a partner and motion for him to join us on the dancefloor. The kings are bewitched, and every man who is selected as a dance partner grins as he comes side to side with his mysterious lady. I, of course, choose George, and Anne beckons to François, both happy to oblige. I watch François as he winds his arm about Anne's waist – maybe a little too snug – which won't bode well with Henry, as he's not in the habit of sharing his toys with others. One of the other ladies chooses the King of Navarre, and Honor selects Henry – Anne's English king. Barely have we completed one galliard when George, filled with excitement, wraps his arm around my waist, brushing his hand 'accidentally' across my breast as he guides me, much to Jane's disgust, and she thuds around the edge of the dancefloor in a temper. It must be obvious to Jane that it is me behind this face covering.

Filled with exuberance at the climax of the masque, Henry dances over to Anne and whisks the mask from her face, revealing her identity to François. Following his lead, the other dancers remove their masks, as do I, and we all watch excitedly as Henry crows, "Voilà, mon frère François! Stunning feminine beauty is not the sole dominion of the Frenchman!"

With that, he traces Anne's cheek with the back of his forefinger, and, with one last lingering look, releases her back into François' company, while he gazes on with pride. My cheeks flush as George winks at me. Of course, he knew it was me. My clumsy dancing must have given me away! He leans in and kisses my cheek.

"You did well, Beth!"

"I felt nervous!"

"If you were, you hid it well." George chuckles, and we stand together watching François takes Anne's arm, guiding her to a small adjacent chamber for some privacy, where, relaxing on padded chairs and sipping cups of spiced wine, they laugh and converse for over an hour as the dancing continues.

I observe the revels from a distance, with George standing beside me. I wonder what the French king thinks of Anne's proposed marriage to our English king. While I watch them, they appear to be locked in diplomatic conversation. It's clear that François is assessing Anne, and vice-versa, while, from the corner of my eye, I notice George assessing me. There is no question that François finds Anne attractive, yet I wonder if his attentions have ever been more purposeful in the past with her than she presently allows or shows. Anne would have never slept with the French king.

"Do you think my sister has done enough diplomacy tonight, Beth?" George looks to me, then to Anne, then across to Henry, who watches like a hawk as Anne and François talk out of everyone's earshot.

"The king must be very proud of her, George, do you not think?" I raise a brow at him. "Do you not think that Anne has secured French approval for her marriage to Henry?"

"Undoubtedly." He smiles at me, and I sense his longing to lean in closer, but before he can, his wife approaches and drags him away to fetch her a goblet of wine.

Anne looks delighted, and relieved, as she converses with the French king – just what she needs on this glorious evening. For a time, it seems she has vanquished her rival of Aragon and has enjoyed being the object of desire of two kings. No doubt, all the ambassadors of their respective courts will send a clear message back to their masters that the French king supports Anne Boleyn in her marriage to Henry VIII. She finally seems to have the support she requires to become Queen of England.

This meeting at Calais needed careful planning, and I know who is behind it: Thomas Cromwell. As we all meet in France, the printing press is churning out printed pamphlets – government propaganda dressed up like a 'red top' newspaper – to present Anne in a certain way to the Tudor public.

———————— • ❋ • ————————

Later that night, in the candlelight and after the entertainment has concluded and all is quiet, I help Anne prepare herself for her first full night of passion with Henry. She delves into my makeup bag and asks me which will make her look as beautiful as possible.

"Will you trust me, Anne, to make you look perfect?" I ask, grabbing what I think is suitable. I use a moisturiser on her skin, then kohl on her eyes to widen them, a little blush on her cheeks, and spritz some of my perfume on her décolleté and wrists. Then she rubs some toothpaste on her teeth.

Her hair hangs lose to her waist, and she looks like Rapunzel waiting to be rescued from her tower by a handsome prince. But Anne doesn't need to be rescued, because she is creating her destiny at this moment – to be the queen of England, and mother to one of our greatest monarchs from English history. I stand back and look at her, a ball of emotion in my throat.

"If the king is not bowled over by you tonight, my sweet friend,"—I gaze at my handiwork—"then he never will be!" I lean in to kiss her on the cheek. She smells wonderful – like roses and orange.

"I trust you more than anyone, Beth. No one must know about tonight until my bargain with the king has been sealed."

As she stares at herself in the mirror, she looks pleased with the results of her makeover, and puts her arms through the sleeves of her silk dressing gown as I hold it up for her, then slides her feet into her delicate slippers.

"I will gladly keep your secrets," I say.

"Tonight, is the triumph of the 'scandal of Christendom'." She laughs. "I would that Katharine knew that tonight she loses Henry, forever."

Butterflies flutter in my stomach as she creeps from her chamber. It is time for her to force Henry's hand. A short time later, as I'm lost in a memory of the last dance with George when he led me in a volta, full of intensity and intimate contact, Mary Howard enters the room, perhaps more effervescent than most. She swirls about, replaying having danced with François' son, the young and handsome, fourteen-year-old dauphin.

"Where is the Lady Pembroke?" she asks, looking around.

Not sure what to say, it takes me a moment to answer her. "Anne's whereabouts at this time, is none of your business." I sound rude, but Anne swore me to secrecy about the deal being sealed between her and Henry. She looks puzzled. "There is one thing you need to learn, Lady Mary, and quickly," I continue, "the world is not run from where you think it is." I nod once at her. "Not from fortresses, or even from Whitehall or Windsor. Do not concern yourself!" I'm not going to tell her that the world is run from Henry's bed. In keeping my word, my loyalty will be rewarded eventually, with history playing out as it should.

She looks at me aghast. "Am I not needed then?"

"No, Mary." I shake my head. "Go and get yourself off to bed."

"Very well."

When she closes the door after her, I sit on the edge of Anne's bed, kick off my slippers, remove my dressing gown, and slide beneath her sheets. While the crackling of flames in the hearth comforts me, all I can think about is Anne with the king, and George with Jane, and here I am, all alone.

The door to Anne's bedchamber swings open and, as she walks in, sunlight streams through the gap in the damask curtains and lights her face. There is something about her expression I can't quite grasp as she stands beside the bed. Hmm, maybe I'm expecting too much.

"Beth, you slept here last night?" She sits on the edge of the bed and looks down at me.

"Yes, I thought it best – in case anyone came in – they would see the form of someone in the bed and think it was you."

"That was a good idea, to cover our tracks."

"How was last night?" I whisper.

"Henry told me that François has promised not only to wage war with him against the Turks but that he will unreservedly support my marriage." She smiles. "François has told Henry that he pledges to send forth a message to the pope with reassurances that, backed by France and England, his Holiness does not need to fear the emperor's wrath, as he will make sure that Charles of Spain will follow his lead."

"Then, it seems that Henry is a step closer to fulfilling his heart's desire – his union with you, and the fulfilment of his dynastic aspirations." I smile. "But that wasn't the question I asked, Anne." I stare at her.

She blinks, pulling her dressing gown tighter around her. "If you want to know, I have done just as my mother instructed." And with that, she walks back out of the room.

EARLY NOVEMBER 1532, CALAIS

Anne alights in the main courtyard, accompanied by her gentlewomen and maids of honour. We laugh and chat our way up the great processional stair, making our way to her dressing room. It is a goodly sized chamber, painted with various royal and heraldic symbols on three separate wood panels, the central one depicting the royal coat of arms and the king's motto, Dieu et Mon Droit. There are two decorative panels on either side, one with the initials HR, while the other has only recently been painted with AB in preparation for our visit. There are several fine and sturdy pieces of furniture along with a few mannequins, which display a variety of Anne's most favoured gowns. A lit fire has kept the room warm and welcoming, and a few candles augment the soft glow from the flickering flames in the hearth. I sit in a chair whilst Lady Wallop kneels at Anne's feet to remove her slippers and stockings. Anne listens with some detachment as her ladies good-naturedly tease little Mary Howard about the obvious attentions of the young Duke of Richmond.

Yet, in my mind, I am elsewhere. Although I have spent precious little time with George during the course of the evening, I have not failed to notice how he watches me and feel the palpable and growing sexual tension between us, again pulling, and clawing at our sensibilities, impelling us towards that inevitable expression of our desire: a good shag. I shouldn't word it like that but sometimes I can't shake the modern woman out of me, not even here after all this time.

My thoughts linger on instances when he traced his finger across the back of my neck, or linked hands with me in a surreptitious moment, or placed the gentlest breath of a kiss against my cheek – it might as well have been the deepest and most passionate. God knows how much George turns me on. Rob has never made me feel like that. Not in the same way. I must speak to Anne, and soon, about how she can help me bring about a reconciliation between us. Am I selfish to want George when I know how much he wants me. I know I have to wait until she has spoken to him before I'll feel safe and comfortable to return his attentions in their fullest. I'd be blind not to realise that he longs to be with me with every fibre of his being. The frisson between us is electric, and the way he looks at me is so intense, as if he wishes to devour me. It's a similar look I have seen Henry give Anne on numerous occasions. Sometimes, George stares at me like a lovesick schoolboy. It's endearing, dreamy, and wistful, as if he's hypnotised by a desperate longing.

11TH NOVEMBER 1532

"It has been decided we shall leave Calais today, Lady Wallop," Anne says. "You and Mistress Wickers shall finish packing every casket and trunk ready for our return to England."

She walks to the window and raises her gaze skyward. The clouds are grey, yet not as thunderous as they have been.

"Henry longs to return to England now that the negotiations with King François are over. We are frustrated by the inclement and stormy weather that has kept us here an extra twelve days." She beckons me to her side. "Do you not think we could travel today?"

"Madam, it appears the storms are clearing, and the skies are beginning to turn blue, so perhaps it might be a possibility."

A clarion sounds and the king is announced. He sweeps into the room, filling the air with the scent of his usual walnut soap. His fellow courtiers follow, bowing respectfully as they enter the Lady Pembroke's presence.

"Ladies, we leave for England today. Prepare yourselves for the journey as the fog has lifted and we will send for you within the hour." He pulls Anne closer by her elbow and beams like a schoolboy with a great crush. As he whispers to her, I am just close enough to overhear.

"Then, upon our return, what you have wished for, for so long, will be accomplished and you shall be known as Queen of England."

"Majesty!" She cannot contain herself, and a great smile of delight spreads across her face as she falls to her knees, grasps his hand, and plants a kiss upon one of his ruby rings.

14TH NOVEMBER, FEAST OF SAINT ERKENWALD, DOVER

As we sail for the English coastline, I sit in the knowledge that Anne is about to be secretly pre-contracted to the king. The channel is choppy, the skies grey again, and rolling waves toss and turn the ship like a restless baby in its crib. Anne and I, with some of her ladies, are in her cabin below decks, and I am once again green at the gills. Waves crash against the side of the ship, and the sailors fight with the rigging as the vessel rolls, her decks soaked, the conditions causing mayhem and nausea for most on board.

Anne leans across to me and whispers, "Henry has promised me that, shortly after we land, we will be promised to one another, and that we will have a second marriage service at a later date, just as foreign royal brides of the Middle Ages have done."

"Really?" I try not to sounds surprised. Jane Boleyn, otherwise known as Lady Rochford, is nearby, pretending not to earwig. I've seen Henry's frustration at being stuck in interminable battles with Rome and Spain to try to divorce his post-menopausal Spanish Queen Katharine. Now, with the backing of the English clergy and the French monarchy within her grasp, Anne feels confident.

"I hope for a son," she says, "born in wedlock."

"I hope you have your desired wish." I'm one of the few who knows she has abandoned her much vaunted moral principles and had sex with the man she's famously said "no" to since he first asked. When I asked her about her first time with Henry before, it seemed she didn't want to talk about it. Perhaps she will now.

"What?" she asks, raising a brow at me.

"Well?" I lean even closer, hoping to prize more detail from her. "Is Henry as you thought?"

"Not really." She flicks a look towards Jane. "I was expecting a sweet and gentle lover, but he seemed impatient – the longing games couples play, when laying naked with a mate, were over almost before they had begun. He was overpowering and, at times, a little rough. But I am putting this down to enthusiasm and eagerness, being our first full sexual encounter."

I wish we'd had this conversation after the first night she spent with Henry, but she has been too shy, or maybe embarrassed to share the details, even though we are so close. She is tactful enough not to divulge anything more, but her look tells me she is disappointed, and even a little worried. It reminds me of her ambiguous expression that morning she returned from Henry's bed.

We say no more, aware of Jane Rochford floating around the edge of the cabin, pretending not to listen, trying to collect any fragment of information she can carry back to the duke of Norfolk.

With a good wind, by nightfall we arrive at Dover and head to the castle. When I wake Anne in the pitch dark of the next morning, her eyes are sleep heavy as she searches the shadows, and for a moment she seems unsure of her whereabouts.

She sits up and looks out at the flickering lights of the ships in the misty harbour, some distance from the castle. "I love this time in the morning, when time seems to stop still."

The morning is freezing so I light the candles and stoke the hearth. When I look out of the window, thick snow swirls, doing its best to invade the room. I jerk the window, making sure it's properly closed, and stand shivering in front of the hearth, which is now ablaze. Time to dress Anne for her wedding day.

She steps out of bed and stretches, then sits on the edge of the mattress and yawns.

"I am tired, Beth. I did not sleep well." Her shift drops to the floor.

"Too much excitement," I say. "But by the time I have finished with you, you will look magnificent." I smile to reassure her. I'm already dressed and have grabbed my toiletries and makeup to prepare her for her day.

"'Twas not the excitement," she says, stepping into a bath I've already prepared. "It was the owls. Did you not hear them?"

"No, I did not," I reply.

"I could not have slept if I had wanted to." She sighs, sinking below the waterline, trying to keep her long hair dry. After a quick soak, she dries herself and I hand her roll-on deodorant, which I have shown her how to use. She takes my perfume bottle from me and spritzes herself with its heady scent. Next, I hand her a Holland linen shift, embroidered in black work, her wool stockings, and her petticoats. I pull the lacings as tight as I can, working fast. There is no one here to help us, as, if we have company, they will realise she is up to something, and the king has instructed her to keep their pre-contract secret.

Kirtle now secure, she steps into her wedding gown – an exquisite creation made of silver thread and tissue. She looks radiant as I braid her hair, plaited across her crown. Next comes a black and silver gable hood, which makes her look even more regal, accentuating her elongated neck.

My goodness, how lucky am I, a 21st-century girl, to be prepping the famous Anne Boleyn for her secret wedding to King Henry VIII? I'm tempted to pinch myself to make sure I'm really here, doing this, but I know it's true, so I smile to myself and get on with it.

The only jewellery she wears along with her emerald betrothal ring is the large diamond given to her by Henry, dangling from a golden chain around her neck. Her hair is braided tight against her face, with only her hairline showing, and her face is devoid of cosmetics, save for the tiniest bit of rouge, which I apply to her cheeks just to offset the winter's pallor.

As she readies herself for her pre-dawn rendezvous to promise herself to her dearest love, pulling an ermine wrap about her shoulders, she looks nervous. The time has come. We hurry in silence through the shadowed halls of the sleeping castle, winding our way up the spiral stair until we reach the uppermost chamber. The room seems almost dreamlike in the bright candlelight, with braziers in each of the four corners radiating warmth. It is simple but beautiful, with a soaring ceiling, a stunning marble hearth ablaze on the courtyard side, carved wooden panelling all around, and a bank of eight stained-glass and mullioned windows, four up and four down, overlooking the cobbles.

Anne and I approach the groom and his guests, already present in the chamber: Henry, Henry Norris, Thomas Heneage, and William Brereton. The officiant present is to witness the most significant day in Anne's life – the ceremony where she is pre-contracted with Henry. We wait, breath held, while Henry verifies that the pre-contract is in order. With a look of absolute command, he turns to the officiant.

"Go forth, then, in God's name, and do that which pertained to you."

We all assume our places. Henry stands to Anne's right, both facing the Archbishop. As a witness, I stand to the side, and when George Brown recites the marriage banns, repeating three times, if anyone present knows of an impediment to this marriage, all gazes are lowered to the floor. No one utters a word for fear of retribution from the king. Henry and Anne are asked if they are willing to proceed with the ceremony, and, as is traditional, they both answer, "Yes". Then Henry takes her right hand in his.

Prompted by the Archbishop of Dublin, George Brown, Henry looks into Anne's eyes. "I Henricus Rex, take thee, Anne Boleyn, to be my wedded wife, to have and to hold from this day forth, for better for worse, for richer or poorer, in sickness and in health, till death do us part, according to God's holy ordinance, and thereto I plight thee my troth."

Trembling as she squeezes his hand, Anne's voice is not nearly as strong. "I, Anne Boleyn, take thee, Henricus Rex, to be my wedded husband, to have and to hold from this day forth, for richer or poorer, in sickness and in health, till death do us part, according to God's holy ordinance, and thereto I plight thee my troth."

The delicate golden band is offered on a plate of gilt for the chaplain to bless. Henry picks it up and places Anne's right hand in his. He holds the ring on her thumb: "In the name of the Father," then on her second finger, "and of the Son," then the third finger, "and of the Holy Ghost," then slips the band on her fourth finger, "Amen."

Soft snowfall complements the dawn above Dover. The couple seem pleased to have committed themselves to each other in a pre-contracted and binding ceremony. I feel happy, knowing history has taken the correct turn, and Henry and Anne have made their declarations, in a watertight, legal intent to marry each other, just as I knew they had to. I hope with this specific event over and done with, the cover of the Ives' book will remain in its original form. I'm glad that, at least here, in the sixteenth century, things seem to be on the 'right' track.

After such a ceremony, 16th-century canon law states that it is permissible for the couple to commence sexual intercourse with one another. But I know that horse has already bolted. Tears well up as I witness this most secret of moments, of this couple promising themselves to one another, with the few here assembled, and I'm unable to look away from the royal couple, and the simple gold ring on Anne's hand. She is now a queen awaiting her crown. After years of legal wrangling, Henry holds the woman he has longed for in his arms. This ceremony is private – held in the queen's chapel closet with only a handful of witnesses – and there is no record of a bedding ceremony with her. He is a private man in matters of the heart, and despite his later protestations that it is all about obtaining an heir for England, his marital turmoil is all about his desires.

Henry and Anne's return trip from Dover to London is now an unofficial honeymoon. The journey's progress is aggravated by the weather, with November 1532 being wet and stormy, and the notoriously bad English roads are muddy quagmires.

Our first stop after leaving Dover is at Sandwich, where we all stay for one night. Our lodgings are at the friary, the only location large enough to house the royal retinue. Hosting the king is an honour, but incredibly expensive –

only the largest accommodations will do. Anne has thirty highborn ladies with her. We all then next to Canterbury, where we stay at Lord Feneux's home. Our next stop is at Sittingbourne, where we stay at the Lion Inn before moving onward to Stone Castle, the home of Bridget Wingfield – Lady Tyrwhitt.

Anne feels tense as we arrive, having written a letter to her some days previous. Bridget was widowed when her then husband, Sir Nicholas Hervey, died on August 5th, but she has already remarried, not three months later, to Sir Robert Tyrwhitt, a man who dislikes Anne. I remember Anne commenting about Bridget marrying him, saying she doesn't approve of the man. Both had argued – the reason Anne feels uncomfortable being here. The tension is palpable in the Castle as Lady Tyrwhitt shows the king around.

"Your Grace, a room has been prepared for you here and another down the hall for Mistress Boleyn and her ladies."

"Thank you, Lady Tyrwhitt, you are a gracious hostess, and I am most obliged to you." He nods at her. "However, Lady Anne will be joining me in the rooms you have prepared."

Her brows raise in clear disgust. "Your Majesty, you are a married man!"

"Indeed, I am, Lady Tyrwhitt, and the Lady Pembroke will accompany me in my chambers."

It's so obvious that Bridget doesn't like the idea of Henry and Anne sharing a bed under her roof, believing they will be sinning, unaware that they are now pre-contracted for marriage. Sir Robert's opposition to Anne Boleyn does not seem to make the king hesitate to accept overnight hospitality in Stone Castle. Despite his appearing to enjoy his visit, I feel nervous, knowing from history that Bridget will later make a confession on her deathbed about Anne, evidence that will be transcribed and will help to seal her fate. Someone – either her stepson or her husband – will make a statement before Anne's trial, disclosing a vague description of 'bawdry and lecherous' behaviour. Maybe Anne's stay at their home, on this night, is where this evidence originates from. Knowing what I know, I'm glad we will not be staying here for long.

We arrive at Eltham Palace on November 24th, and, for a time, it appears to the court at large as though nothing has changed – the secret remaining with the select few who have witnessed the pre-contact ceremony. Anne occupies the queen's apartments at Eltham, while Henry occupies his. Unbeknown to most at court, he slips down the corridor to her door in the dead of night with only a few faithful, silent servants, like me, opening it to him.

"Good evening, Your Majesty." I wave him in, to where he can see his wife reclining on a rug by the warm hearth in nothing but an embroidered linen shift. He stands there, so mesmerised by the curves of her flesh that he doesn't say a word for what seems like minutes. The shadows of the flickering flames dance across Anne's silhouette, and I need to remind him to walk through the door and take a seat. I bid them both goodnight and leave them to their lovemaking. One way or another, Henry must move his situation forward.

Now that he and Anne have their hearts' desire, I wish I could have mine. I try not to think of George a few rooms down the passageway, knowing he is with Jane. Being with her, I know he will never disturb me, more's the pity. I must stop thinking of him in that way and heed the words of Professor Marshall. Perhaps, now that history is playing out as it should, I could consider returning home to my own family and friends, even though one of the reasons I jumped here was to see George. Surely, I have proved that my presence here has put any previous crooked history straight? The book cover must be back as it should be. I hope not much time has passed at home, so no one will have time to realise that I'm missing. I think of my parents and my sister often – Jessica, too – and wonder what they are doing.

I look down at the cypher ring, not daring to touch or twist it in case it might propel me out of here in full view of Anne's ladies, bedding down on their palettes in the chamber adjacent to Henry and Anne's rooms. Not a great position to find myself in. I shake my head, then blow out the candle's flickering flame with one puff. I'm exhausted as I thump a dent into my pillow and pull the linen sheet and woollen blanket up over my shoulder. Now is not the time for me to be time-slipping anywhere. If I have to go, I need to give George a credible reason for my absence – maybe having to return to Surrey – unless, of course, there is the possibility of getting with him properly. But then, the professor did emphasise that I had to make sure everything goes 'to plan' with Anne, and the way to do that is to continue being a close-up witness to life around her. Whatever happens, I need to keep my wits about me and appear as much like these Tudors as I can.

Six

Greenwich Palace is preparing for the king's return, and Henry's long absence from court has caused some apprehension. His son, the Duke of Richmond, has stayed on in France. We have heard reports that the French king is pleased to entertain such a promising youth, and Richmond and his followers are proud and pleased to be feted by the French Court. He enjoys the company of the dauphin, François, and his brother, Henri d'Orléans, as well as their sisters. They hunt, play tennis, gamble and, if the rumour is to be believed, behave like teenage hooligans, riding the streets at night, beating people up and raising a riot. The goings-on in Calais have created such a stir that, in the autumn of 1532, two editions have been produced of the work entitled *The Manner of the Triumph at Calais and Boulogne*. Both plays were concerned with all the details of the meeting between the monarchs and were a way of recording for the court what proceeded there.

Anne is excited as she prepares for her return to court, having received a letter from a person of her chambers who went before us to Greenwich to ready her rooms.

"Mistress Wickers, you will be interested to hear that the court has enjoyed some revels in our absence."

"Yes, Mistress?" I fold freshly embroidered linen shifts into caskets.

"An entertainment titled *'The Play of the Weather'* has been performed at Greenwich, designed to address our trip to France."

"Mistress, will it not be difficult to conceal your intimacies with His Majesty?"

"No, I shall act as I always have. No one shall know of the promises made nor that I have lain with the king. The servants are expected to be discreet."

"The court shall never hear of your secrets from me," I say, closing the lid on the large casket. She scans the letter and a wry smile creeps across her face.

"It sounds as if the court is coming to its own conclusions on matters between Henry and me." She nods as she continues reading to herself. "There has been a speech made, within a revel, detailing several important and not very subtle references to the king's marital affairs."

"Really? It seems the court is on tenterhooks awaiting the pope's judgement upon the king's matter."

"Beth, listen to this speech that has been recorded for me to learn off. Merry Report is the character."

I sit on a large cushion by the window and give her my full attention.

> "By my faith, for his lordship is right busy
> With a piece of work that needs must be done.
> Even now is he making of a new moon:
> He sayeth your old moons be so far tasted
> That all the goodness of them is wasted;
> Which of the great wait hath been most matter,
> For old moons be leaky, they can hold no water."

She is somewhat stunned by the ribald words and appears shocked that Merry Report's speech has filled the space of the court with bawdy jokes. With a slow shake of her head, she snaps the page straight and continues.

> "But for this new moon, I durst lay my gown
> Except a few drops at her going down,
> Ye get no rain till her arising
> Without yet need, and then no man's devising
> Could wash the fashion of rain to be so good:
> Not gushing out like gutters of Noah's flood,
> But small drops sprinkling softly on the ground:
> Though they fell on a sponge, they would give no sound.
> This new moon shall make a thing spring more in this while
> Than an old moon shall while a mile go a mile."

She sits on a cushion in silence for some time, and I know she is disturbed, not only about the 'tightness' of the new moon compared with the leakiness of the old but also with the references to Katharine's miscarriages.

I get up and walk around the chamber, tidying things away and packing in readiness for our journey home. During the first year of my degree, I studied that play and debated it with others when picking apart the king's matter. The speech refers to Henry's sexual prowess, and I try not to imagine him in full, physical seduction mode.

Poor Anne's cheeks are red, and she has collapsed back into the cushion on the chair behind her, the words no doubt producing ungodly pictures in her mind. But she continues to reread aloud the speech, her voice shaken by the court's brazenness. The reference to Jupiter making a new moon relates to her pregnant body. It is possible that Merry Report is telling the court that she could be pregnant and confirming in its misogyny, Katharine's complete downfall. The Greenwich revels and entertainments often combine didactic and comic material with specific and detailed topical allusions. As an audience of revels and interludes, the court is practised in adopting different interpretative strategies for aspects of the same entertainment.

"Madam," I say, standing behind her, my hand on her shoulder, "the revel is a jest of a court performance meant simply to be enjoyed, even though it has a specific political charge. Put the letter away and take the revel for what it was, an amusement."

"It seems the court will not take me seriously," she replies. "Perhaps they will when I am declared queen."

Word arrives from Pope Clement threatening Henry with excommunication if he does not leave Anne Boleyn and take Katharine of Aragon back as his wife within one month. However, unbeknown to the pope, Anne Boleyn, the secret queen of England, is already planning for her coronation, and sits listening as Cromwell pores over the plans, making sure everything is done to her taste and the king's approval. As he reads out his list, she seems unsurprised by his manner.

"I have itemised everything, Madame la Marquess, and will send these lists to the king for his signature, if you are happy with my work?"

She looks up at him. "You are being most diligent in these matters. I am most impressed."

"There is more," he continues. "For your apparel, Madam, in consulting the Head of the Royal Wardrobe, we have ordered one and a half yards of crimson satin, three yards of crimson taffeta to line your velvet gown, and two yards of black satin for another gown."

"Go on, Master Cromwell."

He reads the list of bolts of fabrics and embellishments the king has ordered for her.

"I will be very well dressed, Master Cromwell." She smiles over at me, excited by the prospect of such sumptuous costumes at her coronation.

"Madam, the king has assured me that he wants no expense spared." Cromwell nods once, keeping his emotions to himself, as is his norm.

NEW YEAR'S EVE, DECEMBER 1532 – WHITEHALL PALACE

Henry never likes to miss the opportunity for a game but, on this fine morning, he has no idea the game will be played on him, as he and Henry Norris lead Anne blindfolded and by the elbow into her new apartments, and bedchamber.

Anne laughs. "My Lord, where are you taking me?"

I watch as I follow them, with Anne resting each arm over her respective companions, gripping their hands tight.

"My love, this is a surprise – wait and see!" Henry beams at Norris, enjoying the moment of spoiling his wife.

"Sire, are you sure the blindfold is tight enough?" Norris asks. "We cannot let her know what is happening." Anne laughs again.

"Do not worry, Norris, I tied it most securely."

"Your Grace, you tease my Lady so," I say, following this small group like a little duckling skipping after its mother.

The king laughs, turning his face towards me, the twinkle in his eye giving away his delight. He nods to the royal guards, who open the large oak doors, revealing the most exquisite presence chamber, fit for a woman of great majesty. Henry leads Anne to the centre of the room, with Norris hanging back.

"Can I remove the mask now, my Lord?" Anne whispers.

Henry tugs at the silk cloth but does not get the immediate response he expects. Anne blinks and smiles up at the fresco around the edges of the room, taking in the brilliant and illuminated colours, which, to my 21st-century eye, is impressive but gaudy. She walks over to the ornately decorated fireplace, with its H and A cyphers carved into the woodwork. The ormolu clock Henry gifted her as a wedding present has already been placed on a large, ornately carved table, and it chimes its bright song as she stands beside it. It's much bigger in 'real life' and 'real time' than the replica housed at Hever. I know that England's current monarch will keep Anne's clock most securely on display in private apartments at St. James's Palace.

I stare at the tapestries which adorn the walls, depicting scenes of nature, animals, and children, their rich gilt threads so magnificent in the sunlight. Every convenience has been thought of, as Henry takes her hand and leads her into her privy bedchamber. A huge walnut bed dominates the room, adorned with soft silken sheets embroidered with entwined H and A initials. Drapes covered in the embroidery of fruits, animals, and children hang from the large four posters, ready to shut out the night when sleep or procreation beckons.

Anne seems to realise that she hasn't shown as much astonishment and delight as Henry was expecting, and now makes a great play of swooning. She recovers fast and kneels at his feet, thanking him profusely and professing her love.

He leads her back to the New Year's Eve feast, with Norris and I following, where courtiers note his inexplicably content expression, and Anne no doubt hopes that it will be observed and recorded by all the European ambassadors, who will report back to their masters.

EARLY JANUARY 1533 – GREENWICH PALACE

The convent at Greenwich was a favourite refuge for Henry until he began to obsess about his annulment from Katharine. On more than one occasion, he has written to Pope Leo X to extol the virtues of the Observant Order, and its convent at Greenwich, declaring his deep, devoted affection and admiration for the friars' Christian poverty, sincerity, and charity. The convent had for some time provided the confessors for Queen Katharine, and many others at the royal court. Rome has wanted to interview Henry personally over the case of the desired annulment, but he categorically refuses to comply. One of the pope's predecessors granted permission for the king's marriage to Katharine in the first place, and the current pope is unwilling to overrule that decision, even if it merits the possibility of a different decision being reached. All signs are that the final word from Rome is, at last, imminent — and negative — and Henry is moving to establish himself as the final arbiter in matters religious within his kingdom. He has since decided to pre-empt any final decision from Rome by asserting the independence and supremacy of his authority over the Church in England. Even though I know what is coming, it is still astonishing to witness events and see how they develop in real time.

JANUARY 25TH, 1533 – WHITEHALL

In the pre-dawn darkness of St Paul's, Henry and a few of his closest confidants gather in the upper chamber of the Holbein Gate of Anne's splendid new palace at Whitehall. Doctor Rowland Lee, the king's chaplain, is waiting nervously for the bride to appear.

It's bitter cold as Anne, Nan Savage – now Lady Berkeley – and I walk towards the Holbein Gate.

Anne leans closer to me. "We must hurry – Henry will be waiting for me!" Her voice comes in an excited whisper. The frosted gravel crunches under our feet, and we're serenaded by the dawn chorus of starlings and sparrows as we make our way to meet the matrimonial party.

"Yes, and the priest will be waiting too," Lady Berkeley says, trying to keep up.

"I had thought to marry at Westminster. Not over the king's gate."

"You will have Westminster when you are crowned, Lady Pembroke."

Anne nods at that, then looks at me. "I think the priest will ask for a licence from the pope."

"Henry does not care," I say. "Besides, no one can deny him. Not even you."

"Henry's terrible in rage, and he's got his response revised if anyone asks. He's going to say he truly has a licence, whichever was seen with discharges all. The priest will not dare to cross him."

"No," I say, doing my best not to show any foreknowledge in my eyes.

"Yet, I know in his heart he still looks for, and seeks papal approval." She quickens her pace, and we follow her up the stairway, trying to stop her dress snagging on the stonework.

The flame of Lady Berkeley's candle flickers in its holder as we hurry through the darkness. This hushed wedding is so secret that even Cranmer does not know of the arrangement. The only people present are Henry Norris, Mr Heneage, Lady Berkeley, Rowland Lee, me, and, of course, the royal couple.

As far as all of Europe knows, Henry is still married to his first wife, Katharine of Aragon. The pope has not yet made a ruling on whether the marriage is valid, or whether Henry can have the annulment he seeks.

As we stand outside the chamber door, I hear Roland Lee broach the subject of marital law, trying to be as tactful as possible.

"Sir, I trust you have the pope's licence, both that you may marry and that I may join you together in marriage?"

"What else?" Henry lies.

Lee asks to see it. "This matter touches us all very near, and therefore it is expedient that the license is read before us all, or else we run all – and I, deeper than any other – into excommunication in marrying Your Grace without any banns being asked, and in a place unhallowed, and no divorce as yet given of the first matrimony."

We listen in trepidation as Henry pretends to be outraged.

"Why, Master Rowland, think you me a man of so small faith and credit?" He claims he does have the licence, but has it stored in a secure location, and to go fetch it at this hour would cause a stir of gossip, so orders Roland Lee to proceed, and he would take any consequences on his head.

With no other choice but to obey, Lee bows in acquiescence. Henry turns, awaiting the entrance of his bride. Having overheard his argument with the chaplain, Anne's anxiety hits her as we step into the chamber. I cup her elbow to support her, but she seems to calm on seeing Henry and they exchange the most intimate of looks. At this moment, at her wedding promised by the pre-contract back in November, she is at the height of her power. She says she is not yet certain if she is pregnant but has missed a monthly bleed. I know she has said nothing to anyone, except me, and is glad that being with child already is not the motivating factor for Henry securing their pre-contract with marriage.

I watch with amazement as they exchange vows and rings once more, counting my blessings to be in attendance in the early dawn of January 25th, 1533, when Henry VIII and Anne Boleyn are officially married.

As soft snow blankets the awakening city of London, I find myself unable to tear my eyes from the simple golden ring on Anne's hand. With everything I've seen in my time-slip travels, I cannot believe I have just witnessed the most important wedding in history. Anne is married. Everything has been done to make sure her title of Queen is unimpeachable. Indeed, everything has been done in the proper form, set out in the bible of ceremony known as The Royal Book. It will be these customs that will govern Anne and Henry's actions over the next few months.

FEBRUARY 1533

Thomas More is accused of being complicit with Elizabeth Barton, who opposes Henry's break with Rome. More refuses to accept the king as head of the Church of England, which he believes will disparage the power of the pope. Meanwhile, George Boleyn – who is now always at court, having been called to parliament – and Thomas Wyatt stand together in the Great Watching Chamber of the palace, watching the skirts of Anne Boleyn, now Queen of England, rustle along the floor. They dip deep bows as she and I glide towards the king's privy chamber. Without warning, Anne stops in her tracks and takes my elbow.

"Mistress Wickers, I believe I need to speak with my brother and Master Wyatt." She turns back towards them. "Brother." She smiles, offering her hand. "Thomas."

The two men move to stand before her. George bows and smiles.

"Sister." He kisses her hand. "Mistress Wickers." He goes to take my hand to kiss it, and, to my surprise, Anne doesn't stop him. My cheeks burn as he gazes up into my eyes and chuckles.

"Yes, Lady Pembroke?" Thomas Wyatt asks.

"Do you know something, Master Wyatt?"

"What is it, Anne?" George asks.

"Over the past few days, and especially at night, I have found I have the most enormous hankering for fresh apples that I haven't stopped eating them."

Thomas looks at her in confusion, not understanding her meaning.

"Sister?" George leans forward. "Does this mean…?"

Anne arches her eyebrows. "Brother, I have found myself of an evening down in the stores demanding apples."

George's mouth falls open. "Anne?"

"The king says my desire to eat apples is a sign I am with child, but I have told him that could not possibly be. What say you?" She lets out her famous laugh as she watches his expression, which cannot conceal his amazement.

"You cannot be with child, surely?"

"George, I think it is true." She giggles at him, then looks at me. Thomas just stands there, his mouth agape.

"Does the king know?" George asks, his eyes still wide.

"He hopes."

"Then you are with child!"

"Yes, Brother!" She cannot hold her laughter back.

"The future king of England!" he exclaims.

Anne claps once, the sound soft. "Your nephew!"

"Your son!" He holds her shoulders. "Darling Sister, I told you heaven willed it. But I thought this wedding in January was your contract – your virginity, the prize!"

On hearing this, Thomas Wyatt strides off in disgust, not looking back. George pulls Anne and me to a nearby window seat. Anne sits between us.

"Brother, the promise was made in November in Dover," she says, keeping her voice low, "on the way back from Calais. We were fugitives from the storm, remember?"

"You never said a word to me!" he moans.

"Brother, first the snow, then the wind and the rain seemed as if it would go on forever. It held us in prison, like Dido and Aeneas and the cave."

"But, Sister, you did not wait…?" His eyes are wide once again.

"It was not a rash hot moment." She rests her hand on his forearm in reassurance. "Lord knows, the king has had many of those over the last six years, which I have held at bay. 'Twas a considered thing. You said yourself, with the submission of the clergy and Cranmer revealing that leading the church, the opposition of Rome is crumbling. As Marchioness of Pembroke and with the tacit approval of King François, I could not consult with you, Brother, but in my heart, I did – and ultimately, I put myself in the hands of God. He has thus repaid my trust."

"You have risked so much!" he says, glancing around to make sure other courtiers are not within earshot.

"Binding vows were made, George, in Dover. The walls were hung with green velvet and embroidered wonderfully – it seemed to be saying that my time for change had come." She smiles, still trying to reassure him. He looks worried, but elated at the same time.

"We made great vows."

"Henry made great vows," I add. "I witnessed their ceremony of pre-contract."

George stares at me, his disappointment at being left out of the secret clear.

"All right," he says. "I had been dreading the thought of finally letting you go, only to find it's already happened."

"You must understand, Brother, it changes nothing between us."

"There will be ceremony enough for me to witness at your coronation."

"Oh, George, the king has taken me to see the royal treasure room!"

He laughs. "I am sure he has!" He pats the back of her hand, and I long for him to do the same with me, and more. "You know I am to leave in March to France, on a diplomatic warrant with King François, to raise with him the differences between England and Scotland?"

"Yes," Anne says.

"I am your champion, Sister. I am your round table knight of legend." He smiles. "No one will deny me in France – I will promote you tirelessly, my sister, as my sister – my queen – and now the mother of my future king!" His face radiates his pride. "They will not turn me down!"

"Who could deny you anything, George?" I say. As we get up, I squeeze his hand, unable to hold back. Anne notices but says nothing, then we walk away, leaving him standing there, while other courtiers whisper behind their hands. Now the court will be awash with more gossip about Anne. She is elated at her condition, and later, in her chamber, I ask of her certainty of being pregnant.

"How long is it since your last bleed, Madam, and how do you feel?"

"Weeks, I have had no wallops for weeks, and my breasts feel tender. Is that not a sign?"

"Yes, it is. But, then again, it might be a sign that Henry is not being as gentle as he ought in the bedchamber."

"Gentle or no, I think, Beth, I am with child." She strokes her belly and looks out of the window. "The king always desired me, but with this child in my belly, I will now be valued as well, you see, and that makes my position at Court different."

"Have you told Henry?"

"No, not yet, but I think I am over two months gone, and I wanted to be sure before breaking the news of the pending birth of a son."

"Then why did you confide in George, and then blurt out your secret to Master Wyatt?"

"What the court does not know, they talk about anyway, so I thought I would add some fuel to the fire – and with a bit of luck, it may get back to the Spanish Katharine!"

26TH MARCH 1533

In the run-up to the official annulment, there is much consternation at what is known of the king's plans, and opportunities for decrying or opposing them are not wanting in those who have the courage. The Observant Friars, not just of Greenwich but also across the country, are in the forefront of spiritual and theological opposition to Henry's clear will in his matter.

For Anne – on March 26th, after six years of waiting, of being the king's love but not his wife, first lady but not queen, and after months of secretly being a married woman – is finally to be publicly presented as Queen of

England and Lady of Ireland. At the same time, throughout the kingdom, she will be publicly prayed for in church services as a member of the royal family for the first time.

As she enters the chapel at Greenwich, at her husband's side, she shows no hint of nerves. Month by month, her status increases with the size of her belly, cementing even tighter the bond between her and the king. She thrives on attention, and now steps into a space packed not only with people who have worked feverishly to make this day possible but also those who have worked with equal vigour to prevent it. Eustace Chapuys, the Spanish ambassador to London, along with the assembled Catholic courtiers, upon seeing her occupying the Queen's chair at Mass, look like they don't know whether to laugh or cry. I, for one, feel proud as I watch from the courtiers' pew as my dear friend takes her rightful place.

Gertrude Courtenay, Marchioness of Exeter, on the other hand, looks disgruntled. She is about the same age as Anne and is a homely looking woman – Rubenesque, but not a beauty – and men have been known to weaken at the knees at the sight of her bosom. I know, as a Catholic, that she takes on the Catholic side of the debate, having to suffer Anne Boleyn in the Queen's seat, and now looks as though she's eaten something foul by the way her face is screwed up. Others of Henry's court are in favour of Anne's elevation and seem relieved that all the confusion of the past few years has been quelled.

No one can deny that she looks every inch the queen as she sweeps majestically through the rainbow-coloured puddles of light created by the stained-glass windows. As she processes through the bowing crowds and clouds of Catholic incense, sixty immaculately dressed maids of honour follow her, headed by her beautiful young cousin, Lady Mary Howard, who has the honour of carrying the queen's train.

For once, I am an observer, enjoying the spectacle as Anne reaches her seat and the officiating priest begins the Mass with the blessing of the altar. A short time later, head bowed, she speaks aloud to the congregation, making her first public words as Queen of England:

"*Sicut erat in princípio, et nunc, et semper, et in sæcula sæculórum. Amen.*"

The Latin translates to "As it was in the beginning, is now, and ever shall be, world without end. Amen."

Considering Anne's pious and religious beliefs, the words are deeply appropriate and comforting for her. Paschaltide is the holiest of seasons in the Christian liturgical calendar and almost anybody and everybody in the Tudor Court attends the High Mass being celebrated today. This is a new beginning for her and for so many others. The day before marked the start of the calendar on the Feast of the Annunciation – the most opportune time to unveil Anne Boleyn, Marchioness of Pembroke, as queen consort.

31ST MARCH 1533 – CHURCH OF THE OBSERVANT FRIARS AT GREENWICH

Henry attends Holy Mass at the Observant Friars' abbey in Greenwich on Easter Sunday, only a few weeks, it seems, before he settles this business of the annulment through a compliant Cranmer. No doubt, he is aware of the friars' already expressed resistance to his known will. Cromwell has his spies in the abbey, and I must be careful in all that I say, as I know the man has informers everywhere.

The three individuals foremost in their opposition to the king's annulment at the monastery are friars Peto, Elstow, and Forest. Friar Peto is to preach today, and I wonder whether the presence of the king will encourage or deter him. Henry and Anne take a prime position before the pulpit, right under Peto's nostrils, as the choir fills the cloisters with echoes of *'Christe Jesu, pastor bone'*. Peto's words are like fire and brimstone of ancient times as he ploughs into his sermon, undeterred by the presence of royalty.

As he continues his strong denunciation of Henry, the congregation is stunned. Instead of focusing on the Easter story and Christ's resurrection, the friar, who supports Katharine of Aragon, speaks on 1 Kings, 22, in which he compares Henry VIII to Ahab, drawing comparisons between Anne Boleyn and Jezebel, Ahab's wife, who replaced God's prophets with pagan priests, as Anne is promoting men of the New Religion – a new religion she supports. I want to shrink back into my seat as I see her squirm. Henry's eyes are like organ stops as he glares at Peto.

Peto glares back at the king. "And if you continue to behave like Ahab, then it might come to pass that after your death, dogs will lick your blood, as they had licked the blood of Ahab!"

Many of the congregation begin to cough, for those who know their Old Testament know this is strong stuff indeed.

"Ahab's life is not a good or happy one, and his death is shameful," the friar continues.

The congregation shift in their pews, not knowing where to look, as to meet the king's gaze in his anger may bring retribution on their heads. However, the friar doesn't falter. Anne flicks through her prayer book, I suspect to find something that will counteract Peto's sermon, but she is so incensed with his self-righteousness that she slams the small book shut. She juts her chin out in defiance of the friar and sits on the edge of her pew, her small hands drawn into fists. Henry looks on in disbelief.

"So, the king died and was brought to Samaria, and they buried him there. They washed the chariot at a pool in Samaria, where the prostitutes bathed, and the dogs licked up his blood, as the word of the Lord had declared."

Peto wants to set Henry on the right path. He wants him to abandon Anne, with her heretical views, and return to Katharine of Aragon. Henry leans into Anne and I can hear him whisper, "I will persuade him that my marriage to Katharine is invalid."

Anne turns her shoulder towards him, her mouth curling in anger. "Majesty, you cannot let him get away with this, surely? He talks of your death, by comparing you to Ahab!"

Henry pats her slender shoulder in reassurance, but she will not be silenced.

"My Lord, he has compared me…to Jezebel!" She frowns. "Peto implies that I am how the devil attacks man. I am the new Eve. That is his opinion, My Lord, not mine!"

"I am his nemesis, and I will change his mind. Maybe the best way to change his views about you will be whilst he is on the rack!" He stands, offering his arm to Anne. Next moment, he orders the guards to arrest the treasonous priest.

Peto has preached a dangerous sermon, and we watch in horror as he is manhandled from the pulpit and frogmarched out of the church, no doubt to be taken to the Tower and tied to the rack to repent his controversial sermon. Anne looks livid at the complete and utter audacity of this so-called humble and religious man who slanders her and the king before his court. I know Peto will be imprisoned for a few months, on Henry and Cromwell's orders.

People are afraid. Henry VIII's version of reform means retaining all Catholic ideals and rituals but plundering the abbeys of their wealth. On the flipside, whilst in office, Thomas More was a man who has delighted in torturing and burning Evangelicals. The Tudors did not invent the burning of heretics, as this was a method previously sanctioned by the Catholic Church several centuries earlier.

Thomas More will be stripped of most of his wit, gentleness, and warmth, at his execution in a few years, but, for now, he is a gentle man full of warmth and compassion, until he is challenged on matters of religion. Looking around at the throngs of people in the pews, I feel so guilty for knowing some of their fates and wish I was able to help both Catholics and Evangelicals alike, even More, Cromwell, George, and Anne, evade death, but what damage would it cause in the long-term? No, for now, I will just observe, support, and take note.

Everyone notices the king turn to look at Cromwell, who sits aghast at the audacity of this friar, no doubt wishing the man had held his tongue.

There is unrest in the cities as well as from the pulpits, as the citizens of England are truly afraid of breaking with Rome. The real impact on the social climate – with thousands made destitute, hungry, and homeless when they no longer have the abbeys to employ, feed, and heal them – will have a devastating knock-on effect on their lives. Later persecutions will also effect Evangelicals because Henry will always be a Catholic at heart.

Anne is not responsible for this religious upheaval, but she will be blamed for it. The king is responsible because anything Henry wants, Henry will have, and he will blame everyone else for the change in the Church and its religion, and his ordering executions of Catholic and Protestant friends will be blamed on others.

Seven

THURSDAY, 4TH APRIL 1533 – WHITEHALL PALACE

I have been summoned to the king's privy chamber, and fidget as I wait in the Great Watching Chamber, my gaze never shifting from the guards at the door which leads to Henry's apartments. Anne is already with him, and I have no idea why I have been called here. Butterflies flutter through my stomach, as if in panic at being trapped indoors. Sunlight streams through the high stained-glass windows, their colours illuminating the wooden floor.

Anne's most trusted ladies wait with me: Nan Cobham, Lady Lee, and Lady Mary Howard. Across the room, Lady Exeter is in a huddle with her faction, her bosom much raised as she holds court with all the men.

After waiting for what seems like an eternity, and having not seen him in some time, my heart races when George enters the chamber. He is dressed smarter than normal, wearing a velvet cap in which flies a large plume. As he comes closer, he removes his bonnet and bows.

"What goes on here?" he asks, looking rather perplexed. "I have been summoned too."

"So, you don't know what this is all about then?"

"I have no idea." He shrugs one shoulder. "All Anne told me was to dress in my best and be here early this morning."

"Anne told me to wear my best, too," I say. Nan Cobham has trussed me up in an emerald-green gown, with a black kirtle and matching gable hood. I press my stomach with both hands. "I am nervous, George."

"No need to be nervous. How could you possibly offend the king?" He leans in, stroking the back of my neck with a surreptitious finger, which sends a delightful quiver down my spine. "No harm will come to you while I am here – all will be well."

At last, the doors to Henry's apartments are opened by the guards and Cromwell steps out into the gathering – a cockpit, as George likes to call it. To my surprise, Cromwell strides towards me, his steely gaze on me alone. My tummy flips in another wave of butterflies. He waves aside other petitioners trying to get in his way and stops feet away from George and me.

"Mistress Wickers, the king has asked you to attend on him today." He glances at George. "Lord Rochford may come, too, I suppose."

He purses his lips as if sucking a lemon, his dislike for me and George clear. It's his loss. As we follow him, my hand brushes George's, and a current of sexual energy shoots between us. He winks at me, giving me a cheeky smile.

We walk into the presence chamber and find both Henry and Anne enthroned on the dais, with Thomas Boleyn – the Earl of Wiltshire – stood alongside them. Cranmer is at the window, arms behind his back, looking out as the sun climbs higher in the sky.

Henry glances at Cranmer, who turns to face us. He is a thin man with a kindly face, who, as a friend of the Boleyns, is now comfortable in his office, having been Archbishop for over sixth months. He steps up to the dais, and Henry hands him a rolled parchment that's fixed with a large wax seal.

Cromwell approaches the king and bows. "Mistress Wickers is here, Your Majesty."

I curtsy low, and George joins his father behind Anne on the dais. His father whispers something to him, evoking a knowing smile.

Henry fixes his gaze on me as I rise. "Mistress Wickers, I have invited you here for your contribution to the happiness of my beloved Anne." He smiles. "In keeping my wife happy, you are keeping the kingdom happy, and in keeping my realm happy, you make your king happy."

"I am and have always been loyal to Your Majesties."

"In this matter, this is why you have been summoned here." I look at him, then Anne, my butterflies not letting up. "Come closer," he orders. "Cranmer, read out the patent."

"Patent, Your Majesty?" I ask, my voice croaking.

"Yes, Mistress Wickers. What power does the king hold if he cannot reward his subjects?" He nods once to me. "Archbishop Cranmer is here to bestow the title of Viscountess Beaumont upon you, as is mine and my wife's wish." He smiles at Anne and squeezes her hand as it rests in his. "This title is to be conferred on you, in your own right."

I don't know what to say and feel overwhelmed as, in a deep, clear voice, Cranmer begins to read the patents to be conferred upon me. First, I am awarded a small holding in Surrey, not far from where Nonsuch Palace will be built in the future. Trumpets fanfare before Cranmer continues. The king is giving me two patents, one of my creation, as Viscountess, and the other of 250 pounds a year – a lot of money in this age.

There is a momentary silence as Henry stands and comes down from his dais. The Earl of Wiltshire hands him a small coronet, surmounted with pearls. Anne now steps down from the dais, removes my gable hood, and watches as her husband, with reverence, places the coronet on my head. He then hands me my letters patent.

Thomas Boleyn steps closer and kisses me on the cheek. "Congratulations, Viscountess."

"My Lord." I smile, somewhat stunned by the experience.

Anne embraces me. "Viscountess."

"Your Majesty." My face burns, not believing what is happening.

Cranmer looks on with an approving smile. He knows I am of an evangelical persuasion. Cromwell says nothing, just observing – keeping his counsel.

George strides from the dais and envelops me in an exuberant embrace. "Congratulations – I had heard whispers that such a reward was afoot!"

I glare at him. "You said nothing."

"I was asked to say nothing." He smiles at Henry and Anne, moving aside as the king stands in front of me again.

"Perhaps now, Viscountess, we should find you a husband!"

Anne and I are strolling in the gardens, without company for a change, when we are joined by Master Cromwell. He removes his hat. The man is overweight, with a pronounced nose and thin lips. I have noticed before how tiny flecks of spittle escape from his mouth if he becomes agitated. He has a permanent frown, as if constipated, and his eyes are dark and piercing. I chuckle to myself at the thought that he resembles his descendant, the actor Danny Dyer, around the eyes.

He stares at me. This man misses nothing. He is, in fact, the all-seeing eye of the Tudor Court.

"Your Majesty." He bows to Anne, then looks back at me. "Viscountess."

Anne acknowledges his arrival. "Last week, at Greenwich, Secretary Cromwell, you were there when the friar preached to us about the good king who was corrupted by the wicked Jezebel. She built a pagan temple and let the priests of Baal into the palace. She ended up being thrown out of the window. I am the Jezebel, you see, and *you* are the priests of Baal."

Hmm, I know who I'd like to fling out of a window – Jane Boleyn!

"I see," Cromwell replies. "I heard that sermon too. I watched the guards drag the friar out."

"It seems, Master Cromwell, that our shared ideas upset many people."

"Majesty," I say, "any new learning and ideas are viewed as radical by those of the old faith."

Anne nods. "I know, Viscountess."

Cromwell views me with a wary eye, probably wondering if he can trust me. When courtiers of rank address me by my title, I still can't get used to being exalted in such tones. I find it unnatural to be put on a pedestal, hobnobbing with the nobility. With Anne, it's different, as, having known her before her meteoric rise, she is like an old friend, and at times, when we are alone, I need to remind myself of her position as queen. She smiles at me, then glances up at Cromwell as she plays with her leather gloves.

"The Viscountess is of the new faith, Cromwell. Indeed, you can say anything in front of Beth."

"Majesty, I came to you with these petitions, which I feel, as they are charitable causes you support, might best be replied to by you."

"Very well." She takes the bundle of vellum from him. "Attend me in my chambers and we shall go through them together." She looks at me. "Are you coming with us, Viscountess Beaumont?"

"If you do not mind, Majesty, I would like to take a turn about the garden for a time and enjoy the sunshine."

"Very well – I shall be in my chambers."

I curtsy to her. Cromwell nods at me, and they walk away, back down the gravel path, towards the palace.

Alone, I walk in the opposite direction, through the knotted hedges of the queen's privy gardens. Tucked away in one corner is a bench which is shaded in the boughs of an oak tree. As I get closer, my tummy fizzes on seeing George, sat alone, reading. He hears the gravel crunch beneath my feet and looks up. When he sees me, his face lights up. He puts the book down, gets to his feet, and makes a quick bow.

"Viscountess."

"My Lord, it sounds strange when you address me so." I grimace. "Please, do not change towards me – we have known one another a long time. Continue to call me plain Beth."

"Beth – you are not plain!" He laughs. "And you never will be." My cheeks burn. He steps closer and takes my hand. "I know not how to make sufficient demonstrations of my affection. I have stayed away, just as you instructed." He looks like a lost puppy, craving attention.

His hand is warm. "I am glad I have found you here because that's exactly what I need to talk with you about."

"How so?" he asks, hope rising in his voice.

"Has your sister spoken with you about me?"

"Yes," he replies. "But I had not dared hope that you would be open to the idea of being my mistress, because of Jane." He leads me to the base of the tree to shade us from prying eyes that might look down upon us from chamber windows.

My legs are trembling, and I'm glad he can't see them. "Anne made the point that you might be happier in your marriage if you had a mistress."

His eyes widen. "On consideration, I think she has a point. Even though it would be frowned upon at Court, I'd rather be your mistress than anyone else's wife."

His mouth falls open. "Well, I was not expecting that!" He touches my chin. "You never cease to amaze me, my love."

I raise a brow at him. "It can never be said that I am predictable."

"There is only one thing that is predictable when you are around, and that is the unusual." His sweet breath caresses my cheek. "Kiss me, Beth?" he says, his ardour spiked.

"Will we not be seen here?" I ask, a little anxious.

He glances about, up at the windows of the palace, and around the garden. "We are alone – I cannot see anyone about."

"George, does this not remind you of when we sheltered beneath the tree, in the gardens at Hever, within sight of Mary's casement windows, and when we overheard and saw Anne's first meaningful conversation with the king?"

He chuckles. "It does. He asked Anne to be his mistress."

With that, his gaze bores into mine, then on my mouth as he bends to brush my lips with his. His tongue parts my lips and he pulls me in as his kisses crush me.

"Will you be my mistress?" he asks, breathless.

"George, how could I say no?"

"Beth!" he whispers, pinning me against the tree trunk.

This time, I don't hold back, driving my tongue into his mouth, exploring with passionate enthusiasm. His soft hand cradles the back of my neck, making me weak at the knees. His other hand is about my waist, pulling me tighter to him, and the intensity of our unexpected liaison makes me know that, in his heart, he considers me the centre of his universe.

As our passion rises, the sound of tranquil birdsong is broken by the crunch of approaching footsteps. We break our embrace, my breasts and cheeks burning. Then I see Thomas Culpeper.

"What goes on here, Boleyn?" he asks, smirking. "Are you attempting to rape the Viscountess?"

"Leave us be, Culpeper!" George snarls. "Entertain yourself elsewhere. You are a beggar on horseback and your presence is not welcome here."

"I wonder what Lady Rochford would think if she discovered you both like this?"

Culpeper is only a young lad, but even I can see he's on dangerous ground.

George's eyes narrow. "It is very difficult to run and tell tales when one's legs are broken. You are forgetting your position – now fuck off back to your duties. Go wash the stains out of your coat!"

Culpeper continues smirking as he skulks off, muttering to himself. "Let me know what her cunny tastes like when you get there. She is a whore who could be fucked for a pennyworth of fish!"

It's clear he didn't think we would hear him. How wrong he is. George chases him down the path. When he catches him, he grabs him by the collar of his shirt.

"You have been warned, boy. I will make you apologise to the Viscountess in front of Queen Anne."

I come out from under the shade of the tree and lift George's book from the bench, watching open-mouthed as Culpeper is frogmarched back towards the palace.

By the time we arrive at the door of Anne's apartments, Culpeper is red in the face and about to burst into tears. George looks stony-faced as the usher announces us. He enters his sister's chamber much like the victor in a boxing match, still grappling with the scruff of Culpeper's shirt. I follow, saying nothing. A few of Anne's gentlewomen look up from the books they are reading, alarmed by the commotion. Anne and Lady Rochford rise to their feet, and George thrusts Thomas Culpeper under Anne's nose, then bows.

"Husband?" Jane says, her eyes wide.

"I shall deal with George, Jane. Now, go!" Anne dismisses all company around her, besides us, and the usher closes the door.

"What is going on here, Brother?"

"Your Majesty, I would ask you to bring a case of slander before the ecclesiastical courts because I have heard Master Culpeper insult Viscountess Beaumont, calling her a whore."

Anne's eyes harden, her mouth a thin line. "How dare you call one of my gentlewomen a whore! I surround myself with goodly women and friends. If you insult my ladies, Master Culpeper, you insult me. You are too free with your words – you will guard your tongue from now on, and only speak when you are spoken to, otherwise you will find yourself in very hot oil."

Even her lapdogs cower under her skirts at the tone of her voice. However, it's clear that she's less than happy at having to give Culpeper a right royal slap down.

"Yes, Your Majesty."

"If you cannot keep your council, I will inform the king, and believe me, he is less forgiving than I."

A look of fear creeps across Culpeper's face as he bows and walks backwards towards the door. Hopefully that's the end of that, though I'll be sure to keep an eye on him in future, and George and I will have to be more careful when in a dangerous liaison.

APRIL – 1533

I have overheard categorical news that Rome's decision is what Henry has feared it would be. Cardinals have concluded by seventeen votes to three that his marriage to Katharine is lawful and good, and the pope has ratified that decision. Henry is fuming, with the marriage having to be annulled under his own authority. No one questions his bigamous marriage in his presence; however, there is much whispering behind his back.

He is having an interview in his privy chamber with Eustace Chapuys, the Imperial Ambassador. Many are present in the Watching Chamber, and I wait with bated breath as this unprofessional audience spills over into the outer rooms. Chapuys' snooty air infuriates the king, with his presence irritating Henry when they are mere metres away from each other.

The feathers in Chapuys large hat wisp as he follows Henry from the inner rooms into the bright daylight of the large chamber. In full view of the court, he decides to point out a few facts to the king.

"Majesty," he calls, "a new wife to replace Queen Katharine by no means guarantees children."

I look on while jaws drop around the great room.

Henry glares down on Chapuys. "Am I not a man like other men?" he demands. "Am I not?"

The ambassador looks somewhat stunned. "I have no reason at all to deny this, Your Majesty."

"Ambassador, you are not privy to all my secrets!"

The fiery anger in Henry's eyes reduces Chapuys to size. He doesn't know that Anne is now four months pregnant, and Henry no doubt wants to keep it secret in case it causes an early catastrophe if courtiers find out about it before time. It is tempting providence. He doesn't know the gossips talk of it already. The only comfort for him is that it cements his virility and sexual potency in his mind, and the mind of his courtiers, knowing he can father more children.

THURSDAY, 29TH MAY 1533
THE PALACE OF PLACENTIA – GREENWICH

The court is in no doubt that the king loves Anne more than all women, as he spends almost every waking moment with her. He is about to set the royal crown on her head and make her queen and has commanded a magnificent feast to be prepared for it. The whole of the city of London is out in the streets to watch the procession of their new queen-in-waiting.

Nan Gainsford – now Lady Zouche – Mary Carey, Honor Lisle, and Bridget Wingfield are helping to dress Anne on this auspicious morning, and I observe as they decorate her long hair in preparation. She takes it all in her stride, as she does with everything. Each lady-in-waiting is assigned a task and they turn this way and that in their endeavours.

"Are you prepared for today?" I ask her, looking at her swollen feet and ankles as she steps into her gown.

"Yes, I am. This ceremony is of the upmost importance to Henry and me. I told one of my chaplains that the monarchy on earth represents an outward shadow to our people of the glorious and celestial monarchy to which God, the governor of all things, exercises in the firmament. I needed to justify to the chaplain why the treasury is spending this amount of money the king has laid out in paying for my coronation."

"What did the chaplain answer?"

A corner of her mouth curls in a half-smile. "Well, he could not answer, for he knew I was right."

Her feet already look heavy, and she has yet to journey to the Tower. Sitting on the barge, being rowed down the Thames for a couple of hours, will do her ankles no good.

"My Lady Pembroke," I say, my excitement bubbling over, "are you sure you will be well enough to cope with the next few days? Have your doctors not warned you about overexerting yourself?" While I know things will work out fine, I'm still concerned by her condition, worried she will soon be exhausted by the energy required to carry out the events ahead. Her pregnancy is progressing well but the last thing she should be doing is putting herself under pressure.

At just after 3 p.m., Henry meets her. He seems in a jovial mood and is undaunted by proceedings. As king, he is used to such pomp and ceremony, and takes the events of the day in his stride, relaxed and happy as he escorts our party to the wharf, whereupon several ladies-in-waiting join us on the barge. The queen's brigantine is decorated with Anne's emblems and colours and looks glorious in the May sunshine. Anticipation pounds in my chest as we set off to take our place amongst the splendid parade of watercraft as it makes its way down the Thames.

Many-oared boats sport gargoyles and monsters that breathe fire and create a frightful noise. The mayor follows in his barge, with the bachelors' barge trailing him.

Delightful melodies of the minstrels on board waft on the breeze, and swathes of gold tissue and silks shield us all from the wind and bright sunlight. I sit on deck gazing about, while Anne's party giggle with delight as we watch scores of craft bob on the sparkling water. The barges are all shapes and sizes, with their flying standards raised high in the rigging. It is a breathtaking sight of allegiance, a colourful extravaganza, and a warm-up for what is to come.

Our barge rows past bankside landmarks I do not recognise, probably because most will later be destroyed in the Great Fire of London. A salute of gunfire is discharged, and the crowds ashore wave as we pass. No one seems to be jealous or cruel amongst the people, which surprises me, as tales are told down the centuries that Anne was jeered and heckled on the way to be crowned.

We must make a spectacular sight, as a four-gun salute gives notice from Wapping Mills that we are approaching the Tower. I can't help smiling as Anne waves. But her gentlewomen clasp their hands, squealing in playful terror as the guns are fired from the shore. Anne looks radiant, and I feel so alive as we journey around the final corner and the Tower comes into view.

The magnificent fortress looks even more foreboding than on visits in my modern life, as its architecture dominates the skyline here, not crowded out by skyscrapers, The Shard, and the like. Barges filled with nobles of the realm escort us as more cannon fire marks our arrival.

Once we come alongside the wharf, we are helped to disembark by the Lieutenant of the Tower, Sir Edward Walsingham, and its constable, Sir William Kingston, who I remember from when I time-slipped to the wrong year. I'm hoping this is the last time I will meet him. The sight of Kingston, not to mention the Tower, triggers visions of George's demise. Seeing Sir William again sends a shiver down my spine, as, according to the proper history, he will be the man responsible for guarding Anne in the Tower after she is arrested in 1536.

Anne, for once, looks stunned as she steps ashore, stroking her pregnancy bump for comfort as the cannon shots echo across the Thames.

"Madam, are you well?"

"Yes, Viscountess, quite well. But I think the sound of the cannon awoke the boy in my womb, for I can feel his movements."

As we proceed along the cobble path, the heralds serenade us while officers at arms stand to attention. Many gentlemen of Henry's court follow in Anne's wake, as does the Dowager Duchess of Norfolk in her designated role to carry her train. I walk alongside the duchess, proud to be a reassuring presence should she need any assistance. As we reach the Byward Gate, before Anne enters the Tower, she turns to the mayor, officials, and crowd.

"Lords. Ladies, and Gentlemen, I give you thanks for the magnificent celebrations you are staging for me this day. I will never forget it for so long as I live."

She radiates vitality and warmth as she addresses the throng, then I follow her and the duchess as we make our way through the gate. The king greets us just inside the doors, and plants a huge, loving kiss on Anne's lips.

"I offer thanks to the gentlemen and women of the court for your service today. You shall be well provided for, and lodgings shall be made available to you this night."

His eyes glitter as he looks upon his wife. He is like an excited child with a new toy, too exuberant to hold his feelings in check. We make our way along Water Lane, with Henry, Anne's hand on his, leading. I look up to see the massive twin towers of the Coldharbour Gate, and inner wall – the entrance between the palace ward and the bailey by the south-west corner of the White Tower. In my day, it will lie in ruins, the foundations concealed for centuries by later buildings until re-exposed in 1940 by Second World War bomb damage. It feels so strange to see this part of the Tower in its full splendour. I'm also troubled by flashes of George being decapitated. I can't shift that from my mind.

My eyes adjust to the change in light, which dims as we proceed through the entrance of the Great Hall. I am stunned by the sight of the interior, as it no longer exists in my time. To see it in its contemporary setting, transformed into an ornate and exquisite apparition, takes my breath away. A gleaming riot of colour and decoration adorns the walls, looking over long tables set out with linen cloths and shimmering candelabra, offering up a festive supper for all the invitees. The tables must be groaning under the weight of the gold plate, piled high with foodstuffs, sweetmeats, and peeled pears, ruby-red after being boiled in heated and sugared red wine. It's wonderful, and I inhale the inviting scents, knowing how, when consumed, they will tingle on my tongue.

"What think you of this, Viscountess?" Henry asks.

"It is beautiful, Your Grace."

Anne stands by his side, surveying the glorious sight, and he guides her by her elbow towards the doorway leading to a small presence chamber, and beyond, to their separate private apartments. As we parade into these rooms, I glance out of the windows to see the Jewel Tower across the courtyard.

"These are the new apartments I ordered to be built for your use, my love. Beyond our private chambers is a gallery where you may take your exercise, and to the right of these rooms is a garden for your delight." He points to the window on the right of Anne's chambers. I peer out to the garden below, seeing freshly planted rose bushes, their green buds swollen, waiting to bloom.

"How do you like your chambers, sweetheart?"

"Henry, your designers have done a magnificent job."

His face lights up with a huge smile. With everything coming to fruition, he seems proud of his achievements, and rightly so. He loves praise.

"How did you enjoy your day, my love?" he asks with keen anticipation.

"It has been incredible. I have never seen anything as wonderful as the river pageant today. The fire on the water was miraculous. The dragon was adorable. How on earth did they create that?"

"I have a way of knowing the right people to engage to do the job. I know how to make things happen." He smiles again, then turns to me.

"Beth, would you help Anne out of her finery and make her more comfortable." This is not a question.

"Yes, Your Grace."

"I will join you both for supper in the Great Hall, for we will sup early, and then you, my love,"—he looks directly at Anne—"must retire early, as you must sleep well, for you have important days ahead and you and our son need all your strength."

FRIDAY, 30TH MAY 1533 THE ROYAL APARTMENTS, HIS MAJESTIES FORTRESS, THE TOWER OF LONDON

Today, Anne is at leisure to do as she wants. Lady Zouche and I decide to let her sleep until mid-morning, as I'm concerned that she needs to build up her strength for what lies ahead. When we wake her, she looks rested and refreshed. Bridget and Mary, on the other hand, look tired when they come to attend on her. They've been busy preparing her clothes for the ceremony due is unfold over the next few days. Nevertheless, they dress Anne with great exuberance before organising breakfast. We all sit together at the table, excited by the prospect of being involved in these important events. 6

In the eyes of many of his contemporaries, Sir Thomas Boleyn is a callous opportunist, willing to sacrifice his daughter on the altar of his own ambition. Little does he know, as he enters Anne's chambers, that he helps to create more intrigue around his family with the things he does.

The Boleyns have risen even further because of their ambitions. Some courtiers whisper that they rise too far above their station. But I don't see Sir Thomas as the villain of the piece, widely derided as a heartless, grasping courtier who stops at nothing to advance his own interests.

It's Katharine of Aragon's supporters who despise the Boleyns, especially Anne, and they have put about the idea that Thomas uses his children to enhance his status. Having witnessed for many years how he is with his family, I'm surprised that others don't see the reality. Over time, these accusations will stick. Yes, he intended his daughter to take a prominent place at the English court, but I know he never raised her to share the king's bed, and Anne was clever enough to refuse Henry's advances initially. In the end, Thomas, who is now fifty-five years old, seems resigned to his daughter being queen. The king's wishes have prevailed, and Thomas knows he cannot defy him, so he stands in his daughter's presence chamber, aware that he has no option but to support her marriage, and her new role as queen.

His eyes show his exhaustion. Henry's annulment of his marriage to Queen Katharine is deeply unpopular, and is putting a strain not only on his relationship with Anne but on her relationships with close family members. On the eve of her coronation, she is inspecting the ceremonial gown her ladies have been altering. I try to stay out of the way, tidying things up.

"Father, will you not sit?" she asks, rubbing her belly.

"I have come to speak with you." He looks at me from the corner of his eye.

"Do not mind Beth, Father – what do you want to discuss with me?" She glances up, preoccupied with the clothing laid out before her. "I hope it is important because I have greater things to worry about than what may trouble you. I will be walking down the aisle of Westminster Abbey – all alone. All eyes will be on me. With this child growing so quickly in my belly, I am worried my coronation gown won't fit. What could be more important than how your daughter looks when she is crowned tomorrow?"

With her being heavily pregnant, it's no surprise she is self-conscious and uncertain.

"We have already let out my gown a few weeks ago, so I do not want to be letting it out again."

I turn away to fold a linen shift. In this moment, she sounds like a spoilt child. I'm sure her nerves are grating on her.

"Leave the gowns as they be!" Thomas shouts. "Anne, you should be thankful to God for the state you are in." He walks over to her gown, eying it on the mannequin, examining the extra panel of fabric that's just been adjusted on her kirtle. "You should take away the piece you have put on this." He points to the front of the gown, then strokes his beard. "Why have you made it bigger?"

"To accommodate my impending motherhood," she snaps. "I would not want the kirtle to be too tight. Besides, I am in a better plight than you would have wished me to be, Father."

I snap out the shift and fold it again, shocked at how she is talking to him. With the crushing expectation that the baby she carries will be the male heir Henry craves, it appears tempers are fraying. I wonder how Anne and her father would be reacting if they only knew the truth, and the future, as I do. Baby Princess Elizabeth hasn't got long to go before she meets the world.

WHIT SUNDAY, 1ST JUNE 1533 - WESTMINSTER ABBEY

Anne intends to follow the ordinances for the coronation precisely, as she doesn't want to disappoint Henry. In preparation for today, over the last few weeks, she has shown me, digested, read, and re-read the 'articles ordained by King Henry VII for the regulation of his household'. The book contains explicit instructions for the coronation of a queen. This has stood her in good stead because, as she wakes, she doesn't seem nervous. She stretches against the sheets as I pull back the cover, then steps out onto the Turkish rug.

"How are you feeling this morning?" I ask.

"I feel emotional. I cannot believe this momentous day is finally here! Today, I become Queen of England." She frowns. "I am sure you knew this would happen from the first day we met, but you would never tell me."

"If I had told you at that time, you would never have believed me, would you?"

"Definitely not!"

"Then I did the right thing by holding my tongue, did I not?" I smirk.

She smiles. "I suppose you did."

"It has been a long journey, hasn't it?" I turn at a noise and see Margaret Lee entering, to help me attend on Anne.

"Look at me now," Anne says, standing in her linen shift and stroking her belly. "Carrying the king's son. Who would have thought when Henry asked me to be his mistress in the rose garden, that this day would arrive?"

She blinks at the pale sunlight streaming through the casement windows, holding her in a dreamlike state as we draw her rosewater bath in the adjacent closet.

"We are kindred spirits, the king and I," she says as she walks to the bath, keeping her shift on as she steps into the crystal-clear water. She sinks so the waterline covers her breasts, the shift floating away from her curves. Despite being pregnant, she has such a glow about her. It's not difficult to understand why the king fell in love with her. Her long, dark hair fans around her shoulders as she leans back against the end of the bath. The other gentlewomen hurry back and forth between her chambers and the great wardrobe, where her coronation gown and robes have been stored.

In this moment of isolation, she looks up at me. "I cannot believe you knew this would happen all along." She frowns as she eyes me. "How you kept from telling me such a secret is beyond me."

"Do you not see now that I could never tell you, in case this day never came to pass?"

She stares at me. "That is why you lied?"

"I never lied. I just…omitted information. This day had to happen – it is written in the history books."

Her eyes are black, and wide. I don't think she knows quite what to say. It's probably best she says nothing.

"Perhaps, from now on, Beth, I should trust in your time-travelling tales." She chuckles to herself.

"What is it?"

"Imagine if you had met Henry instead of me. He fancied you before me – imagine if you had time travelled just as he had become king, what then?" Her mouth hangs open in a gaping smile. "What would you have done then?"

"Anne, stop it! The king did *not* fancy me first, he always had his eye on you." I glance behind to make sure we're alone. "I don't even wish to consider what I might have done. Turned him down again, most probably. Then he would still have married Katharine."

"My friend, do not be so sure about him not fancying you first – I have seen the way he looks at you." She laughs, the sound carrying through her chambers. Then she sinks under the water, the overflow drenching the floor.

The moment is broken by the return of Bridget, Nan Zouche, and Margaret Lee, tutting at Anne as the water runs down the sides of her bath and over the closet floor. Fresh towels are fetched to mop up the mess. At least their presence stops the conversation in its tracks. They are animated and excited as they continue preparing Anne for her great day. There are moments in life so momentous, and Anne Boleyn has awaited this one for so long that, now it has arrived, it is difficult to believe it.

"I tell you, ladies, today is unquestionably God's will!"

"Just as you predicted in your book of hours, my Lady," I say.

"I could not have predicted this – that is for sure. But do you remember a few years ago, the Venetian diplomat had been taken aback by the depth of my certainty regarding my elevation as being divinely ordained?"

"I remember that," Margaret Lee pipes in.

"God has his hand in so many things," Nan Zouche adds.

"Do you not remember your supporters comparing you to Esther from the bible?"

Anne beams. "Yes, I do! Is it not funny that they compare me to a young virgin, chosen by a mighty monarch from amongst his subjects to replace his haughty and arrogant foreign queen?" She laughs again, the sound floating on the breeze from the open window, causing a royal guard to look up from the courtyard below.

"Today, my destiny will become manifest. I will be crowned Queen, not as a consort but as Queen, anointed by God, never to be withdrawn until my death."

I shudder at her words, and she notices.

"What is it?"

"It is nothing, my Lady. Come, we must prepare you."

Her wet shift clings to her every curve. She now stands on a rug as her gentlewomen fuss about her, drying her hair, changing her into a fresh, clean linen shift with goldwork embroidery. They flit around her like butterflies attracted to buddleia as they work their magic. Once fully dressed, Anne rubs cochineal rouge into her cheeks and lips for colour and a little charcoal to elongate her eyes. It's necessary as, on the day that's in it, I forgot to bring my cosmetics.

"Margaret, what time is it?" she asks, standing before us all in her great splendour.

"Seven of the clock."

The early morning sunlight slants through the windows of the Royal Apartments, catching the golden floss stitched into her gown. Its long train trails out over the floor, making her look every inch a queen.

"We must away to the abbey!" she cries.

Her gentlewomen flutter about her, making the finishing touches to her coronation robes so she looks nothing but perfection.

By eight-thirty in the morning, we process through the streets, inside the city walls. The crowds have turned out in their thousands but are largely silent, and their welcome seems frosty. I watch, walking behind Anne and the rest of her entourage, as they wave to the people. Few caps are removed, and even less cry out "God save Your Grace!"

Jayne Fool walks beside me, looking worried, her gaze darting this way and that. Maybe she doesn't like the noise of the horses or the clarions.

"My Lord Mayor!" she shouts without warning, making me flinch. "My Lord Mayor! Why do you not command the people to make the customary shouts?" Her face has reddened as she glares at the mayor.

"Jayne Fool, I cannot command people's hearts," he replies, turning to us and walking backwards. He holds both arms out. "Even the king could not make them do so!"

Anne looks back from her litter, attached to horses front and back, to see what all the fuss is about. "What goes on there?"

"It is nothing, Your Grace," the mayor says, giving a sharp nod towards Jayne.

"Well, it ain't nothing to me, Lord Mayor!" Jayne snaps, shaking her head at him. She looks out at the crowd and shouts at the top of her voice, "I think you have all scurvy heads and dare not uncover!"

Onlookers laugh at her remark. A bad example of ableism. It disappoints me to see how the crowd is treating Jayne, after being impressed previously at how Tudor society, and the royal court in particular, treat disabled people. Jayne is scowling as she walks along, her arms folded in front of her.

"Pay them no heed," I say, smiling. "They are ignorant, and do not know Anne Boleyn as we do."

She nods, then lifts her head high, probably in the realisation that she is a best friend to the queen of England.

All the members of the clergy await Anne, and the mayor, sheriffs, and many of the nobility stand uniformly dressed in crimson and gold cloth. As she stands under the golden cloth of estate, everyone bows in unison. Before her is an outstretched royal-blue carpet, upon which she walks barefoot, through the hall and on into the abbey to stand at the high altar. Everyone assembles in order of rank. As part of the lower nobility, I hang back, but I'm close enough to see the proceedings and have to pinch myself. I notice George, who looks splendid in his robes. Will we ever get it together now? Perhaps that incident with Culpeper has dampened his enthusiasm for me and sent him scurrying back to his wife. What would Rob think if he could see me now? What would he say? He'd never believe me. The only person who'd believe me is Professor Marshall. Is he wondering how I'm getting on? Then again, while I've been here quite a while, it's possible only a few hours have passed in my time.

I pull my attention back to this royal extravaganza as members of parliament pass by in their ceremonial robes, followed by the city of London officials, then the archbishops, bishops, and abbots close behind. I've seen so much in my time here, but this is astonishing. I feel like a young child at the most fantastic parade in the world, and have to hold myself back when I'm tempted to clap as the procession passes me.

The knights of Bath are followed by the barons, viscounts, earls, marquesses and dukes, then counts and countesses. I can't remember everyone, but the usual nobility is here…those that are allowed to wear it, are all decked out in ermine. Even I'm wearing noble colours, but I refused to walk through the abbey in the procession. That was too daunting. Everyone who is anyone is present. The earl of Arundel, the earl of Oxford, and the high chamberlain of England, carrying the crown of St Edward.

Henry's best friend, the duke of Suffolk, doesn't look happy, despite the fact he's holding the ceremonial ivory rod.

Anne walks far ahead of me under the gold canopy of the cinque ports, and I wonder if the Dowager Duchess of Norfolk is still managing to cope with carrying her train, as the path is long, and the train must be heavy.

Mary Carey is helping Anne, but I recall that she doesn't stay at court after the Coronation, and will only occasionally visit her sister. Perhaps Anne doesn't want her here, a constant reminder that she, too, may be the mother of the king's children.

If Mary had not been here, I might have offered my services to Anne, if I wasn't so nervous about it. I did wonder why she didn't pick me for this office, considering I've been at her side for just about everything else. Perhaps she was trying to please the old noble families and the king.

I take a covert look around for Henry, who is hidden from view so as not to overshadow his wife's special day and solemn rite. Smoke rises and swirls from a multitude of torches and candles, and the sharp, biting scent of incense lingers on the air, almost singeing my nostrils. The clergy swing the burning incense from chains, as if carrying handbags to the service.

The ritual sends the crowd into a hypnotic state as they watch Anne approach the high altar, where she ascends the steps and seats herself in the gold-painted coronation chair. It looks gaudy and bright, not faded, and jaded as it is in my time, after centuries of being used to crown monarchs.

I catch a glimpse of Henry behind a lattice screen placed high above the congregation and wish I was standing next to him with the other ambassadors of the court, as his vantage point has such a better view.

Raised voices ascend into the cloisters as they sing their melodic chant, fading as Anne descends the few stairs to present herself before the altar, where she lowers herself with the help of her ladies-in-waiting and lies prostrate before the Archbishop of Canterbury, Dr Cranmer. As she lies beneath the dense cloud of florid incense, the archbishop prays over her, then offers her his hand and helps her to her feet, to resume her seat in St Edward's chair. Cranmer places into her hand the decorated sceptre, and in the other, a rod of ivory, before resting the small crown of St Edward on her head. He changes it then for a lighter and more bearable crown, shuffling them as if playing a game of poker. It is almost as if he has crowned many queens before.

The cloisters resonate with the sound of the Te Deum as Cranmer recites the liturgy, and the choir, with their ethereal voices, lift the words of the psalms. My gaze is fixed on Anne as she walks to the shrine of St Edward with an offering. Before the ceremony is complete, every duchess and countess raise their arms in unison to exalt Anne's Queenship, and I almost chuckle as they, and I, fumble with coronets as we place them on our heads.

Sir Thomas Boleyn and Lord Talbot support her on the recessional to leave the abbey. I look up and see Henry's face pressed to an opening in the lattice screen, his broad smile visible as he watches Anne exit.

It doesn't take long to arrive at Westminster Hall, which has been prepared to host a magnificent coronation banquet and looks warm and grand as Anne presides under its hammer-beam sky. The walls are covered in Henry's great tapestries, with their vibrant red, blue, and gold threads reflecting the candlelight. Anne sits in front of four great tables extending the length of the hall. She has at her feet two ladies, seated under the table to serve her secretly with what she might need, and two others near her, one on each side, who often raise a great linen cloth to hide her from view when she wishes for privacy. I'm tempted to chuckle at such palaver but control myself, aware that this is the way of things in this wonderful time, and it is my honour and duty to take it all in as best I can.

Looking down the length of the hall, I'm reminded of when the late Queen Elizabeth II was lying in state, and Mum, Dad, and I queued for hours – overnight, in fact – to see her, and say goodbye, while she was honoured by so many from across the world. Seeing the Imperial State Crown up close, as it is when it's on display in the Tower, was magnificent. I will never forget it. Neither will I forget seeing members of the modern royal family, presiding over a vigil of the queen, headed up by her heir, Charles. What a moving tribute for so great and dutiful a monarch.

My thoughts snap back to my present. Half of the first table is taken up by those of the realm who have charge of the doors. Below them, at the same table, are many gentlemen, with the second table occupied by the archbishops and bishops, the chancellor, and many lords and knights. The two other tables are on the far side of the hall, seating the Mayor of London, his sheriffs, the duchesses, countesses, and ladies.

The duke of Suffolk is arrayed with many stones and pearls, and rides up and down the hall and around the tables upon a courser caparisoned in crimson velvet, as does Lord William, who presides over the serving, and keeps order. The king has stationed himself in a place where he can see without being seen, and the ambassadors of France and Venice are with him. At the hall entrance are conduits pouring out wine, and brass and woodwind sound at each course, with heralds crying "largesse!"

I'm exhausted from the day and try not to stretch my weary bones as I witness the continuing celebrations. While the banquet is enjoyable, I'm feeling so full from all the rich food and wine that I can't wait for bed. Goodness knows how Anne feels. It must be worse for her, being so far gone in her trimester. I'm longing for her to decide to retire soon, so both of us can get some much-needed rest.

JUNE 1533

During this unexpected gift-giving season in the early summer of 1533, Anne's husband sends her many presents to mark her coronation as Queen of England, most of which seem to be for the decoration of her new apartments.

They are a lot more practical than the gifts she received a few years earlier, and include a decorative piece of a silver platter, which the Tudor upper classes like to display in their main audience chambers. The chamber is filled with so many gifts, an outsider might think it was Christmastide.

I trace my fingers across a gilt chafing dish, which will be used if Anne wants a late-night snack in her apartments. She has an eye for design and beautiful things, and commissioned the young German artist, Hans Holbein, to make a small solid-silver fountain to sit in the centre of her dining table so she can splash rosewater into its basin to allow her and her guests to wash their hands before, during, and after the meal. When I see anything, Holbein has designed, I'm reminded of my portrait in the National Gallery, and wonder when I will meet this ingenious artist.

The fountain is exquisite and beyond expensive, and as we take supper in Anne's chamber a few days after the ceremony, George, Margaret Lee, Henry Norris, Thomas Boleyn, Anne's mother, and others sit around it, sipping wine and picking over gourmet food served on gilt plates, talking amongst themselves. They discuss the new faith, and various scandals they have heard from the courts of Paris, Madrid, and Vienna. The shifting sand of European diplomacy dominates the conversation as the intrigues of Eustace Chapuys, the future of the monasteries, the new theologies, and the political ideas all seem to be up for discussion. Some are brave enough to discuss More's account of Henry being akin to a lion who does not know his strength. All conversations aside, Anne is triumphant, and the only thing that stands in her way now is Katharine.

19TH AUGUST 1533

The queen's staff is extensive now she has been crowned. Stewards, secretaries, and chaplains are assigned to her, to assist with all her stately and political duties as well as fine-tuning the running of her household. She has her all-male council, whose members perform such practical tasks as directing and supervising the care of her extensive properties. Along with them, she has her Lord Chancellor, her Master of the Horse, her secretary, her chaplain, and a host of male servants, as well as needlewomen, chamberers, and ladies-in-waiting.

Henry and Anne are in good health, and happy with it. On Thursday next, they are due to travel by water from Windsor to Westminster. Anne is well-on now, and is more often troubled with back pain, shortness of breath, and even false labour pains, as the baby's head engages. Her gentlewomen observe her closer, as does the king, but the other men don't. To them, pregnancy, and labour, as well as the safe delivery of a child, is solely a woman's domain.

Rather than discuss her condition, the relatives surrounding her at this time talk about names instead, in preparation for announcements to be sent out.

"I cannot decide if we should name him Henry or Edward," Henry says to her and a select gathering of friends. I watch from my seated position, and notice he is in high spirits, as if a great weight has been lifted from his shoulders.

"Henry is a good name, My Lord. Our son should be named after you."

"Very well, Madam. Henry he is." He smiles, rubbing her belly as they sit beside the hearth fire.

"I agree, Niece," Norfolk quips from his position by the window, breaking his conversation with George.

"Norfolk, if the French Ambassador drops the boy at his christening, it will mean war!"

"Ah, your Grace, it will never come to that!" Norfolk replies, his face creased with a smile.

This is only the second time I have seen him smile. I groan inside at being the only one with the knowledge, again, that this child will never be a 'Henry', and I must endeavour never to allow Anne to see that in my eyes.

26TH AUGUST 1533 – PALACE OF PLACENTIA, GREENWICH

I wait in a huddle with the other ladies-in-waiting who are to be with Anne during her lying-in period. We watch as the king kisses her, then Thomas Cranmer blesses and prays for her. We are to play a vital role as the queen takes to her chamber as September approaches. There is no pretence that Henry and Anne expect a prince to be born soon. I have helped her ladies make her rooms ready with many comforts. Inside, we have placed two specially made folding tables, one for breakfast and the other to play cards on. Each has been made with tiles entailed with fretwork.

Her ormolu clock ticks on a deep-carved mahogany table. It's the clock Henry gave her on their wedding day. Sometimes, I stare at it, knowing that during my lifetime it will be in the hands of our monarch, in the care of the Royal Collection, displayed on a marble plinth at St James's Palace. To get within a hair's breadth of such an artefact, with its weights engraved with 'H' and 'A' – true lovers' knots – and the mottoes *'Dieu et Mon Droit'* and *'the most happy'* brings tears to my eyes and a lump to my throat.

Announcements of a prince's arrival are drawn up ahead of time. Henry's confidence is based on an astrologer's prediction that Anne will give birth to a male child. Would either of them have had any reason to doubt such a prediction? Anne and I have often sat and discussed the issue, with her convinced of the sex of the child growing in her belly.

"Anne, astrologers can be proven wrong. You must be prepared for a daughter as well as a son."

We sit in the window while she finishes off embroidery for her baby's christening gown. She knows that I *'know things'*, being from the future, and I wonder why she has been so well behaved of late, not pressing me about my possible foreknowledge. Why hasn't she tried to pull that information about her child's sex from me? I laugh inwardly to cover what I'm thinking, something I've become fairly experienced at, fobbing Anne off. I'm proud of that, because it means I'm keeping to my mission, making sure everything stays on track.

"Beth, you are quiet. What vexes you?"

"Nothing," I say, hoping she doesn't hear the lie in my voice.

"Do not have a care about my baby. I know not to even ask you to confirm that it will be a boy, because you will try to convince me that you know not. Am I right?"

"Your Majesty, as I said previously, the child could be of either sex. I am no astrologer and will say no more."

She laughs, and I stare at her. "Why do you laugh?"

"I shall repeat what I said: a daughter is not an option." She glares at me, then rests her needlework in her lap and stretches, pressing her left hand against her lower back.

"Anne, are you well?"

"Yes, just a little back ache. This prince grows bigger by the day. I am glad my time approaches."

"I am certain all will go as it should for you and the baby, Your Majesty." I rest my hand on her shoulder. She relaxes once more, and picks up her needlework again.

"The baby is a *son*, Beth. I have promised the king a son – I know our first child will be a boy, and we shall name him Henry."

"But, Madam, these predictions you have been given may not come true. You must put your trust in God."

"I do try," she reassures me, picking up another strand of ivory silk thread to prepare for her needle.

"They are propagandists as well as predictors of the future," I say, wishing she would take on what I'm suggesting. It's often the case that propaganda is more useful than a correct prediction, as it inspires well-timed fear in the enemy and hope amongst allies. Of course, the more accurate one's astrologer is at making predictions, the more useful the propaganda, but the creation of fear is a tremendous boon on its own account. Also, the Tudor propaganda mill is working overtime, suggesting to the country that when a prince is born it will validate Anne's marriage to Henry. I cringe at the thought of what I know is to come, and the closer we creep to her downfall, the more uncomfortable I become.

"The king has taken the astrologer's predictions to heart," Anne continues, threading her needle and sliding it into the silk, teasing an intricate design into place.

"That is a mistake," I say, knowing from my modern viewpoint how easy it is to make in my time, where astrology is often viewed as trickery. However, it is not a con in the Tudor era, nor is it incompatible with religion. Indeed, it is considered a way to understand God's divine plan, and is viewed to be a grounded science, like that of the study of the changing seasons. For Henry and Anne, the astrologer's prediction of a male child is one they look on positively. The royal couple hoped for this prediction, and the months Henry persisted in the belief that a boy would be born is enough to buy him time and advantage with those he deals with. It has justified his proceedings against Katharine of Aragon and his marriage to Anne. Everyone at court understands the urgency that accompanies his need for a male heir, as it has been a favourable verdict to royalty for generations before Henry VIII became king.

Royal etiquette demands that a pregnant queen takes to her chamber, isolating herself from male company and the world outside for up to a month and a half before her child's birth. Of course, I already know when the child will be born and realise that, as Anne takes to her chamber, it is just twelve days before Elizabeth's birth. Anne has selected a tapestry displaying the legend of Saint Ursula, one of Christianity's most beloved virgin-saints, to hang in her birthing chamber. Knowing when she will go into labour emotionally drains me, and it is difficult to always be alert, to never give any hint of what I know to anyone. It's a constant struggle, knowing so much yet not being able to divulge it.

I look up from the hand of cards I'm holding. "What date is it today? I have no idea what day we are in, being confined in here without word from anyone."

"'Tis the seventh day of September, I believe." Jane Rochford looks up from her hand of cards, realises it's her turn, and slaps her card down on the table. With her answer, I realise that today is the day Anne will go into labour with Elizabeth. The hairs on the back of my arms stand up. My goodness, I'm to witness the birth of England's 'Gloriana'.

Anne is sat at the table with me, as are Jane, and Nan, when the colour drains from Anne's face.

"Are you well, Your Majesty?" Jane asks.

"Something has happened," she says in a quiet voice, dropping her cards on the table.

"What?" I ask, knowing well. "What has happened?"

She looks down, then at me, her dark eyes glazing over. "My privy parts and shift are wet."

"I think your baby is coming."

Quick as a flash, the midwife comes over. "I think it is time we get you to your bed, Your Majesty."

She supports Anne's elbow and I take the other, then we help her walk to the four-poster, a snail trail of fluid left in her wake.

"Is this normal?" she asks the midwife as we undress her. Her voice is shaky, showing her anxiety.

"This is perfectly normal," the woman replies, helping Anne up onto the bed. "You are in the best of hands, Your Majesty."

During the next few hours, the pains are intermittent, and Anne is lulled into a false sense of security, thinking this is the extent of the pain she will have to put up with.

"I can cope with this," she says. "The pains I am having are bad, but not beyond my endurance."

The midwife looks at her, no doubt knowing the pains are going to get far worse, and Anne will not be able to subdue her cries of anguish for much longer. My sister Joanna told me it was like shitting a red-hot hedgehog when she had her child, so I know things are going to get messy. I remember what it was like helping Mary Carey in her birthing chamber. Things are going to get a lot worse before they get better.

Anne's clock chimes the hour, but it's not until more have passed before the contractions come swift and regular.

Royal ladies of the court – married ones – who have witnessed births or had children themselves, run around trying to keep Anne's spirits up as she goes into labour. They try to comfort her, encouraging her to obey what her body is telling her to do. Other devout women in the chamber pray over their rosary beads, hoping God will intervene should a crisis emerge.

The midwife offers Anne a cup of cloudy liquid from a small receptacle. "Majesty, this will take the edge off your pain." She must be administering a kind of laudanum.

Anne wretches on sniffing the fluid. "Will this not make me sick?"

"Hopefully not," the midwife replies.

She takes small sips, wiping her mouth each time.

I step forward. "Your Majesty, I have heard that the alchemist Paracelsus devised what I think has been prepared for you. Is that not right?" I say to the midwife, who just glances at me and smiles, continuing to mop Anne's forehead with a damp linen cloth.

"It will not be long, Your Majesty," she says.

"'Tis opium dissolved in alcohol, isn't it?" I ask.

"Yes," the woman answers. "It is administered sparingly, and, please, do not tell Archbishop Cranmer or the king, as it is a practice very much frowned upon."

"Majesty, would you not prefer us to move you to the birthing chair?"

"No!" she screams. "I cannot move. The pain is too great!"

Jane and Nan are now perched either side of her, and she has her arms around their shoulders, resting on her knees as the pains accelerate, the contractions coming at a swift and regular pace. The ladies rub her back as her screams reverberate through the low-lit chamber, to the point where the sound vibrates in my chest. We urge her to press down against the mattress, to ease the contractions.

"I cannot, it will tear me in two!"

"Go with the pain, Your Majesty – push when the pain starts."

She screws her face up and bears down for all she is worth, letting out a mixture of scream and grunt at the same time. While she is doing her duty, Margery Horsman and others fetch fresh linens and warm rosewater. The windows are boarded up and covered with tapestries, to shut out the light, with flickering candles illuminate the chamber.

A shadow of desperation wafts across Anne's face and she turns to the midwife. "I…I need to use the house of easement!"

"No, Your Majesty, the baby's head is coming. It is the reason for that sensation."

Anne bears down yet again and cries out as if her life depends on it. Her gentlewomen hold her tight as the baby's head crowns.

"You are nearly there, Your Majesty!"

I catch sight of the baby's head, and its little face looks blue. A lump forms in my throat and tears well in my eyes. I don't know whether this is due to Anne's suffering, or because I'm witnessing a new life coming into the world – and not just a new life, but the future Elizabeth 1.

Sitting on the side of her bed, I encourage and comfort her, while the experienced women instruct her until the safe delivery of her child is guaranteed.

"The pain is coming again!" she screams. "Good God help me!" Jane and Nan hold her upper body even tighter.

"Push, Your Majesty!" the midwife shouts as she supports the baby's head.

Anne releases a final, piercing scream as the baby slithers out onto the fluid-stained sheets. The ladies lay her back on the comfort of her pillows as her ormolu clock strikes 3 p.m., and the second midwife begins to clean her up.

One more push and the placenta is delivered. She closes her eyes, thanking God the ordeal is over.

"Is it a boy?" she asks, her voice weary. The midwife doesn't hear her as the baby is crying. "I said, is it a boy?" Her agitation is clear.

"It is a healthy girl, Your Majesty," the midwife replies.

Anne brings both her hands up to her face, covering her eyes. "How am I going to explain this to Henry?"

I move closer and put my arm around her. "You have such a beautiful little girl. The king will not be anything but delighted."

She looks at me, real fear in her eyes. "You do not know him as well as I do. I do not think 'delighted' is a word that will describe his emotion when he realises, I have not given him the son he has longed for.

In a split second, her expression changes. Her accusing eyes narrow as her gaze fixes on me. I can't look her in the eyes, sure she is disgusted at me.

"Viscountess," she snarls. "Do not look away! You had to know the outcome of my labour pains. You knew this baby would be a girl. You knew the truth, and I am disgusted at you for not sharing that with me!"

"Anne, lower your voice!" From the faces of some of her gentlewomen, I know they've overheard. Some frown because they don't understand what's going on. Jane Boleyn rushes over.

"Sister, do not vex yourself, it will do you no good."

"Jane, leave me be!"

"Calm yourself, Anne," I say, lowering my tone. "You are upsetting yourself, and you will distress your baby."

She turns on her side, away from me. "Remove Viscountess Beaumont from my sight."

With a victorious look, Jane Boleyn herds me out of the bedchamber, into an adjoining chamber where a wet nurse is swaddling the baby in linens.

My face feels hot, but I try to bite back the humiliation as I sit watching the wet-nurse cradle the new princess. It seems my foreknowledge is always going to get me into trouble, whether I say anything or not.

Eight

SEPTEMBER 7TH, 1533 – GREENWICH PALACE

Anne promised Henry a son ever since they were engaged to be married. In return, he has bestowed favour after favour on her and her family. He cast off his first wife and, over the objections of the pope and the rest of Christendom, made her his queen, raising her above all others.

Walking past the open door of Henry's presence chamber, I hear his voice rise above everyone.

"Elizabeth, she has called the child Elizabeth?" I can imagine his incredulous glare. "Cancel the celebrations, Cromwell!"

I scurry past the open doorway, hoping I won't be spotted.

"Viscountess!" he bellows, his ushers directing me into his chamber.

I walk towards him. Cromwell says nothing – still as stone as I approach the dais.

"Your Majesty." I curtsy.

He looks me up and down in his usual fashion. "How is the queen?"

"It was a difficult labour, Your Majesty, but the queen fares well."

He sniffs. "And the child?"

"Healthy, Sire." I keep my gaze lowered, as I have no wish to see the disappointment in his face at his new-born not being a boy.

"Tell Her Majesty I will come and visit her and the child shortly."

With a flourish of his hand, he shoos me away. Chapuys will report in days to come of Elizabeth's arrival, declaring that the child is thriving, which will indicate to the court that future healthy children are likely to follow. But, for now, Henry knows it is back to business as usual.

I feel anxious walking back into Anne's chambers. Her reaction to me made me nervous. She's in bed, holding her daughter as her ladies attend her, and she glances up as I enter her bedchamber.

"Viscountess?"

"Your Majesty." I curtsy.

She beckons me to approach her. "Beth," she whispers, "forgive me for my outburst. I was overcome with emotion."

"Majesty, there is nothing to forgive."

She pats her bedcovers. "Sit with me."

It's not a request. I watch her as she cradles her baby in her arms. It's not hard to see the bond growing between mother and child. The sex of the baby has been a terrible shock to her, and I wish I could have done more, for her to avoid feeling hurt and disappointed, but sharing my knowledge wouldn't have changed the outcome. I know it will be a great disappointment to both the king, and to Anne's parents, but also a subject of ill-contained glee to their many opponents. However, being here, witnessing the birth of the princess Elizabeth, I hope it's not quite the death-knell to Henry and Anne's marriage that tradition will later suggest, and I hope Henry won't let it affect his treatment of his wife.

"I was grief-stricken," she whispers. "I realise you could not have told me what you know, especially when you might be unsure of how I might react? Again, forgive me, and let me show you, my daughter."

I smile, then lean over the bed to get a closer look, peering over the linens that swaddle her little girl.

"See her eyes," Anne says. "They are sapphire blue, like her father. Her skin is as white as the moon, and her hair is a crown of gold."

"Just like the king, Madam."

"You know I named her after you?" she whispers, looking up at me. Her proud expression melts my heart.

"I had assumed you named her after both of her grandmothers?"

She gestures me even closer. "That is what I shall tell His Majesty when I receive him, but you know the truth of it."

I am truly honoured and almost speechless. The Virgin Queen, named after me! Fancy that – how incredible. I smile as the child wriggles her toes underneath her swaddling. It's such a relief that things have gone well, especially for Anne during labour, though I'm not sure there is any such thing as an easy delivery. The thought of pushing something the size of a watermelon out of my undercarriage almost brings water to my eyes. But Anne has survived, and looks well, if a little tired. The last few months of her pregnancy were difficult for her – something common to many thin women – and as July and August rolled on, her health had suffered. The court's summer progress was cancelled, and the king was so concerned about his new wife's well-being that he ordered all news which might upset her be withheld.

As a result, she had been locked away from the world, not knowing that the pope has ruled about Henry's marriage, determining that he is still legally wed to his first wife, and, as such, not only is Anne's queenship illegal but her child is considered a bastard by those of the Catholic faith. Characteristically, the pope's edict has come too late to save Katharine, but just in time to cause serious trouble for Anne, which, no doubt, was his intention.

What matters to all sides, is that Elizabeth has joined the royal nursery and is healthy. Had she been a boy, of course, her mother's newfound title would have been unassailable. Even opponents of her marriage, like Sir Thomas More, have been prepared to wait and see on the issue of her offspring. If she had produced a longed-for son and heir, then all the criticisms of her would have evaporated and her predecessor will be regarded as a cantankerous irrelevance. More let it be known, if the new queen produced a prince, then it would be 'to the rest, peace, wealth, and profit of the entire country'.

No matter how much anyone liked Katharine of Aragon, they would have loved a Prince of Wales. Although, a son would render the queen untouchable and the king vindicated, a daughter is not a complete disaster, and the royal couple ensure that everything will be done to mark her birth with the splendour customary for that of a princess.

As we watch Elizabeth writhe and wriggle in her mother's arms, an usher announces the king's arrival.

Anne greets her husband, and he settles beside her.

"My Lord, I have named her after your mother and my mother."

Henry nods his approval, having no idea that this little babe in arms is destined to be their only living child together, and will arguably become the single most famous woman in her country's history.

"And is the child healthy?" he asks.

She cannot meet his gaze, but he must see the fear in her face. I've no doubt she feels she has failed him in the one thing she promised. After a long moment, she raises her head to nod at him, acknowledging that the child is well, knowing how he must feel her betrayal.

"You and I are both young," he says, "and by God's grace, boys will follow."

He is a capricious father, and will, in time, alternate between indifference and indulgence, whilst Anne is and will always be a devoted mother who adores her daughter.

"Yes," she whispers, her voice somewhat feeble, "next time we will have a son, Your Grace. I am sure of it."

His jaw clenches. Poor Anne will probably face a storm of discontent the next time she and her husband are alone. I don't envy her being on the receiving end of his wrath, and as he struggles to hide his disappointment, or show his disdain, he refuses to move closer to kiss her or his daughter, to give them his blessing.

"Will you not kiss the child, Your Grace?" she asks.

"No, I will kiss the child when she has a brother!"

An ominous panic rakes through Anne's eyes as Henry takes his leave. Maybe he believes he has given up a lot for her, and all he has to show for it is, in his opinion, yet another useless daughter. I have no doubt Anne will want to get pregnant again, and fast, to produce a son, though I know it will never happen.

"Lady Zouche," Anne says, as she watches Nan go to the door after the usher announces someone, "I asked for a period of silent contemplation. Why do you continue to fail in your respect of the wishes of your queen?"

"I beg your pardon, Your Majesty, but there is a gentleman to see you."

"What?" She groans, sitting up in her bed.

"He is outside, Your Majesty. He says he must be allowed in."

"Anne releases a long sigh that borders on a growl. "Who is it?"

"I did not like to say 'no' to him." She steps back inside the bedchamber, smiling. "He was right forceful." She curtsies, and my tummy does a flip at the sight of George standing behind her. Nan returns to her duties, and as George approaches the side of Anne's bed, I realise my legs are like jelly.

"George," Anne says as he takes her hand and kisses it.

"Your Majesty, I could not wait any longer." He smiles.

"How do you fare?" she asks, smiling back. "We have missed you at Court, with you being away on diplomatic duties with our uncle." She glances at me, knowing how much I've been pining to see him.

"I am well, Sister, but should I not be asking you how you fare, under the circumstances?" He smiles, brushing a hand through his hair. "I have seen little Elizabeth. She is goodly – a little Henry!"

Anne sighs again, this time without the anger. "She misses one thing..."

"Courage, Anne." He touches the back of her hand. "Next time."

"Yes."

"And, really – are you well?"

She grimaces. "It is an undignified affair, and painful."

"You are lucky to be so healthily delivered."

"Weeks before were worse. Your letters have been a great comfort. Though, I must say, your predictions, like those of others, were wrong."

"For now." He gives a wry smile.

"I heard from the midwives that Henry was beside himself, George. Apparently, when he heard my cries, I believe he prayed for the death of the unborn child, if that might release me from any danger."

George's eyes widen. "The king said that?"

"In his grief for my pain, he did."

He chuckles, a sound I love about him. "You have the power to sway continents, Sister!"

"But Henry is cold in his disappointment – and he's cancelled the 'Great Joust'."

He snorts. "Oh, that is a shame. I was looking forward to bringing down a few of those fellows." He rubs his hands together. "But there will still be bonfires and fountains of free wine."

"Stay away from the wine, Brother." She giggles. "I know what you are like when you drink a little too much."

"I must celebrate the birth of my niece."

She shakes her head, the action slow. "We were so sure, George. All the astrologers said it would be a bonny prince. I was so sure in my heart that I was carrying a boy. Cromwell had the proclamations drawn up in readiness. I heard he had to hastily rewrite them – turning prince into princess. I wanted to scratch out all debate. Another princess is what they are saying. I wanted to obliterate Princess Mary." She groans to herself. "I know Henry still calls her *Daughter* but I would like to give her a good boxing on the ears for the bastard she is." Her cheeks redden as she pulls her mouth back in a thin line. "I would make her a maid in my household if I had my way, or better still, marry her off to some varlet and be rid of her for good."

George raises one eyebrow. "Anne, you know Mary is no match for you!"

"Did you know the Spaniard refused to let me have the royal christening robe?" Her blood is up. "Refused! How dare she!" Her nostrils flare. "I do not want the cursed thing for my child. It would bring us bad luck!" She stares at the boarded-up windows, still blocking out the sunlight. "George, I am longing for some fresh air. I wish I could get out of this dungeon and see Elizabeth's christening tomorrow."

"I will be there in your stead. I am part of the entourage, carrying the canopy of estate over our most dear Princess Elizabeth. Father will be there too." His gorgeous face lights up with pride. "As I came here, I saw them laying a carpet of fresh, green rushes. Worry not, Sister, I will bring her back to you afterwards." He pats the back of her hand. "It will be wonderful. The procession is to be lit with five hundred flaming torches."

Anne pulls herself up against her pillows. "Brother, pretending to be overjoyed is wearing me away."

"Do not pretend with me – you do not have to."

"Thank you." She reaches for his hand and squeezes it.

He looks around the room, then at the bed. "This is a fine bed." He rubs his hand over the walnut carving of one of the posters. "I have not seen it before."

"It is French," Anne says. "We brought it out of the treasure room. It was the ransom for a captured nobleman. Imagine the people who may have slept in it."

"I'd rather not!" He chuckles.

"Henry insisted I had it."

"Elizabeth will speak good French, then." He chuckles again. "It seems my niece has practically been born in France."

She frowns. "Now you are being foolish. But what about you, George? When are you going to set about getting an heir?"

He stares at her, then glances over at me. "It is not for me – my union sickens me. Jane Parker—"

"Boleyn, you mean," she says, wagging a finger at him.

"Always Parker to me. We are the Boleyns – you, me, Mary, Mother, Father, and…" He glances at me again, and my legs shake. It's a good job Jane isn't in the room – she'd be furious.

"Do not say her name, George," Anne whispers, glancing over at me.

"Jane Parker will never be the mother of my children. I've told you – any nephew will be my heir."

"George, are children not the greatest consolation in this world?"

"I do not think Uncle Norfolk has ever seen it that way. Nephews and nieces are the greatest advancements for him." He sighs, exasperated. I want to grab him, hug him, and never let him go.

"Anne, I almost forgot – have you heard?"

"Heard what?" she asks.

"I am being given the palace of Beaulieu." He smiles now, like a little boy with a plan. "There is enough room for Jane Parker to get lost in, and I am having it fitted with wall hangings and running water!"

"Wonderful."

He nods to himself. "The Essex palace to be proud of."

I know the site of the palace well, in my modern time. It's not far from Colchester. But in the 21st-century, Beaulieu is long gone, apart from a sign advertising a modern development of new-build houses that cover the location. It upsets me how all that history will be built over.

"George," Anne says, pulling me back to the moment, "I look forward to being received in state."

"You will, Sister – you will."

"You are a brother to be very proud of."

He bows, then stands strong.

"Of body small,
Of power regal,
She isn't sharp of sight,
Of courage halt,
No manner fault,
Is this falcon white!"

He bows again. "There is plenty of time for giving birth to princes, Sister."

"Brother, I pray God in heaven, it is so."

WEDNESDAY 10TH SEPTEMBER 1533 – GREENWICH PALACE

The state occasion in procession today is acted out to humiliate Anne's critics and still their wagging tongues. I join in, leaving her recovering in her chambers as the procession walks over green rushes between hangings of arras from the Great Hall at Greenwich to the church of the Observant Friars. The arrangements are lavish, much like those made later for the baby boy Jane Seymour will bear the king. The whole event reminds me of the programme the BBC filmed called *Britain's Tudor Treasure: A Night at Hampton Court*. The crazy thing is, I still have to pinch myself, realising that I am observing real life.

In the church, the splendour is exemplified by the magnificence of those taking part in this christening. The marquis of Exeter is called upon to carry 'the taper of virgin wax', and the duke of Suffolk escorts the child more from duty than liking. John, Lord Hussey, Lady Mary's chamberlain, and George, carry the gold canopy of state. Most striking of all, Katharine's friend, the marchioness of Exeter, is one of the godmothers, and it is common knowledge that she wanted to have nothing to do with this occasion but took part so as not to displease the king. From all accounts, she loathed having to buy a christening gift for the princess, but it is an impressive present, namely three engraved silver-gilt bowls with covers.

Among the twenty-one participants are, of course, Elizabeth's grandfather, Thomas Boleyn, her Uncle George, and eight Howard connections, while Thomas Cranmer becomes godfather, and there is one person linked to William Brereton and another to Thomas Cromwell. I'm standing among the throng when someone nudges my shoulder.

"Mistress Wickers, do you not think Master Cromwell has prepared and arranged everything very well?"

I turn, and my face goes cold in astonishment. Professor Marshall is looking down on me, dressed from head to toe in dark-brown velvet and fox hair.

"Sir, what are you doing here?"

"Shhh," he whispers. "Don't draw attention to the fact we know each other."

"But why are you here?"

"Now Elizabeth is born,"—he smiles—"I'm here to support and serve her."

"Like me with Anne?"

"Exactly."

"Have you helped plan the christening?" I ask.

"No, Cromwell is largely responsible for the success of this event."

I look across to Cromwell, who is an omnipotent observer of proceedings.

"Have you been introduced to the queen?"

"Yes, when she publicly announced her pregnancy to the court."

"But I wasn't there."

"No, you were probably off chasing George Boleyn!" He scowls at me.

"No, sir, it's the other way around – he chases me." My face flushes with the realisation that he has heard court gossip about me and George.

"I never saw you," I say. "Why didn't you come and speak with me?"

"I didn't want to draw any attention to you. I wasn't even sure you were still here."

I nod. "Ah, right. You think I'd miss this? Never!"

He smiles in agreement.

"But Anne said nothing to me about you," I say. "That you were here."

"I asked her not to," he replies, matter-of-fact.

I'm relieved our conversation ceases when I have to fall into line as the procession makes way, with Elizabeth being brought back from the ceremony this autumn afternoon. George looks as beautiful as ever as he helps to carry the Canopy of Estate. And he was right, the procession is illuminated by what looks like hundreds of lighted torches. Maybe I exaggerate, but however many there are, they make the whole occasion perfect. Nothing has been left to chance. Goodness, I can't believe Professor Marshall is here. Not just that, he's been here for ages, and I never noticed him. I hope things don't get complicated. Well, any more than it already is.

OCTOBER 1533 – GREENWICH PALACE

Anne's ladies-in-waiting and I escort her from her apartments, leaving her confinement behind, all relieved that her time of seclusion has ended. She has had to be 'churched' in the Chapel Royal, as custom dictates, before her re-entry into court society and the king's bed. Following Mass, one of Henry's body servants enters the chapel unannounced.

He bows. "Your Majesty, the king has requested an audience with you."

Anne finishes her prayers and gets up from the royal pew, leaving all her ladies, bar me. We follow the servant with a certain amount of trepidation and make our way to Henry's privy apartments. What will be said between the two of them? Anne has been dreading the time when she will be truly alone with him, when there will be no pretence for the sake of appearances, and when she will witness in grisly detail the true extent of the damage done in the wake of Elizabeth's birth.

One of Henry's gentlemen, Sir Richard Page, escorts us to the entrance of the three-storey donjon that contains the king's most private of rooms. Anne takes her leave of me and goes to meet with Henry in his library, located on the second floor. Sir Richard indicates that I should wait, and I watch Anne ascend the narrow, spiral staircase, running her left hand against the rough surface of brick, whilst lifting the hem of her gown with her right.

As I await her return, anxious to hear how Henry was with her, courtiers walk past me, locked in a discourse on matters of state, discussing Thomas More's refusal to sign the oath in favour of the Act of Succession that has just been written and declared. Others discuss the Holy Maid of Kent, Elizabeth Barton, who has talked of having access to heaven, hell, and purgatory. She has supporters, but some think she is mad, and it is all about politics – the politics of religion that festers and brews under Henry's feet.

"Some say she has sworn the king will not reign for more than a month after Elizabeth's birth, and will die," a lady says to her husband, eyeing me as they walk by.

The man scowls at her. "Deliberating on the king's death is treason, Wife, and Elizabeth Barton will be seen for the lying harlot she is. They should send her back to the whorehouse before she says anything more to offend the king's majesty. You must have a brain the size of a flea. Give no credence to what the Lady Exeter discusses in private."

Ah, his wife is a friend of Lady Exeter, who has received the Barton prophet on occasion.

My heart jumps when George enters, in conversation with his uncle. He has returned from matters of state abroad and has just arrived back to court. When he sees me, he makes a hasty excuse and heads in my direction.

"Viscountess," he says, his face lit with his wonderful smile. "How are you?"

"Very well, George." I struggle not to jump into his arms. "And you?"

"I have come to see my sister, as we have plans to consider for my niece's upbringing. Is she with the king?" He looks towards the staircase and the heavy oak door at the top. It is fitted with an elaborate golden lock and is ajar. Without warning, Henry's vitriolic tones filter down to us:

"It is your fault, Anne! Have I not born a son with Elizabeth Blount, and your sister? Am I not like any other man? You promised me a son and you did not deliver. I gave you everything, and what do I have in return? Nothing. I look like a fool afore the whole of Christendom!"

George blanches at the ferocity of Henry's attack. It is unfair. Anne went to Henry wanting to apologise and to show him her love and loyalty, and yet this is how he speaks to her.

"Perhaps if you had managed to get yourself a divorce from Katharine earlier," she bites back, the full force of her anger escaping through the open door, "there would be no question of the validity of our marriage. Perhaps God is angry that it took so long for you to get out of that unholy union.

Perhaps, if I hadn't been so distressed for months – no, years – wondering if we would ever be together, then all would be well, and we would have a son by now. In fact, many sons!"

Her rant sounds illogical and irrational, but her intemperance is no bedfellow of logic, as she is swept up in a primitive desire to lash out at Henry and defend her new-born daughter.

George looks around, and I'm thankful there are no other around to hear this.

"You refused to bring either Katharine or your *daughter Mary* to heel," Anne continues, "and in the meantime, what was I supposed to think? How do you imagine that makes me feel?"

"Wait here for me," George says, "I'll go and rescue her." He takes the stairs two at a time as Henry's voice booms through the doorway.

"Madam, it seems you forget yourself – yet again. You are my wife and my queen…and I will not tolerate your insolence!" This comes as a rising, thunderous crescendo.

Before he can continue, George is pushing the door in. He shuts it behind him, and I'm left waiting on tenterhooks. It's only a ten-minute wait but feels like a lifetime before I see the familiar silk of Anne's slippers descending the stairs, with George taking her arm. She looks shaken but tries to remain stoic, holding her head high as she reaches the bottom step, letting go of George's arm to take mine.

"Madam, are you well?" I ask, tucking my arm through hers.

"I have been better," she states, matter-of-fact.

"She has wounded his pride," George whispers. "His Majesty is hurt. All my sister need do is surrender herself to the king's will, allow his ego to conquer her once more, and all will be well, you will see." He smiles, and it's like he's trying to reassure both himself and his sister.

With the cooling of her temper, Anne listens to him, nodding in agreement. I'm hoping this is a sign that she can soften her sharp tongue, rein herself in, and begin to achieve what is expected of all female monarchs: to stay quiet; to support her husband; and produce male heirs. She will need to pull herself together, to conduct herself as expected with Henry, now she is queen. And that means committing to rebuilding his bruised pride and bringing him back to her bed.

Once she returns to her chambers, George stops me, grabbing my wrist in a vicelike grip and preventing me from following her.

"See what happens when women do not keep their husbands happy?" His brows are furrowed in a deep frown.

"Yes, I do indeed," I reply.

"Now, do you understand why I prefer you?"

"No, tell me," I whisper.

"Because a man likes to be the centre of a woman's world, and I am that to you."

Don't I know it. "But you know Anne feels that way about the king."

"Yes, I do – but the trouble is, I am not sure that he believes it." He looks at my wrist but maintains his grip. "Watch over my sister – the times are disordered, and she sees enemies everywhere."

"So, she should, they are waiting for her to fail. She said she would give Henry a son. That is what the king expected." I wince, trying to pull my arm free. "George, you are hurting me."

His hand snaps open. "I do not mean to. Stop her from failing! If Anne does not give Henry a son, all the old families are waiting their turn. I am worried about her. She needs protecting."

I nod, understanding his concerns. At this moment, he frightens me – I've never seen him angry like that. Perhaps he is picking up in his spirit what his fate may be? Who knows?

"I am sorry," he says, his temper cooling. "I did not mean to scare you, but dealing with the king is not easy sometimes." He rubs my wrist where he held it. "Did you hear about the Barton woman?"

"Yes, her prophecies are absurd. Cromwell will have the matter in hand, surely?"

"Cromwell is a friend of our family and my sister, and he will support us, as he should." My observations of Cromwell are somewhat less positive than those of the Boleyns. My foreknowledge leaves an ominous distaste in my mouth because I am well aware that Secretary Cromwell will be of no help to George, or Anne, in the end. I thank God George has no idea what is to come.

LATE OCTOBER 1533 – GREENWICH PALACE

Anne's maids of honour are repeating Henry's brazen remark that he loves the queen so much that he would beg alms from door to door rather than give her up. The two are merry again and Henry keeps her, as always, in selective touch with diplomatic affairs, and I'm glad to say, they visit little Princess Elizabeth often.

This morning, Anne's rooms are filled with bright daylight streaming through the windows. Henry sits with her, baby upon his arm, as she pulls out miniature smocks and green, embroidered silk coifs for the princess. The fine silks shimmer in the cool air when she holds them up for his inspection.

"What think you of this, Husband?" she asks, showing him a dainty smock embroidered with intricate patterns in silk threads. "Isn't it sweet? It has just come from the embroiderer. Our little Elizabeth shall wear it well, shall she not?"

Henry smiles and rocks Elizabeth in his arms. "She shall, Madam, she shall." He looks up at his wife, then back to Elizabeth. "Our daughter is to have her household at Hertford. Her governess shall be Lady Bryan."

"Yes, My Lord. You will be giving our child a household befitting of her royal status – therefore, I have been preparing such items for her trunk."

"Once the princess has her own establishment, we can think of bringing her a brother, can we not?" He hands the baby to her wet nurse, who places her back in her royal crib.

An usher announces the arrival of Lord Rochford, who performs a deep bow to the royal couple. Today, I see a side to George I haven't witnessed before. He takes Elizabeth, unwraps her from her swaddling, and cradles her in his arms. He's a natural, it seems. The nearly two-month-old squirms and squeals thrilled it seems to be picked up by someone other than her wet nurse. I get up and walk next to him and peer over his arm at the princess.

"Fatherhood would suit you, Lord Rochford."

He shakes his head at me. "Only if I was a father to your children," he whispers, rocking his niece. Her eyes widen as he looks at her, cooing at her while she gurgles with delight back at him. When he's finished playing with her, I go back to sit in my seat. He hands her back to her nurse, who leaves the room with the infant. George watches the woman walk away, his eyes full of sadness.

This afternoon, in Henry's private chambers, Anne, George, and I are discussing political matters with the king. George turns to Henry.

"Your Majesty, Ambassador Chapuys has sought out His Grace, the duke of Norfolk, and Master Cromwell, and complains bitterly of what he perceives to be the unfair treatment of the Princess Dowager and the Lady Mary. In particular, he fears that with the proclamation of your legitimate daughter, my niece, as Princess of Wales, the rights of the Lady Mary might be impaired, depriving her of her lawful succession to the throne. Chapuys felt that you might wish to intervene."

"I hate ungratefulness," Henry says. "The Princess Dowager has had much from me since the death of her husband, my brother. Staying rent free in my homes. Gifted of The Old Manor, at Hazdor, Droitwich. The woman has been gifted other houses, monies, clothing. Her needs have been paid for since she was a young woman. She is a guest in our country and her daughter shares in her abundance."

Anne stands beside him as he pores over the Act of Succession that Cromwell has drawn up for them to agree. I long to see this original document – itching to get my hands on it – but it's not my place to read it, so, instead, I sit back, observe, and listen.

Cromwell has now entered the chamber, bowing low as he is announced. Clutching his leather-bound set of papers, he awaits Henry's response, his eagerness clear in his eyes. Anne reads the bill over Henry's shoulder.

"The Bill of Succession has been drawn up," Cromwell says, "recognising Queen Anne as your lawful wife, and your children you have, and will have, as your legitimate heirs."

"Hmm, good." Henry devours every word on the parchment.

"The bill will succeed before parliament, My Lord, and to seal the act, we would like to add an oath, so that every person may confirm their loyalty, beyond doubt."

"Very well." Henry looks up, scrutinizing Cromwell. Anne is still tracing each point with her long forefinger.

"You mention the possibility of my demise," she says to Cromwell. He stares back, showing no emotion. "If it shall happen that your said dear and beloved true wedded wife, Queen Anne, do decease…"

"I cannot exclude the possibility, Madam. It might happen." Cromwell probably thinks she will die in childbirth, no doubt. How wrong he is.

"You say that, if I die, the king can put another wife, and queen in my place?"

Henry grips her hand as she leans over the desk beside him, her shoulder brushing against the fur of his coat. "I cannot imagine another wife, or queen, in your place, sweetheart." He looks up at her, holding her hand to his chest. I wonder if he's ever uttered similar words to the Princess Dowager. Probably. "Darling, this is only a precaution." He's trying to show her a kindness, to reassure her. "It is the notion of your death, only."

"I thought it treason for anyone to imagine my death, Henry?"

"No, Anne. It is only treason if anyone imagines my demise." He glares at her for a moment. Has he had a premonition of what's to come? I shudder at the thought.

"And what if a new wife, and queen, has a son after my death? That son would inherit, and what would happen to my daughter and her claim to the throne?"

"Elizabeth would still be a princess of England. Look, it says it here." He points to the said passage, still gripping her hand.

"Where does it say Spanish Mary is illegitimate, and a bastard?"

Cromwell nods at the document. "As the king has asked me to write the Lady Mary out of the line of succession, the inference is clear. This law has been written sparingly, so it does not seem personal."

"This is a personal attack against me and my children, Cromwell."

"Do not argue against Cromwell, Anne. He serves us well, darling, and others have been disloyal, like Buckingham, before your time." Henry turns back to Cromwell. "Now we have other names to add to that list, such as Gardiner, and others. They have all turned against me in their disobedience."

Anne blinks at him, staying silent.

"Your bill against Elizabeth Barton, that Nun of Kent," he says as Cromwell turns away, "you should add traitors like Thomas More to the list of the guilty." He taps the document. "I hate his disloyalty too."

"Believe me when I say, Sir Thomas More was not involved, Your Majesty. He came to me before Barton was arrested."

"I asked you to add the man to the list – it may make him sign the oath and agree with the bill."

Worrying about what Thomas More thinks of him could be seen as a weakness. Anne has urged him in private to secure her right as Queen and draw up this bill to ensconce Elizabeth in the line of succession. I can see her argument, as factions move against her, waiting and watching for her demise. Indeed, I can see it all, and there doesn't seem to be anything I can do about it.

31ST DECEMBER 1533 – THE PALACE OF PLACENTIA, GREENWICH.

Outside, sunlight bounces off the crisp white snow and streams through the windows, illuminating the great hall. The air is astir on this bustling afternoon with industrious stewards, yeomen, and kitchen staff. They hasten to ready the massive chamber once again for a large holiday gathering – a festive celebration – the second in a week. On New Year's Day, King Henry VIII, his family and chief courtiers, are to exchange gifts, as is the custom. And this observance of the New Year will be accompanied by feasting and merriment.

Within the hearth, the yule log continues to smoulder and crackle. It had been dragged into the hall on Christmas Eve and lit, its flame nurtured by the kitchen staff, and will be kept alive and guarded through to Twelfth Night.

Fresh, aromatic rushes are being spread on the floor, and for the special day, the mix is heavy with rosemary, sage, sweet fennel, and lavender. The citrus scent from the cloved oranges hangs in the air. Many slippered feet tread upon the herbs, crushing them until they release a heavenly bouquet of fragranced delights. Fresh candles are being placed in the many candelabra positioned about the room. The buffets are situated to allow ease of service for all the guests once the feasting commences.

Henry and Anne's dais is laid with a beautiful Turkish carpet, with gilt chairs of estate and the royal dining table placed upon it. At the front of the room, a stage has been constructed where, during dinner, the minstrels and choir will create music.

I rush back to Anne's closet to assist with her preparations. Velvet gowns are being shifted about, and a silk kirtle is set at her stockinged feet, ready for her to step into. The room is buzzing with anticipation as we prepare the queen consort for her New Year appearance. She insists she will not be overshadowed by her husband, and with that notion in her head, she selects a gown of deep emerald and green velvet, accented with white satin and powdered ermine.

"Your Majesty, which hood would you prefer?" Lady Lee asks.

Anne points to the velvet hood in Margaret's left hand, beckoning her to bring it forward. I have to say, she looks magnificent today, wearing a carcanet of diamonds around her neck, with rings of emerald and gold on her fingers. The silks of my skirts crush beneath my knees as I help her into her velvet slippers.

Ready, at last, her gown laced and pinned, she glides through the long galleries, accompanied by the most loyal ladies of her closet, who chatter with excitement behind her. Her dogs nip at their heels, no doubt hoping for treats. I stop to look through a mullioned gallery window, its icy chill biting at my fingertips as I press against it to view the falling snow. In that moment, I reflect on how long I've now been here, and wonder how things might be back at home. I'm hoping it's only been a day that's passed, and that I'm not being missed.

We watch and wait until Henry appears, striding towards us, accompanied by Henry Norris and George. He enters the hall to a fanfare of sackbuts and cornets, with delighted applause from all the guests awaiting him. There is great anticipation among them, for this gathering marks the exchanging of gifts with his closest subjects. It starts with the bishops, then the dukes and earls.

I'm amazed watching the king being gifted parmesan cheese, various birds and beasts, gold and silver objects, homemade items, and the always welcome, if unimaginative, present of money. And, in return, he will give them silver plate and pots as tokens of his esteem and gratitude. Many waiting are nervous, fiddling with their doublets. Henry may not be gracious with every gift given to him, and his degree of appreciation will serve as a marker of one's level of good standing with him.

Anne honours him with a deep curtsy. His eyes twinkle and brighten, and he raises her to a standing position by taking her hand, which he then lifts to his lips. It is clear to all that he is still much in love with her. Together, they move to the dais. Their exchange of gifts took place in his privy chambers earlier this morning, during intimate time alone.

At the signal of the chief steward, the many gentlemen ushers rush to an adjoining anteroom to bring forth the king's gifts, while the courtiers form a receiving line to process past the royal couple. The first assemblies are the dukes and earls of the realm: Lord Chancellor Thomas Cromwell, the dukes of Richmond, Norfolk, and Suffolk, the Lord Marquess Exeter, the Lord Steward, and the earls of Oxford, Northumberland, Westmoreland, Rutland, Wiltshire, Huntingdon, Sussex, Worcester, Derby, and Essex. To them, Henry presents gilt cups, bowls, and silver and golden basins. In exchange, each nobleman bows, offering him their gift. Cromwell presents him with a beautiful walking staff, wrought with gold. The duke of Norfolk gives him a wood-knife, a pair of tables and chessmen, and a tablet of gold. Henry's close friend Brandon, the duke of Suffolk, smiles as he presents a gold ball which holds a waxy perfume. The Marquess of Exeter offers a bonnet trimmed with aglets, buttons, and a gold brooch. The earl of Shrewsbury gives a nine-ounce flagon of gold for rosewater. The earl of Oxford provides ten sovereigns in a kidskin glove. The earl of Northumberland and many others come before him, bearing gifts just like the three wise men to Jesus.

I watch George as he waits in line to present his gift. As I do, I flick a look around, not wanting Jane to catch me eyeing him. I'm not sure if he's seen me. He wouldn't have bought me a gift, would he? No, Jane wouldn't allow it. My feet ache, standing in procession for so long.

Next come the lords. The ushers step forward to assist in the gift exchange. One by one, they move past the king and queen, bowing and offering words of greeting and good cheer on the holiday. They each receive gold and silver-gilt bowls, salt cellars, cups, goblets, and trenchers. In exchange, they present gifts of great value and even greater creativity – all wanting to provide *the* gift of the festive season. Creating a growing pile in one corner are satin purses, beautiful carpets, gold swords, books, and fine shirts sewn of cambric.

Next, it's the turn of the waiting duchesses and countesses. This is going to take forever! I feel as if I'm going to faint. Some wine would be perfect right now.

Now it's time for the ladies. Jane Boleyn steps forward and offers the king two velvet and two satin caps. He gives them a quick look over.

"Thank you, Lady Rochford." He nods, then waits for the next person in the procession. More ladies. More pain in my feet. I need to sit. This event makes me think of the royal court in the eighteenth century, where King George III used to make everyone stay standing all the time, even if they needed to use the lavatory. According to one television historian, some courtiers would have to do their business, and stand in it, because they weren't allowed to move. I'm so glad I time-slipped to now rather than a Georgian Royal Court, or the French Royal Court of Versailles.

I really do need to focus on this moment and stop my mind wandering. Next come the Chaplains, and then, at last, it's the gentlewomen – the line I'm in. Hold on, maybe I got it wrong. As a titled woman, perhaps I should have been in the procession with the duchesses and countesses, or maybe with the ladies? God knows. Tudor protocol sometimes confuses me.

My turn comes, and the king looks at me, beckoning me forward. I curtsy with as much grace as I can and, with nerves jangling, step forward and offer Henry a folded linen shirt with a black-worked collar I have sewn myself. One of his usher's hands it to him, and he unfolds it in front of everyone, examining the thread work.

"Viscountess Beaumont, this is very fine work – I am well pleased!" He hands the shirt to the chief steward.

I already gave Anne a linen shift early this morning, which I embroidered for her under the watchful instruction of Nan, and she wears it now under her gown. She nods in appreciation, signalling to me that Henry is pleased with my efforts. He signals to his steward to step forward, closer to me, and he holds a small, dark, wooden casket out towards me.

"For me, Your Majesty?" My face burns.

The steward opens the lid of the intricately carved box.

"Yes, Viscountess." Henry replies. "I hope you like it." Inside, is a delicately worked silver goblet nestled in a bed of blue velvet.

"Your Majesty!" I exclaim, barely wanting to touch the goblet. "I see it has my new coat of arms on it!" The item takes my breath away. "I shall treasure this for ever." I must remember to take this back home with me, when I next return to my time, in Carshalton.

Henry beams at me, pleased with my reaction. The steward hands my casket to one of the gentlewomen, who says she will take it to my chamber.

Not long after, with the parade completed, the servers lay the tables with food for the hungry and thirsty guests. Adding to the wonderment and excess of the day, the end of the meal is marked by a special mummers' performance. The actors, dressed in disguises of feathers and elaborate masks, entertain the crowd with mimes and stories of Christmas and the saints. Jests and jokes are added, and the guests laugh uproariously, thoroughly enjoying themselves.

As darkness falls, the day of festive introduction into the New Year draws to a close. Some wander outside afterwards to breathe the crisp air and to throw snowballs, continuing their evening's entertainment.

The staff clear the hall of the remains and the riches, needing to prepare the palace yet again for the final celebration of the Christmas season – Twelfth Night, held on the eve of the 5th of January. As the harbinger of a promised good year, there was no more magical place to be than in the court of Henry VIII of England on January 1st. However, all I can think about is the fact that we are almost one year closer to Anne and George's unjust and brutal demise.

FEBRUARY 1534 – HATFIELD HOUSE

I accompany Anne on a visit to five-month-old Princess Elizabeth, and she is delighted at seeing her daughter. She cradles her in her arms and asks Lady Bryan how the princess fares.

"Your Highness, you must know she is a princess already, for she is well behaved."

"I am glad she is of good temper, Lady Bryan. And has she a good appetite?"

"Yes, very good, Your Highness. The princess eats a hearty breakfast and is still being fed by her wet nurse."

"I am very pleased." Anne smiles, but the delight on her face dissipates when Lady Mary enters the chamber. She passes Elizabeth back to Lady Bryan and stands in front of Henry's first born, waiting for her to curtsy in respect, but she doesn't. Mary is a small, plain young woman – pious, much like her mother: clever, brave, and stubborn. Her dislike of Anne is obvious, for she will not even look her in the eye.

"Lady Mary, I would gladly be a kind and generous stepmother – I would even go so far as to speak with my husband to reconcile you to him, being he is your father, if you would acknowledge me as his wife, and queen."

Mary doesn't even look at her. "*Lady Pembroke,* I would accept you as my father's bedfellow, however, I will never accept you as his true and lawful wife in the eyes of God. I could never accept you as queen. My mother is Queen of England. Understand that I know no other queen but Katharine. However, if you, as the king's paramour, would intercede with him on my behalf, I would be thankful."

Her refusal to acknowledge Anne as queen, and by denying her half-sister's precedence, she is letting Anne know that she thinks she is still first in line to the English throne.

Even after this offensiveness, Anne tries again before leaving the house, but Mary will have none of it, and Anne vows to me that she will repress such impudence. From what I observe, this is no ordinary family feud.

Mary's failure to accept Anne is one problem, but it is linked to another: an increasing opposition to the queen among the elite and the nation at large. There is no doubt that a good deal of her unpopularity is on account of Mary and the repudiation of Katharine. This sentiment is often found among women such as Margaret Chanseler, from Bradfield St Clare in Suffolk, who demonstrates such hate when she says that Anne is a "goggle-eyed whore".

Feelings are usually kept beneath the surface among the elite, and Anne must notice the readiness of courtiers, who accompany her to see Elizabeth, to slink off to pay their respects to Mary. Much of the hostility is associated with a dislike of Henry's recent policies, namely taxation and interference with the church. As Anne makes her way to leave, she ushers Lady Bryan to one side.

"Lady Bryan, under no circumstances should Princess Elizabeth be left alone with the Lady Mary. And I do mean, under *no* circumstances. Do we understand each other?"

Lady Bryan just nods in acknowledgement of the queen's command. Neither of them realises that Lady Mary is standing in the doorway a few feet away, and I know she heard everything.

Nine

MARCH 1534

"Your Majesty, I have it on good authority that the pope has given a definitive answer in the matter between yourself and the Dowager Princess."

Henry gives Cromwell an expectant look. "And?"

"Sir, it appears it is not an answer in your favour."

The king frowns. "Thomas, did you really expect it to be?"

"'Tis rather strange, because I heard the news on the very day that parliament passed the First Act of Succession."

"How Clement VII can declare my marriage to Katharine valid, I dare not understand. If the pope thinks I will treat either Katharine or the Lady Mary any differently, then he is much mistaken. Mary may suffer ill-health, but the pope cannot force me to take Katharine back or restore Mary to the succession. The matter has been finalised."

"The Roman Catholics can complain all they like. No doubt Andrew Boorde, the physician, traveller, and writer will continue to keep me informed of any news from Europe."

"Changing the subject, Thomas, I have other news."

I hear a smile in Henry's voice, even if I cannot see his face now that I'm at the open door.

"Other news?" Cromwell looks bemused. "What can possibly be more important than what is happening in Europe, sir?"

"Anne has missed her monthly bleed," Henry announces. He rushes to Cromwell with open arms, and they embrace but move apart just as fast, though his hands remain on his secretary's shoulders.

"This time for sure, it will be a boy, Thomas!" he declares, exalted in the news of Anne's pregnancy, so soon after the birth of Princess Elizabeth. "What say you, my good fellow?"

I rush down the corridor, holding my skirts up to stop them rustling. Everyone will hope Anne can keep the baby to term and that it will be a boy to bring about a golden age for England, but I alone know different, and that knowledge weighs on me like nothing else.

APRIL 1534

Anne cannot resist beaming with pride, sitting on the dais in her chamber of presence as the Master of the Royal Mint, Sir William Blount, 4th Baron Mountjoy, bows before her. He is dressed in dark wool, decorated with pewter buttons, and trimmed with rabbit fur – the attire of a typical English courtier, scholar, and patron of learning. Blount has been master of the mint since 1509 and was Chamberlain to Queen Katharine. He had the unfortunate duty of office to inform the dowager of Henry's intention to divorce her. Jane Rochford told me he signed Henry's letter to the pope, in which the king threatened to turn his back on the Roman Catholic Church unless the divorce was granted.

At fifty-six, he is frail, his hair greying at the temples, and he wobbles a little as he rises from his low bow. He signals his master craftsman, who steps forward, holding out an open velvet box.

"Your Majesty," Blount says, "the King has commissioned his Royal Mint to strike this medal. He has asked me for your approval before we manufacture copies to go out to all the people of London."

Jane cranes her neck to peer over Anne's shoulder as she lifts the medal from its bed of velvet.

"Will the copies be made in lead?" she asks, running her fingertips over the raised carving.

Blount nods. "Yes, Your Majesty."

"It looks a little like you, Madam," Jane says.

"I'm not sure that His Majesty would approve of my raised bosom," Anne says in jest, "but the depiction is fairly accurate."

Blount squirms as he points out the carving with his blunt forefinger. His face is sallow, drawn, and thin. "Your Majesty, we have depicted you in this condition because the medal has been struck to commemorate your pregnancy, in the hope of a prince."

Anne is shown in a pedimental headdress, with large veil at the back, a cross hanging from a necklace, and a square-necked, low-cut dress, with a mantle over her shoulders. Also showing are her initials. The medal's inscription is squeezed around the outer edge: THE MOOST HAPPI – ANNO 1534. The most likely interpretation of the letters A R is that they refer to Anne as ANNA REGINA. The cast is from a carving in hone-stone.

"If you approve, Majesty, you may keep the original, as we have the carving to work from."

"That is most kind of you, Sir William. Please convey my gracious thanks to His Majesty. I am very pleased with your work."

He nods, failing to hide a slight groan as he bows again, then shuffles out of the chamber, his servant following.

Anne turns to me, smiling. "No matter what Lady Jane here says, I think this a pleasing likeness and one I am most proud of." With that, she places the medal back in the box and snaps the lid shut. I struggle to hold back a wry smile when Jane flinches.

Lady Shelton, known as Madge, arranges flowers in a vase while Lady Lee fusses about Anne, who is struggling to fit into gowns now that her belly is beginning to show. Madge is the queen's cousin, the daughter of Sir Thomas Boleyn's sister, Anne, who is married to Sir John Shelton. Queen Anne seems to favour the Sheltons, which I do find odd, when some of them don't get on with their royal relative.

George Zouche raps on the door, announcing the entrance of Thomas Boleyn, 1st Earl of Wiltshire, who beams at his daughter. He takes her hand and kisses it.

"Papa."

"Your Majesty – you look very well. And I see you are already showing." He glances down at his daughter's belly, his eyes full of delight.

"Only a little, Father." She nods and smiles.

"How is Henry? He must be pleased with your present condition. Tell me he is pleased?"

"He is happy. We both hope for a son this time." Her gaze lowers, as if worried that if she doesn't vocalise the king's wishes, she will not encourage her longed-for male heir to continue to stir in her belly.

"But?" her father says, not missing anything.

"Everything is good," she assures him.

I plump the cushions on her chair, motioning her to sit. Her smile lights up her chamber as she reclines against the soft velvet, her arms resting on the arms of a chair.

"I am worried, for when I was last with child, did you know that Henry took a mistress? Papa, I am concerned he will take another. I hear rumours he has taken a fancy to a woman called Joanna Dingley. Since I must be careful, for the sake of my son,"—she rubs her abdomen—"I cannot allow my husband to enjoy his conjugal rights."

Thomas draws closer to his daughter, smiling at me, then her, and rests his hands against a walnut table, his expression serious as he looks into her face. "It is natural for a man, when his wife is in your condition, and unwilling or unable to lie with him, to…find some temporary consolation elsewhere – and for kings, it is properly accepted, as the thing to do."

I watch, mesmerised at the change in him as he manipulates his daughter's emotions, making suggestions he thinks will alleviate her concerns. He drops to her level, his eye contact strong, so he is assured of her attention.

"Sweetheart, please listen to me," he says, his voice at a whisper. "The danger to you and us is not that the king takes a paramour, but that he takes the wrong one." He strokes her hand. "This woman will not be involved with Henry for love, but entertainment purposes only – and we must choose this source of entertainment that will be conducive to our needs. Someone we can control but, more importantly, someone we can also trust with this most delicate of matters."

I'm standing close by with Lady Shelton and Lady Lee, and we watch aghast as Anne and her father's gaze falls on each of us in turn.

"A lady who would not seek power or advancement, nor to control the king," Anne whispers.

"Precisely," Thomas says. "If you suppose he is to take another woman to his bed, then you need to make sure that she is your choice, and never his. You have got to be sure the king does not cultivate a yearning for her nectar."

"Yes, Papa," she replies, nodding once, her lips pursed. Crickey, I have a sickening feeling in my gut at what's going to come of this conversation. Madge Shelton catches my eye, and I frown, trying to remember who it was that became the king's mistress at this point in Anne's history. Was it Madge Shelton?

"Now, Your Majesty," he says, getting to his feet, "I must take my leave of you and attend the king." He bows and smiles, like the true statesman he is. "Viscountess Beaumont, Lady Shelton, Lady Lee." He nods at us and departs, leaving us all with much to think about. I wonder if he is beginning to regret allowing Anne to marry Henry. Not that there is anything he could have done about it – the whole of Tudor England orbits around the will of their king.

"Lady Shelton, Lady Lee, would you please leave us," Anne commands as Madge prods the last flower into the vase.

"Yes, Your Majesty." They both curtsy before leaving the two of us alone. Anne watches me as I place more kindling in a basket beside the hearth, then beckons me to her side.

"Beth, I need to talk to you."

Her tone is shallow. Goodness, I hope she's not going to ask me to bed Henry? No, surely, she wouldn't.

"What is it, Anne?"

"I need to ask you something."

Oh, God, here it comes. She's going to ask *me* of all people to sleep with her husband.

"Yes?"

"What is the sex of this child?"

I visibly exhale with a puffing of my cheeks as she stares at me. What a relief to know she hasn't asked what I thought she would. But, even so, this is still a problem.

She sits next to me, rubbing her belly. "What is the fate of my unborn baby?"

I squirm, wishing she wouldn't ask me to share my foreknowledge with her about this pregnancy.

"I cannot tell you."

"I never asked you for your truth with Elizabeth." She whispers so we won't be overheard. "But I am asking you now."

"Your Majesty, you are impossible!" She gives me a knowing smile. "Forgive me, but I am going to say no, again. I mean it! Do not press me for answers you might not be able to accept."

She smirks. "Now who is being impossible?"

I jump up and grab a basket. "I will not give in. You must put your trust in God."

"You are stubborn, just like me." She laughs. "If you will not share your foreknowledge, then do something else for me?"

I turn back to her. "Yes, what is it?"

"You heard what my father suggested to me?" She looks more serious than I have ever seen her.

"I did, Your Majesty," I say, putting the basket down and sitting on a cushioned stool beside her. Oh God, she *is* going to ask me. I thought I'd had a lucky escape.

"You are like a sister to me. And out of all the women about me, it is you I trust most."

"My Lady, I appreciate that, but I know what happened to your sister. I do not want to be used in such a way – it's not a path I wish to walk down. I feel flattered that you would think of me, but it cannot be."

I think of George and know that I couldn't shag Henry, no matter how loyal I feel to Anne. I grimace, crossing my hands in my lap.

"We are like family, and I know you have an admirer in my brother."

"Yes, but I always remember what you told me in the beginning about not encouraging him. Until of, course, you gave us your approval. Though, I will say, neither of us have taken things to their ultimate, intimate conclusion… since…" Oh no, I shouldn't have said that.

"Since?" Anne asks, her eyes narrowing.

"Since you told your household about setting a standard and not being lewd or crude." I sigh with relief, happy that I've managed to worm my way out of

163

confessing that George has already been unfaithful to his wife, with me. I smile. "And I know, in the past, that you wanted me to keep George at arm's length. I have kissed him but nothing more." I push back the guilt at lying to her.

She raises a brow, looking displeased. I'm sure the untruth is written all over my face. I am useless at lying.

"I did give you and George my blessing – that is true – but I am glad you both have not acted upon it as yet, because you also have another admirer. The king."

"Anne, it is not true! I turned his head away from me, and deliberately towards you, remember?"

"Yes, I do, but he has always admired you, since his first visit to Hever. He told me so. He chased you but never caught you, remember?"

I groan inside. What a lucky escape that was. "Who are you trying to persuade, Anne, that this is the right thing for me to do – me or yourself?" I grimace. "I do not have such physical affections for the king."

"Beth, that is my point! Do you think I did, initially? As you do not have those affections for Henry, you will never be swept away by his arduous attentions. Women *love* powerful men. It may surprise you even more if I told you that I will give you my blessing to keep the king's attention whilst I am with child – so much so, that the king's eyes do not wander in any other direction."

Oh, goodness. "What have I got to do to keep his attention?"

"Anything you have to."

"But I was never educated at the French Court!"

"This is easy – you are a woman of the world." She leans forward. "I know George had you – he told me."

My jaw drops, and my face burns red hot. "Anne, I'm so sorry I lied to you. I love your brother – I cannot sleep with the king."

"Regarding George, I gave you both my blessing. Now, while I am with child, I give you my blessing to sleep with His Majesty, as he needs to be able to lie with another woman. He is a passionate man, and I need him to be with a woman I can trust. You, I can trust. Like me, you are a reformer. You are no staunch Catholic. You believe in the same things as me, and you are the winning horse because he has an affection for you already."

She straightens in her seat. "I have seen women put themselves in Henry's way more times than I care to mention. You, Beth Wickers, are the better choice. You are a Viscountess now, and are going to share Henry's bed, and that's an end to it!"

"Majesty, like many at Court, as you know, when the king suggested it, I gladly signed the Oath of Supremacy, which Cromwell decreed to show allegiance to your marriage with the king, and his supremacy over the church." I take a deep breath. "You know I am loyal to you both, but, surely, even with our friendship, this is too much to ask of me?" I shrug and leap for the last thing I hope will save me. "George will hate me for it!"

"It is because of our friendship, and your love for my family, that I trust you, so, upon my command, you will go willingly to the king's bed. I will deal with my brother."

17TH APRIL 1534

Jane Rochford enters Anne's bed chamber with a flourish. "Majesty." She curtsies.

"How do you fare, Jane?" Anne asks, as she watches me pin the placard on the front of her gown. She looks at her reflection in a large mirror. "That looks very well."

Jane stands next to the dressing table, fingering through a string of pearls that are piled in a jewellery box. "I must tell you some news, Madam." She continues fiddling with the pearls. "George has relayed to me that Thomas More has been sent to the Tower today, having been found guilty of treason."

Anne nods once. "It seems that Thomas has been forced to choose between the two great forces in his life – his God and his king, and God has won."

MAY 1534

It is too late for me to do Anne's bidding, for Henry has set up a 'new mistress'. I find Anne distressed when I enter her chambers on this bright crisp morning. Warmth is not to be found as ladies-in-waiting hustle and bustle about, trying to keep out of her way, for she is in a foul mood.

"What ails you, Your Majesty?" I ask, wondering why she is so incensed.

She paces her room back and forth. "I cannot talk to anyone. With George gone, I do not know what to do."

If George were here, I know she would have confided in him, but he is away in France, on his fourth diplomatic mission, to ask François to adopt similar legislation against the pope as that taken in England, and to arrange a meeting between the two kings, his sister, and François' sister.

"Can you not tell me what troubles you?"

"I am so used to confiding in George, as well as you," she says. "It is always better to have two opinions, rather than one."

"Go on…" I urge, sensing her frustrations bubbling over.

"Henry, I have heard, is in love with another lady, and it is not you!" Her eyes are wide, her mouth pulled back into a thin line as her anger radiates, her silk sleeves flying like a whirlwind around her delicate frame.

"Are you certain?" I ask.

"Of course, I am certain!" Rage flashes from her eyes, and I wish I could either duck out of the way or wrap her in my arms for reassurance, but all I can do is continue to watch her mounting distress.

"My Ladies have told me that the girl in question is not of noble birth, but they say Henry seems to like her."

"What's her name?" I ask, as if I hadn't already heard the rumours.

"Joanna Dingley. I wonder if Henry still cares for her." Her words come slow, as if she's considering her options. "I think she is low in rank, enough for her not to be a risk politically. She's royal laundress, so I've been told, and the girl was raised by a John Malte, one of the pattern cutters in the king's wardrobe."

Whatever advice Anne's father has given her, she now appears to allow herself to be swept against it, as conclusions trip from her lips.

"The king, I have heard, is entertaining this mistress well, and Mistress Shelton tells me that many lords help him with his conquest, in the hope of separating him from me." She chokes the venom back, her shoulders rising and falling as she fumes.

I know from history that she will never embrace her queenship, think of her unborn child, or shut her eyes as Katharine did before her. All she will ever do from now on is challenge Henry. I bite my lip and await her decision.

"I shall go to the king," she says, her frown showing her determination. "I shall ask him to put her aside."

"Instead, Sister, we could always find a way to get rid of her," Jane Boleyn says, making her presence known.

"Jane,"—Anne raises one eyebrow—"that is not a bad idea, but do you not think I should speak to the king first?"

"If it were me, I would not." Jane's reply is curt as she returns a discarded book to the bookcase.

My mind races at the thought of Anne launching into a tirade of invective against her husband, and I long to pull her back in line, but it is not my place.

"Perhaps," she suggests, "it would not be a bad idea to send my most loyal friend to my husband, to placate him, and take his mind away from the Dingley girl?"

She looks at Jane, then back to me, and both stare at me with a knowing look that I understand too well. For Jane, the arrangement would be perfect, as it might take George's mind off me. A shiver of foreboding runs down my spine. Who better to be the mistress of a king than a woman who knows him better than anyone else, because of hindsight?

As Anne and I walk through the palace gardens, we try to stifle our giggles, seeing poor Jayne Fool struggling to keep Purkoy under control. Even when on a lead, he pulls and tugs away from her so he can pick up on the scent of the peacocks, or perhaps roll around on his back in fox poo. Every now and again, Jayne shouts, trying to attract his attention away from where his nose pokes the grass.

"Pur-koy! Do not be doing that – come back 'ere!" She groans. "Stop rubbings yourself in that soil, you naughty dog!" She tries to pull him back, but he continues to roll in the grass, his lead tangled around his legs as he gets muddier and filthier. She turns to look at us, pleading for help with her eyes.

Purkoy jumps up, walks on for a bit, his nose to the ground, smells a fresh, pungent scent, and starts digging.

"Purkoy!" Jayne shouts again. "Pur-koy! Why you be doing that? Pur-koy, stop!"

Anne laughs out loud. She can't help herself. It's not that she wants to be unkind to Jayne, but her little dog does amuse her.

"Why does Purkoy do that?" Jayne asks. She looks at Anne and blinks, still holding the lead.

"Because, my sweet fool, his name means *'why'*." Jayne looks confused. "Dear girl, Purkoy means 'why' in French."

Jayne smiles, then laughs. It's infectious, and now we are all laughing.

"Your Majesty, I have understood your joke!"

Anne steps closer to her. "If he is of trouble to you, let me take him." She stretches out her hand to take Purkoy's lead but Jayne looks sad. "Jayne, you have not upset me. Please do not be afraid. Purkoy is a little troublesome, is all. I will walk him with Viscountess Beaumont, and you can catch up with Lady Rochford, if you prefer?"

"Thank ye, Anne." Jayne tries her best to bob a curtsy, then walks away to catch up with Anne's other gentlewomen, strolling ahead of us a few yards away.

Anne tugs Purkoy to heel. Realising he's now with his mistress, he's much better behaved, which is a relief. The gravel crunches underfoot as we stroll through the gardens. With a gable hood on, the spring sunshine is warm on the back of my neck. It reminds me of when George strokes that spot with the tip of his finger, and always so no one will see. I miss his touch.

The gentle scent of violets and primroses fill the air, now they are in full bloom. Budding roses show their healthy greenery, but not their colour. Sadly, it's a bit early for us to admire them.

I squint into the sun, and see Jayne has now caught up with the other ladies, with Jane Boleyn walking beside her, chatting, which is lovely to see. Maybe she isn't as bad as I make her out to be.

"Beth." Anne says.

"Yes?"

"I did not take Lady Rochford's advice."

"About?"

"I went to talk to Henry, and asked him to remove… No, I demanded he banish Joanna Dingley from Court immediately."

"You did?" I ask, as if I didn't know that she is never one to back away from a challenge. "What else did you say?"

"I complained to him that the Dingley girl did not treat me as a servant should, with due respect, as her queen, in words or deeds."

"How did the king take that?"

"I infuriated him." There's a silent pause, and I glance at her. "He complained loudly of my importunity and vexatiousness."

"What will you do now?"

"Perhaps I should ask my brother's wife for assistance, and then take matters into my own hands."

JUNE 1534

George is away again, attending the French court on diplomatic duties, this time to rearrange a meeting between the French and English kings, because of Anne's pregnancy. She thinks it's wonderful that her brother is being awarded more and more responsibilities, as do I, and that Henry loves and trusts him. I'm glad he is away from court at this time, because I wouldn't want him to witness his sister's continued scheming in trying to manoeuvre me into her husband's bed.

"When we go down for the evening dining, you must put yourself in the king's way, in a manner that he cannot refuse. Heat his blood so much so he wants to finish the evening with you in his bed." She stares at me, unblinking.

"That is a big request, Your Majesty!"

"What I ask of you, Beth, is considered a privilege – one that many women here long for – that you should be so singled out to be called mistress of the king."

"I feel as if I am prostituting myself, like one of the women from the stew houses, except I am not taking payment for my services!"

"Now, Beth"—she places her hand on my shoulder, her touch soft—"this is not so – the favour you do is to me. You must keep the king's thoughts and attentions on me. What you do is a political act, for the benefit of me, and for this realm." Her corners of her mouth curl into a reassuring half-smile. "Lady Shelton and I will dress you. You may wear one of my best gowns." She nods at Madge, and they strip me out of my gown, down to my shift.

"Yes, that will be a sure way to catch his attention." Anne nudges Madge, and they both laugh.

"What?" I ask, my face burning. "Am I to go and dine in my underwear?"

"No!" Anne laughs again. "Do not be foolish – I told you, I shall put you in one of my gowns."

"Oh." I giggle, but the thought of what I am about to try gives me the shivers. What the hell have I got myself into and how am I going to pull this off? My heart thunders as I stand in my shift, flattered and terrified at the same time. How many women can say they've been to bed with the King of England? Not many, that's for sure.

The gown Anne has chosen for me is in the French style, low cut and not leaving much to the imagination. She has made certain I'm going to stand out, wearing crimson velvet with gold habiliments and a black gable hood. The two women circle me like wolves, checking every detail is perfect, and it's no surprise that I feel like a sacrificial lamb. Anne dabs a bead of perfume on my décolleté and steps back, nodding her satisfaction.

"That will do nicely."

The late June breeze filters through the open casements as Anne and her entourage make their way to the banqueting hall. I follow on, my nerves jangling. She takes her place at the king's side at the high table, and he nods at me as I waft past him to my place. I believe he recognises the gown.

"You look rather fetching this afternoon, Viscountess Beaumont – anyone might think you try to outshine the queen."

Anne covers her mouth, trying to stifle a giggle.

I look over at Joanna Dingley, who is acting as an usher, and not a royal laundress today. Suddenly, I feel triggered by the sight of a man stood beside Joanna at the end of the hall. He looks familiar. Where have I seen him before? Then, as I watch him changing a keg of ale, I remember. He's the Geoff Capes lookalike, who was talking to a woman called Joanna on their way to watch George's execution. Paxton, something. What was his name? Merril. That's it. She must have been the royal laundress that smelt of urine! And didn't someone mention she had a daughter by the king? Considering all the people I have met, and what I've been through, my memory is still good. Joanna and Paxton glance around the room while they chat together. Her gaze rests on me, but if looks could kill, my neck would be on the block. She finally turns away, handing out goblets filled with wine to the noblemen. Has Anne noticed her? My cheeks flush at being the focus of all the men present, including Paxton. Surely, he wouldn't know who I am, because according to the present timeline, George's execution hasn't happened, yet. I try to avoid eye contact with many in the hall. I feel conspicuous, as if everyone has guessed Anne's plan. She is a devious one, having asked the Comptroller of the Household to seat me within Henry's eye line.

Minstrels play Consort No.12 from the gallery, high above our heads. I recognise it from a downloaded album made by David Skinner and Alamire. Listening to the real thing, during the actual period these musical pieces were written, has the hairs on the back of my neck standing.

Large racks of lamb, pork, beef, various subtleties, and pastries are carried out and placed in the centre of the top table, then moved to lower tables of the nobility around the king.

A pewter plate, piled with seasoned asparagus, surrounded by Manchet bread rolls, is placed in front of me. I fold a linen towel and lay it over my left shoulder, as is the way, take a sip of ale from my goblet, and wait for Henry and Anne to begin eating.

I don't know what comes over me but, as I dunk the end of the asparagus into a small bowl of sweet vinegar, an idea comes to me. It's as good a time as any, I suppose. I slip the tip of the vegetable into my mouth and caressing the tip with my tongue. It doesn't take much for Henry to notice, his eyes widening as his pupils dilate. He watches me loop my tongue in slow motions around the asparagus tip, then slipping the stalk all the way in before drawing it out, repeating the action several times, my eyes rolling in the process.

The poor man is aghast, unable to look away as I bite into the vegetable, my teeth bared. Mouth hanging open, he lets out a deep groan, which catches the attention of those sat closest to him. To me, as he squirms, it looks like he's sitting on something uncomfortable, and it takes serious effort not to laugh.

Anne gives me a wink and smiles before excusing herself to her apartments. Her job in this matter is finished, and it is now down to me. The game is on, the hare has been released, and the hound is sure to follow.

A few hours later, after dining and dancing, it comes as no surprise when I am summoned to Henry's chamber. This is it! Anne and her ladies prepared me for what lies ahead. I have been bathed in rosewater from head to toe, hair brushed over a hundred strokes, then clothed in the most beautifully embroidered linen shift. I venture forth, my tummy alive with a mixture of dread and excitement. The torchlight flickers, lighting my tentative footsteps as I make my way across the shadowy twilight of the courtyard and up the secret stairway leading to the king's privy bedchamber.

Cool air brushes at my ankles and I wrap my dressing gown tighter, my heart pounding in my mouth at the realisation of what I am about to do. My loyalty and friendship to the queen have gone too far. Haven't they? Is Anne testing me? Or is it down to her genuine trust in me? Oh, goodness, I can't believe I am expected to be in the king's bed tonight. But it's not for me. No, it's my mission, to divert him from other women at court who would try and turn his loyalties away from his wife – my dear friend.

As the usher shows me to Henry's innermost sanctum, I cannot believe that I am about to be bedded by His Majesty.

I've no need to worry about an unwanted pregnancy, as I'm protected by my implant, which I only had fitted not long before I time-slipped. Even though time has passed here, my health and looks never seem to be affected, which is fortunate. For me, no matter how long I spend here, the only thing that matters biologically is the amount of 21st-century time that has passed, so friends and family haven't missed me when I time-slip back. How the cypher seems to work, with, and against time, is beyond me.

A shiver runs through me, as if someone has just walked over my grave. I need to pull myself together and keep my mind focused on my mission. And here I am, waiting to be presented to the king, like some kind of prize ornament.

When I enter, I find servants preparing the room for Henry's entertainment. Rose petals are strewn over the covers of the bed, just like when I first visited him in his bedchamber before he began courting Anne. Plates of cut apricots, asparagus, cut-open pomegranates, and subtleties dress the table near the roaring fire in the hearth. Great bunches of roses fill vases about the chamber, lending the air their heady scent. A page places empty goblets and a flagon of watered-down wine alongside the prepared food.

"Good evening, Viscountess. The king will be with you shortly. Please make yourself comfortable."

The usher bows to me and leaves the chamber. I sit on the edge of a chair and wait for Henry's arrival. I have never felt more uncomfortable in my life, and keep repeating *"I'm on a mission"* in my head.

As I wait – the clock ticking in the background – my mind drifts to thoughts of Bessie Blount, Mary Boleyn, and Anne herself, Joanna Dingley, and all who have gone before me. I want to cry at the predicament my loyalty has brought me to, but I need to keep my wits about me and remember that I can influence the king tonight, keeping his heart loyal to his wife throughout her pregnancy. It's my duty and I need to be quick-witted and wise. From beyond a private door, left ajar, I hear the king's page.

"Your Grace, what time should I awaken thee to break your fast in the morning?"

"Seven of the morning clock."

Through the opening, I see him pat his page on the shoulder.

"Wait – make that seven of the clock…next Tuesday!" He winks at the boy and chuckles.

"Tuesday? But today is only Sunday."

"Be gone – I will summon you if needed."

I must look like a rabbit caught in headlights, not that Henry would know what that is. The woody notes of his cologne precedes his entrance, and the door swings wide open as he enters the bedchamber. I rise to my feet fast but say nothing to break the silence. He seems smaller in frame without his finery, though never insignificant, even when relaxed.

"Good evening, Mistress – what think you of my robe? 'Tis a gift from the ambassador of France. I am unsure if the colour suits me."

Another dressing gown. How many does he own? It is a garment of blue and gold damask, tied loose about his waist with a silk sash. He holds out his arms as he paces about the room in his nightwear. I want to laugh and say something that would be out of place for a Tudor woman, but I bite it back, knowing better.

"You look very fine in it, Your Majesty."

He smiles, appearing pleased with my answer as he stands opposite me in the low light of the flickering flames. This is my opportunity to ask anything of him, to get the answers all historians must yearn to know, from the horse's mouth, so to speak. But my mouth is dry, parched from nervousness. He must realise my feelings, for he stands closer.

"After all these years of knowing me, do I still frighten you, Viscountess?" He reaches out for my hand and entwines his fingers in mine.

"No, Your Grace," I lie, not taking my eyes from the patterns on the floor rug.

"Surely, we know each other well enough now?" He caresses the back of my hand with his thumb. "And you have been in my bedchamber before." He touches my shoulder and, no doubt, can feel me shiver.

"I think you lie to me – I think you are still afraid of me, even now." He bends his knees, trying to catch my gaze. "You must think of me as a man, hmm?"

"Yes, Your Grace," I whisper, a thousand thoughts racing through my mind. Soon, I am going to be closer to the king than any historian has ever been. I know I am going to be the only one to experience him sexually. What is Anne thinking, knowing that I'm with her husband tonight?

He wanders to the table and picks up a stick of asparagus, holding it between his fingers.

"I wish you to show me again how you handled that piece of asparagus earlier. I found it most…enjoyable."

He waits in anticipation at the end of his bed, gripping the post, wearing a long, embroidered linen nightshirt under his dressing gown. My attention is drawn to the intricate design, and as I look down to the sash which holds his gown closed, my optical journey is interrupted by an enormous bulge. My goodness, he hasn't still got his nether-stocks and codpiece on?

I snap my gaze up but it's too late – he's aware.

Oh, God, what am I supposed to do now? How am I to think of him as just a man and not the King of England?

"Sir?" I ask, all innocent.

"Forgive me whilst I gaze upon your beauty, my Lady, for I have not forgotten just how lovely you are."

Heat radiates in my cheeks as he comes closer, and I'm halfway through curtsying when his hand cups my chin and raises me to his level.

"Sit on the bed." He still has the asparagus in hand. "Close your eyes and open your mouth!"

"Y-Your Grace?"

"Please, no formalities here – I am just Henry."

I do as he asks, and he slides the tip of the vegetable between my lips. I caress it with my tongue, as before, taking the stalk into my mouth three times before biting the end off in a slow and deliberate movement, maintaining eye contact all the time. A modern girl knows how effective that can be.

He groans, the sound deep and lingering. "I wonder what else you could do with those lips." He wiggles his eyebrows as he eats the rest of the asparagus, then leans in for a kiss, his hot breath insistent.

"Do I have permission to ravage you?" he asks before delving into my mouth with his strong tongue. He cups one of my breasts in his hand, giving it a gentle squeeze. His breathing becomes heavier, and he shakes as his passion mounts. Everything is moving so fast, but, for now, I'm happy he had enough with the asparagus.

"I am putty in your hands, Viscountess," he says, looking into my eyes.

"Your Grace," I reply, cupping his balls through his shirt, "in my hands, nothing turns to putty." I can't believe I just did that, but the game really is on, so I have to go with it.

He picks me up as if I'm weightless, carries me around the four-poster, and lays me across the bed. His dressing gown falls to the floor, and through the sheerness of his embroidered shirt, it is obvious that he is more than ready to take me. However, I'm not sure I'm ready for him. He climbs on top of me, caressing my inner thigh with gentle enthusiasm, his fingers warm against my flesh. His kisses grow persistent, his beard prickling as he moves from my mouth to my neck. I close my eyes, banishing my inhibitions, for there can be none if my mission is to succeed.

As he enjoys the mysteries of my body, I'm somewhat surprised to find myself warming to his passionate endeavours. Is it wrong to enjoy what Professor Marshall has forbidden me to indulge in? I remember the old adage: forbidden fruit always tastes the sweetest. My God, how true that is. I try not to think of the professor, or George, as Henry manoeuvres my shift up, so it is bunched under my chin, leaving me naked in the flickering candlelight, beneath Henry VIII.

"Beth," he whispers, continuing to plant wet kisses on my neck, "if only you knew how long I have waited and wanted this!"

With his passion rising, he moves down to kiss and caress each breast in turn, sucking on each nipple with amorous abandon, and, as he does, I pull his shirt up over his shoulders and head. The man is in good shape, and he knows how to use his mouth, his hot tongue sliding down my abdomen, then between my thighs, evoking a low but delightful growl from me as I run my fingers through his hair. So much for historians thinking he was a prude. Or maybe he just feels freer with a mistress. With me.

All too soon, he moves back up and pushes his tongue hard into my mouth, making me taste myself, and I open my thighs as he presses against me, with both of us groaning out loud as he enters me.

This is it! I'm shagging Henry Tudor! Oh – my – God!

As he drives into me, his groans of passion fill the room, and I can't help wondering what the usher stood outside the door can hear. How embarrassed I will be leaving these chambers in the morning because I know I won't be able to look him in the eye. No doubt Anne will want a detailed report of what has gone on here tonight. Do I tell her I enjoyed it? Make her think I slept with her husband for Queen and Country?

As far as Henry is concerned, it appears he has hit the jackpot, continuing to thrust towards his intended destination – a journey, it seems, he has long waited for. He's not the only one enjoying the experience. While I can't keep George's face from my mind, I'm not finding it difficult to meet Henry's passion head on, wrapping my legs around his waist as his endeavours quicken, my voice in his ear urging him on and on, until his whole body stiffens, the muscles in his shoulders flexing, and he lets out a euphoric cry, beads of perspiration running down his face as my whole body pulsates beneath him.

With that, he lays upon me in a contented heap.

"Are you satisfied?" he asks in a low voice.

I sigh. "I am, indeed, sir."

"You will certainly go to heaven after that!"

The effort not to laugh nearly kills me, but I'm well aware of the danger I would be in if I did.

As he catches his breath, he tilts his face towards mine, our heads resting against the bolster pillows. "I have admired you since I first saw you at Hever. Why we have never spent any time alone before now, like this, is beyond me."

"It is a pity." I smile, working the lie, knowing full well my loyalty has always been with Anne.

He takes my hand, stroking my skin with his ringed fingers. "I am glad tonight is a chance for us to rectify matters." He gets up from the bed and walks naked to the table, where he pours us both a glass of wine. As he holds my drink out to me, I pull myself up against the pillows, averting my eyes. He slides beneath the coverlets and furs, pulling the linen sheets over us both to protect my modesty. I take a sip of the wine and place the glass on the nightstand, then snuggle into him as his arms wrap about me.

"Why are you not yet married?" He gives me what can only be described as an adoring look. "I am puzzled that a woman as beautiful as you, has not been promised to another. Now I have bestowed you a title, I thought you would have had a long line of suitors plying for your hand."

"I have admirers, Your Grace, but, alas, it is not my hand they are plying for – and I must tell you here and now, I am fussy about what I put on my feet, never mind what I allow near my privy parts."

He shakes as he lets out a raucous laugh. "You have a way with words!" A cheeky smile sharpens his cheeks. "I wonder,"—he looks down at me—"some time ago, I saw a woman of the court being taken by a courtier, and I wondered if it was you, splayed across an office table, being ravished by an unknown gentleman."

My heart is back in my mouth. "Where, sir?"

"In the cloisters, during a dance, when Brandon, Norris, and I were looking for somewhere quiet to gamble and play cards." His brows knit together. "Was it you?"

"I, Your Grace – surely you are mistaken?" I snuggle into him, not about to be honest with him about my entanglements with George, knowing how prone to jealousy he is, and being well aware that, in admitting it, it may cause more trouble than it is worth. "I have been pursued in the past, sir, but never caught – until now."

A wry smile crosses his lips, and he bends his head and kisses me with passion. Please God, not round two – I don't think I could take it – not yet anyway.

He looks puzzled as his finger traces my cheek. "You cannot blame men for admiring your beauty, married or not." He chuckles as he pulls me against him once more, his breath warm on my face as we cradle each other.

I stare up at the inside of the bed's embroidered canopy, hardly believing that I have the King of England's arms wrapped around me. Butterflies kick in at the enormity of what has just happened. My goodness, I've just shagged Henry VIII!

It isn't long before he's fast asleep, his snoring soft. The candlelight is gentle, and the flickering fire in the grate has all but extinguished itself. Henry's chest rises and falls against me as he slides off into his dreams, which I hope include Anne, not me. The stillness of my thoughts is broken by the sound of him farting in his sleep, and I can't help giggle as I realise that Henry VIII, King of England, is just a man, like any other – the only difference being, he holds the realm of England and the heart of Anne Boleyn in his hands.

Today, Anne wears a crucifix hanging from a long gold chain. She gives it a nervous tug when she sees me, before tucking her hands inside her sleeves. That tugging action is becoming a habit with her, and I wonder if she does it out of anxiety or because she is saying her prayers under her breath. It has taken some time on her part to persuade me into Henry's bed, and now that I've made a few visits there, she wants to know all the details.

"So, did the king have you last night?" she whispers, so her ladies don't overhear.

"Yes," I answer, bordering on a sheepish grimace.

"Several times?" Her gaze almost penetrates my soul.

I don't answer, feeling as if I have betrayed their love.

She senses my remorse. "It was *I* who suggested it." She takes my hand. "You can tell me – I promise I will not be angry."

I press my toes into the floor to steady myself. "Yes, he had me more than once."

"If he requests to spend time with you again, we must make sure you do not become pregnant."

"There is no chance of that, Your Majesty." I lower my gaze, my face heating.

"What are you suggesting? Is there something wrong with the king's virility?" She pulls me to the corner of her chambers where we sit together out of earshot of everyone else. The servants eye us as we whisper.

"Anne, there is nothing wrong with the king," I say. "I have my ways to avoid ending up being with child."

"Ah, like a sponge soaked in vinegar?"

I grimace inside at the thought of it. "No, Madam. Something from my time. Something placed beneath my skin."

She stares at me, unable to comprehend. I take her hand and trace her fingertips over the spot in my upper arm where the implant is, and she looks at me wide-eyed as I explain how it works.

"How I would love to come to the twenty-first century, to experience all it has to offer. I wonder whether the future could help me conceive a son – beyond any doubt."

"Trust me, Anne, there is as much good and bad in my time as there is in yours. If we have God, we have all we need, in both timeframes. Sadly, less than half the population in England and Wales now describe themselves as

Christians, and believers in God, never mind saying they are Catholic or Lutheran." Her eyes widen. "I know, the idea seems foreign to me too." I'm one of those rare people of my time who is not embarrassed to say I have a strong faith and belief in God.

Anne shakes her head. "Let us not talk of faith. Not now. At Court, that is what all the divisions are about. Tell me more about how the king was with you."

Before I can speak, an usher approaches.

"Your Majesty, Secretary Cromwell is here."

Cromwell is close behind. He removes his hat, then bows before the queen. "Your Majesty."

"Secretary Cromwell." She gets to her feet, beckoning me to stand with her. "What news have you for me?"

"Sir Thomas More will not sign the oath."

"He is stubborn. Why will he not sign?"

"Madam, I am questioning him during his imprisonment." He twists his fingers around themselves. Other than that, he is motionless, unflinching, and speaks to the point, the darkness of his wool and velvet clothes almost as dense as the secrets he keeps. I have not often been this close to him, and he comes across as the calmest person in the room – the best man in a crisis.

"Thomas More's motives are hidden behind a barrier of writing, eluding wit and eloquence," he says. "He seems to have made his choice, and there is nothing I can do to dissuade him from it."

I think about Thomas More's face, which is ceaselessly mobile, unlike Cromwell's impassive mask, but, in its way, just as inscrutable. Conscience, Anne has heard, is what More protests and what stays his hand from signing the two words that will save him. Conscience is something Cromwell appears to lack. He makes up for this with his robust confidence, which he holds in reserve, ready to be unleashed like an invisible pit bull if required. It is with this confidence, however, in defiance of Anne, that he refuses to add More's name to the list of those who have subscribed to the mad prophecies of the Holy Maid of Kent, Elizabeth Barton.

"Madam, More says that he is clear of anything relating to the Barton woman, but he does not believe the king should have the title 'Head of The Church in England', and that is what irks him."

"Then, perhaps, Secretary Cromwell, you need to find a way to persuade More to concede and let go of his objections of his king."

He looks at her for a long moment, never blinking. "Madam, we do not do that. Never torture."

She glares at him, like a petulant child. Court politics is getting to her – perhaps her queenship is not what she expected. She growls in the back of her throat.

"Your Majesty, More's wife has requested an audience with me and comes to Court today."

"Then, Cromwell, you need to give Lady Alice your best advice." She nods, somewhat calmer, realising her frustration does not affect her husband's first minister.

No doubt, Alice will come to implore Cromwell to save her husband from the king's wrath. Will she ask him to take her to see Henry? Would Cromwell agree to it? Thomas More is stubborn. He leaves his wife and son without advice, and his precious, educated daughter, Margaret, without protection by going against the king.

JULY 1534

The month has started in a strange way because Anne's ladies treat me different now that rumours of my dalliances with the king are rife about the court. It fascinates me how courtiers are affording me more reverence, acting on rumour alone. Thank God I haven't been approached by Anne's enemies, looking to depose her as Queen.

Anne, Lady Zouche, Margery Horsman, Nan Cobham, and other ladies-in-waiting have been walking about the gardens, picking roses, sitting in arbours, soaking up the ambience of the mid-summer sun while taking in the delights of the swallows as they swoop and swirl overhead. The sun's warmth caresses my face as I daydream about life back home. I miss my family.

George is here, and I'm glad because he's been away in France so much, meeting François to defer an audience between both kings. The timing is wrong, from some reason, probably something to do with Anne.

My heart breaks at his reunion with Jane, and as I watch them together, I presume she must have told him about me going to Henry's bed. She's done it to make sure he will lose interest in me. Anne wouldn't have said anything – she's too loyal for that. As they walk together, he gives her his full attention, and she soaks it up.

While Anne and I recline on a garden bench, Margery teases Purkoy with a stick. Anne doesn't question me any longer but knows full well I've continued to visit Henry. She is confident of my loyalty and trusts me without question.

Jane Boleyn's sister, Alice Parker, and Lady Worcester, directed by the gardener, pluck pink rose blooms for Anne's apartments, while George walks arm in arm with his wife across the grass towards us. He hasn't plucked up the courage yet to ask me about the rumours. Perhaps his heightened interest in Jane is because he knows he will never be able to have his way with me again. By walking over, arm in arm with Jane, he is rubbing salt into my wounds, and Jane appears to be loving every minute of it. The distance between us hurts, as he has been a good friend – a friendship I do not want to lose. Perhaps I will find the chance to explain all that is happening so he will know the truth and understand that I do things out of support and love for his sister and her family. Or maybe he has changed his mind, and wants to give his marriage another try? Or his father has insisted that he produce an heir for the Boleyn estate. Worse than that, perhaps he is looking to heal the rift between himself and Jane. I suppose it's about time. While my heart dips when I see them together, it is not my place to interfere, and I need to encourage them to stay together and work things out for the greater good. It's not like they have years ahead of them.

Anne's second baby is due soon: a second September baby, no doubt why her trip with Henry to see François has been put off. Her swollen belly pulls the silks of her dress this way and that as she tries to maintain a comfortable position on the bench. I secure a cushion into the small of her back to make her feel at ease. It is early July, and she is hot and flustered, as the baby has not made much movement today, and I am in the unfortunate position to know why.

We head for her chambers, with Jane, George, Margery Horsman, Jayne Fool, and Lady Zouche following, when, halfway up the stairs, Anne stops dead in her tracks and grips her swollen belly with both hands. She lets out a deep moan and turns to me.

"Get me to my chamber," she whispers, "as quickly as possible."

When we arrive in her rooms, she dismisses everyone apart from me and George.

"What ails you?" I ask, knowing what's coming, and struggling to keep it from my eyes.

"Something is wrong," she cries, her eyes rolling in her head. She still clutches her belly, looking distressed. "The baby is not moving!"

"Sister, he's probably asleep – do not concern yourself."

"But, George, it's been five days since I felt any real movement. He hasn't stirred in my belly for five days."

"Anne, you must rest," he says. "All will be well."

"George, I know in my heart all is not well." Her face creases in a deep grimace. "I feel the boy is gone." She looks at me, her eyes glazed in terror. "Unlace me, quickly!"

I start to unlace her gown as George goes to pour her a glass of wine.

"I know the child has died, and Henry is turning away from me even before he knows the truth about the baby."

"Now you are being hysterical!" George says.

"Henry has taken other women to his bed," she says, glancing at me, "while my body has been doing its business!"

179

That was your idea, I think to myself – don't try to make me feel guilty about it.

"Sister, it is all for show. You have his heart in your hand – you always have done. He told me, and the others, not weeks since. Mark Smeaton was there playing the virginal – Henry said I'd rather beg alms door to door than leave my pretty queen."

"You are wrong," she cries, "he gazes at other's pretty duckies like a man possessed."

"To Henry, it's just a game." He turns to me as I help Anne out of her gown. "I mean no disrespect, Beth."

"None taken," I reply, placing the gown over the back of a chair.

"Sister, Henry is not serious about other women – no more serious than a game of tennis or billiards."

Her eyes darken. "What should I do if the babe is born dead?"

"You worry too much!" he says. "If that happened, you would conceive again."

As they continue, I undress her down to her shift, the sight that meets me causing me to swallow back my nerves. George and I stare at the lower part of her linen shift, which is soiled with heavy bloodstains.

"Your Majesty, I need to remove your shift."

"Why?" she asks. "What is wrong?"

She lifts her arms as I remove it, and looks at me in horror on seeing the bloodstains.

"Should I summon the midwife?" I ask, grabbing a clean shift from a nearby trunk and putting it over her head.

"No! Do not summon anyone – no one must know." She slips her arms through and pulls the fabric down over her body. The colour drains from her face right before she collapses onto her bed. She crawls over the coverlets and curls up.

"If I lose this child, Henry will leave me like he did the Spaniard. He's terrified of infant deaths." Her face is wet from tears. She stares at the stains on her shift. "He sees an event like this as a sign from God."

"I do not mean to be a prophet of doom, Sister, but not all babies live. This,"—he looks at her stained shift—"is not a sign from God." He looks helpless as she lies on the bed. "I am glad I was not born a woman."

I ask him to fetch extra linens so I can place them underneath her, to prevent her staining the bedclothes with the loss. Somewhat frantic now, he searches through a nearby drawer to find what I need, and looks worried as he hands the linens to me. I pack them beneath Anne's shift, under her bottom. She is losing the baby – there's no doubt about it. I try to gauge the time of the contractions, but I know it won't be long. She's distressed but doesn't moan unless a contraction pulls her into the covers. George stands at the side of the bed, his face wracked with concern. He grips her hand, trying to comfort her, but she snatches it away and buries her face, her cries muffled in the thickness of her linen pillows as another contraction grips her. These are full-blown, and the child is on its way. Seeing her in so much agony, I wish I had some of the laudanum mixture the midwife gave her when she was birthing Elizabeth, but I have nothing but gentle reassurance for her, that all will be well. But I know in my heart what is about to happen.

"Will all be well?" George asks.

"It is in God's hands!" I answer, touching his shoulder. He flinches away as Anne cries out once more, and then she grows silent.

As I wipe her brow, she looks at me, her eyes filled with fear. "I need to use the house of easement."

I have heard this before when she was last in labour.

"George – this is bad."

I get him to help me lift her between us, suspending her on her knees. Her whole body is shaking, her perspiration seeping through her shift.

"All is going to be well," I say, trying to calm her. George looks at me, and he knows by the look on my face that I'm lying.

"Beth, I should not be here!" he cries.

"It's too late, George, you have to stay."

"For goodness' sake, will you both stop arguing and help me?"

Her breathing is ragged, as if she is hyperventilating, and, as the pressure to push comes, her face is deep red with the strain. She presses her lips together, trying to quell her screams, knowing as well as I that this must be a silent delivery, as no one must ever know.

With the last push, the baby frees itself from her body. It flops on the linen beneath her, its skin shiny, grey, and transparent. The poor thing lies deathly still. It is perfectly formed, down to its eyelashes, and the little nails on its fingers. George and I wait for it to cry but the sound doesn't come. It is plain to see the baby is a stillborn boy.

"Oh my God!" George cries, though it comes as a harsh whisper.

"God help me," Anne gasps. "I am undone."

Time to think fast. I need to get her cleaned up and make sure everything is as it should be. And George has to get out so she can finish the birthing process.

"George, get a linen cloth and move the child." I keep my voice low but firm, as it's clear he's in shock.

He stands there transfixed, his gaze glued to the tiny form lying between Anne's thighs.

"He looks so perfect," she says, sobbing. "Why does God not help me?" She lies back in the bed, in a state of exhaustion, and I cut the umbilical cord to free the child from her.

"George, I need to clean Anne up."

"What do I do with the babe?" he asks, his voice quivering along with his bottom lip.

"I do not know," Anne cries. "Bury him in the gardens – throw it in the river – I cannot bear to have him near me!"

"But, Sister—"

"Get him out of my sight and let not a soul see what you are about."

Without a word, he swaddles the baby and leaves the room, nodding to me as he exits. The poor man is shaken. I know what I must do, remembering what the midwives did at Elizabeth's birth. With one hand on Anne's swollen belly, I push down. A long moment later, she delivers the placenta, through silent tears. I check the heap of flesh isn't broken, and no bits are missing. It seems that all is as it should be. However, I know that, from now on, history will never play out in the way I wish it could.

The king is inconsolable, with the news of his stillborn son hitting him hard. He sits on his throne in his presence chamber, his face like thunder and his countenance like the Antichrist. Nobody dares speak to him. Cromwell and other courtiers make a hasty exit after relaying the news from his wife. No one wants to be the whipping boy to this gargantuan tragedy.

A short time later, as he enters Anne's room, he waves every usher, page, and lady-in-waiting out. I hide in the corner, hanging back in the shadows, keeping dead quiet as his discontent unravels. Matters from the last few days have weighed heavy on his mind.

"I'm sorry, Henry," Anne says when he's finished. "It was our boy."

"I know." It takes all his muster to say this. "This is what I went through with Katharine, but at least the Duke of Cornwall lived, for even just a short time."

"I was most careful with myself – but the child seemed to have stopped moving for a time, sir." She walks towards him, reaching for his hand. "There was nothing I could do."

I remain like a statue, not wanting to attract Henry's attention. Relief floods through me when he embraces Anne, enveloping her in his arms.

"It is not your fault," he says. "We can try for another."

They stand together, with him stroking her long hair. His anger has vanished, or perhaps he doesn't want to show her how devastated he feels about the loss of his son. I slip out of the chamber to give the couple their privacy.

SEPTEMBER 1534

I'm snapped out of my reverie at the sound of pounding footsteps. It's Henry, and he acknowledges only me.

"Viscountess." He stares at me with fervour, pulling me closer by the elbow, his musky fragrance almost drawing me under his spell. "Tonight," he whispers, and I nod once, understanding what he wants. As he walks away, I feel Anne glaring, her disdain burning into my back.

I walk over to her, ensuring nobody is within hearing. "Madam, please place no great stress on the king's words."

"Do not worry, Beth, I know perfectly well how to deal with him."

I nod once again. Hmm, perhaps I do too.

The usher shows me to Henry's privy bedchamber – his inner sanctum – which I am now quite familiar with. As I enter the room, I inhale the heady, woody scent from the fire that has been burning all evening. It's weird but it feels normal to be here after visiting him so many times whilst Anne was pregnant. His temper earlier today makes me nervous about being in his company, though he became tender with Anne later, so I hope he's a bit more at ease.

To my astonishment, I find him already lying on his bed, in a casual manner, dressed in his linen shirt and a long velvet dressing gown. He is sipping wine in the dim candlelight, the gloom making him look younger, and not so intimidating. I dip a deep curtsy, keeping my focus on him as servants dart about, placing gold plates heaped with a delicious array of cut apricots, sweetmeats, and other delicacies on the table for our enjoyment. The page adds empty goblets and a flagon of ale.

Henry's usher pokes the fire back to life, bows to us, and leaves the chamber. The fire crackles in the hearth as he beckons me to him. I sense this is not going to be the only fire lit in this room by the end of this evening. As I draw closer, I catch a hint of orange flower water on his skin, providing a powerful allure. It would be easy to fall under his spell, but I am here with a clear objective in mind: to smooth things over between him and Anne.

"I am glad you are here." He smiles. "Come and lay next to me. Make yourself comfortable."

That sounds like a reasonable start to the evening. He moves to the opposite side of the bed, and the ropes groan under the mattress as I climb up next to him. I know my intention is to smooth things over between him and his wife, yet maybe it will be better for Anne if this evening is about satisfying him, so his pent-up energies don't feed his foul mood tomorrow? Okay, I'll go with that.

I run a light hand across his thigh. "Would you like me on top, Your Grace?" I curse myself for forgetting not to push him. He's not as prudish as I once thought, but he still has limits.

"Perhaps later," he replies, his eyes narrowing in thought. "Lie back." He leans over me, moving my shift up.

"Open your legs…a bit wider, yes?"

I do as I'm asked, and he begins with deliberate slowness to pull off his dressing gown and hitch up his nightshirt. Releasing a suggestive sigh, I shift my bum, preparing to avoid getting cramp in case I'm in the same position for too long. Now naked, he abandons any pretence of a delay as he climbs on, eyeing me with approval.

"Hold onto me," he says, and I run my nails in soft lines up and down his hairy back. It excites him, and he throws his head back and arches his spine. I wrap my legs around him, moving with him, encouraging him, and his shoulder blades flex as he gets into a strong rhythm, powering into me. He is rather rough with me tonight, more determined to enjoy himself, and I close my eyes, continuing to urge him on, more to get it over with than anything else, though I make all the right sounds – it doesn't take long to become good at that – and it's only a few minutes before he reaches that peak, his breath hot on my neck as he groans out my name. He collapses onto me, his chest heaving, then slips out and shifts over to spoon against me.

"You have done me great service tonight, Viscountess," he whispers. "And to look upon your face brings me great pleasure." He leans up and brushes a stray hair from my face, then kisses the tip of my nose. "I would love to have your image immortalised by Master Holbein, so I may look at your hidden delights any time I choose." His gaze is intense, and I'm hoping he doesn't see anything in my eyes, as I remember Rob finding the sketch in the gallery. I pull myself back to this moment.

"You do me a great honour, Your Majesty, but I could not sit for Master Holbein in a state of undress. I must sit as all well-born ladies do for their portraits – fully clothed."

He shifts up, looking from one eye to the other. "I meant it as no insult. I had hoped to keep such a portrait private, for no one else to look upon – for my sole enjoyment."

"Every time you close your eyes, Sire, you can imagine what delights my attire hides."

He smiles, taking a deep breath through his nose. "But you would still do me this service and sit for your portrait?"

"I will do whatever Your Majesty commands. It will be an honour to do your bidding."

He nods once. "Very well, have it your way – clothed it shall be. I will send word to Master Holbein. I will summon him on the morrow to arrange it." He puts his arm around me, and I snuggle into the golden hair on his broad chest. It doesn't take long for him to fall into a deep slumber. In the darkness, his snoring keeps me awake and I look at him, realising this powerful being really is just a man, looking for something in me that he already has in his wife.

EARLY AUTUMN – 1534

This morning, Anne is not yet dressed. She sits in her dressing gown and coif in a relaxed manner as we discuss with her daughter's governess, Lady Bryan, the designs she is dispatching to the princess and how she is to be brought up. The ladies of her household spend considerable amounts of time sewing clothes, which are to be taken on progress and distributed to the poor at each stopping place, with a shilling a head, by arrangement with the local priest and two parishioners. We also discuss the decorating of George's palace at Beaulieu in Essex. He has taken his wife back home for allegedly conspiring with Anne to have her rival, Joanna Dingley, removed from court. It's nice to have her out of the way, but I miss George. We also talk about Holbein's latest portrait, the most recent court entertainments, as well as Anne's newest gowns.

The peacocks in the royal gardens are creating a racket and Anne gets up to look through the window, screwing up her face in disgust.

"Those birds must be removed from the garden, as I cannot take rest in the mornings for the noise of them. I shall complain to His Majesty."

Her favourite dog, Urien, a greyhound given to her by William Brereton, pads around her skirts, nudging her for attention. The dog is named after Brereton's brother, who is a groom of the privy chamber.

Someone taps on the door, and the usher announces the court painter, Master Holbein, into our presence.

"Your Majesty, I have come here this morning – the king has commissioned me to draw your image."

He speaks with a strong German accent, and I have to push John Cleese's comedy sketches out of my mind. Anne doesn't seem phased that she's still wearing casual attire.

"Get on with it, then," she says.

She's not in the mood for small talk so sits in a position of Holbein's choosing, and he sets up his easel and gets to work. He doesn't say a word but, every few minutes, leans around the prepared paper, taking his measurements. The dogs yelp and bark around Anne's gentlewomen, begging for sweetmeats, and I get up from my seat and walk behind Holbein, looking over his shoulder as the lead glides across the sheet. He is so focused, and the marks he makes look easy, though I know they can't be. It's amazing to be here witnessing him work her image onto the paper. This is how Anne must have felt when she met Leonardo. Hmm, what would Dr Janina Ramirez ask Holbein if she was in the same room as him?

I almost jerk back when he looks at me.

"What do you think of it, Viscountess?"

"Sir, you are a genius – your drawing is exquisite."

Anne sits up. "Beth, do I look well in it?"

"Beautiful, Your Majesty."

"Then, Master Holbein, you are a genius!" She laughs and returns to her pose.

After an hour more of sitting, she wriggles in her seat. "Holbein, are you finished?"

"Yes, Madam, I am, but I am here a while longer, as His Majesty has asked me to draw Viscountess Beaumont's portrait."

"Has he?" She looks at him, eyebrows raised. He nods, though it comes more as a nervous shrug. "If that is the case, then, Master Holbein, you best make a start." She scans the room, her gaze landing on Nan Cobham and Anne Saville.

"Ladies, I cannot sit around in my nightclothes all day, come and dress me."

"Yes, Your Majesty!" they reply in unison, and walk off into the bedchamber in a huddle, with the lapdogs following.

Holbein directs me. "Viscountess, I would like you to stand…"—he waves his right hand—"right there, in the window."

As I walk over, all I see is John Cleese doing his *German* thing in Fawlty Towers, and it takes real effort not to giggle.

"Fix your gaze on a certain point – and hold it."

"Very well," I answer, straightening my gable hood and making sure my partlet is secure. I look out of the window to the river beyond, trying to remember the details of my pencil sketch in the gallery, glad now that I know the context of its rendering.

Holbein gets to work, peering around the boarded paper every few seconds, using his lead to measure my form. My legs feel heavy and stiff from standing in the same position for such a long time but, after about an hour and a half, the artist has finished.

"Would you like to take a look?" he asks, folding his arms as he stands behind his easel.

I smile. "I would, very much." I walk around to stand next to him, and am blown away by its beauty, and not a little gobsmacked at the reality of standing in front of the sketch Rob and I examined at the National Portrait Gallery.

"With your permission," Holbein says, "I shall take the drawing to His Majesty."

All I can do is curtsy in agreement. Wait till Professor Marshall hears about this.

Walking into Anne's presence chamber, I meet Nan Cobham, who is carrying a bundle of fresh linens. Anne's dais is empty, and I see Sir Francis Bryan, the Sir Thomas Boleyn, and the Duke of Norfolk standing in a holy huddle, discussing at length a family matter. The ushers stand transfixed at one end of the room.

Francis Weston hangs around badgering for gossip but nearly jumps to attention when a clarion sounds, and stewards of the body announce:

"The King! The King!"

Henry enters the chamber with more than a flourish, breaking up the little group. Cromwell, like a faithful lapdog, follows a few paces behind.

Weston steps away, fiddling with his signet ring and laughing with Francis Bryan. They don't seem to notice me.

"The queen's sister, Mary, she is..." Weston laughs again. "She finds herself—"

"With a belly full of bastard," Bryan says, chuckling.

Henry nods to his courtiers but doesn't enter conversation and heads straight for Anne's private apartments.

Sir Thomas Boleyn turns to Cromwell, stopping him in his tracks with his hand on his forearm. Cromwell seems perturbed at being prevented from following the king.

Thomas turns his back to the gossiping group. "Cromwell, I need to discuss my daughter Mary with you."

"Yes, My Lord." Cromwell isn't happy to be here.

"She claims the child's father is William Stafford. And she has married him because she is with child!" It's clear he's not impressed that his daughter has failed to ask the king or queen for their consent to marry.

"I see," Cromwell says. And that's it – he says nothing more. No surprise considering the man always wants to know the full details before committing himself to anything.

"Shall we go in, gentlemen?" Cromwell says. "Viscountess Beaumont, will you go and see to your mistress?"

As I follow him, I feel sombre in my cocoa-coloured gown of silk and velvet, which matches my mood. Before we walk through the open door, Anne's raised voice filters out.

"Now we find out she is pregnant!"

"She is a member of the household, Anne," Henry responds.

"Humph! I know she is a member of the household. But she has not been a member of my household much since I married you! Maybe you make a mistake, Henry, and think my sister is a part of yours?"

She is flustered, a swirl of red satin and silk as she bangs heads with Henry.

"And where has William Stafford come from?" she asks, squaring up to him, as if about to commence a duel.

For her slight size, she packs a punch, and Henry knows it. With her miscarriage still raw, his latest dalliances, and the pressure of trying to conceive again, is it any surprise she's become so angry when her sister causes the Boleyn family reputation to slide? She probably cannot fathom what has made Mary forget her place and not ask permission to be married. A match with William Stafford would have been out of the question, and Mary's audacity has hit a raw nerve. As usual, when she feels surrounded and harassed, Anne lashes out at the people closest to her: her family and her husband.

"I don't believe the baby is William Stafford's," she declares.

I watch from the wings, sighing to myself, wanting so much to drag her from the room before her mouth runs away with her.

"Whose is it then?" Henry asks. "Madam, do you blame me for this pregnancy? I have not touched the lady since before I knew you!"

He holds his stance in defiance of his unhappy wife. When Sir Thomas nudges past me, along with Weston and Bryan, Cromwell turns to him.

"Boleyn, can you not control either of your two daughters, hmm?"

"Mary has done this to spite me," Anne shouts. "She thinks she can glide around the court, with her round belly showing, and laugh at me because I have recently lost my last child." She coughs, almost choking on her frustration, failing to hold back the tears.

"I'm sure if we—"

"Oh, Father, please get out!" Anne roars like a banshee, her eyes flashing, matching the red satin of her gown. "All of you, please leave!"

Henry raises his eyes heavenwards, hands still on his hips, not knowing quite how to deal with his wife. He, too, is frustrated, and walks out of the room without so much as a by-your-leave.

"And you, Cromwell,"—Anne jabs a finger at him—"tell my sister that she will never come to Court again. I do not know her. She is no longer considered a Boleyn." Her temples bulge with rage. Once everyone is gone, she collapses on her fur-covered chaise longue, mentally exhausted.

"Do you want me to speak with Mary?" I ask, sitting with her.

"No!" she snaps. "I can do no more for her. Let her soldier husband provide for her."

"Should you not consider preventing her from becoming an embarrassment?"

"Is that what Cromwell thinks?" She sniffs. "I think my sister has already caused the embarrassment, all by herself." She rubs her eye. "She has been an embarrassment all of our lives – she has no pride in herself, nor any sense of decorum." She grimaces. "Or loyalty."

"I think it's romantic," I say, wishing her the best of luck.

She glares at me. "Romantic? Humph! Let her great love sustain her – much good it will do her." She huffs. "No matter. And no matter more when Elizabeth has a brother." She rests her hands in her lap and sighs. Never a dull moment in this household.

Mary thrashes around in the chamber, sorting through her gowns, ready to pack for her banishment to the country. As I enter the chaos, her trunks are open, her chattels and goods strewn all over the place.

"William Stafford, eh?" I say as she flaps around the room.

"You may be my sister's friend, but that does not give you any entitlement to pass comment on my affairs."

I look at her, not knowing what to say. Hmm, there goes any friendship we had.

"Excuse me, Viscountess," Nan Cobham says as she glides around the room, helping Mary pack. Mark Smeaton hangs around, trying to make himself useful by carrying trunks and heavy cargo, taking it down the stairs and out towards the courtyard to load the litter ready for its journey back to Kent.

"Nan, have you seen my silk shoes?"

"I think they have been packed, Mistress Stafford," she answers, folding another gown. "But you'd best be quick, for your royal sister is out for your blood. She doesn't believe you would give yourself to a man as penniless as William Stafford."

"What would my sister know about taking a man because she likes him?" Her face reddens, the lines over her forehead knotting in frustration. She kneels on the floor, searching through the last of her belongings, then pulls a trunk over.

"I'm not sure I can use this. It has the Boleyn badge all over it."

The black bulls' heads accentuate the lid and curvature of the casket, showing clear ownership.

"If they see me with this, they may turn me out on the road. What think you, Viscountess?"

"I'm certain you can disguise it with other things on top."

The poor woman is flustered by the uncertainty of having anything much of a future.

"When George comes back from Essex, he will speak for me. He will not see me banished and cut off."

"I am certain he will speak up for you," I say. "You cannot help who you fall in love with." I'm not sure my words are soothing her mood.

"At least, Viscountess Beaumont, I am married to the man I love, which is more than I can say for you, with my brother!"

Her insult hits me hard but I must make allowances for her. I hold my tongue.

"Before I go, Viscountess, would you accompany me to an audience with Secretary Cromwell?"

"Of course, Mary." Out of loyalty to the Boleyn family, I oblige.

As we enter Cromwell's rooms, he motions Mary to sit in a high-backed walnut chair in front of his desk. She looks like a startled rabbit, caught in front of a blocked burrow by a pack of wild dogs.

"Please sit, Mistress Stafford."

"Master Cromwell," she whispers as she perches on the chair, back straight and round belly swelled against the gathers of her gown.

"I am surprised you are married," Cromwell says as he takes his seat on the opposite side of his desk.

"I wish to be reconciled with my sister. I confess freely that in my dealings with the world, love overcame reason. That is my fault and I beg her forgiveness. After all, she above everyone should know about marrying for love."

"Lady Mary, forgive me, but you should not presume upon the queen's good graces. Nor ever assume that forgiveness is likely given."

"I do not so presume... Only..." She looks to me for reassurance.

Cromwell grunts. "I cannot say but it may be that the queen is not minded of forgiveness in this matter."

"But you will ask her? You must ask her... Then, perhaps, Master Cromwell, you can tell Her Majesty that I might have had a man of greater birth, but I could never have had a man that loved me so well. And tell her that I would rather beg my bread with him than be the greatest queen alive."

Silence falls on the chamber for what seems like a lifetime as Cromwell stares back at her, no doubt conjuring up a reply that will send her back to the country, to no longer bother him with what he sees as a trivial family matter.

Nan Cobham lights the candles around Anne's rooms, illuminating the apartments in a soft glow. The peacocks, I'm glad to report, have grown silent as dusk falls. I try to discuss Mary, who has now left court, having been found guilty of misconduct.

"Why are you not pleased for your sister?"

"William Stafford is a man far beneath Mary's station in life, with only a small income. He may be a gentleman usher to the king, but his occupation before that was one of a soldier. Mary has married without her family's permission, and with her brother-in-law being the King of England, she cannot marry far below her status."

Anne is readied for bed. As she stands naked, Nan hands her a clean linen shift.

"Not only is Mary now married to a man below her status, *but she* is also pregnant."

"You can't disown her, Anne."

"I have not," she says as she slides her toes into her silk slippers. "She has displeased me greatly. Am I to smile at her, knowing that she disgraces our family? I had to reprimand her severely, otherwise, others may do the same, and marry without mine or the king's permission."

"You have been most lenient in this matter. People have been thrown in the Tower for less."

"I know Mary's situation is very tight since Papa stopped her allowance."

"I know how desperate your sister is," I say, helping her into her black silk dressing gown gifted to her by Henry. "She went to Thomas Cromwell asking for help, and before she left, she asked me to deliver a letter to him."

"Really?" She looks at me for a long moment. "Have you read it?"

"Of course not."

"Then get it for me and I will read it."

When I return, I hand her the letter, which is tied with a thin piece of satin ribbon. She tugs at it, opens the letter, and scans the writing, then folds it back up, retying the ribbon around it.

"Take it to Master Secretary Cromwell on the morrow."

I walk to Cromwell's chambers to deliver the letter and discover Master Sadler writing lists and preparing petitions for Cromwell to sign, though he is nowhere to be seen.

"I am sorry to disturb you," I say, "but I have a letter to deliver to Secretary Cromwell from the Mistress Stafford."

Rafe Sadler, a slim, pasty-looking youth, glances up from his writing. He rests his quill in the ink receptacle and rises from his seat. For his tender age, he appears older than his years. He has a studious nature and seems a man of integrity. Being Cromwell's chief clerk, it's no surprise he is sober and shrewd.

"Viscountess, I shall make sure Secretary Cromwell gets it." He allows a polite smile as he takes the letter from my outstretched hand, then places it upon the mountain of paperwork that decorates the desk.

"Will that be all?" he asks, as he returns to his seat.

"Yes." I nod, feeling like I shouldn't be in such a hallowed room as this, for it seems that anything to do with the king, any matters of state, pass over this desk before Henry knows of it, and it leaves me feeling somewhat uncomfortable. As I turn to leave, Rafe opens Mary's letter, no doubt to decide if it is important or should be discarded to the side.

I find my way through the corridors of power, back to Anne's rooms. One of her gentlewomen is tidying away pewter plates from breakfast, and Anne is now at her desk, poring over state papers.

"I have heard the king has written to George, asking him to contact Papa about helping Mary."

"Is that not a good thing? At least Mary will get some support."

"The king, in his generosity, says he will give her and Stafford the manor of Rochford, in Essex, and to add to Stafford's land at Grafton, Staffordshire."

I nod once. "The king is very kind."

"Hopefully, my sister will now retire, and remain quiet."

"What of your niece and nephew, Your Majesty?"

"Henry Carey will remain in my wardship, and he shall be educated by Nicholas Bourbon."

I find it fascinating hearing her plans, as she still seems to care for her sister, despite the disastrous marriage – a trait I know her daughter will copy when she becomes queen.

The tranquillity in the chamber is broken as the king is announced. He stands there in all his splendour. Anne offers him a cup of wine, which he accepts.

"What think you of Beth's portrait by Master Holbein?" she asks, all innocence.

"I think it is a true image of her," he replies, sitting on a chair

"And my portrait, My Lord, what do you think of mine?" She takes another sip of wine.

"Again, it is a true, and a good likeness of your fair features, but it does not show what lies within."

She stiffens. "What do you mean by that, sir?"

"The exterior can be fair on a woman, but the interior can be a dark dungeon."

"I find that an unfair comment, sir." Her lips thin as she pulls them back. "I am only a dark dungeon when I am sad that you have taken mistresses."

He rises from the chair. "What are you talking of, Anne?"

"Such as Joanna Dingley – and the others…"

He glances at me, then looks down at Anne. "Why, Madam, did you have Joanna Dingley removed from Court?"

"She tried to steal from me." Her face once again full of innocence.

Henry's mouth opens, then closes. "Are you certain of this?"

"Yes, My Lord, I had the evidence – she was caught in the act." She flares her nostrils. "It hurts me when you take mistresses. It makes me feel I am not doing my wifely duty."

"It is a king's right to be able to pick whichever flowers he wishes in his garden."

"That may be the case, My Lord. However, I think it not right that you think you can cultivate seedlings, as you did with Bessie Blount."

Henry's face turns puce. "Again, you forget yourself, Madam. It is a sad day when I must answer to my wife."

"Sir, I trust Viscountess Beaumont around you, but no one else."

"It is no wonder I take mistresses, Anne, when you do not do your wifely duty by giving me the son you promised!"

He sees me in the shadows and offers me his outstretched hand so I can kiss his ring. I oblige him and am dismissed with a wave. As I leave the chamber, I can still hear them arguing.

"Joanna Dingley, Madge, and Beth will never love you as I do!" she shouts. "And don't you realise I love you ten thousand times more than that Spanish cow ever did?"

"Enough!" he bellows. "I have heard enough of your rantings. You should be concentrating on getting a son and keeping your end of the bargain!"

I can imagine flecks of anger flash in his eyes, the likes of which Anne will have never seen before.

"And don't you realise very well, Madam, that you ought to be satisfied with what I have done for you, for I would certainly not do as much if we were to start over again!"

I'm about to leave after a despondent silence, thinking the argument has run its course, but Henry's starts up again.

"You ought to consider where you come from, as I can lower you from your position as quickly as I raised you." Something slams, possibly his wine cup on the table. "Do not meddle in my business again, Madam. I had Lady Rochford banished in your place because you did not know when to stop interfering in my business!

Ten

OCTOBER 1534

George seems carefree since his wife has left court to go to their home in Essex – I can't quite believe how relaxed Anne's chambers feel since Jane's been gone, no longer here moping about like a depressed spectator. Anne is entertaining some of the ladies and gallants of the court in her presence chamber. Smeaton and the other musicians are providing the music, and tables and furniture have been dragged to the sides of the room so the men with their partners can learn some new dance steps. George notices me from across the room, his gaze transfixed as he strides through the dancing partners.

Heat rises in my cheeks as he approaches, and it's clear that he's happy to see me. Perhaps the cause of my embarrassment is the warmth accumulating in the room from all the bodies crowded together in a small space, or perhaps, when I look at George, I realise I'm still head-over-heels in love with him.

To me, he embodies my idea of what I consider perfect, unfaltering masculinity. He is stoic, brave, and pragmatic. The man makes me laugh, is a capable diplomat, able to lead, as well as being incredibly handsome. What is there not to like, with his mesmerising eyes and dark hair? His only fault being, when I first met him, he was a bit immature, but at seventeen, what does a girl expect? What hasn't helped, is that he was placed in an alliance of incompatibility, which, at times, makes him unhappy. He's now thirty-one, and far from the boy he was, but then I have changed, too, at twenty-seven, and my education is almost complete, which has me wondering how things are back home. How much time has passed since I've been away?

"Viscountess." He bows, giving me a wry smile. "How do you fare?"

"Well, Lord Rochford – thank you." My heart beats faster as he stands closer, and I inhale the heady scent of nutmeg, cloves, and cumin on his clothes.

"Beth, can we go somewhere?" he whispers. I raise a brow. "Alone." His expression is hopeful as he awaits my answer.

"Why, George?" I ask, conveying pure innocence.

"I need to talk with you." He brushes his hand through his hair.

"I think it's best if we just stay here, otherwise we may be missed. We don't want any unwelcome attention, especially when your wife is not here. We would end up adding to the gossip." I glance around. "And talking of gossip, you seemed to be getting along well with your Jane before she left for Essex."

"And I heard you were getting on well with the king." He frowns. "Jane told me."

Hmm, just as I thought.

He gulps back some of his wine. "I was jealous with rage about you, and Jane was happy you were growing closer to the king."

"George, what you don't seem to understand is, I wasn't happy. You didn't speak to me for weeks. I felt hurt." Maybe I shouldn't be so hard, but I don't want to show any weakness.

"I stayed away from you because I could not bear the thought of the king's hands on your flesh – it upset me so." He puts his goblet down on a table, then steps back in front of me. "How do you think I felt, having to keep you at arm's length for the sake of the king?"

"I didn't go behind your back with him to hurt you," I whisper.

"Yes, but I bet he went behind yours." He winks.

"If you are going to start talking like that, I'm leaving."

"Now, now, no need to be like that. It's a gargoyle-eat-gargoyle world." He chuckles.

"It certainly is. Talking of gargoyles, how long is Jane going to be away?"

He raises his brows in shock. I can't believe I've just said that – it's the 21st-century coming out in me.

"For however long His Majesty deems fit – now don't be spikey." He straightens to his full height. "If you're going to be like that, I'm going to be the one leaving."

"Then, before you leave, My Lord, what about the rumours I hear of you sleeping with other women?" I purse my lips. "Does that not matter?"

"As you have just said, the stories are just rumours, promoted by Cavendish. The man does not know me." He frowns. "For the time being, Jane's absence suits me – and it might suit you too." He runs the tip of his tongue across his bottom lip. "Does this not allow us to be together? Is this not what you wanted? And Anne said she would allow it."

"Yes," I say, letting my sarcasm flow, "it's been my life's dream since childhood to be someone's mistress."

He shrugs. "What else am I to do?"

"I don't know – but what about Jane?"

"What about her?" He rolls his eyes. "Jane is my wife – she will do as I say. Hang Jane!"

"George, you can't say such a thing."

He picks up a jug of wine from the table, refills his goblet, and gulps back its contents. "God, I needed that!" He can hold his drink, I'll give him that. "I have been unhappy for years, and you know it."

"I'm sorry about that."

He refills his goblet. "And I am sorry that the king feels he can take you, and other women to his bed, which hurts my sister."

"Please, George, let's not talk on this anymore." He's standing as close as he physically can, and my heart is pounding ten to the dozen.

"Is it over with you and the king?" he asks, his eyes wide like saucers.

"One minute I am the answer to his prayers," I answer, matter of fact, "and the next, he will not give me the time of day. Once he has had his way, the novelty wears off – you know what the king can be like better than most." I maintain eye contact. "I'm glad Henry has tired of me – it suits me, as your situation with Jane now suits you."

He sighs. "Thank God."

"I have missed you," I say.

"And I you. Let us bury our differences."

"I don't see why not, My Lord." I know well what he wants to bury.

His face lights up. "Does this mean you are prepared to relent and come to my bed?"

"Well…we are wasting valuable time."

He licks his bottom lip again, picks up his goblet, and swigs the whole lot back. Before I can say another word, he grabs my hand and leads me around the edge of the room, passing courtiers and tables, trying to avoid knocking over wine goblets and empty glasses. We leave the revelry and make our way down adjoining halls and passageways, which takes us to an area of the palace I have never been before – George's private chambers.

"My Lord," his servant John says when George opens the door.

We walk in, and I feel anxious about being in the rooms he and Jane normally share. The space is richly decorated with tapestries, silver plate, and rows of leather-bound books.

"These are charming," I say as I examine a set of small, delicate miniatures in oils hanging on the white-lime walls, depicting George and Jane.

John walks around the room with a long taper, lighting candles in candelabras, creating a soft, warm glow. He bows to me, nods to George, then leaves.

George turns to me, grinning. "Mine own darling, you are not here to admire my décor."

Hmm, you're right, I'm here for you. A fire burns deep within the hearth, as does the flame within George's loins. Before I can say another word, he pulls me to him, his lips crushing against mine. He presses against me, grinding with his hips, his kisses burning with passion, and I give as good as I'm getting – I've been waiting for this for so long.

Without a word, he steps away, takes a sip of wine, places the goblet back on the table, then kisses me, allowing the wine to fill my mouth and trickle down the back of my throat. No wine has ever tasted so sweet.

He pushes my hood back off my head and throws it in the direction of a chair beside me, then grips my head and plants hot kisses up the side of my neck.

"I want you right now!" he says.

I pluck the pins from my placard, removing it from the front of my gown. He reaches down to tug the lacing on the front of my dress, and, as he does, I'm sure he sees the look of anticipation on my face. Butterflies are swirling through my stomach like the swallows of summer. He growls like a predatory cat and looks up, the laces now between his teeth, and pulls his head back as he tugs at them. When he stands, he thrusts his fingers under my lacing and pulls hard, and my breasts leap, escaping their restriction, as we have escaped the restriction of the courtly gaze.

"Are you ready for this?" he asks. "Because I know I am!" He pushes my gown off my shoulders, and it falls at my feet, then grabs for the lacing on my kirtle and begins undoing them.

He groans, then laughs. "Why do women's clothes need to be so complicated?"

"Don't worry," I whisper, "it will be worth it."

With that, he picks me up, my kirtle half undone, and kisses me hard. I feel sick with passion as, being this close, I can smell his lusty masculinity. He kicks the door of his bedchamber wide open as he carries me through, then lays me on the furs of his four-poster bed.

The ropes strain beneath the mattress as we writhe about in the full throes of passion. He's shaking in his excitement as he touches me, but we must stop as I pull and tug my kirtle, and petticoat over my head. As I do, he pulls down his nether stocks and kicks them off. The only barrier between us now are two layers of flimsy linen. His shirt sticks to his sweaty torso, showing his pecs and the toned muscles of his abdomen. He's like a stallion wanting to mate with his mare, and I am not going to make him wait any longer.

His excitement is visible through the thinness of his shirt, and he wastes no time in removing it, adding it to the pile of clothes and shoes on the floor. Shadows from the dancing flames of the fire flicker across his skin, and his erect shaft stands strong.

My God, I want him now, like I have never wanted anything before in my life. My hands tremble as I sit on the edge of the bed in front of him, and I run them down the front of his chest, kissing his skin, tonguing his flesh with circular motions. As I look up at him, the anticipation in his eyes hooks me, and he moistens his lips with his tongue, probably wondering how far I am going to take this. Little does he know.

The saltiness of his perspiration turns me on even more. I shuffle off the side of the bed and rest on my knees in front of him, his member throbbing inches from my eyes. He trembles beneath my fingers as I trace them down his abdomen, taking his erection in my hand. The man has no idea what's coming. His cock pulses as I kiss its base, licking and tonguing for a short time before running my wet tongue up its length, evoking a choked groan from him when I flick it over the tip and graze his glans with my teeth.

"Stop! Stop!" he cries.

I gaze up at his face, and he stares down at me, looking as if he's about to explode. Stopping is the last thing on my mind, and I take him in both hands and lick his tip in circular motions, working my hands in quick time, maintaining eye contact all the time. It doesn't take long before it becomes too much and he stiffens, crying out as he releases his load over my face, its heat almost taking me over the top.

He flops on the bed, his chest heaving. "Oh my God, where did you learn that?" His eyes are wide in amazement. I grab my shift from the floor and quickly wipe it over my chin. "You were going to put my tackle in your mouth, were you not?" The very thought of it must be too much for him. Some men can't even cope with the idea of it – it turns them on so much. "Were you in France with my sister?" He grins. "No wonder the king wanted you."

"This is an experience only for you, and not for others. I don't want to be the next queen." I crawl up on the bed beside him and stroke his chest, his cheek, then forehead, hoping to calm him.

"That was truly amazing," he whispers.

We are lying next to each other in the candle glow, and as he presses his nakedness against me, I stroke his chest, my touch gentle and light. He leans over me, his kisses deep and loving as he caresses my breasts, tweaking my nipples, sending gorgeous shards of ecstasy through my pelvis and down my legs. I bite his bottom lip and drive my tongue into his mouth as he reaches down to cup my secret parts with his hand before slipping his fingers inside me.

I break free from his hot kisses and gasp beneath his touch, grinding into his hand as his explorations bring me to heights of pleasure I haven't experienced in a lifetime. When I reach down for his cock, I'm delighted to find it ready for action again. That's my boy!

As I lie back beneath him, he places himself between my thighs. Christ! I growl when he squeezes my buttocks, pulling me towards him, rubbing his shaft against me, my desire burning to have him inside me. He keeps rubbing, hitting the right spots – working me into a frenzy.

By God, George is going to make it his business to fulfil my every need, just as I am doing for him. I wrap my legs around his waist and can't help squealing as he plunges into me. He bites my ear, whispering his love before drawing back, teasing me as he kisses my face, neck, and shoulders, then driving in again, deep, and delicious.

Is this real? Am I dreaming? He continues his little game, with both of us trembling as our desire builds to such a level that we can't hold back, and I urge him on out loud as he increases his rhythm, and now he is that stallion, and I am his mare, and we are galloping at a speed beyond my imagination.

He raises himself, arms straight, his head thrown back, the sweat on his chest and face glistening in the candlelight as we work ourselves higher and higher, the intensity of pleasure raging between my thighs as his thrusting increases. This is not like the quickie in the office within the cloisters. I am in another world altogether.

I close my eyes, clinging to him, driving my nails into his back as waves of ecstasy build, and I have no intention of holding back, not caring who or what hears us. He's lost in the moment and, as he looks down on me, I see that it's not going to be long before he climaxes. I cry for him to give me more, meeting his thrusts as they increase in persistence and speed, the fire inside me scorching through every nerve, until we both cry out, reaching that glorious pinnacle in an explosive release.

He collapses against me, and we gasp, breathless, covered in each other's sweat and love. Fantastic!

"I could never feel like that with anyone else," he says, kissing my ear.

"Me neither, my love," I whisper back, struggling to catch my breath.

Afterwards, we lie in a pleasant tangle, the linen sheets knotted around our ankles, with the light in the room coming from slight shafts of moonlight glowing through the gap in the curtains, and the few flames from the remaining candles. I feel a strange tinge of guilt being in his marital bed.

"What are you thinking about?" I ask, flouncing onto my side to face him.

"How much I love you."

"My heart belongs to you, and only you," I whisper.

"And mine yours."

With that, he plants sweet kisses on my lips, his body crushing against me as he begins his lovemaking again. This time it is gentle and slow, and once we are spent, we lay back against the pillows.

"You puzzle me," he says. "You always have."

"How so?"

"You are not like the other women at Court. You're different. Why is that?"

"You tell me." I laugh, rubbing my free hand over my eyes. I reach out for him and rest my palm on his chest. "George, can I ask you something?"

"Yes, anything."

"Do you love Jane?"

"Love?" He snorts. "No, not in the way a man should love his wife. Jane was chosen by my father, and Lord Morley paid him so that I would marry his daughter."

"Why have you never had children?"

"Believe you me, it is not for the want of trying, but I do not love Jane, and I am sure she does not love me. Once Anne became queen, I felt it my duty to produce a Boleyn heir, for Father's sake. Jane has been 'with child' a few times, but her pregnancies last for a couple of months and then she miscarries."

His eyes glisten, and I feel devastated that he hasn't had the gumption to share this with me before.

"I have lost all interest in my marriage," he says, forlorn. "Let's change the subject, dear Beth – you say I have your heart, but who is it that you love?" He stares at me. "I know you have been with the king on many occasions. Do you love him?"

"George, you must know I do not love the king, even as his mistress." I look at him in silence for a long moment. "I was asked to keep Henry's mind on Anne. I did what was expected of me out of loyalty and love for your family."

"For that reason, I could never be angry with you." He brushes an errant lock off my face. "Do you really love me?"

"George, I think you know the answer to that."

"I may do," he says, taking me in his arms again.

NOVEMBER 1534

When it comes to public relations, Cromwell is a visionary. Due to the break with Rome, he is encouraging printed propaganda to be distributed against the pope and traditional religion. He has also commissioned Hans Holbein the Younger to make anti-papal woodcuts and is subsidising playwrights to publicise the Protestant message. Along with that, he was involved in introducing a new bill curtailing the right to make appeals to Rome. The Act in Restraint of Appeals was passed in April last year, ensuring reform of the church. He is playing a major role in making sure the pope is attacked in official propaganda, and is involved in further measures such as writing the Act of Succession of 1534, the Dispensations Act, the Act for the Submission of the Clergy, and the Act in Restraint of Annates, which stops the pope from taxing the clergy.

Cromwell's power and influence have increased dramatically now he is appointed principal secretary and chief minister. He is deeply involved in social reform, intending changes in education, agriculture, trade, and industry, and he is known for his ruthless enforcement of the Acts of Succession.

He's just introduced the Act of Supremacy, which punishes those who refuse to swear the Oath, like Bishop John Fisher and Sir Thomas More. The Act of Supremacy infers that the signatory recognises Henry as the only supreme head on earth of the Church of England. He's also introduced a new

Treason Act, one that will eventually be used against Anne and George, unless I interfere. The Treason Act stipulates that anyone who maliciously wishes, wills, or desires, by words, writing, or by craft, imagines, invents, practises, or attempts any bodily harm to be done or committed to the king's most royal person, the queen's, or their heir's apparent would be guilty of high treason. This is serious stuff. As I know Anne's story, it's easy to understand how this treason act is applied to her in her final months.

"Madam, I am prepared to crush anyone who is perceived to be a significant threat," he says to her during a discussion in her chamber. "Most incidents of rebellion that came to my attention in the last year originate from ordinary people, Your Majesty."

"These reports, Secretary Cromwell, have you dealt with them? Are you dealing with these people?"

As I observe him standing motionless before the queen, all traces of the blacksmith's boy are gone; he is no longer the ruffian of his youth, and the rough diamond is now polished. From the obvious poverty of his childhood, he now knows more than modest prosperity, thanks to his patron, the king, and has sampled what money can buy. He seems comfortable in his shoes, learning from every situation he has experienced, and, at this moment, seems flexible, pragmatic, and shrewd. The man is widely read, understands poetry and art, just like Anne. Indeed, they have much in common. Whilst they discuss religion and churchmen, I wonder if he has found God – his views are relatively unknown, like many things about him, apart from the fact that he now sympathises with reformers. From what I can tell, his religious feelings are genuine and strong.

"Yes, Madam, however, an elderly friar during his sermon asked the congregation to pray for Queen Katharine rather than yourself, an easy mistake to make as he is in his seventies."

I am unsure whether he would torture a seventy-year-old unless, of course, reasons of the state demand it and Henry agreed.

"Ah well, Cromwell, we can forgive that," she says with a flick of her hand, possibly remembering my advice to be more gracious to those around her.

NOVEMBER 1534

Preparations are being made for the arrival of the Admiral of France, who is bringing an imperial suggestion for a settlement between King Charles V and King François I, which involves the marriage of Henry's daughter, the Lady Mary to the Dauphin. This has shocked Anne because it implies that her patron, François, considers Mary to have a better claim to the English throne than Princess Elizabeth, and matters are being made worse by France's lukewarm attitude to Henry's counterproposal for a marriage between Elizabeth and François' third son. Anne acts cool towards the French envoy, and his feeling towards the Queen is mutual. George, with his diplomatic career continually rising, has been asked to meet the Admiral in a bid to smooth things over. Meanwhile, while Jane stays banished at Rochford Hall in Essex, I spend most nights in his bed.

Anne sits at her writing table in her chamber, signing off petitions and penning letters to her mother and sister. As I walk in and curtsy, she looks up, her expression serious.

"Viscountess, come and sit with me." She motions to the chair beside her as the other women go about their allotted tasks.

"How do you fare, Beth?"

"I am very well, Your Majesty!"

"You have some colour in your cheeks," she whispers, a cheeky smile lighting her eyes. "As does my brother." She glances about. "Are you responsible for that?"

"Perhaps."

"There is no 'perhaps' about it, and you look good on it." She signs a missive and lays it aside. "It is good to see my brother with a rosy hue in his cheeks and a glint in his eye." She leans closer. "I have noticed him sending for you almost every night."

"Please, Anne, don't be angry with me."

Her eyes widen. "I am not. I am happy that George is happy, and the fact that Jane is not here is most convenient." She gives me a knowing nod.

"I feel guilty about it."

"Do not be. Jane must learn to do as she is told."

"George has left to meet the French Admiral, hasn't he?"

"Yes, and I'm sure he can smooth things over with them."

"Even though you leave the bulk of diplomatic relations to him, you must try to improve your position with the Ambassador, for the sake of European relations and diplomacy."

She looks up for a couple of seconds, then meets my gaze. "I thank you for your advice, Viscountess, but I am certain George and I have things in hand."

"I mean no disrespect."

"I understand. Now, take these letters to my usher so he can send them to the courier."

"Yes, Your Majesty." I take the letters to the door and hand them over, knowing how things with France will turn out. Cromwell can try his best to work behind the scenes, to improve relations with Henry and the other heads of Europe, but I know it won't work. The delicate, diplomatic dance may be a subtle one to Cromwell, but for many, it's a difficult game to master, which, at times, seems to cast a shadow over Henry and Anne's relationship.

I can hear Cromwell and Henry in a side room. They are deep in conversation, and I strain to listen as I wait for Anne to process down to the Great Hall.

"How are matters proceeding with our negotiations for a match between the Princess Elizabeth and Charles, the Duke of Angoulême?"

"Under way, just as you directed, but I have had no decisions relayed about your behest."

Henry groans. "That will frustrate Anne."

"Your Majesty, hopefully, we will make progress this evening."

Just before Cromwell steps into the hall, I move away from the open door and look like I'm inspecting the decorations on the table. Henry has probably gone to meet Anne before they are both announced. I'm aware of Cromwell's suspicious look as he passes me, but I pretend to be too busy to notice him.

Tonight, the Tudor Court entertains the Admiral at the final great banquet. Anne sits at the dining table on the dais next to her French guests. I sit a few places down, next to George. With Jane still banished, no one thinks it unusual that he flirts with any of Anne's ladies-in-waiting. He gets up from his seat and goes and speaks with his sister, while Henry seeks out Gontier, the ambassador's secretary – a man of considerable influence.

Diplomacy aside, the talks will not work because, two months later, Monsieur Gontier will return to England with an answer to the proposal about Elizabeth's betrothal, and it will be a disappointing 'no'.

DECEMBER 1534

"Why do the French delay?" Anne questions me in her chambers. "Am I not Queen of England? Have I not produced a Princess of England?"

She is not happy about the time it is taking for the French to come back with an answer regarding Princess Elizabeth's betrothal. I know the delay, and the refusal of a betrothal, will arouse all Henry's suspicions about his marriage to Anne, and Princess Elizabeth's legitimacy.

"Madam, please be patient, otherwise you will make your position impossible."

She stares at me for a long moment, and I fear she's wondering what I know.

"I feel my position more precarious than ever before I was married."

I glance about to make sure we're not overheard. "You cannot write to the envoy, for the king will find out. You must say no more, as the court is watching, and the eavesdroppers wait for you to make a mistake."

JANUARY 1535

The palace is lit with a plethora of candles to guard off the winter gloom. Little Princess Elizabeth takes her first tentative steps across the Turkish carpet towards her mother, who bends to her level, arms open wide, and scoops her up before she falls.

"My little one!" she cries, hugging her close to her breast. "You may leave us now, Lady Bryan," she instructs, and I sit watching Elizabeth nuzzle into her mother's neck. She is an affectionate child and enjoys the maternal warmth.

Purkoy, given to Anne some time ago by Lady Honor Lisle, wife of the governor of Calais, sits on my lap, knowing he will get no attention from Anne when her daughter is around. Instead, he tries to lick my hand while I rub his stomach, which is round and full because he ate too much bread today. As Anne told Jayne Fool, his name derives from the French word 'pourquoi', meaning 'why', because the pup tends to tilt its head when you look at him, as though he's asking a question. His doleful expression is so full of love, and he has such a gentle nature.

Elizabeth leans over from her mother's lap and lets him lick her hand too. Anne pulls her back, not wanting him teased. However, Elizabeth is used to such animals, as courtiers live here with their lapdogs.

I won't have a dog at court, as I don't want to become too attached, in case I must return home to my 'real' life. Many ladies have obtained the king's permission to bring their pets with them when they live at court, but they must keep them in the kennels provided so the palace remains sweet, wholesome, clean, and well-furnished, as is to be expected for a royal residence. Ladies are also allowed singing birds. Henry keeps canaries and nightingales in ornamental cages hanging in windows at Hampton Court, and he keeps ferrets, although he forbids his courtiers to do so.

His favourite pets are his dogs, especially his beagles, spaniels, and greyhounds; the latter is considered a noble breed. Over the years, he has sent hundreds of such dogs as gifts to the Holy Roman Emperor and the King of France. His dogs wear decorative collars of velvet – permitted only to royal dogs – and kid leather, fashioned with or without spikes of silver and gold; some are adorned with pearls or the king's crest, and his portcullis and rose badges. His dogs' coats are of white silk, and they have their fur regularly rubbed down with a haircloth.

Anne's dogs are kept in the same condition, with jewelled collars, and bread is given to them rather than meat, to discourage them from developing hunting instincts. Two of Henry's dogs, 'Cut' and 'Ball', are growing old, which means they are prone to getting lost, and Henry pays out huge sums in rewards to those who bring them back to the palace.

MAY 1535

Cromwell's power within the church has escalated following his appointment as Viceregent in spirituals. His involvement in religious reform and monastic visitations is more active. Although he is an independent political figure, important in his own right, he maintains his links with Anne, and to outward appearances is still her man.

The Carthusian monks of the London Charterhouse – the monastery of the Carthusian order in central London – are being put to death, the first of which happened yesterday, May 4th. The method of execution is hanging, followed by disembowelment while still alive, then quartering. I'm aware from my study of the period that this will go on until September 1537. Others not executed will be imprisoned and left to starve to death. In total, eighteen men will die, which will lead to them being formally recognized by the Catholic Church as martyrs.

Not content with having Anne as his legal wife, and Princess Elizabeth now being his heir, Henry still wants everyone to sign the oath, agreeing he is Head of the Church in England, and that Anne Boleyn is his true and lawful wife. At the outset of the king's Great Matter, the government was anxious to secure the public acquiescence of the Carthusian monks, since they enjoyed great prestige for the austerity and sincerity of their way of life. When this attempt failed, the only alternative was for the State to annihilate the resistance. This is now taking the form of a long process of attrition.

The sun feels warm on my face as George, and I walk arm in arm in the palace gardens. He's explaining what has been going on with religion and politics in London.

"I know I can talk to you about such matters," he says, giving my arm a gentle squeeze. "Anne seems to have no compassion when it comes to Henry's political decisions, because she feels she must take the king's side, especially when matters involve her."

I look up at him, knowing that will change in a year from now. "What matters do you talk of?" I ask, pretending not to know.

"The monks of the London Charterhouse are held in high esteem, and have considerable influence among the people."

"Yes, and?"

"Many consult the Carthusians for spiritual advice, but in the last few days, the authorities…" He looks to the sky, as if searching for something.

"You mean, Thomas Cromwell?"

"Yes." He nods. "He sent them to their death at Tyburn,"

"That's terrible!"

"Yes, I know – three leading monks – a John Houghton, Robert Lawrence, and Augustine Webster, along with a Bridgettine monk, Richard Reynolds of Syon Abbey, and a secular priest, John Haile." The gravel crunches underfoot as we walk. "Richard Reynolds should have known better, being that he was educated at Corpus Christi, Cambridge, and was the only English monk well versed in the three principal languages of Latin, Greek, and Hebrew. But he refused to sign the Oath of Supremacy."

"What else do you know of him?"

"He was the most renowned spiritual counsellor of the Syon community, and was consulted by Elizabeth Barton, the Holy Maid of Kent, who, as you know, was executed at Tyburn over a year ago now for speaking out against the king's marriage to my sister."

I nod once to convey my understanding. "Did Reynolds not arrange a meeting between Elizabeth Barton and Thomas More?"

"Yes." He looks at me, surprised by my knowledge on the matter. "It was his connection to Barton that particularly compromised him in the view of the Crown officers."

"Elizabeth Barton was foolish."

He laughs. "Like Reynolds, Barton attempted to dissuade people from submitting to the king's authority."

I glance behind. "Many of the monks have claimed that the Dowager Princess is still the true queen."

"Yes, I believe so. Reynolds denied that he declared an opinion against the king, except in confession."

"George, it is mad to speak against the king's marriage to Anne. Those men were foolish, but did they deserve to die?"

He looks down at me, strokes my cheek, then bends to kiss my lips, his touch so gentle.

"Beth, it was treason," he whispers. I shudder as he continues, knowing he will tread the same path in the near future. "Apparently, Thomas More, still in the Tower, saw the three Carthusian friars being dragged to Tyburn."

"I know what he would have said."

As we walk, I put my arm through his, enjoying the fresh air and our closeness.

"What would Thomas More say?" he asks.

"He would think that these blessed fathers be now as cheerfully going to their deaths as bridegrooms to their marriage."

He shakes his head, probably thinking how stubborn Thomas More is for not signing the oath of supremacy.

"I doubt the king would see it that way!" He grimaces. "Anne told me that Henry went to the monks in disguise, and asked them if they would sign the oath."

"Really? No one recognised him?"

"No, it appears not, because each and every one of them denied him as head of the Church."

"They dared say no to Henry? His costume must have been very authentic!"

"I imagine it must have been. Father, myself, my uncle, the Duke of Richmond, Henry Norris, and forty of the king's bodyguard watched to see John Houghton as the first to be executed. After he was hanged, he was taken down alive and the process of quartering him began. As the executioner tore open his chest to remove his heart, he prayed, 'O, Jesus, what wouldst thou do with my heart?'"

"Please, George, don't tell me anymore!"

"Beth, have you never been to an execution?"

"No." I shake my head, flashes of his execution burning behind my eyes. "And I never want to." I shudder as I look at him, not liking all this talk of death. It's as if a ghost gazes down at me when I look into his eyes because he's on borrowed time. I really need to do something to save both him and Anne. Tears well in my eyes, and he notices.

"Whatever is the matter?" He grabs my hands. "Mine own darling, what is wrong?"

I can barely look him in the face. "My heart feels full of sorrow for those poor, religious men."

"Beth, you have a compassionate soul. It's just one of the many things I love about you." He pulls me into his arms and hugs me for the longest time.

20TH JUNE 1535

It is a good job Anne is some distance from central London and is not swept up in the furore surrounding the Carthusian monks. A second group has been executed after spreading gossip about the morals of the Boleyn family and the falseness of Henry's claim to be the Supreme Head of the Church. Naturally, like the group before, they refused to sign the Oath of Supremacy. Anne has heard that it is this group who spread cryptic prophecies that a queen would be burned. This reminds me of seeing that sketch in Anne's chambers of Queen Katherine, King Henry, and a beheaded Anne Boleyn, way back during another time-slip.

She is pacing her chamber, unhappy with the discontent being reported back to her.

"Anne, you must calm yourself," I say. "Henry has turned the world upside down to have you as his queen."

"You think I do not know that?" she snaps. "Henry cannot get a son for the fear of not getting one!"

"Am I not like any other men, am I not?" George mimics the king.

"Come on, a prince!" Anne cries. "We need a prince. The prince – silver cradles and precious stones – and baby clothes of copper gold. The prince's lodgings, the prince's wet-nurse, all for the love of the prince's eyes, prince's ears, and nose!"

"Your time will come, Sister," he says. "We and our supporters are gaining strength all the time. All resistance to you and His Majesty will be swept aside by Cromwell's Succession Act. We will make them all sign. All will submit and confirm Henry and your successors are the sole heirs in England, and that Henry is supreme head of everything in our land."

"Will that make a difference?" she asks.

"When we have brought the bible to the people in their own tongue and swept away for the common good the vile corruption of the monasteries, Henry will see the wisdom of his actions." He raises both eyebrows. "Come, Sister, you must be strong."

"I see the Courtneys and others – their hatred for me plainly in their expressions, and in their hearts – wanting me to fail, wishing evil on my daughter."

"And what care we?" he asks.

"Nothing."

"You are strong, Anne," I say. "Pay no heed to rumours and hatred, spread by others who would not wish you well."

George holds his arms wide. "You see, we care nothing. And we are strong. You have my whole heart, Sister – my support – and I am one with a King who loves and trusts me. I have heard Henry is to appoint me the Warden of the Clinque Ports, and Constable of Dover Castle – let's not trust others with our hearts, whoever they may be."

"No?" She looks hard at him. "Not even Cromwell?"

"Especially not Cromwell," I answer.

"Why?" they ask in unison, staring at me.

"Trust me. You can both trust me."

Anne gives me a knowing look, and George just nods.

"I do not think we can trust our sister Mary either," he says. "She complains about her position in life all the time. I think she and her William Stafford should be silenced."

"Send her whatever is in my purse and your purse combined."

"Very well." He goes and stands by the window looking over the gardens, closing his eyes as he begins to pray. "Lord, from ill deliver us, as these days and times are dangerous and disordered. Save us from everlasting death. Save us and give us a blessed end in this life. Bequeath into thine hands our souls for you to gladly receive."

He opens his eyes and leans against the sill. "Lady Rochford has truly disgraced herself now."

"How so?" I ask.

"Herself – and me."

Anne steps closer. "She must be silenced, George. She must owe you her obedience as your wife – her behaviour cannot be tolerated."

"She owes me nothing," he says.

"You must go to her and her father – if his sympathises are so strong for the Spanish – for the shame of my own brother's wife pleading and demonstrating in the streets for that brat Mary. Calling her Princess. Is she mad?"

He chuckles. "Yes, she is mad – we both know that."

"Can we change the subject?" I ask. "It makes me feel uncomfortable." I look at him. "Where did you go yesterday? I couldn't find you."

"I saw more of the Carthusian monks die yesterday."

"Good," Anne says.

I glare at her. What a terrible thing to say.

"No, not really," George replies, his tone hushed.

"Why are you moping over those traitors?"

"My God – moping? You weren't there!" he shouts. It makes me jump. I wasn't expecting him to raise his voice.

"And, Brother, if I had been, I should have been glad to see justice carried out! You were part of this – you said you were injured by their ingratitude and their gross disloyalty. Why are you so squeamish suddenly? You have been present at executions before, have you not?"

"Not like that!"

"Like what? Being hanged and drawn is the penalty for treason and heresy – the monks were given every opportunity to recant, were they not?"

"They did not want to recant!" His voice fills the room.

"I cannot believe you sympathise with them."

"Sympathise?" he shouts.

I wring my hands. "Please, can the two of you just stop arguing?"

"No, Beth – Anne needs to understand that of course I sympathise. We are not talking about some debauched and treacherous old abbot making prostitutes out of children."

"George!" Anne snaps.

"Sister, you do realise these men were true men of conscience?" He glares at her. "If Henry has no heart,"—he points his forefinger at her, "—then surely there is a vestige of kindness left in you?" He steps away from the window. "Henry wept when told that Sebastian Newdigate would die."

Anne's eyes are wide. "You mean he cried with frustration!"

"Because he cannot always have his own way – the king is like a child!"

I step towards him. "Hush, George!"

"No!" he snaps at me, his face red. He sucks in a deep breath. "The King loved Newdigate especially – they were friends. Newdigate was educated at Court. Studied at Cambridge. He became a member of Henry's Privy Chamber, and he had enjoyed the king's favour."

"Brother, did his sister Jane not express concern about his suitability for the strictness of monastic life after his early years here at Court?"

"Yes, I remember, she did, but despite her misgivings, he remained at the charterhouse. He was ordained a deacon in fifteen-thirty-one, and when Henry required all to take the Oath of Succession recognizing you as his lawful wife, Newdigate signed it, 'in as far as the law of God permits' this time but a year ago."

"So why was he arrested?" I ask.

"Because the Carthusian community at the Charterhouse refuses to accept the king's assumption of supremacy over the Church." He walks over to a table and pours himself a goblet of ale. "Newdigate and two other monks, Humphrey Middlemore and William Exmew, were arrested in May and imprisoned in the Marshalsea, where they were kept for fourteen days bound to pillars, standing upright, with iron rings around their necks, hands, and feet."

"He was then brought before the Privy Council," Anne says, "and sent to the Tower of London, where Henry again visited him, but was unable to change his mind. Henry visited him, in person – in disguise! He offered to load the man with riches and honours if he would only conform."

"Yes, true," George says.

Anne crosses her arms. "Foolish man."

"But the problem was, Sister, he did not want to sell his immortal soul, eh?"

"There were others, weren't there?" I ask, knowing full well a list would later be displayed at their execution site.

Yes," George answers.

"You sat in judgement on them, not me," Anne says.

"I know," he whispers, still upset. He's shaking. "I am ashamed to show my face for what I have done."

"It is too late for that, Brother."

This is getting out of hand. "Anne, did you not say this was done for a great purpose, and it is God's work?"

"Yes." She sighs, turning to George. "How many times have you said that yourself? God's work can often be ugly and difficult for those who lead the way. We lead the way – reforming the old faith."

"How can we be so sure that what we do is God's will?"

"Trust in the truth," I say. "Trust in the future." They both stare at me again, as if I'm some kind of oracle. Maybe I shouldn't involve myself in their religious politics.

"George, you forget their superstitions, their evil rantings. They said I will be burnt, and that Henry is Merlin – calling me his wife for fornication and likening the king to a filthy sap."

"Anne, you go too far," I say. "All those monks wanted was to be excused from accepting Henry as the Head of the Church and from signing the act."

"You are right," George says, "Henry did not have to ask them."

Anne looks to the ceiling, and it's clear her patience is dwindling. "The monks had to lead by example."

"Sister, they were the most pious and devoted of men."

"Exactly," I say, backing him up.

"No, obstinate is what they were."

"Determined," he says. "They often said they refused to comply with His Majesty, not out of obstinacy, malice, or a rebellious spirit, but solely for the fear of offending the supreme majesty of God."

She holds both arms out to her sides. "So, the monks got what they wanted!"

"Please, calm down, both of you," I say.

"No, Beth, Anne needs to hear this." He tugs at his cuff. "They hacked an arm off each monk and nailed them to the Charterhouse door!"

"Those monks had the choice, Brother, and you know it."

"Yes! Yes – they went to their deaths singing!" He still won't calm down.

"Deranged, you mean!" she shouts.

"Anne, stop it!" I plead.

"Beth, George, and I said we would leave it to Cromwell – and so we did. Do you think Thomas Cromwell is puking in disgust?" I think not."

I shrug. "Master Cromwell has a strong constitution."

She giggles. "Beth, you are my comfort in all things – you are very wise. And, George, you are my guide."

He nods once. "The executioner used extra-thick ropes so they would not die straight away from their hanging. Did you know that?"

My face goes cold. "I don't want to hear this, George – it turns my stomach."

Anne glances behind. "This may turn you stomach, Beth, but nothing upsets Cromwell."

"It is all that fighting he did in Italy," George explains. "He watched while the executioners cut out the monks' hearts, while the poor fellows were still alive, and rubbed their own beating flesh in their faces!"

"George, please stop!" I say, hand over mouth.

"Those monks wanted martyrdom," Anne cries. "In allowing this to happen to them, for you to witness their deaths, they knew it would rock your steadfastness – to intervene in your great work and your service of the future. They wanted to harm you, and me!"

"I do not pretend to know what those monks thought they would achieve or know what they wanted – but their executions were on a higher plane than that." He glares at her. "Than the rattish court politics of a blacksmith's boy, or perhaps a queen's vanity!"

Her eyes bulge. She steps closer and slaps him across his face. "How dare you suggest me vain!"

"You, Sister, are not above God's law!" He holds his cheek. "You have benefited from my rise in almost equal measure to myself."

"I know," she replies, her tone calmer.

"Waiver now at your peril."

"I am sick of you both quarrelling," I say. "It is not like you."

"I am sorry, Beth, but my brother needs to understand that Henry threatens me." She raises a brow at me, then turns to George. "You know he does. He has told me he can lower me as much as he has raised me – he has told me many a time. The country is buckling. The harvest will be in ruins, and, no doubt, I will be blamed for it. The plague is everywhere."

George snorts. "While the heads on London gates turn black in the sun."

"I hate you for failing me!" she says through gritted teeth.

"I feel nothing, Sister. Hate me if you prefer, if it makes you feel better."

"I need to feel better – there are people who will have rejoiced when my boy child died inside my belly."

He scrunches up his brow. "That concern was with God, not with you. I told you that at the time, remember? Do you not understand that?"

"God's blood, George, I never thought I would call you a coward, but a coward you are! Your tears for these monks will cost you dearly, my brother. Whatever. I shall have a prince soon and none of you,"—she glances at me, then him—"will criticise me then. When I am the mother of the future king, no one, not either of you, will dare sympathise with my own enemies."

I say nothing in response, but I'm worried for her, knowing her temper will be her downfall. Thomas Cromwell will continue to monitor every possible source of discontent with his armoury of statutory weapons, such as the Succession Act. The King also asked him to create another Act, which has now been passed, extending the definition of treason to cover anything spoken, written, or done to deprive the king of his title, or seriously defame him. Of course, all the factions at court whisper that Anne is responsible.

Eleven

LATE JUNE 1535 – WINDSOR CASTLE

If history plays out as it should, Anne and George have less than a year to live. She has become bitterly anti-French, and now that George has returned from diplomatic duties in Europe, he visits her before reporting to the king himself.

"Anne, the French say that your morals have lowered the temperature of Anglo-French relations,"

"Why?" she snaps. "Because I married the man I love, and who loves me?"

"Although the French once loved you as theirs, King François will never verify your marriage valid, no matter how much I plead. He does not want to be drawn into an argument."

"Hang the French, what do they know of love?" She watches him walk over to me.

"I know more than enough of love." He stands behind me and wraps his arms about my waist, trying to kiss my neck.

"Stop, someone will see!" I say.

"George, leave Beth be – 'tis better to wait until you both have some privacy."

He releases me from his embrace, chuckling. "You spoil all our fun."

"No, Brother, I have encouraged it!" She smiles. "Now, go. I have matters to attend to."

"Your Majesty." He smiles and bows, then turns to me, his mouth at my ear. "Come to my bed tonight?"

I nudge him out and close the door behind him. Anne stands amongst piles of sumptuous silk gowns, linens, ribbon, slippers, and headdresses as her maids go about packing her trunks for the summer progress. Summer in Tudor times means the court will leave the heat, stench, and potential plague of London to travel around the countryside. Progresses are scheduled during the 'grass season', when the hay is cut, while other work done is minimal, and the hunting ideal. A pared-down complement of courtiers will accompany the king and queen to the royal residences and manor houses on a route that is carefully decided in advance so chosen courtiers can prepare for a royal visit. It is a great honour to host the court, though also a great responsibility.

Anne's gentlewomen dance this way and that in between conversations, reading her holy book, sipping wine, and grabbing apricots soaked in honey. The chaos is further heightened by the arrival of Thomas Cromwell.

"Master Secretary Cromwell, Your Majesty," George Zouche announces.

"Madam, I have come with an itinerary of the king's progress to Wiltshire, Somerset, and the West Country." He ignores all, stepping through the preparations and packing, then reads out a list of dates and places we are to travel to. The summer progress of 1535 is the longest and most politically charged Henry has yet undertaken, with he and Anne due to spend fourteen weeks travelling through the West Country, greeting the English people, and hopefully winning their support for their religious reforms. This is Anne's first official progress as queen – and I know the trip will bring them to Wolf Hall, the ancestral home of the Seymour family. Hmm, I wonder if this visit will be the start of Henry's affair with Jane Seymour. I shudder at my negative thoughts, remembering that my job is to observe – to let history play out as it should.

"We are to leave Windsor for Reading Abbey, a favourite of the king's, then onward to Ewelme Manor, Abingdon, Langley, Sudeley Castle, Tewkesbury Abbey, Painswick, Miserden, Leonard Stanley, Berkeley Castle, Thornbury, Acton, Little Sodbury Manor, Bromham House, Wolf Hall, Thruxton, Hurstbourne Priors, Winchester, Bishop's Waltham and so on."

Cromwell sounds like he missed his vocation. Had he been born in my time, he may have been employed as a staff member on the London Underground, as his voice would be excellent for announcing destination arrivals at each and every stop.

He hands Anne the list, bows, then steps back, leaving her tracing her forefinger down the page.

She laughs. "That is an exhaustive list, Secretary Cromwell."

"Why are you laughing?" I whisper.

"Cromwell, you may leave us."

He removes his hat, bows, puts his hat back on, then walks to the door and closes it behind him. I often wonder if he stands at keyholes on the other side of important doors, listening in to other people's conversations.

"Beth, I am laughing about going to Wolf Hall. You must have heard about Sir John Seymour?"

"No," I lie, looking down at the list.

"Do you not know he was caught in the hayloft with his son Edward's wife!" She snorts out a giggle. "You must have heard the stories?"

"No, Madam." I'm such a bad liar but I'm trying my best.

"The Seymours can tell a tale or two. Sir John has had his daughter-in-law so many times, Edward had to send her to a nunnery."

"No wonder Sir John has not been seen at Court," I say.

"I tell you, Viscountess, those sinners at Wolf Hall could teach the likes of Boccaccio a story or too."

"What of Jane Seymour?" I ask, holding down my nerves. "She seems very unassuming."

"The pasty-face girl? It will be her best bet to get sent to a nunnery, too, as no one will want to marry her when her family has such a reputation."

I stay silent. She stares at me, probably wondering why I don't respond.

"I have heard another rumour too," she says. "It seems that the king's 'beautiful' laundress, Joanna Dingley, has given birth to a bastard girl."

"By the king?" I enquire in hushed tones.

"I am unsure if the child has been fathered by the king – and no one dares ask. Etheldreda is the child's name. She is but a month old, having been born on the twenty-third of May."

She looks rather pleased that Henry's former mistress has given birth to a daughter, but no one knows who the father this.

"A couple of my ladies have heard rumours that once the bastard girl has finished being wet nursed by her mother, she is to be raised as the daughter of one of the cutters in the king's wardrobe. A tailor named John Malte. Have you heard such rumours?"

I cough into my hand and lean closer. "No, I have not. I have met John Malte, though. He works with Skutt and Paul Cotton, does he not?"

"Yes. You have a good memory, Beth."

"But I did hear of another rumour, that Henry got rid of the laundress because she practised unnatural acts within the bedchamber, which the king objected to."

"What kind of unnatural acts?" she asks, her eyes wide.

"I heard the gossip from among your ladies – I can't believe you don't know. Apparently, she is partial to some posterior intimacy, but Henry refused her on numerous occasions. Only a woman like that, from the stew houses, with loose morals, would stoop so low!"

From her expression, I'm not sure she believes me. She shakes her head. "Please, Beth, tell me no more. I cannot take it."

I giggle. "Indeed, Mistress, we can leave that kind of encounter for men held at Berkeley Castle, the likes of King Edward II!"

"Shhh, Beth. I know you know your history!" She smirks, "What you speak of is a perverse sexual act or, in King Edward's case, one of murder – something I did not learn at the French Court."

I try to stifle a giggle, then get serious. "Mistress, I must say, you have taken this news about the child very well."

"It is not the king's child, and even if it was, it would be a bastard. Never mind, we will make the entertainment at Wolf Hall. The king needs no more mistresses. Haven't the king and I always been merry?"

"Yes, Majesty, you have."

"And that is the way it will stay, with God's good grace."

I bite my tongue, knowing too well her god has other plans.

Henry and Anne are leaving Windsor on their summer progress, where the sport is reported to be good, particularly the hawking. The king has not hunted the area for some years, and after a few weeks away from the stress and blood of recent events, he is in tremendous form. So is Anne, who accompanies him throughout, and we all notice how they enjoy their time together. If history plays out its hand without change, this will be the only progress that will be made by the royal couple and their retinue.

This progress is the first time Henry will venture outside of London to promote the reformation. Anne, the committed reformer, will visit the households of several pro-reformers during this trip alongside her husband. Plans have been drawn up to start on progress through South-West England from July 8th, carrying onwards to Reading Abbey, then to Ewelme Manor, Oxfordshire on July 12th, moving to Abingdon Abbey on July 14th for two days before arriving at the Old Palace of Langley, then transferring five days later to Sudeley Castle, as detailed by Cromwell.

SUDELEY CASTLE – JULY 21ST - 26TH 1535

Now we are at Sudeley, Anne is Queen of the Cotswolds. The king is to meet with Thomas Cromwell at Winchcombe Abbey to begin to put their plan into place for the dissolution of the monasteries. Anne has sent her chaplains to Hailes Abbey to investigate a renowned relic of the Holy Blood of Christ that has previously made the Abbey one of the most popular places of pilgrimage in late-medieval England. Henry has asked them to investigate how corrupt the church is.

Before Cromwell arrives, we settle ourselves at Sudeley, just a stone's throw from the little village of Winchcombe. Richard III had once been an owner of Sudeley, and during his time, a magnificent banqueting hall with splendid oriel windows and adjoining staterooms was built. Henry walks arm in arm with Anne, telling us in animated terms about the castle's history, turning to me with pride as we walk its palatial rooms.

"When Richard the Third was defeated and killed in the battle of Bosworth in fourteen-eighty-five, by my father, bringing to an end the 'cousins' war', he left all this,"—he indicates with a wave of his hand—"to my great-uncle, Jasper Tudor, Duke of Bedford, who held it until his death when it reverted to the crown."

The trees rustle in the wind as I look out of the window, towards the small chapel. Sir Francis Weston is relaxing alone on a garden bench, enjoying the glow of the midsummer sunshine. His cap is off, his coat lies beside him, and his doublet appears to be unbuttoned.

"Your Majesty, may I take my leave of you and your beautiful wife?"

"Viscountess, please go and enjoy the fresh air and the grounds," he says, having seen me peering out of the window and happy to let me go so he can be alone with Anne. She still excites him, even when she infuriates him.

Walking down the stairs to the resplendent garden, I muse to myself that the chapel will one day be rebuilt to be the final resting place of Henry's last wife, and Sudeley will be the home of Princess Elizabeth for a time. My shoulders shudder at the thought, as I realise that unless I do something, Anne only has ten months, if that, to live. So does the man who now stands up and begins to walk towards me with his coat over his arm.

"Mistress, it is warm today, is it not?" Weston smiles, charming as ever, and I wonder which of my fellow ladies-in-waiting he is bedding, behind his wife's back. Perhaps he is influenced by George, for the two are inseparable. Like George, Weston is a good athlete, musician, and a show-off. The only thing that differs between them is that Weston has run up huge debts because of his regular gambling, mostly losing his hand at cards to Henry Norris and the Queen. At court, Francis is one of the men who are always in and out of Anne's apartments. He flirts with everyone, bedding women, despite having a young son.

"I saw you from the window. I thought I would come and join you."

We proceed onto a gravel path, which runs along a row of rose bushes. Their July fragrance hangs on the air, intoxicating the moment as Weston plucks a pale-pink bloom, handing it to me to be gallant.

"Francis, would you mind if I offer you a little advice?" I tilt my face, taking the beautiful rose from him, hoping that my little tête-à-tête may influence a different outcome for his life. "Please stay out of the way of Secretary Cromwell."

"Why, Mistress?"

"Not so long from now, he may draw you into a plot he will concoct for his political scheme. There are courtiers Cromwell detests, and I have a feeling he will sweep out anyone from the King's nest who happens to look at him sideways."

"I have been warned, thank you," he says, giving me the suspicious eye.

"Please heed my advice, Francis." I'm not sure he will be able to stand up to the pressure Cromwell will apply. He seems sincere in his sentiment, although I would not consider him particularly bright. Our conversation is interrupted as Anne and her entourage approach, all smiles, and pleasantries.

"What are you two discussing behind my back?" She raises a questioning brow as Jane Boleyn, who has joined Anne's party on this trip, steps up to her side. It seems she is forgiven. Margaret Shelton, Lady Worcester, William Brereton, and Henry Norris all look on. Sparrows dart and swoop from turret to window ledge about us, and the green cushion of the grass prompts us all to tread its welcoming path.

"Nothing of importance, Your Majesty," Weston says as she stares at the rose in my hand, glancing at my face, then to Weston.

"Your Majesty, I have heard that Francis Weston enjoys flirting with ladies of your privy chamber," Jane Boleyn says. "It is a shame he does not pay enough attention to his wife! Indeed, it will not surprise me if he flirts with Viscountess Beaumont."

The circling group chuckle in agreement as Weston's cheeks redden. He remains silent.

"Sir Francis, it seems you spend too much time flirting, not only with Lady Shelton, ignoring your wife and leaving her at home. And now you flirt with Beth?" Anne smiles, clearly amused at the situation.

"My wife has just had a child, Majesty, as you know – she cannot attend Court."

"Nevertheless, you keep Henry Norris away from Lady Shelton by showing your attention to her." Her reprimand is not sharp.

"I think you will find that Sir Henry Norris is more interested in other ladies of the court, other than Madge Shelton."

"It seems everyone thinks I have secrets?" Norris says in rapid response.

Anne looks at him in disbelief, then her brows furrow with suspicion. "Do you, Sir Henry?"

"No!" he says, matter of fact.

"I cannot speak for Norris, Your Majesty," Weston interjects, "but I love a lady much more than either my wife, or Madge Shelton."

"Who might that be, Francis Weston? Do tell me. Could it be Lady Worcester, or Viscountess Beaumont?" She laughs as she looks around the party, as if searching for clues.

"No, Madam," he replies, "I cannot say."

"Rather, you will not say?" Stunned for a moment, he isn't sure what to reply.

Jane Boleyn's ears prick up and she leans closer to hear what is transpiring. Madge Shelton has shrunk away from the group and is turning on her heels back to Anne's chambers.

I smile to myself. "Perhaps you should kick him, Norris, to reproach him for insulting the ladies-in-waiting of the Queen of England?"

Norris, ever the gallant, remains composed, the corners of his mouth turning up in a small, admiring smile. This kind of flirting is another display of the romantic, chivalric game that Anne herself has introduced to court. Her old mentor, Margaret of Austria, was highly adept at such things, but Anne seems to be far less successful. While such behaviour works for a single, widowed princess of high rank and an impeccable reputation, it seems to do nothing for a flirtatious queen, with a jealous husband. She is the object of the attention of Henry Norris, Henry VIII, and now, it seems, Sir Francis Weston, judging by his demeanour. They are all in love with her.

Early the next morning, Henry comes blustering in from his rooms, with Anne on his arm. He's decided to take everyone out on a hunt. It's a last-minute decision. To be honest, after the late nights we've all had, and with all the travelling, I feel drained, as though I've got jetlag, and I haven't even been on a plane. All I want to do is stay in my bed and sleep.

"Come on," Anne says. "You will enjoy it once we get out there. Besides, it will put the King in good humour – it is pleasant to see him doing something he enjoys, and that is conducive for all of us."

I pick up my gloves and cloak, doing as I'm told, and make my way down to the courtyard, where Henry and his entourage are now already mounted on their horses. To my regret, I haven't had breakfast, and the smell from the horses rises in my nostrils – the scrapping of their shoes against the cobblestones filling my head. They and our party are raring to go.

George is holding the bridle of Anne's horse as she climbs the mounting block, and he holds her stirrup while she slides her foot into the metal and curls her other leg around the pommel. He mounts his horse, and, with a flash of the whip, they all take off. Madge Shelton, Jane Boleyn, Mark Smeaton, Henry Norris, and I climb up into the litter and the driver follows along. It's tight but at least I'm not riding a horse – I don't think I could handle it today.

Not too long after, the barking hounds signals they have picked up on a scent. Henry lets out a cry, and all the horses take off like hares in pursuit of what is probably a stag.

"That is the last we will be seeing of them for a while," Henry Norris says, looking at me. "It looks like we will have to make our own amusements." He wiggles his brows.

"Steady on there, Master Norris, or you will give yourself a nosebleed."

He sits back against the panelling, laughing away to himself. His comment takes me by surprise – he has a bit of a cheek talking to me in that way in front of Madge. I thought he was kind of heart, but is obviously like every other man. Maybe he just wants to get a rise out of me. However, that's the last thing I want from him.

Madge gives me a filthy look. It's not my fault if she can't keep her fiancé under control, if that's what he is. I smile in an effort to appease her, and look out at the open countryside, trying to spot Anne and the rest of the party.

When we arrive at a clearing, several small tents have been erected. A campfire has been lit, and a spit made ready for wild boar or venison. Servants bustle around as we alight from the litter. I hand Smeaton his lute – it's time for him to start entertaining us until the rest of the party re-joins us. The servants bring goblets and fill them with wine, and it doesn't take long before the full-bodied, crimson liquid goes to my head, no doubt because I rushed out without breakfast.

Jane Boleyn and Madge Shelton sit beside me on one of the wooden benches in a tent, relaying the latest court gossip.

"Master Norris pays you no attention considering he is supposed to be your betrothed," Jane, the troublemaker, says. "What have you to say to that?"

"Maybe it's catching, Lady Rochford, as, along with myself and the rest of the court, your husband pays you no attention either!"

I nearly choke on my wine at the look on Jane's face, like she's sucking on a crab apple.

"George Boleyn is a Gandermooner," Madge continues, taking no quarter, "which is not difficult to understand, considering every strumpet is putting themselves in his and Norris's way. It does not allow us to have a happy relationship with them."

She casts a look at me, as though it's meant to mean something.

"Maybe they are not that interested in either of you?" I suggest. "Let's face it, neither of you are renowned for being the life and soul of the party, are you?"

"Is that not unkind?" Jane says, her nostrils flaring.

"No, it's the truth – learn from it!"

"An unmarried, uncontracted woman is a dangerous one!" she says. "That is what I have learnt."

Madge nudges her arm. "Best not argue."

No, I'm up for an argument. "Lady Rochford, you'd cause trouble in an empty house. Save your breath to cool your porridge."

Her mouth curls in disgust, and she is about to respond when Henry Norris comes bounding in with a large flagon of wine.

"Now then, ladies, who would like a top-up?"

Well now, trust Norris to save the day, jumping in to stop a full-blown row from kicking off. Madge sticks her arm out, pressing her goblet right under his nose.

"Is it not polite to offer the guests a drink first, dearest?" He smiles at me as she pulls her goblet back, her face like a bulldog sucking a wasp.

After he fills my goblet first, she gets up and walks outside, with Jane following, no doubt to stir the pot with Madge. If she does, I will make her lick the spoon. I've had more than enough of her.

An hour or so passes, and with goblet after goblet of wine drunk, the mood has lifted. Norris comes and sits beside me.

"You should not be sat here all alone. Where are Madge and Jane?"

"Oh, they went off scheming." I get up and point to the clearing, then step outside the tent, and not without a bit of a wobble. The vibrations from Smeaton's lute music fill the air, and I feel dizzy and a little sick. I wish George would hurry back because Norris is making himself rather too familiar. Being more than a little drunk, I am now finding it difficult to hold him at bay. I move away from him, the sky swirling, and I'm afraid that I'm about to faint.

"Pray, take Mistress Wickers back to Sudeley," he calls to the servant who drove us here in the litter. "I think she is unwell." He grabs my upper arm, quite hard. "I shall accompany her to make sure she is returned safely." He turns to Smeaton. "Please let their Majesties know that Viscountess Beaumont is unwell and is going back to Sudeley. I think she needs her bed. I will call the physician if necessary."

"There is no need for that!" I cry. "I am quite capable of getting myself back to Sudeley." I burp, and vomit rises in the back of my throat. The branches of the trees seem to spin as the wind swirls around me.

"That may be, but what kind of gentleman would I be if I let you return alone?"

"I cannot argue with that," the servant says, and Norris boards the litter with me and we set off back to Sudeley.

The heat from the sun, and the movement of the litter makes me feel even more nauseous. My stomach is churning, and my head is spinning. Norris puts his arm around me to prevent me being thrown about with the rocking of the litter.

"We will be back soon," he says.

He is being gentlemanly, which is what I expect from him, but I can smell the vapours from the wine on his breath. I think he can take his alcohol better than me. The journey is a haze of greenery, buzzing bees, floating pollen, and the rising temperature of the midday sun.

"Do not worry, your lady will have you tucked up in bed in no time," he reassures me when the litter circles into the courtyard. "You will soon feel better, Viscountess."

He alights onto the cobbles before me and turns with his arms outstretched, ready to lift me down at my waist. As he manoeuvres me off the litter, my frame brushes against his body, and I look up, our gazes meeting. He smiles but I think nothing of his gallantry, or how he supports me to make my way back to my chamber. As I walk through the door, I stumble to my washing bowl on my nightstand, and promptly throw up.

Norris lurks in the corner, watching me as I try to rinse my mouth out with a goblet full of ale, he has handed me. However, as I sip the golden liquid, it makes me feel worse. I'm dizzy, unable to balance, and stagger backwards onto my bed.

"Viscountess, are you well?" he asks.

I try to mumble an insult to suggest how stupid he is, but the words don't come as they should. The room is spinning and, as I reach to stop it, everything goes black.

When I wake, the room is dark. I have no idea what time it is, but it feels as if hours have passed. My head is pounding. Someone, I don't know who, has come in and lit a single candle, because its flame is all I notice, flickering on the mantle. I almost jump out of my skin when I see Henry Norris leaning over me. What the hell is going on? I look about, noticing another empty goblet beside mine. He looks more intoxicated than when we first arrived back, and I can smell the vapours of stale ale lingering on his breath. My own breath catches when I look down and notice the placard of my gown is unpinned, and the forepart of my bodice has been unlaced. My kirtle feels loose, its straps askew. Worse, though, is part of my bosom is exposed, as if he's been trying to free it from the neckline of my shift and kirtle. I watch, paralysed, as I feel him rucking my skirts up to my waist, his hands rubbing up my inner thighs.

"W-what are you doing?" I blurt out, panic gripping my throat. I grasp at his forearms to prevent him getting any closer.

"I came in to check on you, but you were unconscious. I could not stir you, so I thought I would undress you and try to make you more comfortable, so I could put you to bed."

I blink at him. He's lying. His cheeks are flushed, and his doublet is unbuttoned. His clothes look almost as dishevelled as mine. He takes my outstretched arms as an invitation but he's wrong – this is not an invitation – he should realise I'm trying to push him away. Instead, he clamps his hand over my mouth.

"Please, do not make a sound."

The weight of his body is crushing as he forces himself on top of me. I try to scream, but he presses down and the sound muffles through his fingers.

"Stay quiet! It will be easier on you."

He forces my thighs apart with the weight of his frame, and I gag, my heart thumping in my throat. I glare up at him, hoping he can see my hatred for him as he looms over me. I'm unable to move, frozen by a helpless terror coursing through me. I try to fight through it, to fend him off in a last convulsion, but am gripped by a sudden searing pain as he thrusts into me.

His hand is still over my mouth as I try to scream, but it's no good, he's too strong for me, and I'm sickened and exhausted. All I can do is give in and submit. I clench my eyes shut and scrunch my fingers into fists at my sides, lying as still as I can in the hope that, if I don't resist, my ordeal will be over sooner. Through the horror, I try to take my mind to somewhere nice, like riding out with George, or the sun shining on Dad and me as he prunes his roses in the garden at Carshalton. I imagine the smell of the budding flowers, freshly mowed grass, Dad cracking jokes, or discussing some political programme he's watched on TV. In one visual, we're drinking a freshly brewed cup of tea in the front room. I think of anything I can to take myself away, to escape this nightmare.

As soon as he is finished, he releases my mouth from the clamp of his sweaty palm. He looks at me with a confused expression, his brows twisted. I turn my head away, knowing this was an act performed in contempt, as a symbol of humiliation and conquest. When he gets up, stinking of sweat and shame, he stands at the edge of my bed, tucking himself back into his clothes.

"Did you not love that, Beth?" he asks, his words slurring.

I stare at him in disbelief, not knowing what to say. Even so, my heart hurts with a burning rage, and I fumble with my skirts, feeling filthy as I try to cover myself up.

"That was not love," I shout, shuffling across my bed, away from him, "but defilement. How dare you touch me!"

"Every other man seems to have lain with you. The king, Lord Rochford – how many others, I know not. Why not I?"

"Who do you think you are – my apple-squire?" Light sparks in my peripheral vision from the strain of my scream. Norris thinks he's my pimp. "You believe you can have your way with me because you fetched me for the king in many a middle of the night?" My temples are throbbing as my blood boils.

"You are nothing but a common whore!" He ties the points on his codpiece and re-buttons his doublet. "You are only fit for a stew-house!"

"Leave!" I roar, my legs wobbling as I stand up, jabbing a forefinger at the chamber door. My head feels numb, and I'm disorientated, but I must get rid of him. "If anyone sees you…if the king finds out about this…"

Norris, now red-faced, strides towards me until he's a whisker away. "Say nothing to the king…or to Anne!" He sways, the spittle from his mouth splashing my face. "On your head be it if you tell a soul of what has happened here this day!" He lurches backwards and tugs at the hem of his doublet to straighten it, showing me no deference. The man doesn't care what he has just done, showing no remorse as he staggers out of the room.

I rush to the door and slam it shut, resting my body weight against it as I bolt the latch. My breath is short and rapid, and I can't stop shaking. In my wildest imaginings, I never expected Sir Henry Norris to force himself on me – to rape me. My teeth chatter as a tsunami of shivers race through me. Shock, I must be in shock.

Flashbacks fill my mind as I slump onto my bed. His act of master-taking was a contemptuous possession of me. I fly back through the day to see if at any point I might have encouraged him. No, not once. It's because he's drunk. It has to be. He'd never do anything like this if he was sober.

But I am also drunk. Oh, God, maybe it was my fault? I must be at least partly to blame. I shoot up in the bed. No, Beth, that bastard took full advantage of the situation. Damn you, Henry Norris!

I cringe at the wetness between my legs. The back of my shift feels wet too. I want to recoil from this moment, but there is nowhere to go. This is something I am going to have to deal with myself. I want to rip all my clothes off and soak in a long, hot shower – use some modern toiletries to rid myself of his stench. Norris was supposed to be a good guy, but today he's proven me wrong. So wrong.

Damn it, I want to go home. Not back to one of the royal palaces, but back to Carshalton – to my time, where I'll be safe. But how will George and Anne feel if I leave them to face their fates alone? She would realise I had abandoned her in her hour of need, as would George. I can't bear it – how could Norris traumatise me so? Damn it, what am I to do?

Twelve

I wait in my locked bedchamber for what seems like a couple of hours or so, letting no one in, until I hear George and Anne's voices in the passageway outside. Someone taps on the door, then tries lifting the latch.

"Beth, are you well?" George asks. He taps on the door again. "My darling, open the door."

I get up from the bed, making sure my clothing is straight. When I unbolt the door and step back, George and Anne enter.

"We were told you were unwell," she says.

They look about the room, at the dishevelled sheets on the bed, the upturn goblets, and the empty flagon. The single candle is almost spent. George strides over to the window and opens the shutters.

"Why are you sat alone in the dark, with the door bolted?" he asks, the concern evident in his voice. As he turns to me, I can't help but burst into tears at the kindness in his eyes and the affection in his voice.

"Whatever distresses you so?" Anne asks as George open his arms to me. I rush to him. As he embraces me, I press my face against the fabric of his doublet, and the tears run free as sobs rake through my body.

"Beth, you are shaking," he says, kissing the top of my head.

"I... I have...a headache, is all," I stutter through my tears, lifting my head from his chest. "I think I had a l-little too much wine this morning."

"You have an unusual smell about you." His nose and mouth twist as he looks about the room.

"I just feel unwell," I say, as he looks down at me, an element of doubt in his eyes.

"No, this is more than that." He looks around. "Who has been here with you?"

"No one!" I lie. I don't want to get Norris into trouble, or have him coming after me.

Anne walks to the nightstand. "There are two empty goblets here, and no ale left." She glances at the bed. "It was Sir Henry that fetched you back safely, was it not?"

"Yes, Your Majesty," I whisper, stepping back from George, who is now frowning at me.

"Why have you lied to us about being alone, then?" he asks, his nostrils flaring.

"Please, my love," I plead, reaching out to him, "it wasn't his fault. It was mine – I had too much ale!"

He walks over to the nightstand, picks up an empty goblet and throws it across the room. It seems he has put two and two together.

"By the devil's teeth!" he roars, turning towards the door. "When I get my hands on Norris, I shall kill him!" He storms out of the room, and Anne goes to the door after him.

"Brother, hold your temper!" she shouts. "For God's sake, do nothing – think of Beth – think of the consequences."

I know lesser men have been put in the Tower for fighting. Anne closes the door.

"I hope he heard me," she says, coming over to me. She takes me by my hand and sits me in a chair, taking the seat opposite me. "Has my brother come to the conclusion I have?" She lifts my hand, her touch so gentle. "Look at you. Your gown is disordered – your hair hangs loose." She frowns. "This is not you." She looks about the room. "What on earth has happened here?"

I squeeze her hand, drawing her attention back to me. "Anne, you must never tell a soul. Ever. Do you promise?"

"Whatever your secret is, I shall keep it," she replies, her voice soft.

"Even from your brother?"

"Even from George."

I'm still shaking, and the tears come again. "Norris f-forced himself on me!"

"Raped you?" Her eyes are wide.

"Yes," I whisper.

"Sir Henry would never do that!" she says. "He is a gentleman."

"That is what I thought. Gentleman, my arse!" I let my head fall back and release a sob of rage and despair. Anne grips both my hands, and the contact helps. I straighten up and look at her. "But…I think the drink got the better of him, for he accused me of being the King and George's whore, and he thought he was welcome to me – that it gave him an invitation to defile me!"

Anne releases my hands, stands up, and begins pacing the floor.

"This is shocking!" She holds a hand to her mouth and turns to me. "Did he hurt you badly?"

"I've had better days, Madam, and I'm certain there will be bruises. And, with the force that he took me, perhaps…" I can't say it.

"A little blood?" she suggests. I nod. "Then we must get you cleaned up." She walks to the door, opens it, and calls for Lady Lee. Within moments, Margaret appears and curtsies.

"Your Majesty?"

"Come in, Margaret. I, we…need your help."

She looks concerned. "Whatever is the matter?"

Anne closes and bolts the door. "Do not ask questions. Nothing must be repeated outside of this chamber. Where is my husband?"

"Taking refreshments, Madam."

"And my brother?"

"He came charging downstairs, raising his voice, looking angry." She looks from Anne to me, then back to Anne. "He kept saying something about Norris, and stormed off to the stables for his horse."

"Did the king see what was happening?" I ask.

"No, Beth – I think not."

"Good," Anne says. "And Sir Henry, where is he?"

Margaret sits on the chair opposite me. "I think he is in the king's rooms."

"Then he is out of sight. Good, I am glad – for his sake." She purses her mouth, nodding to herself. "Lady Lee, I need you to help me bathe the Viscountess and change her into a fresh gown. I need fresh linens, hot water for a bath, and rose oil."

Margaret raises her brow and looks at me. "But, Majesty, do you not need to get out of your hunting clothes?"

"That can wait."

"Very well, Majesty." She asks no more questions and gets on with ordering two of her ladies to fill the bathtub and light the fire. Anne helps me undress.

"Beth, please do not be alarmed," she says, looking down at the back of my shift, "but you have been bleeding." She pulls the shift over my head and shows me.

I knew Norris was rough with me, but I wasn't aware of the extent. It's difficult to look at the stain, with visions of his sneering face flitting behind my eyes. When the bath is ready, I step in and sink below the waterline, escaping from the stench of my defiler, though I cannot banish it from my mind. When I come up, I shake the water from my head and inhale the welcome floral notes of the rosewater.

"That will be all, Margaret," Anne says. "We will call you if we need you."

"Very well, Majesty." She curtsies, and I thank her as she walks out the door, taking the maids with her.

Anne bolts the latch and goes to my personal trunk, unlocks it, and pulls out some of my modern toiletries, like soap and shampoo. Washing the filth and betrayal out of my hair makes me feel a little better, and the soap does its work in removing the physical stains of unwanted intercourse, but it will never get rid of the emotional scars.

Anne sits in a chair, staring out of the window. "What would you like me to do?"

"What do you mean?"

She looks over to me. "Shall I tell Henry?"

"No!" I snap. "The King must never know – and neither must George."

"I think my brother has already guessed. Yes, that horse has bolted."

"Then you need to stop him acting against Norris. I mean it, the last thing he needs is to be thrown into the Tower for months."

"I know – I think he has gone for a ride, to cool his temper. I shall just tell him that you had too much ale. I shall make him believe me – he does not need to know the details."

"Good." I take a deep breath. "You will also need to explain my imminent absence, because I need to go home."

Her hand goes to her chest. "To your time?"

"Exactly." I rinse the shampoo from my hair, savouring the shelter of the soothing water as it cascades over my head.

"At least you are telling me. At least, this time, I can plan what to tell people about you."

"You deserve my honesty," I reply, knowing I can never give her that.

"I am the only one you can be completely honest with." She smiles. "I will think of something to say to George."

"When the progress is over, do you know where the court will be returning to?"

"In October, I know we will be at Windsor. Why?"

"Because, if that is the case – if, and when, I come back, that is when I shall return."

"If?" She gets up and hands me a linen sheet to dry myself. "You cannot leave me now and never come back. George would be heartbroken without you – you must know by now how deeply he loves you."

I sigh. "I do."

She paces the floor. "I have been thinking of this for some time, and I have decided that once I have given the King a son, I shall ask George to go to him and petition for his marriage to Jane Parker—"

"Lady Rochford, you mean?"

"Yes, I shall have George ask Henry if he will allow Archbishop Cranmer to annul his marriage to Jane, and give his blessing for you to marry him."

I stare at her, astonished, as I dry myself. "That could never happen." I wrap the linen sheet around me and sit on the edge of my bed.

"Why ever not?" she says. "God has not blessed George with an heir by her, so why not let God bless you?"

"But I couldn't." I know full well how history is meant to play out. "It would mean me having two lives – one in this present, and one in my time. George would have to know the whole truth. He… He'd think me mad – he'd never believe me."

"He might – for love. Try him."

"Anne, you are impossible."

"You have always known it." Her unmistakable laugh echoes around the chamber.

"How will we explain my absence?" I drop the sheet on the floor and wrapping a dressing gown around myself.

"If you promise you will return to Windsor in but a few weeks, then we can say you have had to return to Surrey."

"For what reason?"

"To check on the holdings patented to you when you were titled?"

I smile. "Now that is a good idea. That would work, wouldn't it?"

"Why do you think I persuaded the king to gift you such properties?" She raises both eyebrows.

"You are a wise woman." I step over and embrace her. "I promise, I will return."

She kisses my cheek. "I should hope so, my dearest friend." She breaks her embrace and walks towards the door. "I need to go and refresh myself and change my clothes. His Majesty will be wondering where I am."

"Yes, Majesty," I say.

She turns back before opening the door. "Safe travels. Stay well – I shall miss you."

Then she is gone. Within moments, a maid is at the door to help me dress. I choose a simple gown from my trunk, and the maid begins to brush and braid my tangled hair. When I look out of the window, I see George galloping back towards the mellow walls of the Castle. He dismounts, and leads his horse to the stables. I'm sorry that I haven't time to say goodbye – it involves too many issues, too much explanation, and truths he doesn't need to know. I know Anne will smooth over the issue with Norris. She must.

I shudder in my seat as Margaret brushes my hair, and she looks at me curiously as I drift in and out of my thoughts. I remember seeing Norris on the scaffold, on Tower Hill. I wonder if his rape of me is one reason why his life ends there? Anne might tell Henry, and he may set Cromwell on him. I suddenly feel overwhelmed by disgust and guilt – disgust for what he has just done to me, and guilt for potentially setting him on the path to his execution?

My hair now braided, Margaret comes in and helps me dress, and I feel physically clean, although the physiological effect of Norris's despicable behaviour will never leave me. Margaret finishes, and I bolt the door after her, then grab my linen holdall and take the most precious items I need, stuffing them into the bag: my mobile phone, toiletries' bag, makeup, letters George has written to me, letters from Anne, my book gifted from George, and any modern items that might give my identity away.

I sit on the bed and take a steadying breath. Time to go. I twist the cypher ring and rub the ruby stones. What do I think of? Where do I think of? I want to go back to my time, so where's the safest place I can return to without anyone being suspicious? It's safest to return home when my parents are out at work. The only one left alone in the house will be Rutterkin, and where will he be? As usual, probably comatose on my bed, snuggled up on my duvet, like before, if Mum accidentally let him into my bedroom.

Sat in this locked bedchamber now at Sudeley, I need to think of my own bedroom. Yes, that's it, my comfortable bed, with my warm duvet, and Rutterkin curled up, right in the middle of it. Eyes closed, I visualise my room, thinking about all the things I need to do before the start of my PhD. It's time to go home. I focus as hard as I can: bedroom, bookshelves, bed, duvet, Rutterkin…

My breath catches as my mind swirls and tumbles for what feels like seconds, then everything settles, and I scrunch my toes into the unmistakable fluffiness of my bedroom rug. I open my eyes, look around, and nearly cry on seeing the familiar patterns of my room wallpaper, and hear cars driving down my road. And there's Rutterkin, comatose like a black ball of fluff, curled up on my duvet, his tummy rising and falling with each deep sleepy purr. He must have sneaked in my room when Mum came into collect any washing from my linen basket.

I'm home. It worked. I look to my right and see my Tudor reflection in the dressing-table mirror. Not bad. I don't look too dishevelled, except my eyes are red from all that crying earlier. I face the mirror full on and take myself in. Cornflower-blue suits me, I think. This gown is a favourite of mine, but I'll have to get out of it. My braided hair is still intact, and my leather cow-mouthed shoes are still on. But the most unimaginable headache is pounding through my head.

I put my linen holdall on my bed and dig around the bottom of it, jabbing my fingers against cold metal. I pull out the large silver goblet Henry had gifted me. I stare at is as it shines, as if new, under the electric light in my bedroom. What an antique! I need to hide it. Surely, Mum would think it's some kind of re-enactment accessory. No one will know it's real, except me. Where to hide it? I glance about my room. There's a pile of books on a shelf, I can tuck it behind there, no one will find it. Next, I pull out my phone to recharge it. When I wasn't using it to take surreptitious photographs, I made sure I switched the power off, so I didn't waste the battery. It's so weird how modern-day things work in Tudor time. When I switch it back on now, it comes to life, and I check the photos. There are a dozen shots of Anne I took when we were alone, and some I took of parts of Greenwich and Whitehall as reminders. I flick through them, and my tummy flips when I come across the few I took of George, when we were sleeping together, in his chambers, naked. Naughty to take them, I know, but I'm sure he wouldn't begrudge me such a small memento, as it's the only tangible thing I will have of him, besides my memories, I guess.

As I sit back on my bed, I gaze at his face, thinking of his sweet kisses and tender embrace – thanking God this was no dream, and I've been so fortunate to have these treasured friends, people I love in my life. For the time being, I will miss them so much. This time, though, at least Anne has an idea I might be back. I don't want to leave them, but what Norris has done to me, has put me off ever returning to Tudor England. I don't want to let Anne or George down, but do I need to go back. Hopefully the Ives' book and its cover is now as it should be. I hope when I go back to Professor Marshall's office, I will find I won't have let the history down. I hoped I've completely rectified the history, so there's no need to go back. I hope I haven't kept history messed up with my stupid meddling, either. I will go back to them – eventually. Maybe. Tomorrow, I'll go in and check the Ives' book, to make sure everything is as it should be. Then I'll get on with my life, and my PhD.

Want to carry on Beth Wickers adventure with the Timeless Falcon Dual Timeline Series?

COMING SOON:
Volume Four: An Enduring Legacy.

A NOTE TO THE READER

Dear Reader,
Thank you for reading *A Turbulent Crown,*

Welcome to the world of Beth Wickers. This is my fourth novel, and my third historical novel, which is now part of the A Timeless Falcon Dual Timeline Series. Beth's journey began from my interest in history years ago, with Anne Boleyn and the dramatic story of her fall, reading the likes of Jean Plaidy when I was a child of nine. My study of Anne and history has never diminished. I know that Anne's life history is an interest shared by many: the crowds who visit His Majesty's Royal Palace and Fortress, The Tower of London, who feel compelled to see the supposed site of Anne's scaffold, imprisonment, and eventual judicial murder, or walk around with other visitors who flock to Hampton Court Palace where Anne stayed in the triumphant days of her coronation in June 1533, or even to Hever Castle, which was her family home for a time. The fascination with everything Anne Boleyn is evident in numerous websites on the internet. The insatiable appetite for everything relating to the Tudors, from raunchy television series to opulent films, to the Westend musical, Six! continues unabated.

I have consulted academic works and research on Anne Boleyn and personalities of the Tudor Court by successful historians like Eric Ives, Suzannah Lipscomb, Elizabeth Norton, David Loades and others, to frame a number of real events in Anne's life, to bring her story around Beth to life. Primary sources are also fantastic devices to learn of historical context, and analysing sources is the closest we will get to remove the veil between these historical personalities and events, in order to conclude anything which remotely resembles the truth. The highlight of my research was looking through and holding the twenty-six pages of Anne Boleyn's indictment of her trial, and seeing the indents in the vellum where the Duke of Norfolk had ticked the jury off with his quill as they entered the king's Great Hall at His Majesty's Royal Palace and Fortress of the Tower of London. My primary research included documents from websites such as British History Online, and The National Archives at Kew. The icing on the cake in terms of research, was having the opportunity to sit in the front row of The Aldwych Theatre and watch Ben Miles as Cromwell in the stage adaptations of Hilary Mantel's *Wolf Hall* and *Bring Up the Bodies* — on the last night's performance — and knowing Hilary Mantel was in the audience. What an incredible experience that was. The play was an atmospheric-inducing device, and historical aspects of the drama were thought-provoking.

It is this insatiable appetite by both historians and enthusiasts for Anne Boleyn, that compelled me to write a completely different take on her story, rather than the usual regurgitation of Anne, from her point of view. Moreover, it is my protagonist's story, which enables us to observe Anne in a different light. What would we do if we had the ability to time-travel back to the Tudor period and meet Anne? Would we behave ourselves and not tamper with history as we know it, or would we wreak havoc and try to save Anne from her well-documented downfall? These are the dilemmas that face Beth Wickers. Her story is one I felt obliged to write, and although I include primary events, it will never be close to the truth of Anne's life, as unless we were there at the time, we can never know all the facts relating to Anne Boleyn. I did consider, at times, what I would ask Anne, Henry, or other key players of the Tudor Court, and speculated what I might try and do to change history if I could time travel. In hindsight, would I allow such prominent Tudor personalities to play out their destiny as history intended? This book has been a labour of love and an exciting and fun retelling of Anne's story, as close to the truth of who I imagine Anne to have been. But this is fiction, after all, and I won't pretend any differently.

For those reading Volume Three, we are continuing with Beth Wicker's time-travelling story together; thank you for being here. You have one more volume in the A Timeless Falcon Dual Timeline Series to go, unless I decide to add further stories. For those that haven't read *The Anne Boleyn Cypher* (Volume One), or The Ring of Fate (Volume Two), you can read them to find out exactly how Beth ended up in sixteenth century England from the present day. My protagonist, Beth Wickers, has often woken me up in the middle of the night, screaming at me to finish her story. I think most authors end up with their characters talking in the heads of their creators? Beth has often told me the outcome of her adventures, clamouring at me to get up out of bed, so I would type her thoughts into my manuscripts as they formed in my head.

While researching the key figures of the Tudor period, tracing their journeys through the primary sources, I saw the potential of weaving a modern-day, fictional character like Beth into the Tudor world to represent the eyes and ears of modern readers who love history. I wanted to integrate Beth Wickers into the Boleyn world and simultaneously set her apart from it. I am a great fan of fiction, television series, films, and their prerogatives. It allows writers, authors, television studios, filmmakers, and readers, to transcend the veil of time, space, and reality, providing the ultimate way to escape the routines of our everyday lives. Series such as this can perform a kind of magic in our mind's eyes, and these fictional tales' only responsibility is to themselves, to be good versions of historical fiction. However, authors cannot hope to please every reader simultaneously. As a genre in its own right, historical fiction has its freedoms and limitations. It also offers the greatest thrill of transporting readers to another realm, the closest we can come to witnessing the past. Growing up reading historical novels, I quickly understood how much the genre could also be educative and deeply rooted in the facts of history.

The Wickers family, Rob Dryden, Professor Marshall, and others from the modern world are fictional. Still, I would suggest that Beth Wickers is also representative of many historians who imagine what it might be like living in the sixteenth century. Although Beth is closest to the Boleyns, in more ways than most, I created her by assimilating the lives of many other historical figures around her and how she might interact with them and them with her – this is especially true of Jane Parker, Jane Boleyn, or Lady Rochford, (whatever title you choose to call her) - George's wife.

We all have ideas of what historical figures may have been like based on evidence and sources, but there is little evidence of these Tudor characters. While some writers, film makers, and historians sometimes suggest George was promiscuous, or homosexual, and a bit of a cad, I wanted to show George in a different light. Yes, he enjoys the company of women, and yes, he probably had a few dalliances in his life, (but not many), yet he is NOT homosexual, not in this story anyway. Jane tries to be a good fiancé and eventual wife, by turning a blind eye to his misdemeanours. Still, through his interactions with Beth, Jane observes that there is more to her husband's relationship with Beth than meets the eye. Jane hates the bond Beth has with George, and it makes her angry. She wants to be loved by George the way he loves Beth – that's what makes her spikey.

I had to make Jane Boleyn spikey, but in Book Three, as you read Jane's backstory you will begin to understand why she treats George as she does. Like most women, she makes the best of it. I didn't want to follow the usual tropes about Jane Boleyn, without good reason, however, she's such a wonderful character to write as spikey, and her reasons for being so, are now obvious. I will stress that Jane's backstory, is purely speculation on my part, because unless you were there to actually witness what went on, we will never know the real truth of what happened, but the way I have implied a backstory in George's and Jane's relationship is a good one to explain Jane's later behaviours.

Another figure I took historical liberties with was Jayne Fool because we know so little about Jayne. We do not know when Jayne came to live in the household with Anne Boleyn or how old Jayne was at the time. We only know of Jayne's life experiences through accounts in the records of her attending Anne Boleyn's coronation and the painting of the Family of Henry VIII c.1545 that hangs in the Haunted Gallery at Hampton Court. I had read about disabled people at the Court of Henry VIII through my non-fiction research, writing, and PhD work. I wanted to show how compassionate and open-minded the Tudor Court could be towards disabled people whose experiences are known to us.

Other characters close to Beth are fictional, especially those relevant to the romantic plot line, such as Robert Dryden. The way I have portrayed Henry VIII's character, and other courtiers, allows me greater scope to flesh out their roles without altering what is known about existing people. It is also worth mentioning that, as Beth Wickers is a modern woman, of our time, that she is bound to be far more attractive to many of the men in the Tudor Court, including the king, than Anne Boleyn's contemporaries because of the modern products Beth uses in her hygiene, and beauty regimes, (which rubs off on Anne), and her usual good, healthy diet and use of modern medicines in her own time, that it is obvious Beth, would have many male Tudor courtiers throwing themselves at her.

Whilst I have researched the lives of individuals like Henry VIII, Katharine of Aragon and Anne Boleyn in detail, a gulf remains between biographical works and the creative fleshing out that allows them to come to life as characters in fiction. Thus, there will be times when historical fiction authors have to take the liberty of putting words into their characters mouths, describing their conversations and deeds that they believe are compatible with what is known or can be inferred about their characters, and events over five hundred years. Individual readers' views on Henry, Katharine, Anne, George, and others can often be unshakable, though, surprisingly different. Still, I have tried to change them from these historical characters usual tropes, and show them as well-rounded, actual human beings dealing with the politics of their day. It may be that a writer's presentation of known figures at this moment in their lives does not always fit with that of readers, but writer's always have sound reasons for writing their characters as they do.

The same is true for locations and events of the era, as well as details such as clothing, food, furnishing, protocol, and behaviour. Writers embellish the known facts, fill in the gaps, in keeping with their essence. The Beth Wickers and Anne Boleyn of 1521 will not be the same as their depiction towards the end of the whole series; their characters will grow and change through the experiences of their lives.

Furthermore, I wish to stress that although the historical aspects of this book are loosely based on original sources, digital archives, and academic accounts. Beth's character however, and her experiences in the Tudor period were used as an entertaining device to creatively retell Anne's story, and is written purely for the readers' enjoyment, and to entertain, which I hope, as a reader, you will enjoy.

Best Wishes,
Phillipa Vincent-Connolly

Reviews by readers these days are integral to a book's success, so if you enjoyed *A Turbulent Crown,* I would be very grateful if you could spare a minute to post a review on Amazon, and I love hearing from readers, and you can talk with me through

My website
www.phillipavincent-connolly.com/

or on Twitter (@PhillipaJC)

and follow my author page on Facebook (Phillipa Connolly Historian).

ALSO BY PHILLIPA VINCENT-CONNOLLY

THE TIMELESS FALCON SERIES:

Volume One: The Anne Boleyn Cypher
Volume Two: The Ring of Fate
Volume Four: An Enduring Legacy

Disability and The Tudors: All the King's Fools

ACKNOWLEDGEMENTS

Firstly, I want to thank my readers who have supported me by reading and reviewing this series, for believing in me and my work, and for loving Beth Wicker's story enough to continue reading the whole Timeless Falcon Dual Timeline series. Secondly, thanks to Eamon Ó Cléirigh from Clear View Editing, who made the self-publishing experience just that little bit easier, having persevered and supported me in slowly transforming this volume, and the subsequent volume in the series, into their final incarnations. Thank you for your patience. I'm glad that during the proceedings, I made you laugh out loud, alarming your little dog, Cú into the bargain.

Thank you to Richard Jenkins for his beautiful photography for the cover of the book, and for Megan Sheer for the beautiful design of the covers for the series.

Thank you to John Gillo for his belief in my work, and the support and encouragement he has given me to publish this series.

I also want to thank art historian Dr Janina Ramirez, for allowing and approving a cameo of herself to appear in this book, and for letting me know that she thought that if readers "Love history? Then lose yourself in time, with this intelligent, fast-paced, witty and immersive story." I hope that I depicted you as you truly are, a genuine, warm-hearted, and supportive person, with a love of life, people, and art, whom I admire very much.

I want to thank Gina Clark from Tudor Dreams Historical Costumier for her unwavering sense of humour, continued support, balanced with copious tea and champagne drinking, giving me some witty one-liners, and spicing up some of the sex-scenes, and inventing Paxton Merrill as a minor character, as I was reading the first draft of Volume Three to her. Gina's sense of humour, enthusiasm and love encouraged me to keep going, because we both know, and as Bob used to say, *"Set a goal to achieve something that is so big, so exhilarating that it excites you and scares you at the same time."*

Lastly, thank you to my two boys, Joshua, and Lucas who at times, have run out of patience with me for the amount of time I am glued to my MacBook Pro, in an event to get Beth's story out to readers. When I first started writing this series, they were children, now they are over 18!

Thank you to everyone for your support, as you are all wonderful!

Phillipa Vincent-Connolly,
Poole, Dorset. January 2023

ABOUT THE AUTHOR

Phillipa Vincent-Connolly is an historian, writer, and published author of historical fiction and nonfiction. She is a consultant on many exciting projects across a broad spectrum with a special interest in disability and is becoming the 'go-to' broadcaster on this subject, especially recently with the publication of her book, 'Disability and the Tudors'. Published by Pen and Sword history imprint, currently, this is the first book in a series on disabilities in specific eras and benefits from Phillipa's own experience of living with Cerebral Palsy.

She achieved her degree in History and Humanities in 2011 and her PGCE, QTS, in 2014, and NQT 2019, in teaching (secondary), and part of her MA Graduate Diploma in History in 2020, and is currently working towards her PhD at Manchester Metropolitan University specialising in Tudor disability history. She has spoken at the National Archives and the British library to great acclaim. Her experience in teaching makes her an authoritative and engaging public speaker. She is a Fellow of the Royal Historical Society.

Phillipa has written for History Today, been chief editor of Blitzed Magazine, has been interviewed regularly for BBC radio, and has appeared in mini-TV documentaries.

Among her many interests, she has a deep and abiding love for all things historical, archives, artefacts, architecture, fashion, and royalty. Phillipa is also a keen activist, giving a contemporary voice to disabled people of the past, and those who currently feel disenfranchised. Her own disability has allowed her to identify and empathise with those who have not been heard and she is passionate about equality for the disabled. She lives in Poole, Dorset, but is not solely UK centric, as she has a broad spectrum of knowledge and research on which to draw.

A rising star in historical fiction too, with her eagerly awaited 'Timeless Falcon' historical fiction series of books, Phillipa has both the research and writing abilities to adapt to any project and is the future of the past.

Printed in Great Britain
by Amazon